GRIMMS'
FAIRY TALES

Brothers Grimm

COLLINS
CLASSICS

Harper Press
An imprint of HarperCollins*Publishers*
77–85 Fulham Palace Road
Hammersmith
London W6 8JB

This Harper Press paperback edition published 2013

The Brothers Grimm asserts the moral right to be identified as the author of this work

A catalogue record for this book is available from the British Library

ISBN: 978-0-00-790224-8

Printed and bound in Great Britain by Clays Ltd, St Ives plc

MIX
Paper from
responsible sources
FSC˚ C007454

FSC™ is a non-profit international organisation established to promote the
responsible management of the world's forests. Products carrying the FSC label
are independently certified to assure consumers that they come
from forests that are managed to meet the social, economic and
ecological needs of present and future generations.

Find out more about HarperCollins and the environment at
www.harpercollins.co.uk/green

Life & Times section © HarperCollins*Publishers* Ltd
Gerard Cheshire asserts his moral rights as author of the Life & Times section
Classic Literature: Words and Phrases adapted from
Collins English Dictionary
Typesetting in Kalix by Palimpsest Book Production Limited,
Falkirk, Stirlingshire

History of Collins

In 1819, millworker William Collins from Glasgow, Scotland, set up a company for printing and publishing pamphlets, sermons, hymn books and prayer books. That company was Collins and was to mark the birth of HarperCollins Publishers as we know it today. The long tradition of Collins dictionary publishing can be traced back to the first dictionary William published in 1824, *Greek and English Lexicon*. Indeed, from 1840 onwards, he began to produce illustrated dictionaries and even obtained a licence to print and publish the Bible.

Soon after, William published the first Collins novel, *Ready Reckoner*, however it was the time of the Long Depression, where harvests were poor, prices were high, potato crops had failed and violence was erupting in Europe. As a result, many factories across the country were forced to close down and William chose to retire in 1846, partly due to the hardships he was facing.

Aged 30, William's son, William II took over the business. A keen humanitarian with a warm heart and a generous spirit, William II was truly 'Victorian' in his outlook. He introduced new, up-to-date steam presses and published affordable editions of Shakespeare's works and *Pilgrim's Progress*, making them available to the masses for the first time. A new demand for educational books meant that success came with the publication of travel books, scientific books, encyclopaedias and dictionaries. This demand to be educated led to the later publication of atlases and Collins also held the monopoly on scripture writing at the time.

In the 1860s Collins began to expand and diversify

and the idea of 'books for the millions' was developed. Affordable editions of classical literature were published and in 1903 Collins introduced 10 titles in their Collins Handy Illustrated Pocket Novels. These proved so popular that a few years later this had increased to an output of 50 volumes, selling nearly half a million in their year of publication. In the same year, The Everyman's Library was also instituted, with the idea of publishing an affordable library of the most important classical works, biographies, religious and philosophical treatments, plays, poems, travel and adventure. This series eclipsed all competition at the time and the introduction of paperback books in the 1950s helped to open that market and marked a high point in the industry.

HarperCollins is and has always been a champion of the classics and the current Collins Classics series follows in this tradition – publishing classical literature that is affordable and available to all. Beautifully packaged, highly collectible and intended to be reread and enjoyed at every opportunity.

Life & Times

About the Brothers Grimm

The Grimm brothers, Jacob (1785–1863) and Wilhelm (1786–1859) were German linguists and academics who saw the potential in gathering together fairy tales and folk tales in the German oral tradition and publishing them as a collection in 1812. Their first edition contained 156 stories, but the number steadily grew with each new edition until the seventh edition (1857) which featured 211 stories. The Grimm brothers wrote and edited their own preferred versions of the fairy tales, as fairy tale content varied greatly across the continent, across populations, across communities and even across families in their detail. Following publication of the first edition of *Grimms' Fairy Tales* the brothers heard about many other stories that they hadn't previously encountered in their home country, which is why the collection grew and became so European in its content and its appeal.

The brothers began their project in 1806 and tried as hard as possible to keep the tales in their traditional form in order to preserve their folklore value. Fairy tales were seen not simply as a device to provide entertainment, but to educate, guide and warn children of dangers in the real world. Consequently, the original versions are quite dark and baleful in mood – designed to deliver morals and messages in the manner of fables, although protracted into more elaborate stories. The idea was to capture the child's attention and impact on the memory, by taking then through the gamut of emotions.

Much of this allegory has been lost in the modern age because people's belief systems and cultures have changed so much. For example, people no longer believe in magic and supernatural phenomena in the way they used to. Nor do they believe in witches, giants, mystical animals and so on, or the medieval idea of good in an eternal battle with evil. As a consequence, the stories are taken largely at face value these days, especially as they have been softened by their adaptation into animated cartoons, pantomimes and films. In fact, most of the classic fairy tales that we know and love today were originally given the Grimm treatment: *Snow-white and Rose-red*, *Little Red Riding Hood*, *Hansel and Gretel*, *The Frog-Prince*, *The Golden Goose*, *Rapunzel*, *Rumpelstiltskin*, *The Elves and the Shoemaker* and *Tom Thumb* among others.

Interpretation of the Stories

Scholars have done their level best to interpret these stories in an attempt to understand what they are saying and how they came to be. The stories would have passed down to the Grimm Brothers in a random and arbitrary manner for centuries before they chose to tether them down in one place.

Medieval life was uncertain and usually short. People felt that fate came down to recognizing and avoiding the dangers around them, and the danger of displeasing their god. Put the two together and you have the underlying themes that are addressed in most fairy tales. The overall doctrine was to keep safe in the real world and keep safe in the spiritual world. That way, one might just live a life longer and happier than most.

In effect, fairy tales are analogies, designed to be both interesting and straightforward for a young audience. *Hansel and Gretel* implies that one should not 'take sweets from strangers' while *The Golden Goose* warns against greed. *The Elves and the Shoemaker* teaches to 'be kind to others and they will be kind to you'. *Little Red Riding Hood* cautions to 'be careful not to be tricked by strangers'. *Snow-white and Rose-red* warns children to 'be wary of enemies who pose as friends' and 'make sure you know who your friends are'. Magic, witchcraft, sorcery and evil curses were regarded as real phenomena at the time and appear in many of the stories, although perhaps these ideas are less resonant now as they are not part of the mindset of the modern age.

It would seem that child illness, harm and abduction were ever present fears in medieval times, just as they are today. It is human nature for parents to overreact in response to news of misfortune befalling other children, so one can imagine that the medieval environment would have prompted hysteria and herd instinct. No wonder then, that such safe-guarding tales became part of the culture. The Grimms, however, were not particularly analytical about the meaning behind fairy tales, and took them more at face value as enter-taining children's stories. As literary scholars they were more concerned with the preservation of the tales, fearing they would one day be lost to time if the oral tradition died out. They were right, as their collection has now become the primary source for many of the tales.

The Grimms were not authors in the strictest terms. They may have documented the fairy tales, but they didn't create them. Nevertheless, *Grimms' Fairy Tales* is now recog-nized as an important archive of social history. History tends to record important events and the lives of important people. It fails to record the more prosaic details of lay life, which are so important in building a more three-dimensional model of the past. Fairy tales give insight into the psychology of those who created them and those who passed them down the generations. They might be thought of as cultural archaeology as they allow us to inhabit the mindset of people who are no longer around to interview. Ironically therefore, they are more valuable as they are than had the Grimms created them from their own imaginations. As it is, they tell us something about a whole population living in a particular era. The Grimms also started a trend for documenting folk and fairy tales in other countries. These include other classics that might easily have been in *Grimms' Fairy Tales*, such as *Jack and the*

Beanstalk, Three Billygoats Gruff, Goldilocks and the Three Bears and *Three Little Pigs*.

Although their original purpose may be lost to us, there is no doubt that fairy tales still have their place in the modern world because they are good stories that have been honed and refined by the process of storytelling over the ages. In essence, many minds had collaborated to perfect the stories by the time the Grimms took it upon themselves to record them on paper.

GRIMMS' FAIRY TALES

CONTENTS

The Golden Bird   1
Hans In Luck   8
Jorinda and Jorindel   15
The Travelling Musicians   19
Old Sultan   23
The Straw, The Coal, and The Bean   26
Briar Rose   28
The Dog and The Sparrow   32
The Twelve Dancing Princesses   36
The Fisherman and His Wife   41
The Willow-Wren and The Bear   48
The Frog-Prince   51
Cat And Mouse In Partnership   55
The Goose-Girl   58
The Adventures of Chanticleer and Partlet   65
Rapunzel   71
Fundevogel   76
The Valiant Little Tailor   79
Hansel and Gretel   88
The Mouse, The Bird, and The Sausage   96

Mother Holle	99
Little Red-Cap [Little Red Riding Hood]	103
The Robber Bridegroom	108
Tom Thumb	113
Rumpelstiltskin	120
Clever Gretel	124
The Old Man and His Grandson	127
The Little Peasant	128
Frederick and Catherine	134
Sweetheart Roland	139
Snowdrop	143
The Pink	151
Clever Elsie	156
The Miser In The Bush	160
Ashputtel	164
The White Snake	172
The Wolf and The Seven Little Kids	177
The Queen Bee	181
The Elves and The Shoemaker	184
The Juniper-Tree	187
The Turnip	198
Clever Hans	202
The Three Languages	205
The Fox and The Cat	208
The Four Clever Brothers	210
Lily and The Lion	215
The Fox and The Horse	221

The Blue Light   223
The Raven   228
The Golden Goose   235
The Water of Life   240
The Twelve Huntsmen   248
The King of The Golden Mountain   252
Doctor Knowall   259
The Seven Ravens   262
The Wedding of Mrs Fox   265
The Salad   269
The Story of The Youth Who
    Went Forth To Learn What Fear Was   275
King Grisly-Beard   285
Iron Hans   289
Cat-Skin   297
Snow-White and Rose-Red   303

THE GOLDEN BIRD

A certain king had a beautiful garden, and in the garden stood a tree which bore golden apples. These apples were always counted, and about the time when they began to grow ripe it was found that every night one of them was gone. The king became very angry at this, and ordered the gardener to keep watch all night under the tree. The gardener set his eldest son to watch; but about twelve o'clock he fell asleep, and in the morning another of the apples was missing. Then the second son was ordered to watch; and at midnight he too fell asleep, and in the morning another apple was gone. Then the third son offered to keep watch; but the gardener at first would not let him, for fear some harm should come to him: however, at last he consented, and the young man laid himself under the tree to watch. As the clock struck twelve he heard a rustling noise in the air, and a bird came flying that was of pure gold; and as it was snapping at one of the apples with its beak, the gardener's son jumped up and shot an arrow at it. But the arrow did the bird no harm; only it dropped a golden feather from its tail, and then flew away. The golden feather was brought to the king in the morning, and all the council was called together. Everyone agreed that it was worth more than all the wealth of the kingdom: but the king said, 'One feather is of no use to me, I must have the whole bird.'

Then the gardener's eldest son set out and thought to find the golden bird very easily; and when he had gone but a little way, he came to a wood, and by the side of the wood he saw a fox sitting; so he took his bow and made ready to shoot at it. Then the fox said, 'Do not shoot me, for I will give you good counsel; I know what your business is, and that you want to find the golden bird. You will reach a village in the evening; and when you get there, you will see two inns opposite to each other, one of which is very pleasant and beautiful to look at: go not in there, but rest for the night in the other, though it may appear to you to be very poor and mean.' But the son thought to himself, 'What can such a beast as this know about the matter?' So he shot his arrow at the fox; but he missed it, and it set up its tail above its back and ran into the wood. Then he went his way, and in the evening came to the village where the two inns were; and in one of these were people singing, and dancing, and feasting; but the other looked very dirty, and poor. 'I should be very silly,' said he, 'if I went to that shabby house, and left this charming place'; so he went into the smart house, and ate and drank at his ease, and forgot the bird, and his country too.

Time passed on; and as the eldest son did not come back, and no tidings were heard of him, the second son set out, and the same thing happened to him. He met the fox, who gave him the good advice: but when he came to the two inns, his eldest brother was standing at the window where the merrymaking was, and called to him to come in; and he could not withstand the temptation, but went in, and forgot the golden bird and his country in the same manner.

Time passed on again, and the youngest son too wished to set out into the wide world to seek for the golden bird; but his father would not listen to it for a long while, for he was very fond of his son, and was afraid that some ill luck might happen to him also, and prevent his coming back. However, at last it was agreed he should go, for he would not rest at home; and as he came to the wood, he met the fox, and heard the same good counsel. But he was thankful to the fox, and did not attempt his life as his brothers had done; so the fox said, 'Sit upon my tail, and you will travel faster.' So he sat down, and the fox began to run, and away they went over stock and stone so quick that their hair whistled in the wind.

When they came to the village, the son followed the fox's counsel, and without looking about him went to the shabby inn and rested there all night at his ease. In the morning came the fox again and met him as he was beginning his journey, and said, 'Go straight forward, till you come to a castle, before which lie a whole troop of soldiers fast asleep and snoring: take no notice of them, but go into the castle and pass on and on till you come to a room, where the golden bird sits in a wooden cage; close by it stands a beautiful golden cage; but do not try to take the bird out of the shabby cage and put it into the handsome one, otherwise you will repent it.' Then the fox stretched out his tail again, and the young man sat himself down, and away they went over stock and stone till their hair whistled in the wind.

Before the castle gate all was as the fox had said: so the son went in and found the chamber where the golden bird hung in a wooden cage, and below stood the golden cage, and the three golden apples that had been lost were lying close by it. Then thought he to himself, 'It will be a very droll thing to bring away such a fine bird in this shabby cage'; so he opened the door and took hold of it and put it into the golden cage. But the bird set up such a loud scream that all the soldiers awoke, and they took him prisoner and carried him before the king. The next morning the court sat to judge him; and when all was heard, it sentenced him to die, unless he should bring the king the golden horse which could run as swiftly as the wind; and if he did this, he was to have the golden bird given him for his own.

So he set out once more on his journey, sighing, and in great despair, when on a sudden his friend the fox met him, and said, 'You see now what has happened on account of your not listening to my counsel. I will still, however, tell you how to find the golden horse, if you will do as I bid you. You must go straight on till you come to the castle where the horse stands in his stall: by his side will lie the groom fast asleep and snoring: take away the horse quietly, but be sure to put the old leathern saddle upon him, and not the golden one that is close by it.' Then the son sat down on the fox's tail, and away they went over stock and stone till their hair whistled in the wind.

All went right, and the groom lay snoring with his hand upon the golden saddle. But when the son looked at the horse, he thought it a great pity to put the leathern saddle upon it. 'I will give him the good one,' said he; 'I am sure he deserves it.' As he took up the golden saddle the groom awoke and cried out so loud, that all the guards ran in and took him prisoner, and in the morning he was again brought before the court to be judged, and was sentenced to die. But it was agreed, that, if he could bring thither the beautiful princess, he should live, and have the bird and the horse given him for his own.

Then he went his way very sorrowful; but the old fox came and said, 'Why did not you listen to me? If you had, you would have carried away both the bird and the horse; yet will I once more give you counsel. Go straight on, and in the evening you will arrive at a castle. At twelve o'clock at night the princess goes to the bathing-house: go up to her and give her a kiss, and she will let you lead her away; but take care you do not suffer her to go and take leave of her father and mother.' Then the fox stretched out his tail, and so away they went over stock and stone till their hair whistled again.

As they came to the castle, all was as the fox had said, and at twelve o'clock the young man met the princess going to the bath and gave her the kiss, and she agreed to run away with him, but begged with many tears that he would let her take leave of her father. At first he refused, but she wept still more and more, and fell at his feet, till at last he consented; but the moment she came to her father's house the guards awoke and he was taken prisoner again.

Then he was brought before the king, and the king said, 'You shall never have my daughter unless in eight days you dig away the hill that stops the view from my window.' Now this hill was so big that the whole world could not take it away: and when he had worked for seven days, and had done very little, the fox came and said. 'Lie down and go to sleep; I will work for you.' And in the morning he awoke and the hill was gone; so he went merrily to the king, and told him that now that it was removed he must give him the princess.

Then the king was obliged to keep his word, and away went the young man and the princess; and the fox came and said to him, 'We will have all three, the princess, the horse, and the bird.' 'Ah!' said the young man, 'that would be a great thing, but how can you contrive it?'

'If you will only listen,' said the fox, 'it can be done. When you come to the king, and he asks for the beautiful princess, you must say, "Here she is!" Then he will be very joyful; and you will mount the golden horse that they are to give you, and put out your hand to take leave of them; but shake hands with the princess last. Then lift her quickly on to the horse behind you; clap your spurs to his side, and gallop away as fast as you can.'

All went right: then the fox said, 'When you come to the castle where the bird is, I will stay with the princess at the door, and you will ride in and speak to the king; and when he sees that it is the right horse, he will bring out the bird;

but you must sit still, and say that you want to look at it, to
see whether it is the true golden bird; and when you get it
into your hand, ride away.'

This, too, happened as the fox said; they carried off the
bird, the princess mounted again, and they rode on to a great
wood. Then the fox came, and said, 'Pray kill me, and cut off
my head and my feet.' But the young man refused to do it:
so the fox said, 'I will at any rate give you good counsel:
beware of two things; ransom no one from the gallows, and
sit down by the side of no river.' Then away he went. 'Well,'
thought the young man, 'it is no hard matter to keep that
advice.'

He rode on with the princess, till at last he came to the
village where he had left his two brothers. And there he heard
a great noise and uproar; and when he asked what was the
matter, the people said, 'Two men are going to be hanged.'
As he came nearer, he saw that the two men were his brothers,
who had turned robbers; so he said, 'Cannot they in any way
be saved?' But the people said 'No,' unless he would bestow
all his money upon the rascals and buy their liberty. Then he
did not stay to think about the matter, but paid what was
asked, and his brothers were given up, and went on with him
towards their home.

And as they came to the wood where the fox first met
them, it was so cool and pleasant that the two brothers said,
'Let us sit down by the side of the river, and rest a while, to
eat and drink.' So he said, 'Yes,' and forgot the fox's counsel,
and sat down on the side of the river; and while he suspected
nothing, they came behind, and threw him down the bank,
and took the princess, the horse, and the bird, and went home
to the king their master, and said. 'All this have we won by
our labour.' Then there was great rejoicing made; but the
horse would not eat, the bird would not sing, and the princess
wept.

The youngest son fell to the bottom of the river's bed:

luckily it was nearly dry, but his bones were almost broken, and the bank was so steep that he could find no way to get out. Then the old fox came once more, and scolded him for not following his advice; otherwise no evil would have befallen him: 'Yet,' said he, 'I cannot leave you here, so lay hold of my tail and hold fast.' Then he pulled him out of the river, and said to him, as he got upon the bank, 'Your brothers have set watch to kill you, if they find you in the kingdom.' So he dressed himself as a poor man, and came secretly to the king's court, and was scarcely within the doors when the horse began to eat, and the bird to sing, and princess left off weeping. Then he went to the king, and told him all his brothers' roguery; and they were seized and punished, and he had the princess given to him again; and after the king's death he was heir to his kingdom.

A long while after, he went to walk one day in the wood, and the old fox met him, and besought him with tears in his eyes to kill him, and cut off his head and feet. And at last he did so, and in a moment the fox was changed into a man, and turned out to be the brother of the princess, who had been lost a great many many years.

HANS IN LUCK

Some men are born to good luck: all they do or try to do comes right—all that falls to them is so much gain—all their geese are swans—all their cards are trumps—toss them which way you will, they will always, like poor puss, alight upon their legs, and only move on so much the faster. The world may very likely not always think of them as they think of themselves, but what care they for the world? what can it know about the matter?

One of these lucky beings was neighbour Hans. Seven long years he had worked hard for his master. At last he said, 'Master, my time is up; I must go home and see my poor mother once more: so pray pay me my wages and let me go.' And the master said, 'You have been a faithful and good servant, Hans, so your pay shall be handsome.' Then he gave him a lump of silver as big as his head.

Hans took out his pocket-handkerchief, put the piece of silver into it, threw it over his shoulder, and jogged off on his road homewards. As he went lazily on, dragging one foot after another, a man came in sight, trotting gaily along on a capital horse. 'Ah!' said Hans aloud, 'what a fine thing it is to ride on horseback! There he sits as easy and happy as if he was at home, in the chair by his fireside; he trips against no stones, saves shoe-leather, and gets on he hardly knows how.' Hans did not speak so softly but the horseman heard it all, and said, 'Well, friend, why do you go on foot then?' 'Ah!' said he, 'I have this load to carry: to be sure it is silver, but it is so heavy that I can't hold up my head, and you must know it hurts my shoulder sadly.' 'What do you say of making an exchange?' said the horseman. 'I will give you my horse, and you shall give me the silver; which will save you a great deal of trouble in carrying such a heavy load about with you.' 'With all my heart,' said Hans: 'but as you are so kind to me, I must tell you one thing—you will have a weary task to draw that silver about with you.' However, the horseman got off, took the silver, helped Hans up, gave him the bridle into one hand and the whip into the other, and said, 'When you want to go very fast, smack your lips loudly together, and cry "Jip!"'

Hans was delighted as he sat on the horse, drew himself up, squared his elbows, turned out his toes, cracked his whip, and rode merrily off, one minute whistling a merry tune, and another singing,

> 'No care and no sorrow,
> A fig for the morrow!
> We'll laugh and be merry,
> Sing neigh down derry!'

After a time he thought he should like to go a little faster, so he smacked his lips and cried 'Jip!' Away went the horse full gallop; and before Hans knew what he was about, he was thrown off, and lay on his back by the road-side. His horse would have ran off, if a shepherd who was coming by, driving a cow, had not stopped it. Hans soon came to himself, and got upon his legs again, sadly vexed, and said to the shepherd, 'This riding is no joke, when a man has the luck to get upon a beast like this that stumbles and flings him off as if it would break his neck. However, I'm off now once for all: I like your cow now a great deal better than this smart beast that played me this trick, and has spoiled my best coat, you see, in this puddle; which, by the by, smells not very like a nosegay. One can walk along at one's leisure behind that cow—keep good company, and have milk, butter, and cheese, every day, into the bargain. What would I give to have such a prize!' 'Well,' said the shepherd, 'if you are so fond of her, I will change my cow for your horse; I like to do good to my neighbours, even though I lose by it myself.' 'Done!' said Hans, merrily. 'What a noble heart that good man has!' thought he. Then the shepherd jumped upon the horse, wished Hans and the cow good morning, and away he rode.

Hans brushed his coat, wiped his face and hands, rested a while, and then drove off his cow quietly, and thought his bargain a very lucky one. 'If I have only a piece of bread (and I certainly shall always be able to get that), I can, whenever I like, eat my butter and cheese with it; and when I am thirsty I can milk my cow and drink the milk: and what can I wish for more?' When he came to an inn, he halted, ate up all his bread, and gave away his last penny for a glass of beer. When he had rested himself he set off again, driving his cow towards his mother's village. But the heat grew greater as soon as noon came on, till at last, as he found himself on a wide heath that would take him more than an hour to cross, he began to be so hot and parched that his tongue clave to the roof of his mouth. 'I can find a cure for this,' thought he; 'now I will milk my cow and quench my thirst': so he tied her to the stump of a tree, and held his leathern cap to milk into; but not a drop was to be had. Who would have thought that this cow, which was to bring him milk and butter and cheese, was all that time utterly dry? Hans had not thought of looking to that.

While he was trying his luck in milking, and managing the matter very clumsily, the uneasy beast began to think him very troublesome; and at last gave him such a kick on the head as knocked him down; and there he lay a long while senseless. Luckily a butcher soon came by, driving a pig in a wheelbarrow. 'What is the matter with you, my man?' said the butcher, as he helped him up. Hans told him what had happened, how he was dry, and wanted to milk his cow, but found the cow was dry too. Then the butcher gave him a flask of ale, saying, 'There, drink and refresh yourself; your cow will give you no milk: don't you see she is an old beast, good for nothing but the slaughter-house?' 'Alas, alas!' said Hans, 'who would have thought it? What a shame to take my horse, and give me only a dry cow! If I kill her, what will she be good for? I hate cow-beef; it is not tender enough for me. If it were a pig now—like that fat gentleman you are driving along at his ease—one could do something with it; it would at any rate make sausages.' 'Well,' said the butcher, 'I don't like to say no, when one is asked to do a kind, neighbourly thing. To please you I will change, and give you my fine fat pig for the cow.' 'Heaven reward you for your kindness and self-denial!' said Hans, as he gave the butcher the cow; and taking the pig off the wheel-barrow, drove it away, holding it by the string that was tied to its leg.

So on he jogged, and all seemed now to go right with him: he had met with some misfortunes, to be sure; but he was now well repaid for all. How could it be otherwise with such a travelling companion as he had at last got?

The next man he met was a countryman carrying a fine white goose. The countryman stopped to ask what was o'clock; this led to further chat; and Hans told him all his luck, how he had so many good bargains, and how all the world went gay and smiling with him. The countryman than began to tell his tale, and said he was going to take the goose to a christening. 'Feel,' said he, 'how heavy it is, and yet it is only eight weeks old. Whoever roasts and eats it will find plenty of fat upon it, it has lived so well!' 'You're right,' said Hans, as he weighed it in his hand; 'but if you talk of fat, my pig is no trifle.' Meantime the countryman began to look grave, and shook his head. 'Hark ye!' said he, 'my worthy friend, you seem a good sort of fellow, so I can't help doing you a kind turn. Your pig may get you into a scrape. In the village I just came from, the squire has had a pig stolen out of his sty. I was dreadfully afraid when I saw you that you had got the squire's pig. If you have, and they catch you, it will be a bad job for you. The least they will do will be to throw you into the horse-pond. Can you swim?'

Poor Hans was sadly frightened. 'Good man,' cried he, 'pray get me out of this scrape. I know nothing of where the pig was either bred or born; but he may have been the squire's for aught I can tell: you know this country better than I do, take my pig and give me the goose.' 'I ought to have something into the bargain,' said the countryman; 'give a fat goose for a pig, indeed! 'Tis not everyone would do so much for you as that. However, I will not be hard upon you, as you are in trouble.' Then he took the string in his hand, and drove off the pig by a side path; while Hans went on the way homewards free from care. 'After all,' thought he, 'that chap is pretty well taken in. I don't care whose pig it is, but wherever it came from it has been a very good friend to me. I have much the best of the bargain. First there will be a capital roast; then the fat will find me in goose-grease for six months; and then there are all the beautiful white feathers. I will put them into my pillow, and then I am sure I shall sleep soundly without rocking. How happy my mother will be! Talk of a pig, indeed! Give me a fine fat goose.'

As he came to the next village, he saw a scissor-grinder with his wheel, working and singing,

> 'O'er hill and o'er dale
> So happy I roam,
> Work light and live well,
> All the world is my home;
> Then who so blythe, so merry as I?'

Hans stood looking on for a while, and at last said, 'You must be well off, master grinder! you seem so happy at your work.' 'Yes,' said the other, 'mine is a golden trade; a good grinder never puts his hand into his pocket without finding money in it—but where did you get that beautiful goose?' 'I did not buy it, I gave a pig for it.' 'And where did you get the pig?' 'I gave a cow for it.' 'And the cow?' 'I gave a horse for it.' 'And the horse?' 'I gave a lump of silver as big as my head for it.' 'And the silver?' 'Oh! I worked hard for that seven long years.' 'You have thriven well in the world hitherto,' said the grinder, 'now if you could find money in your pocket whenever you put your hand in it, your fortune would be made.' 'Very true: but how is that to be managed?' 'How? Why, you must turn grinder like myself,' said the other; 'you only want a grindstone; the rest will come of itself. Here is one that is but little the worse for wear: I would not ask more than the value of your goose for it—will you buy?' 'How can you ask?' said Hans; 'I should be the happiest man in the world, if I could have money whenever I put my hand in my pocket: what could I want more? there's the goose.' 'Now,' said the grinder, as he gave him a common rough stone that lay by his side, 'this is a most capital stone; do but work it well enough, and you can make an old nail cut with it.'

Hans took the stone, and went his way with a light heart: his eyes sparkled for joy, and he said to himself, 'Surely I must have been born in a lucky hour; everything I could want or wish for comes of itself. People are so kind; they seem really to think I do them a favour in letting them make me rich, and giving me good bargains.'

Meantime he began to be tired, and hungry too, for he had given away his last penny in his joy at getting the cow.

At last he could go no farther, for the stone tired him sadly: and he dragged himself to the side of a river, that he might take a drink of water, and rest a while. So he laid the stone carefully by his side on the bank: but, as he stooped down to drink, he forgot it, pushed it a little, and down it rolled, plump into the stream.

For a while he watched it sinking in the deep clear water; then sprang up and danced for joy, and again fell upon his knees and thanked Heaven, with tears in his eyes, for its kindness in taking away his only plague, the ugly heavy stone.

'How happy am I!' cried he; 'nobody was ever so lucky as I.' Then up he got with a light heart, free from all his troubles, and walked on till he reached his mother's house, and told her how very easy the road to good luck was.

JORINDA AND JORINDEL

There was once an old castle, that stood in the middle of a deep gloomy wood, and in the castle lived an old fairy. Now this fairy could take any shape she pleased. All the day long she flew about in the form of an owl, or crept about the country like a cat; but at night she always became an old woman again. When any young man came within a hundred paces of her castle, he became quite fixed, and could not move a step till she came and set him free; which she would not do till he had given her his word never to come there again: but when any pretty maiden came within that space she was changed into a bird, and the fairy put her into a cage, and hung her up in a chamber in the castle. There were seven hundred of these cages hanging in the castle, and all with beautiful birds in them.

Now there was once a maiden whose name was Jorinda. She was prettier than all the pretty girls that ever were seen before, and a shepherd lad, whose name was Jorindel, was very fond of her, and they were soon to be married. One day they went to walk in the wood, that they might be alone; and Jorindel said, 'We must take care that we don't go too near to the fairy's castle.' It was a beautiful evening; the last rays of the setting sun shone bright through the long stems of the trees upon the green underwood beneath, and the turtle-doves sang from the tall birches.

Jorinda sat down to gaze upon the sun; Jorindel sat by her side; and both felt sad, they knew not why; but it seemed as if they were to be parted from one another for ever. They had wandered a long way; and when they looked to see which way they should go home, they found themselves at a loss to know what path to take.

The sun was setting fast, and already half of its circle had sunk behind the hill: Jorindel on a sudden looked behind him, and saw through the bushes that they had, without knowing it, sat down close under the old walls of the castle. Then he shrank for fear, turned pale, and trembled. Jorinda was just singing,

> *'The ring-dove sang from the willow spray,*
> *Well-a-day! Well-a-day!*
> *He mourn'd for the fate of his darling mate,*
> *Well-a-day!'*

when her song stopped suddenly. Jorindel turned to see the reason, and beheld his Jorinda changed into a nightingale, so that her song ended with a mournful *jug, jug*. An owl with fiery eyes flew three times round them, and three times screamed:

> *'Tu whu! Tu whu! Tu whu!'*

Jorindel could not move; he stood fixed as a stone, and could neither weep, nor speak, nor stir hand or foot. And now the sun went quite down; the gloomy night came; the owl flew into a bush; and a moment after the old fairy came forth pale and meagre, with staring eyes, and a nose and chin that almost met one another.

She mumbled something to herself, seized the

nightingale, and went away with it in her hand. Poor Jorindel saw the nightingale was gone—but what could he do? He could not speak, he could not move from the spot where he stood. At last the fairy came back and sang with a hoarse voice:

> ''Till the prisoner is fast,
> And her doom is cast,
> There stay! Oh, stay!
> When the charm is around her,
> And the spell has bound her,
> Hie away! away!'

On a sudden Jorindel found himself free. Then he fell on his knees before the fairy, and prayed her to give him back his dear Jorinda: but she laughed at him, and said he should never see her again; then she went her way.

He prayed, he wept, he sorrowed, but all in vain. 'Alas!' he said, 'what will become of me?' He could not go back to his own home, so he went to a strange village, and employed himself in keeping sheep. Many a time did he walk round and round as near to the hated castle as he dared go, but all in vain; he heard or saw nothing of Jorinda.

At last he dreamt one night that he found a beautiful purple flower, and that in the middle of it lay a costly pearl; and he dreamt that he plucked the flower, and went with it in his hand into the castle, and that everything he touched with it was disenchanted, and that there he found his Jorinda again.

In the morning when he awoke, he began to search over hill and dale for this pretty flower; and eight long days he sought for it in vain: but on the ninth day, early in the morning, he found the beautiful purple flower; and in the middle of it was a large dewdrop, as big as a costly pearl. Then he plucked the flower, and set out and travelled day and night, till he came again to the castle.

He walked nearer than a hundred paces to it, and yet he did not become fixed as before, but found that he could go quite close up to the door. Jorindel was very glad indeed to see this. Then he touched the door with the flower, and it sprang open; so that he went in through the court, and listened when he heard so many birds singing. At last he came to the chamber where the fairy sat, with the seven hundred birds singing in the seven hundred cages. When she saw Jorindel she was very angry, and screamed with rage; but she could not come within two yards of him, for the flower he held in his hand was his safeguard. He looked around at the birds, but alas! there were many, many nightingales, and how then should he find out which was his Jorinda? While he was thinking what to do, he saw the fairy had taken down one of the cages, and was making the best of her way off through the door. He ran or flew after her, touched the cage with the flower, and Jorinda stood before him, and threw her arms round his neck looking as beautiful as ever, as beautiful as when they walked together in the wood.

Then he touched all the other birds with the flower, so that they all took their old forms again; and he took Jorinda home, where they were married, and lived happily together many years: and so did a good many other lads, whose maidens had been forced to sing in the old fairy's cages by themselves, much longer than they liked.

THE TRAVELLING
MUSICIANS

An honest farmer had once an ass that had been a faithful servant to him a great many years, but was now growing old and every day more and more unfit for work. His master therefore was tired of keeping him and began to think of putting an end to him; but the ass, who saw that some mischief was in the wind, took himself slyly off, and began his journey towards the great city, 'For there,' thought he, 'I may turn musician.'

After he had travelled a little way, he spied a dog lying by the roadside and panting as if he were tired. 'What makes you pant so, my friend?' said the ass. 'Alas!' said the dog, 'my master was going to knock me on the head, because I am old and weak, and can no longer make myself useful to him in hunting; so I ran away; but what can I do to earn my livelihood?' 'Hark ye!' said the ass, 'I am going to the great city to turn musician: suppose you go with me, and try what you can do in the same way?' The dog said he was willing, and they jogged on together.

They had not gone far before they saw a cat sitting in the middle of the road and making a most rueful face. 'Pray, my good lady,' said the ass, 'what's the matter with you? You look quite out of spirits!' 'Ah, me!' said the cat, 'how can one be in good spirits when one's life is in danger? Because I am beginning to grow old, and had rather lie at my ease by the fire than run about the house after the mice, my mistress laid hold of me, and was going to drown me; and though I have been lucky enough to get away from her, I do not know what I am to live upon.' 'Oh,' said the ass, 'by all means go with us to the great city; you are a good night singer, and may make your fortune as a musician.' The cat was pleased with the thought, and joined the party.

Soon afterwards, as they were passing by a farmyard, they saw a cock perched upon a gate, and screaming out with all his might and main. 'Bravo!' said the ass; 'upon my word, you make a famous noise; pray what is all this about?' 'Why,' said the cock, 'I was just now saying that we should have fine weather for our washing-day, and yet my mistress and the cook don't thank me for my pains, but threaten to cut off my head tomorrow, and make broth of me for the guests that are coming on Sunday!' 'Heaven forbid!' said the ass, 'come with us Master Chanticleer; it will be better, at any rate, than staying here to have your head cut off! Besides, who knows? If we care to sing in tune, we may get up some kind of a concert; so come along with us.' 'With all my heart,' said the cock: so they all four went on jollily together.

They could not, however, reach the great city the first day; so when night came on, they went into a wood to sleep. The ass and the dog laid themselves down under a great tree, and the cat climbed up into the branches; while the cock, thinking that the higher he sat the safer he should be, flew up to the very top of the tree, and then, according to his custom, before he went to sleep, looked out on all sides of him to see that everything was well. In doing this, he saw afar off something bright and shining and calling to his companions said, 'There must be a house no great way off, for I see a light.' 'If that be the case,' said the ass, 'we had better change our quarters, for our lodging is not the best in the world!' 'Besides,' added the dog, 'I should not be the worse for a bone or two, or a bit of meat.' So they walked off together towards the spot where Chanticleer had seen the light, and as they drew near it became larger and brighter, till they at last came close to a house in which a gang of robbers lived.

The ass, being the tallest of the company, marched up to the window and peeped in. 'Well, Donkey,' said Chanticleer, 'what do you see?' 'What do I see?' replied the ass. 'Why, I see a table spread with all kinds of good things, and robbers sitting round it making merry.' 'That would be a noble lodging for us,' said the cock. 'Yes,' said the ass, 'if we could only get in'; so they consulted together how they should contrive to get the robbers out; and at last they hit upon a plan. The ass placed himself upright on his hind legs, with his forefeet resting against the window; the dog got upon his back; the cat scrambled up to the dog's shoulders, and the cock flew up and sat upon the cat's head. When all was ready a signal was given, and they began their music. The ass brayed, the dog barked, the cat mewed, and the cock screamed; and then they all broke through the window at once, and came tumbling into the room, amongst the broken glass, with a most hideous clatter! The robbers, who had been not a little frightened by the opening concert, had now no doubt that some frightful hobgoblin had broken in upon them, and scampered away as fast as they could.

The coast once clear, our travellers soon sat down and dispatched what the robbers had left, with as much eagerness as if they had not expected to eat again for a month. As soon as they had satisfied themselves, they put out the lights, and each once more sought out a resting place to his own liking. The donkey laid himself down upon a heap of straw in the yard, the dog stretched himself upon a mat behind the door, the cat rolled herself up on the hearth before the warm ashes, and the cock perched upon a beam on the top of the house;

and, as they were all rather tired with their journey, they soon fell asleep.

But about midnight, when the robbers saw from afar that the lights were out and that all seemed quiet, they began to think that they had been in too great a hurry to run away; and one of them, who was bolder than the rest, went to see what was going on. Finding everything still, he marched into the kitchen, and groped about till he found a match in order to light a candle; and then, espying the glittering fiery eyes of the cat, he mistook them for live coals, and held the match to them to light it. But the cat, not understanding this joke, sprang at his face, and spat, and scratched at him. This frightened him dreadfully, and away he ran to the back door; but there the dog jumped up and bit him in the leg; and as he was crossing over the yard the ass kicked him; and the cock, who had been awakened by the noise, crowed with all his might. At this the robber ran back as fast as he could to his comrades, and told the captain how a horrid witch had got into the house, and had spat at him and scratched his face with her long bony fingers; how a man with a knife in his hand had hidden himself behind the door, and stabbed him in the leg; how a black monster stood in the yard and struck him with a club, and how the devil had sat upon the top of the house and cried out, 'Throw the rascal up here!' After this the robbers never dared to go back to the house; but the musicians were so pleased with their quarters that they took up their abode there; and there they are, I dare say, at this very day.

OLD SULTAN

A shepherd had a faithful dog, called Sultan, who was grown very old, and had lost all his teeth. And one day when the shepherd and his wife were standing together before the house the shepherd said, 'I will shoot old Sultan tomorrow morning, for he is of no use now.' But his wife said, 'Pray let the poor faithful creature live; he has served us well a great many years, and we ought to give him a livelihood for the rest of his days.' 'But what can we do with him?' said the shepherd, 'he has not a tooth in his head, and the thieves don't care for him at all; to be sure he has served us, but then he did it to earn his livelihood; tomorrow shall be his last day, depend upon it.'

Poor Sultan, who was lying close by them, heard all that the shepherd and his wife said to one another, and was very much frightened to think tomorrow would be his last day; so in the evening he went to his good friend the wolf, who lived in the wood, and told him all his sorrows, and how his master meant to kill him in the morning. 'Make yourself easy,' said the wolf, 'I will give you some good advice. Your master, you know, goes out every morning very early with his wife into the field; and they take their little child with them, and lay it down behind the hedge in the shade while they are at work. Now do you lie down close by the child, and pretend to be watching it, and I will come out of the wood and run away with it; you must run after me as fast as you can, and I will let it drop; then you may carry it back, and they will think you have saved their child, and will be so thankful to you that they will take care of you as long as you live.' The dog liked this plan very well; and accordingly so it was managed. The wolf ran with the child a little way; the shepherd and his wife screamed out; but Sultan soon overtook him, and carried the poor little thing back to his master and mistress. Then the shepherd patted him on the head, and said, 'Old Sultan has saved our child from the wolf, and therefore he shall live and be well taken care of, and have plenty to eat. Wife, go home, and give him a good dinner, and let him have my old cushion to sleep on as long as he lives.' So from this time forward Sultan had all that he could wish for.

Soon afterwards the wolf came and wished him joy, and said, 'Now, my good fellow, you must tell no tales, but turn your head the other way when I want to taste one of the old shepherd's fine fat sheep.' 'No,' said the Sultan; 'I will be true to my master.' However, the wolf thought he was in joke, and came one night to get a dainty morsel. But Sultan had told his master what the wolf meant to do; so he laid wait for him behind the barn door, and when the wolf was busy looking out for a good fat sheep, he had a stout cudgel laid about his back, that combed his locks for him finely.

Then the wolf was very angry, and called Sultan 'an old rogue,' and swore he would have his revenge. So the next morning the wolf sent the boar to challenge Sultan to come into the wood to fight the matter. Now Sultan had nobody he could ask to be his second but the shepherd's old three-legged cat; so he took her with him, and as the poor thing limped along with some trouble, she stuck up her tail straight in the air.

The wolf and the wild boar were first on the ground; and when they espied their enemies coming, and saw the cat's long tail standing straight in the air, they thought she was carrying a sword for Sultan to fight with; and every time she limped, they thought she was picking up a stone to throw at them; so they said they should not like this way of fighting, and the boar lay down behind a bush, and the wolf jumped up into a tree. Sultan and the cat soon came up, and looked about and wondered that no one was there. The boar, however, had not quite hidden himself, for his ears stuck out of the bush; and when he shook one of them a little, the cat, seeing something move, and thinking it was a mouse, sprang upon it, and bit and scratched it, so that the boar jumped up and grunted, and ran away, roaring out, 'Look up in the tree, there sits the one who is to blame.' So they looked up, and espied the wolf sitting amongst the branches; and they called him a cowardly rascal, and would not suffer him to come down till he was heartily ashamed of himself, and had promised to be good friends again with old Sultan.

THE STRAW, THE COAL,
AND THE BEAN

In a village dwelt a poor old woman, who had gathered together a dish of beans and wanted to cook them. So she made a fire on her hearth, and that it might burn the quicker, she lighted it with a handful of straw. When she was emptying the beans into the pan, one dropped without her observing it, and lay on the ground beside a straw, and soon afterwards a burning coal from the fire leapt down to the two. Then the straw began and said: 'Dear friends, from whence do you come here?' The coal replied: 'I fortunately sprang out of the fire, and if I had not escaped by sheer force, my death would have been certain—I should have been burnt to ashes.' The bean said: 'I too have escaped with a whole skin, but if the old woman had got me into the pan, I should have been made into broth without any mercy, like my comrades.' 'And would a better fate have fallen to my lot?' said the straw. 'The old woman has destroyed all my brethren in fire and smoke; she seized sixty of them at once, and took their lives. I luckily slipped through her fingers.'

'But what are we to do now?' said the coal.

'I think,' answered the bean, 'that as we have so fortunately escaped death, we should keep together like good companions, and lest a new mischance should overtake us here, we should go away together, and repair to a foreign country.'

The proposition pleased the two others, and they set out on their way together. Soon, however, they came to a little brook, and as there was no bridge or foot-plank, they did not know how they were to get over it. The straw hit on a good idea, and said: 'I will lay myself straight across, and then you can walk over on me as on a bridge.' The straw therefore stretched itself from one bank to the other, and the coal, who was of an impetuous disposition, tripped quite boldly on to the newly-built bridge. But when she had reached the middle, and heard the water rushing beneath her, she was after all, afraid, and stood still, and ventured no farther. The straw, however, began to burn, broke in two pieces, and fell into the stream. The coal slipped after her, hissed when she got into the water, and breathed her last. The bean, who had prudently stayed behind on the shore, could not but laugh at the event, was unable to stop, and laughed so heartily that she burst. It would have been all over with her, likewise, if, by good fortune, a tailor who was travelling in search of work, had not sat down to rest by the brook. As he had a compassionate heart he pulled out his needle and thread, and sewed her together. The bean thanked him most prettily, but as the tailor used black thread, all beans since then have a black seam.

BRIAR ROSE

A king and queen once upon a time reigned in a country a
great way off, where there were in those days fairies. Now this
king and queen had plenty of money, and plenty of fine clothes
to wear, and plenty of good things to eat and drink, and a
coach to ride out in every day: but though they had been
married many years they had no children, and this grieved
them very much indeed. But one day as the queen was walking
by the side of the river, at the bottom of the garden, she saw
a poor little fish, that had thrown itself out of the water, and
lay gasping and nearly dead on the bank. Then the queen took
pity on the little fish, and threw it back again into the river;
and before it swam away it lifted its head out of the water and
said, 'I know what your wish is, and it shall be fulfilled, in
return for your kindness to me—you will soon have a daughter.'
What the little fish had foretold soon came to pass; and the
queen had a little girl, so very beautiful that the king could
not cease looking on it for joy, and said he would hold a great
feast and make merry, and show the child to all the land. So
he asked his kinsmen, and nobles, and friends, and neighbours.
But the queen said, 'I will have the fairies also, that they might
be kind and good to our little daughter.' Now there were
thirteen fairies in the kingdom; but as the king and queen had

only twelve golden dishes for them to eat out of, they were forced to leave one of the fairies without asking her. So twelve fairies came, each with a high red cap on her head, and red shoes with high heels on her feet, and a long white wand in her hand: and after the feast was over they gathered round in a ring and gave all their best gifts to the little princess. One gave her goodness, another beauty, another riches, and so on till she had all that was good in the world.

Just as eleven of them had done blessing her, a great noise was heard in the courtyard, and word was brought that the thirteenth fairy was come, with a black cap on her head, and black shoes on her feet, and a broomstick in her hand: and presently up she came into the dining-hall. Now, as she had not been asked to the feast she was very angry, and scolded the king and queen very much, and set to work to take her revenge. So she cried out, 'The king's daughter shall, in her fifteenth year, be wounded by a spindle, and fall down dead.' Then the twelfth of the friendly fairies, who had not yet given her gift, came forward, and said that the evil wish must be fulfilled, but that she could soften its mischief; so her gift was, that the king's daughter, when the spindle wounded her, should not really die, but should only fall asleep for a hundred years.

However, the king hoped still to save his dear child altogether from the threatened evil; so he ordered that all the spindles in the kingdom should be bought up and burnt. But all the gifts of the first eleven fairies were in the meantime fulfilled; for the princess was so beautiful, and well behaved, and good, and wise, that everyone who knew her loved her.

It happened that, on the very day she was fifteen years old, the king and queen were not at home, and she was left alone in the palace. So she roved about by herself, and looked at all the rooms and chambers, till at last she came to an old tower, to which there was a narrow staircase ending with a little door. In the door there was a golden key, and when she turned it the door sprang open, and there sat an old lady spinning away very busily. 'Why, how now, good mother,' said the princess; 'what are you doing there?' 'Spinning,' said the old lady, and nodded her head, humming a tune, while buzz! went the wheel. 'How prettily that little thing turns round!' said the princess, and took the spindle and began to try and spin. But scarcely had she touched it, before the fairy's prophecy was fulfilled; the spindle wounded her, and she fell down lifeless on the ground.

However, she was not dead, but had only fallen into a deep sleep; and the king and the queen, who had just come home, and all their court, fell asleep too; and the horses slept in the stables, and the dogs in the court, the pigeons on the house-top, and the very flies slept upon the walls. Even the fire on the hearth left off blazing, and went to sleep; the jack stopped, and the spit that was turning about with a goose upon it for the king's dinner stood still; and the cook, who was at that moment pulling the kitchen-boy by the hair to give him a box on the ear for something he had done amiss, let him go, and both fell asleep; the butler, who was slyly tasting the ale, fell asleep with the jug at his lips: and thus everything stood still, and slept soundly.

A large hedge of thorns soon grew round the palace, and every year it became higher and thicker; till at last the old palace was surrounded and hidden, so that not even the roof or the chimneys could be seen. But there went a report through all the land of the beautiful sleeping Briar Rose (for so the king's daughter was called): so that, from time to time, several kings' sons came, and tried to break through the thicket into the palace. This, however, none of them could ever do; for the thorns and bushes laid hold of them, as it were with hands; and there they stuck fast, and died wretchedly.

After many, many years there came a king's son into that land: and an old man told him the story of the thicket of thorns; and how a beautiful palace stood behind it, and how a wonderful princess, called Briar Rose, lay in it asleep, with all her court. He told, too, how he had heard from his grand-father that many, many princes had come, and had tried to break through the thicket, but that they had all stuck fast in it, and died. Then the young prince said, 'All this shall not frighten me; I will go and see this Briar Rose.' The old man tried to hinder him, but he was bent upon going.

Now that very day the hundred years were ended; and as the prince came to the thicket he saw nothing but beautiful flowering shrubs, through which he went with ease, and they shut in after him as thick as ever. Then he came at last to the palace, and there in the court lay the dogs asleep; and the horses were standing in the stables; and on the roof sat the pigeons fast asleep, with their heads under their wings. And when he came into the palace, the flies were sleeping on the walls; the spit was standing still; the butler had the jug of ale at his lips, going to drink a draught; the maid sat with a fowl in her lap ready to be plucked; and the cook in the kitchen was still holding up her hand, as if she was going to beat the boy.

Then he went on still farther, and all was so still that he could hear every breath he drew; till at last he came to the old tower, and opened the door of the little room in which Briar Rose was; and there she lay, fast asleep on a couch by the window. She looked so beautiful that he could not take his eyes off her, so he stooped down and gave her a kiss. But the moment he kissed her she opened her eyes and awoke, and smiled upon him; and they went out together; and soon the king and queen also awoke, and all the court, and gazed on each other with great wonder. And the horses shook themselves, and the dogs jumped up and barked; the pigeons took their heads from under their wings, and looked about and flew into the fields; the flies on the walls buzzed again; the fire in the kitchen blazed up; round went the jack, and round went the spit, with the goose for the king's dinner upon it; the butler finished his draught of ale; the maid went on plucking the fowl; and the cook gave the boy the box on his ear.

And then the prince and Briar Rose were married, and the wedding feast was given; and they lived happily together all their lives long.

THE DOG AND THE
SPARROW

A shepherd's dog had a master who took no care of him, but often let him suffer the greatest hunger. At last he could bear it no longer; so he took to his heels, and off he ran in a very sad and sorrowful mood. On the road he met a sparrow that said to him, 'Why are you so sad, my friend?' 'Because,' said the dog, 'I am very very hungry, and have nothing to eat.' 'If that be all,' answered the sparrow, 'come with me into the next town, and I will soon find you plenty of food.' So on they went together into the town: and as they passed by a butcher's shop, the sparrow said to the dog, 'Stand there a little while till I peck you down a piece of meat.' So the sparrow perched upon the shelf: and having first looked carefully about her to see if anyone was watching her, she pecked and scratched at a steak that lay upon the edge of the shelf, till at last down it fell. Then the dog snapped it up, and scrambled away with it into a corner, where he soon ate it all up. 'Well,' said the sparrow, 'you shall have some more if you will; so come with me to the next shop, and I will peck you down another steak.' When the dog had eaten this too, the sparrow said to him, 'Well, my good friend, have you had enough now?' 'I have had plenty of meat,' answered he, 'but I should like to have a piece of bread to eat after it.' 'Come with me then,' said the sparrow, 'and you shall soon have that too.' So she took him to a baker's shop, and pecked at two rolls that lay in the window, till they fell down: and as the dog still wished for more, she took him to another shop and pecked down some more for him. When that was eaten, the sparrow asked him whether he had had enough now. 'Yes,' said he; 'and now let us take a walk a little way out of the town.' So they both went out upon the high road; but as the weather was warm, they had not gone far before the dog said, 'I am very much tired—I should like to take a nap.' 'Very well,' answered the sparrow, 'do so, and in the meantime I will perch upon that bush.' So the dog stretched himself out on the road, and fell fast asleep. Whilst he slept, there came by a carter with a cart drawn by three horses, and loaded with two casks of wine. The sparrow, seeing that the carter did not turn out of the way, but would go on in the track in which the dog lay, so as to drive over him, called out, 'Stop! stop! Mr Carter, or it shall be the worse for you.' But the carter, grumbling to himself, 'You make it the worse for me, indeed! what can you do?' cracked his whip, and drove his cart over the poor dog, so that the wheels crushed him to death. 'There,' cried the sparrow, 'thou cruel villain, thou hast killed my friend the dog. Now mind what I say. This deed of thine shall cost thee all thou art worth.' 'Do your worst, and welcome,' said the brute, 'what harm can you do me?' and passed on. But the sparrow crept under the tilt of the cart, and pecked at the bung of one of the casks till she loosened it; and than all the wine ran out, without the carter seeing it. At last he looked round, and saw that the cart was dripping, and the cask quite empty. 'What an unlucky wretch I am!' cried he. 'Not wretch enough yet!' said the sparrow, as she alighted upon the head of one of the horses, and pecked at him till he reared up and kicked. When the carter saw this, he drew out his hatchet and aimed a blow at the sparrow, meaning to kill her; but she flew away, and the blow fell upon the poor horse's head with such force, that he fell down dead. 'Unlucky wretch that I am!' cried he. 'Not wretch enough yet!' said the sparrow. And as the carter went on with the other two horses, she again crept under the tilt of the cart, and pecked out the bung of the second cask, so that all the wine ran out. When the carter saw this, he again cried out, 'Miserable wretch that I am!' But the sparrow answered, 'Not wretch enough yet!' and perched on the head of the second horse, and pecked at him too. The carter ran up and struck at her again with his hatchet; but away she flew, and the blow fell upon the second horse and killed him on the spot. 'Unlucky wretch that I am!' said he. 'Not wretch enough yet!' said the sparrow; and perching upon the third horse, she began to peck him too. The carter was mad with fury; and without looking about him, or caring what he was about, struck again at the sparrow; but killed his third horse as he done the other two. 'Alas! miserable wretch that I am!' cried he. 'Not wretch enough yet!' answered the sparrow as she flew away; 'now will I plague and punish thee at thy own house.' The carter was forced at last to leave his cart behind him, and to go home overflowing with rage and vexation. 'Alas!' said he to his wife, 'what ill luck has befallen me!—my wine is all spilt, and my horses all three dead.' 'Alas! husband,' replied she, 'and a wicked bird has come into the house, and has brought with her all the birds in the world, I am sure, and they have fallen upon our corn in the loft, and are eating it up at such a rate!' Away ran the husband upstairs, and saw thousands of birds sitting upon the floor eating up his corn, with the sparrow in the midst of them. 'Unlucky wretch that I am!' cried the carter; for he saw that the corn was almost all gone. 'Not wretch enough yet!' said the sparrow; 'thy cruelty shall cost thee thy life yet!' and away she flew.

The carter seeing that he had thus lost all that he had, went down into his kitchen; and was still not sorry for what he had done, but sat himself angrily and sulkily in the chimney corner. But the sparrow sat on the outside of the window, and cried 'Carter! thy cruelty shall cost thee thy life!' With that he jumped up in a rage, seized his hatchet, and threw it at the sparrow; but it missed her, and only broke the window. The sparrow now hopped in, perched upon the window-seat, and cried, 'Carter! it shall cost thee thy life!' Then he became mad and blind with rage, and struck the window-seat with such force that he cleft it in two: and as the sparrow flew from place to place, the carter and his wife were so furious, that they broke all their furniture, glasses, chairs, benches, the table, and at last the walls, without touching the bird at all. In the end, however, they caught her: and the wife said, 'Shall I kill her at once?' 'No,' cried he, 'that is letting her off too easily: she shall die a much more cruel death; I will eat her.' But the sparrow began to flutter about, and stretch out her neck and cried, 'Carter! it shall cost thee thy life yet!' With that he could wait no longer: so he gave his wife the hatchet, and cried, 'Wife, strike at the bird and kill her in my hand.' And the wife struck; but she missed her aim, and hit her husband on the head so that he fell down dead, and the sparrow flew quietly home to her nest.

THE TWELVE DANCING
PRINCESSES

There was a king who had twelve beautiful daughters. They slept in twelve beds all in one room; and when they went to bed, the doors were shut and locked up; but every morning their shoes were found to be quite worn through as if they had been danced in all night; and yet nobody could find out how it happened, or where they had been.

Then the king made it known to all the land, that if any person could discover the secret, and find out where it was that the princesses danced in the night, he should have the one he liked best for his wife, and should be king after his death; but whoever tried and did not succeed, after three days and nights, should be put to death.

A king's son soon came. He was well entertained, and in the evening was taken to the chamber next to the one where the princesses lay in their twelve beds. There he was to sit and watch where they went to dance; and, in order that nothing might pass without his hearing it, the door of his chamber was left open. But the king's son soon fell asleep; and when he awoke in the morning he found that the princesses had all been dancing, for the soles of their shoes were full of holes. The same thing happened the second and third night: so the king ordered his head to be cut off. After him came several others; but they had all the same luck, and all lost their lives in the same manner.

Now it chanced that an old soldier, who had been wounded in battle and could fight no longer, passed through the country where this king reigned: and as he was travelling through a wood, he met an old woman, who asked him where he was going. 'I hardly know where I am going, or what I had better do,' said the soldier; 'but I think I should like very well to find out where it is that the princesses dance, and then in time I might be a king.' 'Well,' said the old dame, 'that is no very hard task: only take care not to drink any of the wine which one of the princesses will bring to you in the evening; and as soon as she leaves you pretend to be fast asleep.'

Then she gave him a cloak, and said, 'As soon as you put that on you will become invisible, and you will then be able to follow the princesses wherever they go.' When the soldier heard all this good counsel, he determined to try his luck: so he went to the king, and said he was willing to undertake the task.

He was as well received as the others had been, and the king ordered fine royal robes to be given him; and when the evening came he was led to the outer chamber. Just as he was going to lie down, the eldest of the princesses brought him a cup of wine; but the soldier threw it all away secretly, taking care not to drink a drop. Then he laid himself down on his bed, and in a little while began to snore very loud as if he was fast asleep. When the twelve princesses heard this they laughed heartily; and the eldest said, 'This fellow too might have done a wiser thing than lose his life in this way!' Then they rose up and opened their drawers and boxes, and took out all their fine clothes, and dressed themselves at the glass, and skipped about as if they were eager to begin dancing. But the youngest said, 'I don't know how it is, while you are so happy I feel very uneasy; I am sure some mischance will befall us.' 'You simpleton,' said the eldest, 'you are always afraid; have you forgotten how many kings' sons have already watched in vain? And as for this soldier, even if I had not given him his sleeping draught, he would have slept soundly enough.'

When they were all ready, they went and looked at the soldier; but he snored on, and did not stir hand or foot: so they thought they were quite safe; and the eldest went up to her own bed and clapped her hands, and the bed sank into the floor and a trap-door flew open. The soldier saw them going down through the trap-door one after another, the eldest leading the way; and thinking he had no time to lose, he jumped up, put on the cloak which the old woman had given him, and followed them; but in the middle of the stairs he trod on the gown of the youngest princess, and she cried out to her sisters, 'All is not right; someone took hold of my gown.' 'You silly creature!' said the eldest, 'it is nothing but a nail in the wall.' Then down they all went, and at the bottom they found themselves in a most delightful grove of trees; and the leaves were all of silver, and glittered and sparkled beautifully. The soldier wished to take away some token of the place; so he broke off a little branch, and there came a loud noise from the tree. Then the youngest daughter said again, 'I am sure all is not right—did not you hear that noise? That never happened before.' But the eldest said, 'It is only our princes, who are shouting for joy at our approach.' Then they came to another grove of trees, where all the leaves were of gold; and afterwards to a third, where the leaves were all glittering diamonds. And the soldier broke a branch from each; and every time there was a loud noise, which made the youngest sister tremble with fear; but the eldest still said, it was only the princes, who were crying for joy. So they went on till they came to a great lake; and at the side of the lake there lay twelve little boats with twelve handsome princes in them, who seemed to be waiting there for the princesses.

One of the princesses went into each boat, and the soldier

stepped into the same boat with the youngest. As they were rowing over the lake, the prince who was in the boat with the youngest princess and the soldier said, 'I do not know why it is, but though I am rowing with all my might we do not get on so fast as usual, and I am quite tired: the boat seems very heavy today.' 'It is only the heat of the weather,' said the princess: 'I feel it very warm too.'

On the other side of the lake stood a fine illuminated castle, from which came the merry music of horns and trumpets. There they all landed, and went into the castle, and each prince danced with his princess; and the soldier, who was all the time invisible, danced with them too; and when any of the princesses had a cup of wine set by her, he drank it all up, so that when she put the cup to her mouth it was empty. At this, too, the youngest sister was terribly frightened, but the eldest always silenced her. They danced on till three o'clock in the morning, and then all their shoes were worn out, so that they were obliged to leave off. The princes rowed them back again over the lake (but this time the soldier placed himself in the boat with the eldest princess); and on the opposite shore they took leave of each other, the princesses promising to come again the next night.

When they came to the stairs, the soldier ran on before the princesses, and laid himself down; and as the twelve sisters slowly came up very much tired, they heard him snoring in his bed; so they said, 'Now all is quite safe'; then they undressed themselves, put away their fine clothes, pulled off their shoes, and went to bed. In the morning the soldier said nothing about what had happened, but determined to see more of this strange adventure, and went again the second and third night; and every thing happened just as before; the princesses danced each time till their shoes were worn to pieces, and then returned home. However, on the third night the soldier carried away one of the golden cups as a token of where he had been.

As soon as the time came when he was to declare the secret, he was taken before the king with the three branches and the golden cup; and the twelve princesses stood listening behind the door to hear what he would say. And when the king asked him. 'Where do my twelve daughters dance at night?' he answered, 'With twelve princes in a castle under ground.' And then he told the king all that had happened, and showed him the three branches and the golden cup which he had brought with him. Then the king called for the princesses, and asked them whether what the soldier said was true: and when they saw that they were discovered, and that it was of no use to deny what had happened, they confessed it all. And the king asked the soldier which of them he would choose for his wife; and he answered, 'I am not very young, so I will have the eldest.'—And they were married that very day, and the soldier was chosen to be the king's heir.

THE FISHERMAN AND
HIS WIFE

There was once a fisherman who lived with his wife in a pigsty, close by the seaside. The fisherman used to go out all day long a-fishing; and one day, as he sat on the shore with his rod, looking at the sparkling waves and watching his line, all of a sudden his float was dragged away deep into the water: and in drawing it up he pulled out a great fish. But the fish said, 'Pray let me live! I am not a real fish; I am an enchanted prince: put me in the water again, and let me go!' 'Oh, ho!' said the man, 'you need not make so many words about the matter; I will have nothing to do with a fish that can talk: so swim away, sir, as soon as you please!' Then he put him back into the water, and the fish darted straight down to the bottom, and left a long streak of blood behind him on the wave.

When the fisherman went home to his wife in the pigsty, he told her how he had caught a great fish, and how it had told him it was an enchanted prince, and how, on hearing it speak, he had let it go again. 'Did not you ask it for anything?' said the wife, 'we live very wretchedly here, in this nasty dirty pigsty; do go back and tell the fish we want a snug little cottage.'

The fisherman did not much like the business: however,

he went to the seashore; and when he came back there the water looked all yellow and green. And he stood at the water's edge, and said:

> *'O man of the sea!*
> *Hearken to me!*
> *My wife Ilsabill*
> *Will have her own will,*
> *And hath sent me to beg a boon of thee!'*

Then the fish came swimming to him, and said, 'Well, what is her will? What does your wife want?' 'Ah!' said the fisherman, 'she says that when I had caught you, I ought to have asked you for something before I let you go; she does not like living any longer in the pigsty, and wants a snug little cottage.' 'Go home, then,' said the fish; 'she is in the cottage already!' So the man went home, and saw his wife standing at the door of a nice trim little cottage. 'Come in, come in!' said she; 'is not this much better than the filthy pigsty we had?' And there was a parlour, and a bedchamber, and a kitchen; and behind the cottage there was a little garden, planted with all sorts of flowers and fruits; and there was a courtyard behind, full of ducks and chickens. 'Ah!' said the fisherman, 'how happily we shall live now!' 'We will try to do so, at least,' said his wife.

Everything went right for a week or two, and then Dame Ilsabill said, 'Husband, there is not near room enough for us in this cottage; the courtyard and the garden are a great deal too small; I should like to have a large stone castle to live in: go to the fish again and tell him to give us a castle.' 'Wife,' said the fisherman, 'I don't like to go to him again, for perhaps he will be angry; we ought to be easy with this pretty cottage to live in.' 'Nonsense!' said the wife; 'he will do it very willingly, I know; go along and try!'

The fisherman went, but his heart was very heavy: and

when he came to the sea, it looked blue and gloomy, though it was very calm; and he went close to the edge of the waves, and said:

> 'O man of the sea!
> Hearken to me!
> My wife Ilsabill
> Will have her own will,
> And hath sent me to beg a boon of thee!'

'Well, what does she want now?' said the fish. 'Ah!' said the man, dolefully, 'my wife wants to live in a stone castle.' 'Go home, then,' said the fish; 'she is standing at the gate of it already.' So away went the fisherman, and found his wife standing before the gate of a great castle. 'See,' said she, 'is not this grand?' With that they went into the castle together, and found a great many servants there, and the rooms all richly furnished, and full of golden chairs and tables; and behind the castle was a garden, and around it was a park half a mile long, full of sheep, and goats, and hares, and deer; and in the courtyard were stables and cow-houses. 'Well,' said the man, 'now we will live cheerful and happy in this beautiful castle for the rest of our lives.' 'Perhaps we may,' said the wife; 'but let us sleep upon it, before we make up our minds to that.' So they went to bed.

The next morning when Dame Ilsabill awoke it was broad daylight, and she jogged the fisherman with her elbow, and said, 'Get up, husband, and bestir yourself, for we must be king of all the land.' 'Wife, wife,' said the man, 'why should we wish to be the king? I will not be king.' 'Then I will,' said she. 'But, wife,' said the fisherman, 'how can you be king—the fish cannot make you a king?' 'Husband,' said she, 'say no more about it, but go and try! I will be king.' So the man went away quite sorrowful to think that his wife should want to be king. This time the sea looked a dark grey colour, and

was overspread with curling waves and the ridges of foam as
he cried out:

> *'O man of the sea!*
> *Hearken to me!*
> *My wife Ilsabill*
> *Will have her own will,*
> *And hath sent me to beg a boon of thee!'*

'Well, what would she have now?' said the fish. 'Alas!'
said the poor man, 'my wife wants to be king.' 'Go home,'
said the fish; 'she is king already.'

Then the fisherman went home; and as he came close
to the palace he saw a troop of soldiers, and heard the sound
of drums and trumpets. And when he went in he saw his wife
sitting on a throne of gold and diamonds, with a golden crown
upon her head; and on each side of her stood six fair maidens,
each a head taller than the other. 'Well, wife,' said the
fisherman, 'are you king?' 'Yes,' said she, 'I am king.' And
when he had looked at her for a long time, he said, 'Ah, wife!
what a fine thing it is to be king! Now we shall never have
anything more to wish for as long as we live.' 'I don't know
how that may be,' said she; 'never is a long time. I am king,
it is true; but I begin to be tired of that, and I think I should
like to be emperor.' 'Alas, wife! why should you wish to be
emperor?' said the fisherman. 'Husband,' said she, 'go to the
fish! I say I will be emperor.' 'Ah, wife!' replied the fisherman,
'the fish cannot make an emperor, I am sure, and I should
not like to ask him for such a thing.' 'I am king,' said Ilsabill,
'and you are my slave; so go at once!'

So the fisherman was forced to go; and he muttered as
he went along, 'This will come to no good, it is too much to
ask; the fish will be tired at last, and then we shall be sorry
for what we have done.' He soon came to the seashore; and
the water was quite black and muddy, and a mighty whirlwind

blew over the waves and rolled them about, but he went as near as he could to the water's brink, and said:

> *'O man of the sea!*
> *Hearken to me!*
> *My wife Ilsabill*
> *Will have her own will,*
> *And hath sent me to beg a boon of thee!'*

'What would she have now?' said the fish. 'Ah!' said the fisherman, 'she wants to be emperor.' 'Go home,' said the fish; 'she is emperor already.'

So he went home again; and as he came near he saw his wife Ilsabill sitting on a very lofty throne made of solid gold, with a great crown on her head full two yards high; and on each side of her stood her guards and attendants in a row, each one smaller than the other, from the tallest giant down to a little dwarf no bigger than my finger. And before her stood princes, and dukes, and earls: and the fisherman went up to her and said, 'Wife, are you emperor?' 'Yes,' said she, 'I am emperor.' 'Ah!' said the man, as he gazed upon her, 'what a fine thing it is to be emperor!' 'Husband,' said she, 'why should we stop at being emperor? I will be pope next.' 'O wife, wife!' said he, 'how can you be pope? there is but one pope at a time in Christendom.' 'Husband,' said she, 'I will be pope this very day.' 'But,' replied the husband, 'the fish cannot make you pope.' 'What nonsense!' said she; 'if he can make an emperor, he can make a pope: go and try him.'

So the fisherman went. But when he came to the shore the wind was raging and the sea was tossed up and down in boiling waves, and the ships were in trouble, and rolled fearfully upon the tops of the billows. In the middle of the heavens there was a little piece of blue sky, but towards the south all was red, as if a dreadful storm was rising. At this sight the fisherman was dreadfully frightened, and he trembled so that his knees knocked together: but still he went down near to the shore, and said:

> *'O man of the sea!*
> *Hearken to me!*
> *My wife Ilsabill*
> *Will have her own will,*
> *And hath sent me to beg a boon of thee!'*

'What does she want now?' said the fish. 'Ah!' said the fisherman, 'my wife wants to be pope.' 'Go home,' said the fish; 'she is pope already.'

Then the fisherman went home, and found Ilsabill sitting on a throne that was two miles high. And she had three great crowns on her head, and around her stood all the pomp and power of the Church. And on each side of her were two rows of burning lights, of all sizes, the greatest as large as the highest and biggest tower in the world, and the least no larger than a small rushlight. 'Wife,' said the fisherman, as he looked at all this greatness, 'are you pope?' 'Yes,' said she, 'I am pope.' 'Well, wife,' replied he, 'it is a grand thing to be pope; and now you must be easy, for you can be nothing greater.' 'I will think about that,' said the wife. Then they went to bed: but Dame Ilsabill could not sleep all night for thinking what she should be next. At last, as she was dropping asleep, morning broke, and the sun rose. 'Ha!' thought she, as she woke up and looked at it through the window, 'after all I cannot prevent the sun rising.' At this thought she was very angry, and wakened her husband, and said, 'Husband, go to the fish and tell him I must be lord of the sun and moon.' The fisherman was half asleep, but the thought frightened him so much that he started and fell out of bed. 'Alas, wife!' said he, 'cannot you be easy with being pope?' 'No,' said she, 'I am very uneasy as long as the sun and moon rise without my leave. Go to the fish at once!'

Then the man went shivering with fear; and as he was going down to the shore a dreadful storm arose, so that the trees and the very rocks shook. And all the heavens became black with stormy clouds, and the lightnings played, and the thunders rolled; and you might have seen in the sea great black waves, swelling up like mountains with crowns of white foam upon their heads. And the fisherman crept towards the sea, and cried out, as well as he could:

> *'O man of the sea!*
> *Hearken to me!*
> *My wife Ilsabill*
> *Will have her own will,*
> *And hath sent me to beg a boon of thee!'*

'What does she want now?' said the fish. 'Ah!' said he, 'she wants to be lord of the sun and moon.' 'Go home,' said the fish, 'to your pigsty again.'

And there they live to this very day.

THE WILLOW-WREN AND
THE BEAR

Once in summer-time the bear and the wolf were walking in the forest, and the bear heard a bird singing so beautifully that he said: 'Brother wolf, what bird is it that sings so well?' 'That is the King of birds,' said the wolf, 'before whom we must bow down.' In reality the bird was the willow-wren. 'If that's the case,' said the bear, 'I should very much like to see his royal palace; come, take me thither.' 'That is not done quite as you seem to think,' said the wolf; 'you must wait until the Queen comes,' Soon afterwards, the Queen arrived with some food in her beak, and the lord King came too, and they began to feed their young ones. The bear would have liked to go at once, but the wolf held him back by the sleeve, and said: 'No, you must wait until the lord and lady Queen have gone away again.' So they took stock of the hole where the nest lay, and trotted away. The bear, however, could not rest until he had seen the royal palace, and when a short time had passed, went to it again. The King and Queen had just flown out, so he peeped in and saw five or six young ones lying there. 'Is that the royal palace?' cried the bear; 'it is a wretched palace, and you are not King's children, you are disreputable children!' When the young wrens heard that, they were frightfully angry, and screamed: 'No, that we are not! Our parents are honest people! Bear, you will have to pay for that!'

The bear and the wolf grew uneasy, and turned back and went into their holes. The young willow-wrens, however, continued to cry and scream, and when their parents again brought food they said: 'We will not so much as touch one fly's leg, no, not if we were dying of hunger, until you have settled whether we are respectable children or not; the bear has been here and has insulted us!' Then the old King said: 'Be easy, he shall be punished,' and he at once flew with the Queen to the bear's cave, and called in: 'Old Growler, why have you insulted my children? You shall suffer for it—we will punish you by a bloody war.' Thus war was announced to the Bear, and all four-footed animals were summoned to take part in it, oxen, asses, cows, deer, and every other animal the earth contained. And the willow-wren summoned everything which flew in the air, not only birds, large and small, but midges, and hornets, bees and flies had to come.

When the time came for the war to begin, the willow-wren sent out spies to discover who was the enemy's commander-in-chief. The gnat, who was the most crafty, flew into the forest where the enemy was assembled, and hid herself beneath a leaf of the tree where the password was to be announced. There stood the bear, and he called the fox before him and said: 'Fox, you are the most cunning of all animals, you shall be general and lead us.' 'Good,' said the fox, 'but what signal shall we agree upon?' No one knew that, so the fox said: 'I have a fine long bushy tail, which almost looks like a plume of red feathers. When I lift my tail up quite high, all is going well, and you must charge; but if I let it hang down, run away as fast as you can.' When the gnat had heard that, she flew away again, and revealed everything, down to the minutest detail, to the willow-wren. When day broke, and the battle was to begin, all the four-footed animals came running up with such a noise that the earth trembled.

The willow-wren with his army also came flying through the air with such a humming, and whirring, and swarming that every one was uneasy and afraid, and on both sides they advanced against each other. But the willow-wren sent down the hornet, with orders to settle beneath the fox's tail, and sting with all his might. When the fox felt the first string, he started so that he lifted one leg, from pain, but he bore it, and still kept his tail high in the air; at the second sting, he was forced to put it down for a moment; at the third, he could hold out no longer, screamed, and put his tail between his legs. When the animals saw that, they thought all was lost, and began to flee, each into his hole, and the birds had won the battle.

Then the King and Queen flew home to their children and cried: 'Children, rejoice, eat and drink to your heart's content, we have won the battle!' But the young wrens said: 'We will not eat yet, the bear must come to the nest, and beg for pardon and say that we are honourable children, before we will do that.' Then the willow-wren flew to the bear's hole and cried: 'Growler, you are to come to the nest to my children, and beg their pardon, or else every rib of your body shall be broken.' So the bear crept thither in the greatest fear, and begged their pardon. And now at last the young wrens were satisfied, and sat down together and ate and drank, and made merry till quite late into the night.

THE FROG-PRINCE

One fine evening a young princess put on her bonnet and clogs, and went out to take a walk by herself in a wood; and when she came to a cool spring of water, that rose in the midst of it, she sat herself down to rest a while. Now she had a golden ball in her hand, which was her favourite plaything; and she was always tossing it up into the air, and catching it again as it fell. After a time she threw it up so high that she missed catching it as it fell; and the ball bounded away, and rolled along upon the ground, till at last it fell down into the spring. The princess looked into the spring after her ball, but it was very deep, so deep that she could not see the bottom of it. Then she began to bewail her loss, and said, 'Alas! if I could only get my ball again, I would give all my fine clothes and jewels, and everything that I have in the world.'

Whilst she was speaking, a frog put its head out of the water, and said, 'Princess, why do you weep so bitterly?' 'Alas!' said she, 'what can you do for me, you nasty frog? My golden ball has fallen into the spring.' The frog said, 'I want not your pearls, and jewels, and fine clothes; but if you will love me, and let me live with you and eat from off your golden plate, and sleep upon your bed, I will bring you your ball again.' 'What nonsense,' thought the princess, 'this silly frog is talking!

He can never even get out of the spring to visit me, though he may be able to get my ball for me, and therefore I will tell him he shall have what he asks.' So she said to the frog, 'Well, if you will bring me my ball, I will do all you ask.' Then the frog put his head down, and dived deep under the water; and after a little while he came up again, with the ball in his mouth, and threw it on the edge of the spring. As soon as the young princess saw her ball, she ran to pick it up; and she was so overjoyed to have it in her hand again, that she never thought of the frog, but ran home with it as fast as she could. The frog called after her, 'Stay, princess, and take me with you as you said.' But she did not stop to hear a word.

The next day, just as the princess had sat down to dinner, she heard a strange noise—tap, tap—plash, plash—as if something was coming up the marble staircase: and soon afterwards there was a gentle knock at the door, and a little voice cried out and said:

> 'Open the door, my princess dear,
> Open the door to thy true love here!
> And mind the words that thou and I said
> By the fountain cool, in the greenwood shade.'

Then the princess ran to the door and opened it, and there she saw the frog, whom she had quite forgotten. At this sight she was sadly frightened, and shutting the door as fast as she could came back to her seat. The king, her father, seeing that something had frightened her, asked her what was the matter. 'There is a nasty frog,' said she, 'at the door, that lifted my ball for me out of the spring this morning: I told him that he should live with me here, thinking that he could never get out of the spring; but there he is at the door, and he wants to come in.'

While she was speaking the frog knocked again at the door, and said:

> *'Open the door, my princess dear,*
> *Open the door to thy true love here!*
> *And mind the words that thou and I said*
> *By the fountain cool, in the greenwood shade.'*

Then the king said to the young princess, 'As you have given your word you must keep it; so go and let him in.' She did so, and the frog hopped into the room, and then straight on—tap, tap—plash, plash—from the bottom of the room to the top, till he came up close to the table where the princess sat. 'Pray lift me upon chair,' said he to the princess, 'and let me sit next to you.' As soon as she had done this, the frog said, 'Put your plate nearer to me, that I may eat out of it.' This she did, and when he had eaten as much as he could, he said, 'Now I am tired; carry me upstairs, and put me into your bed.' And the princess, though very unwilling, took him up in her hand, and put him upon the pillow of her own bed, where he slept all night long. As soon as it was light he jumped up, hopped downstairs, and went out of the house. 'Now, then,' thought the princess, 'at last he is gone, and I shall be troubled with him no more.'

But she was mistaken; for when night came again she heard the same tapping at the door; and the frog came once more, and said:

> *'Open the door, my princess dear,*
> *Open the door to thy true love here!*
> *And mind the words that thou and I said*
> *By the fountain cool, in the greenwood shade.'*

And when the princess opened the door the frog came in, and slept upon her pillow as before, till the morning broke. And the third night he did the same. But when the princess awoke on the following morning she was astonished to see, instead of the frog, a handsome prince, gazing on her with the most beautiful eyes she had ever seen, and standing at the head of her bed.

He told her that he had been enchanted by a spiteful fairy, who had changed him into a frog; and that he had been fated so to abide till some princess should take him out of the spring, and let him eat from her plate, and sleep upon her bed for three nights. 'You,' said the prince, 'have broken his cruel charm, and now I have nothing to wish for but that you should go with me into my father's kingdom, where I will marry you, and love you as long as you live.'

The young princess, you may be sure, was not long in saying 'Yes' to all this; and as they spoke a gay coach drove up, with eight beautiful horses, decked with plumes of feathers and a golden harness; and behind the coach rode the prince's servant, faithful Heinrich, who had bewailed the misfortunes of his dear master during his enchantment so long and so bitterly, that his heart had well-nigh burst.

They then took leave of the king, and got into the coach with eight horses, and all set out, full of joy and merriment, for the prince's kingdom, which they reached safely; and there they lived happily a great many years.

CAT AND MOUSE IN PARTNERSHIP

A certain cat had made the acquaintance of a mouse, and had said so much to her about the great love and friendship she felt for her, that at length the mouse agreed that they should live and keep house together. 'But we must make a provision for winter, or else we shall suffer from hunger,' said the cat; 'and you, little mouse, cannot venture everywhere, or you will be caught in a trap some day.' The good advice was followed, and a pot of fat was bought, but they did not know where to put it. At length, after much consideration, the cat said: 'I know no place where it will be better stored up than in the church, for no one dares take anything away from there. We will set it beneath the altar, and not touch it until we are really in need of it.' So the pot was placed in safety, but it was not long before the cat had a great yearning for it, and said to the mouse: 'I want to tell you something, little mouse; my cousin has brought a little son into the world, and has asked me to be godmother; he is white with brown spots, and I am to hold him over the font at the christening. Let me go out today, and you look after the house by yourself.' 'Yes, yes,' answered the mouse, 'by all means go, and if you get anything very good to eat, think of me. I should like a drop of sweet red christening wine myself.' All this, however, was untrue; the cat had no cousin, and had not been asked to be godmother. She went straight to the church, stole to the pot of fat, began to lick at it, and licked the top of the fat off. Then she took a walk upon the roofs of the town, looked out for opportunities, and then stretched herself in the sun, and licked her lips whenever she thought of the pot of fat, and not until it was evening did she return home. 'Well, here you are again,' said the mouse, 'no doubt you have had a merry day.' 'All went off well,' answered the cat. 'What name did they give the child?' 'Top-off!' said the cat quite coolly. 'Top-off!' cried the mouse, 'that is a very odd and uncommon name, is it a usual one in your family?' 'What does that matter,' said the cat, 'it is no worse than Crumb-stealer, as your godchildren are called.'

Before long the cat was seized by another fit of yearning. She said to the mouse: 'You must do me a favour, and once more manage the house for a day alone. I am again asked to be godmother, and, as the child has a white ring round its neck, I cannot refuse.' The good mouse consented, but the cat crept behind the town walls to the church, and devoured half the pot of fat. 'Nothing ever seems so good as what one keeps to oneself,' said she, and was quite satisfied with her day's work. When she went home the mouse inquired: 'And what was the child christened?' 'Half-done,' answered the cat. 'Half-done! What are you saying? I never heard the name in my life, I'll wager anything it is not in the calendar!'

The cat's mouth soon began to water for some more licking. 'All good things go in threes,' said she, 'I am asked to stand godmother again. The child is quite black, only it has white paws, but with that exception, it has not a single white hair on its whole body; this only happens once every few years, you will let me go, won't you?' 'Top-off! Half-done!' answered the mouse, 'they are such odd names, they make me very thoughtful.' 'You sit at home,' said the cat, 'in your dark-grey fur coat and long tail, and are filled with fancies, that's because you do not go out in the daytime.' During the cat's absence the mouse cleaned the house, and put it in order, but the greedy cat entirely emptied the pot of fat. 'When everything is eaten up one has some peace,' said she to herself, and well filled and fat she did not return home till night. The mouse at once asked what name had been given to the third child. 'It will not please you more than the others,' said the cat. 'He is called All-gone.' 'All-gone,' cried the mouse 'that is the most suspicious name of all! I have never seen it in print. All-gone; what can that mean?' and she shook her head, curled herself up, and lay down to sleep.

From this time forth no one invited the cat to be godmother, but when the winter had come and there was no longer anything to be found outside, the mouse thought of their provision, and said: 'Come, cat, we will go to our pot of fat which we have stored up for ourselves—we shall enjoy that.' 'Yes,' answered the cat, 'you will enjoy it as much as you would enjoy sticking that dainty tongue of yours out of the window.' They set out on their way, but when they arrived, the pot of fat certainly was still in its place, but it was empty. 'Alas!' said the mouse, 'now I see what has happened, now it comes to light! You a true friend! You have devoured all when you were standing godmother. First top off, then half-done, then—' 'Will you hold your tongue,' cried the cat, 'one word more, and I will eat you too.' 'All-gone' was already on the poor mouse's lips; scarcely had she spoken it before the cat sprang on her, seized her, and swallowed her down. Verily, that is the way of the world.

THE GOOSE-GIRL

The king of a great land died, and left his queen to take care
of their only child. This child was a daughter, who was very
beautiful; and her mother loved her dearly, and was very kind
to her. And there was a good fairy too, who was fond of the
princess, and helped her mother to watch over her. When she
grew up, she was betrothed to a prince who lived a great way
off; and as the time drew near for her to be married, she got
ready to set off on her journey to his country. Then the queen
her mother, packed up a great many costly things; jewels, and
gold, and silver; trinkets, fine dresses, and in short everything
that became a royal bride. And she gave her a waiting-maid to
ride with her, and give her into the bridegroom's hands; and
each had a horse for the journey. Now the princess's horse was
the fairy's gift, and it was called Falada, and could speak.

When the time came for them to set out, the fairy went
into her bed-chamber, and took a little knife, and cut off a lock
of her hair, and gave it to the princess, and said, 'Take care of
it, dear child; for it is a charm that may be of use to you on
the road.' Then they all took a sorrowful leave of the princess;
and she put the lock of hair into her bosom, got upon her
horse, and set off on her journey to her bridegroom's kingdom.

One day, as they were riding along by a brook, the princess

began to feel very thirsty: and she said to her maid, 'Pray get down, and fetch me some water in my golden cup out of yonder brook, for I want to drink.' 'Nay,' said the maid, 'if you are thirsty, get off yourself, and stoop down by the water and drink; I shall not be your waiting-maid any longer.' Then she was so thirsty that she got down, and knelt over the little brook, and drank; for she was frightened, and dared not bring out her golden cup; and she wept and said, 'Alas! what will become of me?' And the lock answered her, and said:

> 'Alas! alas! if thy mother knew it,
> Sadly, sadly, would she rue it.'

But the princess was very gentle and meek, so she said nothing to her maid's ill behaviour, but got upon her horse again.

Then all rode farther on their journey, till the day grew so warm, and the sun so scorching, that the bride began to feel very thirsty again; and at last, when they came to a river, she forgot her maid's rude speech, and said, 'Pray get down, and fetch me some water to drink in my golden cup.' But the maid answered her, and even spoke more haughtily than before: 'Drink if you will, but I shall not be your waiting-maid.' Then the princess was so thirsty that she got off her horse, and lay down, and held her head over the running stream, and cried and said, 'What will become of me?' And the lock of hair answered her again:

> 'Alas! alas! if thy mother knew it,
> Sadly, sadly, would she rue it.'

And as she leaned down to drink, the lock of hair fell from her bosom, and floated away with the water. Now she was so frightened that she did not see it; but her maid saw it, and was very glad, for she knew the charm; and she saw that the poor bride would be in her power, now that she had lost the hair. So when the bride had done drinking, and would have got upon Falada again, the maid said, 'I shall ride upon Falada, and you may have my horse instead'; so she was forced to give up her horse, and soon afterwards to take off her royal clothes and put on her maid's shabby ones.

At last, as they drew near the end of their journey, this treacherous servant threatened to kill her mistress if she ever told anyone what had happened. But Falada saw it all, and marked it well.

Then the waiting-maid got upon Falada, and the real bride rode upon the other horse, and they went on in this way till at last they came to the royal court. There was great joy at their coming, and the prince flew to meet them, and lifted the maid from her horse, thinking she was the one who was to be his wife; and she was led upstairs to the royal chamber; but the true princess was told to stay in the court below.

Now the old king happened just then to have nothing else to do; so he amused himself by sitting at his kitchen window, looking at what was going on; and he saw her in the courtyard. As she looked very pretty, and too delicate for a waiting-maid, he went up into the royal chamber to ask the bride who it was she had brought with her, that was thus left standing in the court below. 'I brought her with me for the sake of her company on the road,' said she; 'pray give the girl some work to do, that she may not be idle.' The old king could not for some time think of any work for her to do; but at last he said, 'I have a lad who takes care of my geese; she may go and help him.' Now the name of this lad, that the real bride was to help in watching the king's geese, was Curdken.

But the false bride said to the prince, 'Dear husband, pray do me one piece of kindness.' 'That I will,' said the prince. 'Then tell one of your slaughterers to cut off the head of the horse I rode upon, for it was very unruly, and plagued me sadly on the road'; but the truth was, she was very much afraid lest Falada should some day or other speak, and tell all she had done to the princess. She carried her point, and the faithful

Falada was killed; but when the true princess heard of it, she wept, and begged the man to nail up Falada's head against a large dark gate of the city, through which she had to pass every morning and evening, that there she might still see him sometimes. Then the slaughterer said he would do as she wished; and cut off the head, and nailed it up under the dark gate.

Early the next morning, as she and Curdken went out through the gate, she said sorrowfully:

'Falada, Falada, there thou hangest!'

and the head answered:

'Bride, bride, there thou gangest!
Alas! alas! if thy mother knew it,
Sadly, sadly, would she rue it.'

Then they went out of the city, and drove the geese on. And when she came to the meadow, she sat down upon a bank there, and let down her waving locks of hair, which were all of pure silver; and when Curdken saw it glitter in the sun, he ran up, and would have pulled some of the locks out, but she cried:

'Blow, breezes, blow!
Let Curdken's hat go!
Blow, breezes, blow!
Let him after it go!
O'er hills, dales, and rocks,
Away be it whirl'd
Till the silvery locks
Are all comb'd and curl'd!'

Then there came a wind, so strong that it blew off Curdken's hat; and away it flew over the hills: and he was forced to turn and run after it; till, by the time he came back, she had done combing and curling her hair, and had put it up again safe. Then he was very angry and sulky, and would not speak to her at all; but they watched the geese until it grew dark in the evening, and then drove them homewards.

The next morning, as they were going through the dark gate, the poor girl looked up at Falada's head, and cried:

> 'Falada, Falada, there thou hangest!'

and the head answered:

> 'Bride, bride, there thou gangest!
> Alas! alas! if they mother knew it,
> Sadly, sadly, would she rue it.'

Then she drove on the geese, and sat down again in the meadow, and began to comb out her hair as before; and Curdken ran up to her, and wanted to take hold of it; but she cried out quickly:

> 'Blow, breezes, blow!
> Let Curdken's hat go!
> Blow, breezes, blow!
> Let him after it go!
> O'er hills, dales, and rocks,
> Away be it whirl'd
> Till the silvery locks
> Are all comb'd and curl'd!'

Then the wind came and blew away his hat; and off it flew a great way, over the hills and far away, so that he had to run after it; and when he came back she had bound up her hair again, and all was safe. So they watched the geese till it grew dark.

In the evening, after they came home, Curdken went to the old king, and said, 'I cannot have that strange girl to help me to keep the geese any longer.' 'Why?' said the king. 'Because, instead of doing any good, she does nothing but tease me all day long.' Then the king made him tell him what had happened. And Curdken said, 'When we go in the morning through the dark gate with our flock of geese, she cries and talks with the head of a horse that hangs upon the wall, and says:

> *'Falada, Falada, there thou hangest!'*

and the head answers:

> *'Bride, bride, there thou gangest!*
> *Alas! alas! if they mother knew it,*
> *Sadly, sadly, would she rue it.'*

And Curdken went on telling the king what had happened upon the meadow where the geese fed; how his hat was blown away; and how he was forced to run after it, and to leave his flock of geese to themselves. But the old king told the boy to go out again the next day: and when morning came, he placed himself behind the dark gate, and heard how she spoke to Falada, and how Falada answered. Then he went into the field, and hid himself in a bush by the meadow's side; and he soon saw with his own eyes how they drove the flock of geese; and how, after a little time, she let down her hair that glittered in the sun. And then he heard her say:

> *'Blow, breezes, blow!*
> *Let Curdken's hat go!*
> *Blow, breezes, blow!*
> *Let him after it go!*
> *O'er hills, dales, and rocks,*
> *Away be it whirl'd*
> *Till the silvery locks*
> *Are all comb'd and curl'd!'*

And soon came a gale of wind, and carried away Curdken's hat, and away went Curdken after it, while the girl went on combing and curling her hair. All this the old king saw: so he went home without being seen; and when the little goose-girl came back in the evening he called her aside, and asked her why she did so: but she burst into tears, and said, 'That I must not tell you or any man, or I shall lose my life.'

But the old king begged so hard, that she had no peace till she had told him all the tale, from beginning to end, word for word. And it was very lucky for her that she did so, for when she had done the king ordered royal clothes to be put upon her, and gazed on her with wonder, she was so beautiful. Then he called his son and told him that he had only a false bride; for that she was merely a waiting-maid, while the true bride stood by. And the young king rejoiced when he saw her beauty, and heard how meek and patient she had been; and without saying anything to the false bride, the king ordered a great feast to be got ready for all his court. The bridegroom sat at the top, with the false princess on one side, and the true one on the other; but nobody knew her again, for her beauty was quite dazzling to their eyes; and she did not seem at all like the little goose-girl, now that she had her brilliant dress on.

When they had eaten and drank, and were very merry, the old king said he would tell them a tale. So he began, and told all the story of the princess, as if it was one that he had once heard; and he asked the true waiting-maid what she thought ought to be done to anyone who would behave thus. 'Nothing better,' said this false bride, 'than that she should be thrown into a cask stuck round with sharp nails, and that two white horses should be put to it, and should drag it from street to street till she was dead.' 'Thou art she!' said the old king; 'and as thou has judged thyself, so shall it be done to thee.' And the young king was then married to his true wife, and they reigned over the kingdom in peace and happiness all their lives; and the good fairy came to see them, and restored the faithful Falada to life again.

THE ADVENTURES OF CHANTICLEER AND PARTLET

1. HOW THEY WENT TO THE MOUNTAINS TO EAT NUTS

'The nuts are quite ripe now,' said Chanticleer to his wife Partlet, 'suppose we go together to the mountains, and eat as many as we can, before the squirrel takes them all away.' 'With all my heart,' said Partlet, 'let us go and make a holiday of it together.'

So they went to the mountains; and as it was a lovely day, they stayed there till the evening. Now, whether it was that they had eaten so many nuts that they could not walk, or whether they were lazy and would not, I do not know: however, they took it into their heads that it did not become them to go home on foot. So Chanticleer began to build a little carriage of nutshells: and when it was finished, Partlet jumped into it and sat down, and bid Chanticleer harness himself to it and draw her home. 'That's a good joke!' said Chanticleer; 'no, that will never do; I had rather by half walk home; I'll sit on the box and be coachman, if you like, but I'll not draw.' While this was passing, a duck came quacking up and cried out, 'You thieving vagabonds, what business

have you in my grounds? I'll give it you well for your inso-
lence!' and upon that she fell upon Chanticleer most lustily.
But Chanticleer was no coward, and returned the duck's blows
with his sharp spurs so fiercely that she soon began to cry out
for mercy; which was only granted her upon condition that
she would draw the carriage home for them. This she agreed
to do; and Chanticleer got upon the box, and drove, crying,
'Now, duck, get on as fast as you can.' And away they went
at a pretty good pace.

After they had travelled along a little way, they met a
needle and a pin walking together along the road: and the
needle cried out, 'Stop, stop!' and said it was so dark that
they could hardly find their way, and such dirty walking they
could not get on at all: he told them that he and his friend,
the pin, had been at a public-house a few miles off, and had
sat drinking till they had forgotten how late it was; he begged
therefore that the travellers would be so kind as to give them
a lift in their carriage. Chanticleer observing that they were
but thin fellows, and not likely to take up much room, told
them they might ride, but made them promise not to dirty
the wheels of the carriage in getting in, nor to tread on Partlet's
toes.

Late at night they arrived at an inn; and as it was bad
travelling in the dark, and the duck seemed much tired, and
waddled about a good deal from one side to the other, they
made up their minds to fix their quarters there: but the landlord at first was unwilling, and said his house was full, thinking
they might not be very respectable company: however, they
spoke civilly to him, and gave him the egg which Partlet had
laid by the way, and said they would give him the duck, who
was in the habit of laying one every day: so at last he let them
come in, and they bespoke a handsome supper, and spent the
evening very jollily.

Early in the morning, before it was quite light, and when
nobody was stirring in the inn, Chanticleer awakened his wife,

and, fetching the egg, they pecked a hole in it, ate it up, and threw the shells into the fireplace: they then went to the pin and needle, who were fast asleep, and seizing them by the heads, stuck one into the landlord's easy chair and the other into his handkerchief; and, having done this, they crept away as softly as possible. However, the duck, who slept in the open air in the yard, heard them coming, and jumping into the brook which ran close by the inn, soon swam out of their reach.

An hour or two afterwards the landlord got up, and took his handkerchief to wipe his face, but the pin ran into him and pricked him: then he walked into the kitchen to light his pipe at the fire, but when he stirred it up the eggshells flew into his eyes, and almost blinded him. 'Bless me!' said he, 'all the world seems to have a design against my head this morning': and so saying, he threw himself sulkily into his easy chair; but, oh dear! the needle ran into him; and this time the pain was not in his head. He now flew into a very great passion, and, suspecting the company who had come in the night before, he went to look after them, but they were all off; so he swore that he never again would take in such a troop of vagabonds, who ate a great deal, paid no reckoning, and gave him nothing for his trouble but their apish tricks.

2. HOW CHANTICLEER AND PARTLET WENT TO VIST MR KORBES

Another day, Chanticleer and Partlet wished to ride out together; so Chanticleer built a handsome carriage with four red wheels, and harnessed six mice to it; and then he and Partlet got into the carriage, and away they drove. Soon afterwards a cat met them, and said, 'Where are you going?' And Chanticleer replied,

> *'All on our way*
> *A visit to pay*
> *To Mr Korbes, the fox, today.'*

Then the cat said, 'Take me with you,' Chanticleer said, 'With all my heart: get up behind, and be sure you do not fall off.'

> *'Take care of this handsome coach of mine,*
> *Nor dirty my pretty red wheels so fine!*
> *Now, mice, be ready,*
> *And, wheels, run steady!*
> *For we are going a visit to pay*
> *To Mr Korbes, the fox, today.'*

Soon after came up a millstone, an egg, a duck, and a pin; and Chanticleer gave them all leave to get into the carriage and go with them.

When they arrived at Mr Korbes's house, he was not at home; so the mice drew the carriage into the coach-house, Chanticleer and Partlet flew upon a beam, the cat sat down in the fireplace, the duck got into the washing cistern, the pin stuck himself into the bed pillow, the millstone laid himself over the house door, and the egg rolled himself up in the towel.

When Mr Korbes came home, he went to the fireplace to make a fire; but the cat threw all the ashes in his eyes: so he ran to the kitchen to wash himself; but there the duck splashed all the water in his face; and when he tried to wipe himself, the egg broke to pieces in the towel all over his face and eyes. Then he was very angry, and went without his supper to bed; but when he laid his head on the pillow, the pin ran into his cheek: at this he became quite furious, and, jumping up, would have run out of the house; but when he came to the door, the millstone fell down on his head, and killed him on the spot.

3. HOW PARTLET DIED AND WAS BURIED, AND
HOW CHANTICLEER DIED OF GRIEF

Another day Chanticleer and Partlet agreed to go again to the mountains to eat nuts; and it was settled that all the nuts which they found should be shared equally between them. Now Partlet found a very large nut; but she said nothing about it to Chanticleer, and kept it all to herself: however, it was so big that she could not swallow it, and it stuck in her throat. Then she was in a great fright, and cried out to Chanticleer, 'Pray run as fast as you can, and fetch me some water, or I shall be choked.' Chanticleer ran as fast as he could to the river, and said, 'River, give me some water, for Partlet lies in the mountain, and will be choked by a great nut.' The river said, 'Run first to the bride, and ask her for a silken cord to draw up the water.' Chanticleer ran to the bride, and said, 'Bride, you must give me a silken cord, for then the river will give me water, and the water I will carry to Partlet, who lies on the mountain, and will be choked by a great nut.' But the bride said, 'Run first, and bring me my garland that is hanging on a willow in the garden.' Then Chanticleer ran to the garden, and took the garland from the bough where it hung, and brought it to the bride; and then the bride gave him the silken cord, and he took the silken cord to the river, and the river gave him water, and he carried the water to Partlet; but in the meantime she was choked by the great nut, and lay quite dead, and never moved any more.

Then Chanticleer was very sorry, and cried bitterly; and all the beasts came and wept with him over poor Partlet. And six mice built a little hearse to carry her to her grave; and when it was ready they harnessed themselves before it, and Chanticleer drove them. On the way they met the fox. 'Where are you going, Chanticleer?' said he. 'To bury my Partlet,' said the other. 'May I go with you?' said the fox. 'Yes; but you must get up behind, or my horses will not be able to draw you.' Then the fox got up behind; and presently the wolf, the bear, the goat, and all the beasts of the wood, came and climbed upon the hearse.

So on they went till they came to a rapid stream. 'How shall we get over?' said Chanticleer. Then said a straw, 'I will lay myself across, and you may pass over upon me.' But as the mice were going over, the straw slipped away and fell into the water, and the six mice all fell in and were drowned. What was to be done? Then a large log of wood came and said, 'I am big enough; I will lay myself across the stream, and you shall pass over upon me.' So he laid himself down; but they managed so clumsily, that the log of wood fell in and was carried away by the stream. Then a stone, who saw what had happened, came up and kindly offered to help poor Chanticleer by laying himself across the stream; and this time he got safely to the other side with the hearse, and managed to get Partlet out of it; but the fox and the other mourners, who were sitting behind, were too heavy, and fell back into the water and were all carried away by the stream and drowned.

Thus Chanticleer was left alone with his dead Partlet; and having dug a grave for her, he laid her in it, and made a little hillock over her. Then he sat down by the grave, and wept and mourned, till at last he died too; and so all were dead.

RAPUNZEL

There were once a man and a woman who had long in vain
wished for a child. At length the woman hoped that God was
about to grant her desire. These people had a little window
at the back of their house from which a splendid garden could
be seen, which was full of the most beautiful flowers and
herbs. It was, however, surrounded by a high wall, and no
one dared to go into it because it belonged to an enchantress,
who had great power and was dreaded by all the world. One
day the woman was standing by this window and looking
down into the garden, when she saw a bed which was planted
with the most beautiful rampion (rapunzel), and it looked so
fresh and green that she longed for it, she quite pined away,
and began to look pale and miserable. Then her husband was
alarmed, and asked: 'What ails you, dear wife?' 'Ah,' she
replied, 'if I can't eat some of the rampion, which is in the
garden behind our house, I shall die.' The man, who loved
her, thought: 'Sooner than let your wife die, bring her some
of the rampion yourself, let it cost what it will.' At twilight,
he clambered down over the wall into the garden of the
enchantress, hastily clutched a handful of rampion, and took
it to his wife. She at once made herself a salad of it, and ate it
greedily. It tasted so good to her—so very good, that the next

day she longed for it three times as much as before. If he was to have any rest, her husband must once more descend into the garden. In the gloom of evening therefore, he let himself down again; but when he had clambered down the wall he was terribly afraid, for he saw the enchantress standing before him. 'How can you dare,' said she with angry look, 'descend into my garden and steal my rampion like a thief? You shall suffer for it!' 'Ah,' answered he, 'let mercy take the place of justice, I only made up my mind to do it out of necessity. My wife saw your rampion from the window, and felt such a longing for it that she would have died if she had not got some to eat.' Then the enchantress allowed her anger to be softened, and said to him: 'If the case be as you say, I will allow you to take away with you as much rampion as you will, only I make one condition, you must give me the child which your wife will bring into the world; it shall be well treated, and I will care for it like a mother.' The man in his terror consented to everything, and when the woman was brought to bed, the enchantress appeared at once, gave the child the name of Rapunzel, and took it away with her.

Rapunzel grew into the most beautiful child under the sun. When she was twelve years old, the enchantress shut her into a tower, which lay in a forest, and had neither stairs nor door, but quite at the top was a little window. When the enchantress wanted to go in, she placed herself beneath it and cried:

> *Rapunzel, Rapunzel,*
> *Let down your hair to me.'*

Rapunzel had magnificent long hair, fine as spun gold, and when she heard the voice of the enchantress she unfastened her braided tresses, wound them round one of the hooks of the window above, and then the hair fell twenty ells down, and the enchantress climbed up by it.

After a year or two, it came to pass that the king's son rode through the forest and passed by the tower. Then he heard a song, which was so charming that he stood still and listened. This was Rapunzel, who in her solitude passed her time in letting her sweet voice resound. The king's son wanted to climb up to her, and looked for the door of the tower, but none was to be found. He rode home, but the singing had so deeply touched his heart, that every day he went out into the forest and listened to it. Once when he was thus standing behind a tree, he saw that an enchantress came there, and he heard how she cried:

> '*Rapunzel, Rapunzel,*
> *Let down your hair to me.*'

Then Rapunzel let down the braids of her hair, and the enchantress climbed up to her. 'If that is the ladder by which one mounts, I too will try my fortune,' said he, and the next day when it began to grow dark, he went to the tower and cried:

> '*Rapunzel, Rapunzel,*
> *Let down your hair to me.*'

Immediately the hair fell down and the king's son climbed up.

At first Rapunzel was terribly frightened when a man, such as her eyes had never yet beheld, came to her; but the king's son began to talk to her quite like a friend, and told her that his heart had been so stirred that it had let him have no rest, and he had been forced to see her. Then Rapunzel lost her fear, and when he asked her if she would take him for her husband, and she saw that he was young and handsome, she thought: 'He will love me more than old Dame Gothel does'; and she said yes, and laid her hand in his. She said: 'I will willingly go away with you, but I do not know how to get down. Bring with you a skein of silk every time that you come, and I will weave a ladder with it, and when that is ready I will descend, and you will take me on your horse.' They agreed that until that time he should come to her every evening, for the old woman came by day. The enchantress remarked nothing of this, until once Rapunzel said to her: 'Tell me, Dame Gothel, how it happens that you are so much heavier for me to draw up than the young king's son—he is with me in a moment.' 'Ah! you wicked child,' cried the enchantress. 'What do I hear you say! I thought I had separated you from all the world, and yet you have deceived me!' In her anger she clutched Rapunzel's beautiful tresses, wrapped them twice round her left hand, seized a pair of scissors with the right, and snip, snap, they were cut off, and the lovely braids lay on the ground. And she was so pitiless that she took poor Rapunzel into a desert where she had to live in great grief and misery.

On the same day that she cast out Rapunzel, however, the enchantress fastened the braids of hair, which she had cut off, to the hook of the window, and when the king's son came and cried:

> *'Rapunzel, Rapunzel,*
> *Let down your hair to me.'*

She let the hair down. The king's son ascended, but instead of finding his dearest Rapunzel, he found the enchantress, who gazed at him with wicked and venomous looks. 'Aha!' she cried mockingly, 'you would fetch your dearest, but the beautiful bird sits no longer singing in the nest; the cat has got it, and will scratch out your eyes as well. Rapunzel is lost to you; you will never see her again.' The king's son was beside himself with pain, and in his despair he leapt down from the tower. He escaped with his life, but the thorns into which he fell pierced his eyes. Then he wandered quite blind about the forest, ate nothing but roots and berries, and did naught but lament and weep over the loss of his dearest wife. Thus he roamed about in misery for some years, and at length came to the desert where Rapunzel, with the twins to which she had given birth, a boy and a girl, lived in wretchedness. He heard a voice, and it seemed so familiar to him that he went towards it, and when he approached, Rapunzel knew him and fell on his neck and wept. Two of her tears wetted his eyes and they grew clear again, and he could see with them as before. He led her to his kingdom where he was joyfully received, and they lived for a long time afterwards, happy and contented.

FUNDEVOGEL

There was once a forester who went into the forest to hunt, and as he entered it he heard a sound of screaming as if a little child were there. He followed the sound, and at last came to a high tree, and at the top of this a little child was sitting, for the mother had fallen asleep under the tree with the child, and a bird of prey had seen it in her arms, had flown down, snatched it away, and set it on the high tree.

The forester climbed up, brought the child down, and thought to himself: 'You will take him home with you, and bring him up with your Lina.' He took it home, therefore, and the two children grew up together. And the one, which he had found on a tree was called Fundevogel, because a bird had carried it away. Fundevogel and Lina loved each other so dearly that when they did not see each other they were sad.

Now the forester had an old cook, who one evening took two pails and began to fetch water, and did not go once only, but many times, out to the spring. Lina saw this and said, 'Listen, old Sanna, why are you fetching so much water?' 'If you will never repeat it to anyone, I will tell you why.' So Lina said, no, she would never repeat it to anyone, and then the cook said: 'Early tomorrow morning, when the forester is out hunting, I will heat the water, and when it is boiling in the kettle, I will throw in Fundevogel, and will boil him in it.'

Early next morning the forester got up and went out hunting, and when he was gone the children were still in bed. Then Lina said to Fundevogel: 'If you will never leave me, I too will never leave you.' Fundevogel said: 'Neither now, nor ever will I leave you.' Then said Lina: 'Then will I tell you. Last night, old Sanna carried so many buckets of water into the house that I asked her why she was doing that, and she said that if I would promise not to tell anyone, and she said that early tomorrow morning when father was out hunting, she would set the kettle full of water, throw you into it and boil you; but we will get up quickly, dress ourselves, and go away together.'

The two children therefore got up, dressed themselves quickly, and went away. When the water in the kettle was boiling, the cook went into the bedroom to fetch Fundevogel and throw him into it. But when she came in, and went to the beds, both the children were gone. Then she was terribly alarmed, and she said to herself: 'What shall I say now when the forester comes home and sees that the children are gone? They must be followed instantly to get them back again.'

Then the cook sent three servants after them, who were to run and overtake the children. The children, however, were sitting outside the forest, and when they saw from afar the three servants running, Lina said to Fundevogel: 'Never leave me, and I will never leave you.' Fundevogel said: 'Neither now, nor ever.' Then said Lina: 'Do you become a rose-tree, and I the rose upon it.' When the three servants came to the forest, nothing was there but a rose-tree and one rose on it, but the children were nowhere. Then said they: 'There is nothing to be done here,' and they went home and told the cook that they had seen nothing in the forest but a little rose-bush with one rose on it. Then the old cook scolded and said: 'You simpletons, you should have cut the rose-bush in two, and have broken off the rose and brought it home with you; go, and do it at once.' They had therefore to go out and look for the second time. The children, however, saw them coming from a distance. Then Lina said: 'Fundevogel, never leave me, and I will never leave you.' Fundevogel said: 'Neither now; nor ever.' Said Lina: 'Then do you become a church, and I'll be the chandelier in it.' So when the three servants came, nothing was there but a church, with a chandelier in it. They said therefore to each other: 'What can we do here, let us go home.' When they got home, the cook asked if they had not found them; so they said no, they had found nothing but a church, and there was a chandelier in it. And the cook scolded them and said: 'You fools! why did you not pull the church to pieces, and bring the chandelier home with you?' And now the old cook herself got on her legs, and went with the three servants in pursuit of the children. The children, however, saw from afar that the three servants were coming, and the cook waddling after them. Then said Lina: 'Fundevogel, never leave me, and I will never leave you.' Then said Fundevogel: 'Neither now, nor ever.' Said Lina: 'Be a fishpond, and I will be the duck upon it.' The cook, however, came up to them, and when she saw the pond she lay down by it, and was about to drink it up. But the duck swam quickly to her, seized her head in its beak and drew her into the water, and there the old witch had to drown. Then the children went home together, and were heartily delighted, and if they have not died, they are living still.

THE VALIANT LITTLE TAILOR

One summer's morning a little tailor was sitting on his table by the window; he was in good spirits, and sewed with all his might. Then came a peasant woman down the street crying: 'Good jams, cheap! Good jams, cheap!' This rang pleasantly in the tailor's ears; he stretched his delicate head out of the window, and called: 'Come up here, dear woman; here you will get rid of your goods.' The woman came up the three steps to the tailor with her heavy basket, and he made her unpack all the pots for him. He inspected each one, lifted it up, put his nose to it, and at length said: 'The jam seems to me to be good, so weigh me out four ounces, dear woman, and if it is a quarter of a pound that is of no consequence.' The woman who had hoped to find a good sale, gave him what he desired, but went away quite angry and grumbling. 'Now, this jam shall be blessed by God,' cried the little tailor, 'and give me health and strength'; so he brought the bread out of the cupboard, cut himself a piece right across the loaf and spread the jam over it. 'This won't taste bitter,' said he, 'but I will just finish the jacket before I take a bite.' He laid the bread near him, sewed on, and in his joy, made bigger and bigger stitches. In the meantime the smell of the sweet jam rose to where the flies were sitting in great numbers, and they were attracted and descended on it in hosts. 'Hi! who invited you?' said the little tailor, and drove the unbidden guests away. The flies, however, who understood no German, would not be turned away, but came back again in ever-increasing companies. The little tailor at last lost all patience, and drew a piece of cloth from the hole under his work-table, and saying: 'Wait, and I will give it to you,' struck it mercilessly on them. When he drew it away and counted, there lay before him no fewer than seven, dead and with legs stretched out. 'Are you a fellow of that sort?' said he, and could not help admiring his own bravery. 'The whole town shall know of this!' And the little tailor hastened to cut himself a girdle, stitched it, and embroidered on it in large letters: 'Seven at one stroke!' 'What, the town!' he continued, 'the whole world shall hear of it!' and his heart wagged with joy like a lamb's tail. The tailor put on the girdle, and resolved to go forth into the world, because he thought his workshop was too small for his valour. Before he went away, he sought about in the house to see if there was anything which he could take with him; however, he found nothing but an old cheese, and that he put in his pocket. In front of the door he observed a bird which had caught itself in the thicket. It had to go into his pocket with the cheese. Now he took to the road boldly, and as he was light and nimble, he felt no fatigue. The road led him up a mountain, and when he had reached the highest point of it, there sat a powerful giant looking peacefully about him. The little tailor went bravely up, spoke to him, and said: 'Good day, comrade, so you are sitting there overlooking the wide-spread world! I am just on my way thither, and want to try my luck. Have you any inclination to go with me?' The giant looked contemptuously at the tailor, and said: 'You ragamuffin! You miserable creature!'

'Oh, indeed?' answered the little tailor, and unbuttoned his coat, and showed the giant the girdle, 'there may you read what kind of a man I am!' The giant read: 'Seven at one stroke,' and thought that they had been men whom the tailor had killed, and began to feel a little respect for the tiny fellow. Nevertheless, he wished to try him first, and took a stone in his hand and squeezed it together so that water dropped out of it. 'Do that likewise,' said the giant, 'if you have strength.' 'Is that all?' said the tailor, 'that is child's play with us!' and put his hand into his pocket, brought out the soft cheese, and pressed it until the liquid ran out of it. 'Faith,' said he, 'that was a little better, wasn't it?' The giant did not know what to say, and could not believe it of the little man. Then the giant picked up a stone and threw it so high that the eye could scarcely follow it. 'Now, little mite of a man, do that likewise,' 'Well thrown,' said the tailor, 'but after all the stone came down to earth again; I will throw you one which shall never come back at all,' and he put his hand into his pocket, took out the bird, and threw it into the air. The bird, delighted with its liberty, rose, flew away and did not come back. 'How does that shot please you, comrade?' asked the tailor. 'You can certainly throw,' said the giant, 'but now we will see if you are able to carry anything properly.' He took the little tailor to a mighty oak tree which lay there felled on the ground, and said: 'If you are strong enough, help me to carry the tree out of the forest.' 'Readily,' answered the little man; 'take you the trunk on your shoulders, and I will raise up the branches and twigs; after all, they are the heaviest.' The giant took the trunk on his shoulder, but the tailor seated himself on a branch, and the giant, who could not look round, had to carry away the whole tree, and the little tailor into the bargain: he behind, was quite merry and happy, and whistled the song: 'Three tailors rode forth from the gate,' as if carrying the tree were child's play. The giant, after he had dragged the heavy burden part of the way, could go no further, and cried: 'Hark you, I shall have to let the tree fall!' The tailor sprang nimbly down, seized the tree with both arms as if he had been carrying it, and said to the giant: 'You are such a great fellow, and yet cannot even carry the tree!'

They went on together, and as they passed a cherry-tree, the giant laid hold of the top of the tree where the ripest fruit was hanging, bent it down, gave it into the tailor's hand, and bade him eat. But the little tailor was much too weak to hold the tree, and when the giant let it go, it sprang back again, and the tailor was tossed into the air with it. When he had fallen down again without injury, the giant said: 'What is this? Have you not strength enough to hold the weak twig?' 'There is no lack of strength,' answered the little tailor. 'Do you think that could be anything to a man who has struck down seven at one blow? I leapt over the tree because the huntsmen are shooting down there in the thicket. Jump as I did, if you can do it.' The giant made the attempt but he could not get over the tree, and remained hanging in the branches, so that in this also the tailor kept the upper hand.

The giant said: 'If you are such a valiant fellow, come with me into our cavern and spend the night with us.' The little tailor was willing, and followed him. When they went into the cave, other giants were sitting there by the fire, and each of them had a roasted sheep in his hand and was eating it. The little tailor looked round and thought: 'It is much more spacious here than in my workshop.' The giant showed him a bed, and said he was to lie down in it and sleep. The bed, however, was too big for the little tailor; he did not lie down in it, but crept into a corner. When it was midnight, and the giant thought that the little tailor was lying in a sound sleep, he got up, took a great iron bar, cut through the bed with one blow, and thought he had finished off the grasshopper for good. With the earliest dawn the giants went into the forest, and had quite forgotten the little tailor, when all at once he walked up to them quite merrily and boldly. The giants were terrified, they were afraid that he would strike them all dead, and ran away in a great hurry.

The little tailor went onwards, always following his own pointed nose. After he had walked for a long time, he came to the courtyard of a royal palace, and as he felt weary, he lay down on the grass and fell asleep. Whilst he lay there, the people came and inspected him on all sides, and read on his girdle: 'Seven at one stroke.' 'Ah!' said they, 'what does the great warrior want here in the midst of peace? He must be a mighty lord.' They went and announced him to the king, and gave it as their opinion that if war should break out, this would be a weighty and useful man who ought on no account to be allowed to depart. The counsel pleased the king, and he sent one of his courtiers to the little tailor to offer him military service when he awoke. The ambassador remained standing by the sleeper, waited until he stretched his limbs and opened his eyes, and then conveyed to him this proposal. 'For this very reason have I come here,' the tailor replied, 'I am ready to enter the king's service.' He was therefore honourably received, and a special dwelling was assigned him.

The soldiers, however, were set against the little tailor, and wished him a thousand miles away. 'What is to be the end of this?' they said among themselves. 'If we quarrel with him, and he strikes about him, seven of us will fall at every blow; not one of us can stand against him.' They came therefore to a decision, betook themselves in a body to the king, and begged for their dismissal. 'We are not prepared,' said they, 'to stay with a man who kills seven at one stroke.' The king was sorry that for the sake of one he should lose all his faithful servants, wished that he had never set eyes on the tailor, and would willingly have been rid of him again. But he did not venture to give him his dismissal, for he dreaded lest he should strike him and all his people dead, and place himself on the royal throne. He thought about it for a long time, and at last found good counsel. He sent to the little tailor and caused him to be informed that as he was a great warrior, he had one request to make to him. In a forest of his country lived two giants, who caused great mischief with their robbing, murdering, ravaging, and burning, and no one could approach them without putting himself in danger of death. If the tailor conquered and killed these two giants, he would give him his only daughter to wife, and half of his kingdom as a dowry, likewise one hundred horsemen should go with him to assist him. 'That would indeed be a fine thing for a man like me!' thought the little tailor. 'One is not offered a beautiful princess and half a kingdom every day of one's life!' 'Oh, yes,' he replied, 'I will soon subdue the giants, and do not require the help of the hundred horsemen to do it; he who can hit seven with one blow has no need to be afraid of two.'

The little tailor went forth, and the hundred horsemen followed him. When he came to the outskirts of the forest, he said to his followers: 'Just stay waiting here, I alone will soon finish off the giants.' Then he bounded into the forest and looked about right and left. After a while he perceived both giants. They lay sleeping under a tree, and snored so that the branches waved up and down. The little tailor, not idle, gathered two pocketsful of stones, and with these climbed up the tree. When he was halfway up, he slipped down by a branch, until he sat just above the sleepers, and then let one stone after another fall on the breast of one of the giants. For a long time the giant felt nothing, but at last he awoke, pushed his comrade, and said: 'Why are you knocking me?' 'You must be dreaming,' said the other, 'I am not knocking you.' They laid themselves down to sleep again, and then the tailor threw a stone down on the second. 'What is the meaning of this?' cried the other. 'Why are you pelting me?' 'I am not pelting you,' answered the first, growling. They disputed about it for a time, but as they were weary they let the matter rest, and their eyes closed once more. The little tailor began his game again, picked out the biggest stone, and threw it with all his might on the breast of the first giant. 'That is too bad!' cried he, and sprang up like a madman, and pushed his companion against the tree until it shook. The other paid him back in the same coin, and they got into such a rage that they tore up trees and belaboured each other so long, that at last they both fell down dead on the ground at the same time. Then the little tailor leapt down. 'It is a lucky thing,' said he, 'that they did not tear up the tree on which I was sitting, or I should have had to sprint on to another like a squirrel; but we tailors are nimble.' He drew out his sword and gave each of them a couple of thrusts in the breast, and then went out to the horsemen and said: 'The work is done; I have finished both of them off, but it was hard work! They tore up trees in their sore need, and defended themselves with them, but all that is to no purpose when a man like myself comes, who can kill seven at one blow.' 'But are you not wounded?' asked the horsemen. 'You need not concern yourself about that,' answered the tailor, 'they have not bent one hair of mine.' The horsemen would not believe him, and rode into the forest; there they found the giants swimming in their blood, and all round about lay the torn-up trees.

The little tailor demanded of the king the promised reward; he, however, repented of his promise, and again bethought himself how he could get rid of the hero. 'Before you receive my daughter, and the half of my kingdom,' said he to him, 'you must perform one more heroic deed. In the forest roams a unicorn which does great harm, and you must catch it first.' 'I fear one unicorn still less than two giants. Seven at one blow, is my kind of affair.' He took a rope and an axe with him, went forth into the forest, and again bade those who were sent with him to wait outside. He had not long to seek. The unicorn soon came towards him, and rushed directly on the tailor, as if it would gore him with its horn without more ado. 'Softly, softly; it can't be done as quickly as that,' said he, and stood still and waited until the animal was quite close, and then sprang nimbly behind the tree. The unicorn ran against the tree with all its strength, and stuck its horn so fast in the trunk that it had not the strength enough to draw it out again, and thus it was caught. 'Now, I have got the bird,' said the tailor, and came out from behind the tree and put the rope round its neck, and then with his axe he hewed the horn out of the tree, and when all was ready he led the beast away and took it to the king.

The king still would not give him the promised reward, and made a third demand. Before the wedding the tailor was to catch him a wild boar that made great havoc in the forest, and the huntsmen should give him their help. 'Willingly,' said the tailor, 'that is child's play!' He did not take the huntsmen with him into the forest, and they were well pleased that he did not, for the wild boar had several times received them in such a manner that they had no inclination to lie in wait for him. When the boar perceived the tailor, it ran on him with foaming mouth and whetted tusks, and was about to throw him to the ground, but the hero fled and sprang into a chapel which was near and up to the window at once, and in one bound out again. The boar ran after him, but the tailor ran round outside and shut the door behind it, and then the raging beast, which was much too heavy and awkward to leap out of the window, was caught. The little tailor called the huntsmen thither that they might see the prisoner with their own eyes. The hero, however, went to the king, who was now, whether he liked it or not, obliged to keep his promise, and gave his daughter and the half of his kingdom. Had he known that it was no warlike hero, but a little tailor who was standing before him, it would have gone to his heart still more than it did. The wedding was held with great magnificence and small joy, and out of a tailor a king was made.

After some time the young queen heard her husband say in his dreams at night: 'Boy, make me the doublet, and patch the pantaloons, or else I will rap the yard-measure over your ears.' Then she discovered in what state of life the young lord had been born, and next morning complained of her wrongs to her father, and begged him to help her to get rid of her husband, who was nothing else but a tailor. The king comforted her and said: 'Leave your bedroom door open this night, and my servants shall stand outside, and when he has fallen asleep shall go in, bind him, and take him on board a ship which shall carry him into the wide world.' The woman was satisfied with this; but the king's armour-bearer, who had heard all, was friendly with the young lord, and informed him of the whole plot. 'I'll put a screw into that business,' said the little tailor. At night he went to bed with his wife at the usual time, and when she thought that he had fallen asleep, she got up, opened the door, and then lay down again. The little tailor, who was only pretending to be asleep, began to cry out in a clear voice: 'Boy, make me the doublet and patch me the pantaloons, or I will rap the yard-measure over your ears. I smote seven at one blow. I killed two giants, I brought away one unicorn, and caught a wild boar, and am I to fear those who are standing outside the room.' When these men heard the tailor speaking thus, they were overcome by a great dread, and ran as if the wild huntsman were behind them, and none of them would venture anything further against him. So the little tailor was and remained a king to the end of his life.

HANSEL AND GRETEL

Hard by a great forest dwelt a poor wood-cutter with his wife and his two children. The boy was called Hansel and the girl Gretel. He had little to bite and to break, and once when great dearth fell on the land, he could no longer procure even daily bread. Now when he thought over this by night in his bed, and tossed about in his anxiety, he groaned and said to his wife: 'What is to become of us? How are we to feed our poor children, when we no longer have anything even for ourselves?' 'I'll tell you what, husband,' answered the woman, 'early tomorrow morning we will take the children out into the forest to where it is the thickest; there we will light a fire for them, and give each of them one more piece of bread, and then we will go to our work and leave them alone. They will not find the way home again, and we shall be rid of them.' 'No, wife,' said the man, 'I will not do that; how can I bear to leave my children alone in the forest?—the wild animals would soon come and tear them to pieces.' 'O, you fool!' said she, 'then we must all four die of hunger, you may as well plane the planks for our coffins,' and she left him no peace until he consented. 'But I feel very sorry for the poor children, all the same,' said the man.

The two children had also not been able to sleep for

hunger, and had heard what their stepmother had said to their father. Gretel wept bitter tears, and said to Hansel: 'Now all is over with us.' 'Be quiet, Gretel,' said Hansel, 'do not distress yourself, I will soon find a way to help us.' And when the old folks had fallen asleep, he got up, put on his little coat, opened the door below, and crept outside. The moon shone brightly, and the white pebbles which lay in front of the house glittered like real silver pennies. Hansel stooped and stuffed the little pocket of his coat with as many as he could get in. Then he went back and said to Gretel: 'Be comforted, dear little sister, and sleep in peace, God will not forsake us,' and he lay down again in his bed. When day dawned, but before the sun had risen, the woman came and awoke the two children, saying: 'Get up, you sluggards! we are going into the forest to fetch wood.' She gave each a little piece of bread, and said: 'There is something for your dinner, but do not eat it up before then, for you will get nothing else.' Gretel took the bread under her apron, as Hansel had the pebbles in his pocket. Then they all set out together on the way to the forest. When they had walked a short time, Hansel stood still and peeped back at the house, and did so again and again. His father said: 'Hansel, what are you looking at there and staying behind for? Pay attention, and do not forget how to use your legs.' 'Ah, father,' said Hansel, 'I am looking at my little white cat, which is sitting up on the roof, and wants to say goodbye to me.' The wife said: 'Fool, that is not your little cat, that is the morning sun which is shining on the chimneys.' Hansel, however, had not been looking back at the cat, but had been constantly throwing one of the white pebble-stones out of his pocket on the road.

When they had reached the middle of the forest, the father said: 'Now, children, pile up some wood, and I will light a fire that you may not be cold.' Hansel and Gretel gathered brushwood together, as high as a little hill. The brushwood was lighted, and when the flames were burning very high, the woman said: 'Now, children, lay yourselves down by the fire and rest, we will go into the forest and cut some wood. When we have done, we will come back and fetch you away.' Hansel and Gretel sat by the fire, and when noon came, each ate a little piece of bread, and as they heard the strokes of the wood-axe they believed that their father was near. It was not the axe, however, but a branch which he had fastened to a withered tree which the wind was blowing backwards and forwards. And as they had been sitting such a long time, their eyes closed with fatigue, and they fell fast asleep. When at last they awoke, it was already dark night. Gretel began to cry and said: 'How are we to get out of the forest now?' But Hansel comforted her and said: 'Just wait a little, until the moon has risen, and then we will soon find the way.' And when the full moon had risen, Hansel took his little sister by the hand, and followed the pebbles which shone like newly-coined silver pieces, and showed them the way.

They walked the whole night long, and by break of day came once more to their father's house. They knocked at the door, and when the woman opened it and saw that it was Hansel and Gretel, she said: 'You naughty children, why have you slept so long in the forest?—we thought you were never coming back at all!' The father, however, rejoiced, for it had cut him to the heart to leave them behind alone.

Not long afterwards, there was once more great dearth throughout the land, and the children heard their mother saying at night to their father: 'Everything is eaten again, we have one half loaf left, and that is the end. The children must go, we will take them farther into the wood, so that they will not find their way out again; there is no other means of saving ourselves!' The man's heart was heavy, and he thought: 'It would be better for you to share the last mouthful with your children.' The woman, however, would listen to nothing that he had to say, but scolded and reproached him. He who says A must say B, likewise, and as he had yielded the first time, he had to do so a second time also.

The children, however, were still awake and had heard the conversation. When the old folks were asleep, Hansel again got up, and wanted to go out and pick up pebbles as he had done before, but the woman had locked the door, and Hansel could not get out. Nevertheless he comforted his little sister, and said: 'Do not cry, Gretel, go to sleep quietly, the good God will help us.'

Early in the morning came the woman, and took the children out of their beds. Their piece of bread was given to them, but it was still smaller than the time before. On the way into the forest Hansel crumbled his in his pocket, and often stood still and threw a morsel on the ground. 'Hansel, why do you stop and look round?' said the father, 'go on.' 'I am looking back at my little pigeon which is sitting on the roof, and wants to say goodbye to me,' answered Hansel. 'Fool!' said the woman, 'that is not your little pigeon, that is the morning sun that is shining on the chimney.' Hansel, however little by little, threw all the crumbs on the path.

The woman led the children still deeper into the forest, where they had never in their lives been before. Then a great fire was again made, and the mother said: 'Just sit there, you children, and when you are tired you may sleep a little; we are going into the forest to cut wood, and in the evening when we are done, we will come and fetch you away.' When it was noon, Gretel shared her piece of bread with Hansel, who had scattered his by the way. Then they fell asleep and evening passed, but no one came to the poor children. They did not awake until it was dark night, and Hansel comforted his little sister and said: 'Just wait, Gretel, until the moon rises, and then we shall see the crumbs of bread which I have strewn about, they will show us our way home again.' When the moon came they set out, but they found no crumbs, for the many thousands of birds which fly about in the woods and fields had picked them all up. Hansel said to Gretel: 'We shall soon find the way,' but they did not find it. They walked the whole night and all the next day too from morning till evening, but they did not get out of the forest, and were very hungry, for they had nothing to eat but two or three berries, which grew on the ground. And as they were so weary that their legs would carry them no longer, they lay down beneath a tree and fell asleep.

It was now three mornings since they had left their father's house. They began to walk again, but they always came deeper into the forest, and if help did not come soon, they must die of hunger and weariness. When it was mid-day, they saw a beautiful snow-white bird sitting on a bough, which sang so delightfully that they stood still and listened to it. And when its song was over, it spread its wings and flew away before them, and they followed it until they reached a little house, on the roof of which it alighted; and when they approached the little house they saw that it was built of bread and covered with cakes, but that the windows were of clear sugar. 'We will set to work on that,' said Hansel, 'and have a good meal. I will eat a bit of the roof, and you Gretel, can eat some of the window, it will taste sweet.' Hansel reached up above, and broke off a little of the roof to try how it tasted, and Gretel leant against the window and nibbled at the panes. Then a soft voice cried from the parlour:

> 'Nibble, nibble, gnaw,
> Who is nibbling at my little house?'

The children answered:

> 'The wind, the wind,
> The heaven-born wind,'

and went on eating without disturbing themselves. Hansel, who liked the taste of the roof, tore down a great piece of it, and Gretel pushed out the whole of one round window-pane, sat down, and enjoyed herself with it. Suddenly the door opened, and a woman as old as the hills, who supported herself on crutches, came creeping out. Hansel and Gretel were so terribly frightened that they let fall what they had in their hands. The old woman, however, nodded her head, and said: 'Oh, you dear children, who has brought you here? do come in, and stay with me. No harm shall happen to you.' She took them both by the hand, and led them into her little house. Then good food was set before them, milk and pancakes, with sugar, apples, and nuts. Afterwards two pretty little beds were covered with clean white linen, and Hansel and Gretel lay down in them, and thought they were in heaven.

The old woman had only pretended to be so kind; she was in reality a wicked witch, who lay in wait for children, and had only built the little house of bread in order to entice them there. When a child fell into her power, she killed it, cooked and ate it, and that was a feast day with her. Witches have red eyes, and cannot see far, but they have a keen scent like the beasts, and are aware when human beings draw near. When Hansel and Gretel came into her neighbourhood, she laughed with malice, and said mockingly: 'I have them, they shall not escape me again!' Early in the morning before the children were awake, she was already up, and when she saw both of them sleeping and looking so pretty, with their plump and rosy cheeks she muttered to herself: 'That will be a dainty mouthful!' Then she seized Hansel with her shrivelled hand, carried him into a little stable, and locked him in behind a grated door. Scream as he might, it would not help him. Then she went to Gretel, shook her till she awoke, and cried: 'Get up, lazy thing, fetch some water, and cook something good for your brother, he is in the stable outside, and is to be made fat. When he is fat, I will eat him.' Gretel began to weep bitterly, but it was all in vain, for she was forced to do what the wicked witch commanded.

And now the best food was cooked for poor Hansel, but Gretel got nothing but crab-shells. Every morning the woman crept to the little stable, and cried: 'Hansel, stretch out your finger that I may feel if you will soon be fat.' Hansel, however, stretched out a little bone to her, and the old woman, who had dim eyes, could not see it, and thought it was Hansel's finger, and was astonished that there was no way of fattening him. When four weeks had gone by, and Hansel still remained thin, she was seized with impatience and would not wait any longer. 'Now, then, Gretel,' she cried to the girl, 'stir yourself, and bring some water. Let Hansel be fat or lean, tomorrow I will kill him, and cook him.' Ah, how the poor little sister did lament when she had to fetch the water, and how her tears did flow down her cheeks! 'Dear God, do help us,' she cried. 'If the wild beasts in the forest had but devoured us, we should at any rate have died together.' 'Just keep your noise to yourself,' said the old woman, 'it won't help you at all.'

Early in the morning, Gretel had to go out and hang up the cauldron with the water, and light the fire. 'We will bake first,' said the old woman, 'I have already heated the oven, and kneaded the dough.' She pushed poor Gretel out to the oven, from which flames of fire were already darting. 'Creep in,' said the witch, 'and see if it is properly heated, so that we can put the bread in.' And once Gretel was inside, she intended to shut the oven and let her bake in it, and then she would eat her, too. But Gretel saw what she had in mind, and said: 'I do not know how I am to do it; how do I get in?' 'Silly goose,' said the old woman. 'The door is big enough; just look, I can get in myself!' and she crept up and thrust her head into the oven. Then Gretel gave her a push that drove her far into it, and shut the iron door, and fastened the bolt. Oh! then she began to howl quite horribly, but Gretel ran away and the godless witch was miserably burnt to death.

Gretel, however, ran like lightning to Hansel, opened his little stable, and cried: 'Hansel, we are saved! The old witch is dead!' Then Hansel sprang like a bird from its cage when the door is opened. How they did rejoice and embrace each other, and dance about and kiss each other! And as they had no longer any need to fear her, they went into the witch's house, and in every corner there stood chests full of pearls and jewels. 'These are far better than pebbles!' said Hansel, and thrust into his pockets whatever could be got in, and Gretel said: 'I, too, will take something home with me,' and filled her pinafore full. 'But now we must be off,' said Hansel, 'that we may get out of the witch's forest.'

When they had walked for two hours, they came to a great stretch of water. 'We cannot cross,' said Hansel, 'I see no foot-plank, and no bridge.' 'And there is also no ferry,' answered Gretel, 'but a white duck is swimming there: if I ask her, she will help us over.' Then she cried:

> *'Little duck, little duck, dost thou see,*
> *Hansel and Gretel are waiting for thee?*
> *There's never a plank, or bridge in sight,*
> *Take us across on thy back so white.'*

The duck came to them, and Hansel seated himself on its back, and told his sister to sit by him. 'No,' replied Gretel, 'that will be too heavy for the little duck; she shall take us across, one after the other.' The good little duck did so, and when they were once safely across and had walked for a short time, the forest seemed to be more and more familiar to them, and at length they saw from afar their father's house. Then they began to run, rushed into the parlour, and threw themselves round their father's neck. The man had not known one happy hour since he had left the children in the forest; the woman, however, was dead. Gretel emptied her pinafore until pearls and precious stones ran about the room, and Hansel threw one handful after another out of his pocket to add to them. Then all anxiety was at an end, and they lived together in perfect happiness. My tale is done, there runs a mouse; whosoever catches it, may make himself a big fur cap out of it.

THE MOUSE, THE BIRD, AND THE SAUSAGE

Once upon a time, a mouse, a bird, and a sausage, entered into partnership and set up house together. For a long time all went well; they lived in great comfort, and prospered so far as to be able to add considerably to their stores. The bird's duty was to fly daily into the wood and bring in fuel; the mouse fetched the water, and the sausage saw to the cooking.

When people are too well off they always begin to long for something new. And so it came to pass, that the bird, while out one day, met a fellow bird, to whom he boastfully expatiated on the excellence of his household arrangements. But the other bird sneered at him for being a poor simpleton, who did all the hard work, while the other two stayed at home and had a good time of it. For, when the mouse had made the fire and fetched in the water, she could retire into her little room and rest until it was time to set the table. The sausage had only to watch the pot to see that the food was properly cooked, and when it was near dinner-time, he just threw himself into the broth, or rolled in and out among the vegetables three or four times, and there they were, buttered, and salted, and ready to be served. Then, when the bird came home and had laid aside his burden, they sat down to table, and when they had finished their meal, they could sleep their fill till the following morning: and that was really a very delightful life.

Influenced by those remarks, the bird next morning refused to bring in the wood, telling the others that he had been their servant long enough, and had been a fool into the bargain, and that it was now time to make a change, and to try some other way of arranging the work. Beg and pray as the mouse and the sausage might, it was of no use; the bird remained master of the situation, and the venture had to be made. They therefore drew lots, and it fell to the sausage to bring in the wood, to the mouse to cook, and to the bird to fetch the water.

And now what happened? The sausage started in search of wood, the bird made the fire, and the mouse put on the pot, and then these two waited till the sausage returned with the fuel for the following day. But the sausage remained so long away, that they became uneasy, and the bird flew out to meet him. He had not flown far, however, when he came across a dog who, having met the sausage, had regarded him as his legitimate booty, and so seized and swallowed him. The bird complained to the dog of this bare-faced robbery, but nothing he said was of any avail, for the dog answered that he found false credentials on the sausage, and that was the reason his life had been forfeited.

He picked up the wood, and flew sadly home, and told the mouse all he had seen and heard. They were both very unhappy, but agreed to make the best of things and to remain with one another.

So now the bird set the table, and the mouse looked after the food and, wishing to prepare it in the same way as the sausage, by rolling in and out among the vegetables to salt and butter them, she jumped into the pot; but she stopped short long before she reached the bottom, having already parted not only with her skin and hair, but also with life.

Presently the bird came in and wanted to serve up the

dinner, but he could nowhere see the cook. In his alarm and flurry, he threw the wood here and there about the floor, called and searched, but no cook was to be found. Then some of the wood that had been carelessly thrown down, caught fire and began to blaze. The bird hastened to fetch some water, but his pail fell into the well, and he after it, and as he was unable to recover himself, he was drowned.

MOTHER HOLLE

Once upon a time there was a widow who had two daughters; one of them was beautiful and industrious, the other ugly and lazy. The mother, however, loved the ugly and lazy one best, because she was her own daughter, and so the other, who was only her stepdaughter, was made to do all the work of the house, and was quite the Cinderella of the family. Her stepmother sent her out every day to sit by the well in the high road, there to spin until she made her fingers bleed. Now it chanced one day that some blood fell on to the spindle, and as the girl stopped over the well to wash it off, the spindle suddenly sprang out of her hand and fell into the well. She ran home crying to tell of her misfortune, but her stepmother spoke harshly to her, and after giving her a violent scolding, said unkindly, 'As you have let the spindle fall into the well you may go yourself and fetch it out.'

The girl went back to the well not knowing what to do, and at last in her distress she jumped into the water after the spindle.

She remembered nothing more until she awoke and found herself in a beautiful meadow, full of sunshine, and with countless flowers blooming in every direction.

She walked over the meadow, and presently she came

upon a baker's oven full of bread, and the loaves cried out to her, 'Take us out, take us out, or alas! we shall be burnt to a cinder; we were baked through long ago.' So she took the bread-shovel and drew them all out.

She went on a little farther, till she came to a free full of apples. 'Shake me, shake me, I pray,' cried the tree; 'my apples, one and all, are ripe.' So she shook the tree, and the apples came falling down upon her like rain; but she continued shaking until there was not a single apple left upon it. Then she carefully gathered the apples together in a heap and walked on again.

The next thing she came to was a little house, and there she saw an old woman looking out, with such large teeth, that she was terrified, and turned to run away. But the old woman called after her, 'What are you afraid of, dear child? Stay with me; if you will do the work of my house properly for me, I will make you very happy. You must be very careful, however, to make my bed in the right way, for I wish you always to shake it thoroughly, so that the feathers fly about; then they say, down there in the world, that it is snowing; for I am Mother Holle.' The old woman spoke so kindly, that the girl summoned up courage and agreed to enter into her service.

She took care to do everything according to the old woman's bidding and every time she made the bed she shook it with all her might, so that the feathers flew about like so many snowflakes. The old woman was as good as her word: she never spoke angrily to her, and gave her roast and boiled meats every day.

So she stayed on with Mother Holle for some time, and then she began to grow unhappy. She could not at first tell why she felt sad, but she became conscious at last of great longing to go home; then she knew she was homesick, although she was a thousand times better off with Mother Holle than with her mother and sister. After waiting awhile, she went to Mother Holle and said, 'I am so homesick, that I cannot stay with you any longer, for although I am so happy here, I must return to my own people.'

Then Mother Holle said, 'I am pleased that you should want to go back to your own people, and as you have served me so well and faithfully, I will take you home myself.'

Thereupon she led the girl by the hand up to a broad gateway. The gate was opened, and as the girl passed through, a shower of gold fell upon her, and the gold clung to her, so that she was covered with it from head to foot.

'That is a reward for your industry,' said Mother Holle, and as she spoke she handed her the spindle which she had dropped into the well.

The gate was then closed, and the girl found herself back in the old world close to her mother's house. As she entered the courtyard, the cock who was perched on the well, called out:

> 'Cock-a-doodle-doo!
> Your golden daughter's come back to you.'

Then she went in to her mother and sister, and as she was so richly covered with gold, they gave her a warm welcome. She related to them all that had happened, and when the mother heard how she had come by her great riches, she thought she should like her ugly, lazy daughter to go and try her fortune. So she made the sister go and sit by the well and spin, and the girl pricked her finger and thrust her hand into a thorn-bush, so that she might drop some blood on to the spindle; then she threw it into the well, and jumped in herself.

Like her sister she awoke in the beautiful meadow, and walked over it till she came to the oven. 'Take us out, take us out, or alas! we shall be burnt to a cinder; we were baked through long ago,' cried the loaves as before. But the lazy girl answered, 'Do you think I am going to dirty my hands for you?' and walked on. Presently she came to the apple-tree. 'Shake me, shake me, I pray; my apples, one and all, are ripe,' it cried. But she only answered, 'A nice thing to ask me to do, one of the apples might fall on my head,' and passed on.

At last she came to Mother Holle's house, and as she had heard all about the large teeth from her sister, she was not afraid of them, and engaged herself without delay to the old woman.

The first day she was very obedient and industrious, and exerted herself to please Mother Holle, for she thought of the gold she should get in return. The next day, however, she began to dawdle over her work, and the third day she was more idle still; then she began to lie in bed in the mornings and refused to get up. Worse still, she neglected to make the old woman's bed properly, and forgot to shake it so that the feathers might fly about. So Mother Holle very soon got tired of her, and told her she might go. The lazy girl was delighted at this, and thought to herself, 'The gold will soon be mine.' Mother Holle led her, as she had led her sister, to the broad gateway; but as she was passing through, instead of the shower of gold, a great bucketful of pitch came pouring over her.

'That is in return for your services,' said the old woman, and she shut the gate.

So the lazy girl had to go home covered with pitch, and the cock on the well called out as she saw her:

> *'Cock-a-doodle-doo!*
> *Your dirty daughter's come back to you.'*

But, try what she would, she could not get the pitch off and it stuck to her as long as she lived.

LITTLE RED-CAP [LITTLE RED RIDING HOOD]

Once upon a time there was a dear little girl who was loved by everyone who looked at her, but most of all by her grandmother, and there was nothing that she would not have given to the child. Once she gave her a little cap of red velvet, which suited her so well that she would never wear anything else; so she was always called 'Little Red-Cap.'

One day her mother said to her: 'Come, Little Red-Cap, here is a piece of cake and a bottle of wine; take them to your grandmother, she is ill and weak, and they will do her good. Set out before it gets hot, and when you are going, walk nicely and quietly and do not run off the path, or you may fall and break the bottle, and then your grandmother will get nothing; and when you go into her room, don't forget to say, "Good morning", and don't peep into every corner before you do it.'

'I will take great care,' said Little Red-Cap to her mother, and gave her hand on it.

The grandmother lived out in the wood, half a league from the village, and just as Little Red-Cap entered the wood, a wolf met her. Red-Cap did not know what a wicked creature he was, and was not at all afraid of him.

'Good day, Little Red-Cap,' said he.

'Thank you kindly, wolf.'

'Whither away so early, Little Red-Cap?'

'To my grandmother's.'

'What have you got in your apron?'

'Cake and wine; yesterday was baking-day, so poor sick grandmother is to have something good, to make her stronger.'

'Where does your grandmother live, Little Red-Cap?'

'A good quarter of a league farther on in the wood; her house stands under the three large oak-trees, the nut-trees are just below; you surely must know it,' replied Little Red-Cap.

The wolf thought to himself: 'What a tender young creature! what a nice plump mouthful—she will be better to eat than the old woman. I must act craftily, so as to catch both.' So he walked for a short time by the side of Little Red-Cap, and then he said: 'See, Little Red-Cap, how pretty the flowers are about here—why do you not look round? I believe, too, that you do not hear how sweetly the little birds are singing; you walk gravely along as if you were going to school, while everything else out here in the wood is merry.'

Little Red-Cap raised her eyes, and when she saw the sunbeams dancing here and there through the trees, and pretty flowers growing everywhere, she thought: 'Suppose I take grandmother a fresh nosegay; that would please her too. It is so early in the day that I shall still get there in good time'; and so she ran from the path into the wood to look for flowers. And whenever she had picked one, she fancied that she saw a still prettier one farther on, and ran after it, and so got deeper and deeper into the wood.

Meanwhile the wolf ran straight to the grandmother's house and knocked at the door.

'Who is there?'

'Little Red-Cap,' replied the wolf. 'She is bringing cake and wine; open the door.'

'Lift the latch,' called out the grandmother, 'I am too weak, and cannot get up.'

The wolf lifted the latch, the door sprang open, and without saying a word he went straight to the grandmother's bed, and devoured her. Then he put on her clothes, dressed himself in her cap laid himself in bed and drew the curtains.

Little Red-Cap, however, had been running about picking flowers, and when she had gathered so many that she could carry no more, she remembered her grandmother, and set out on the way to her.

She was surprised to find the cottage-door standing open, and when she went into the room, she had such a strange feeling that she said to herself: 'Oh dear! how uneasy I feel today, and at other times I like being with grandmother so much.' She called out: 'Good morning,' but received no answer; so she went to the bed and drew back the curtains. There lay her grandmother with her cap pulled far over her face, and looking very strange.

'Oh! grandmother,' she said, 'what big ears you have!'

'The better to hear you with, my child,' was the reply.

'But, grandmother, what big eyes you have!' she said.

'The better to see you with, my dear.'

'But, grandmother, what large hands you have!'

'The better to hug you with.'

'Oh! but, grandmother, what a terrible big mouth you have!'

'The better to eat you with!'

And scarcely had the wolf said this, than with one bound he was out of bed and swallowed up Red-Cap.

When the wolf had appeased his appetite, he lay down again in the bed, fell asleep and began to snore very loud. The huntsman was just passing the house, and thought to himself: 'How the old woman is snoring! I must just see if she wants anything.' So he went into the room, and when he came to the bed, he saw that the wolf was lying in it. 'Do I find you here, you old sinner!' said he. 'I have long sought you!' Then just as he was going to fire at him, it occurred to him that the wolf might have devoured the grandmother, and that she might still be saved, so he did not fire, but took a pair of scissors, and began to cut open the stomach of the sleeping wolf. When he had made two snips, he saw the little Red-Cap shining, and then he made two snips more, and the little girl sprang out, crying: 'Ah, how frightened I have been! How dark it was inside the wolf'; and after that the aged grandmother came out alive also, but scarcely able to breathe. Red-Cap, however, quickly fetched great stones with which they filled the wolf's belly, and when he awoke, he wanted to run away, but the stones were so heavy that he collapsed at once, and fell dead.

Then all three were delighted. The huntsman drew off the wolf's skin and went home with it; the grandmother ate the cake and drank the wine which Red-Cap had brought, and revived, but Red-Cap thought to herself: 'As long as I live, I will never by myself leave the path, to run into the wood, when my mother has forbidden me to do so.'

It also related that once when Red-Cap was again taking cakes to the old grandmother, another wolf spoke to her, and tried to entice her from the path. Red-Cap, however, was on her guard, and went straight forward on her way, and told her grandmother that she had met the wolf, and that he had said 'good morning' to her, but with such a wicked look in his eyes, that if they had not been on the public road she was certain he would have eaten her up. 'Well,' said the grandmother, 'we will shut the door, that he may not come in.' Soon afterwards the wolf knocked, and cried: 'Open the door, grandmother, I am Little Red-Cap, and am bringing you some cakes.' But they did not speak, or open the door, so the greybeard stole twice or thrice round the house, and at last jumped on the roof, intending to wait until Red-Cap went home in the evening, and then to steal after her and devour her in the darkness. But the grandmother saw what was in his thoughts. In front of the house was a great stone trough, so she said to the child: 'Take the pail, Red-Cap; I made some sausages yesterday, so carry the water in which I boiled them to the trough.' Red-Cap carried until the great trough was quite full. Then the smell of the sausages reached the wolf, and he sniffed and peeped down, and at last stretched out his neck so far that he could no longer keep his footing and began to slip, and slipped down from the roof straight into the great trough, and was drowned. But Red-Cap went joyously home, and no one ever did anything to harm her again.

THE ROBBER BRIDEGROOM

There was once a miller who had one beautiful daughter, and as she was grown up, he was anxious that she should be well married and provided for. He said to himself, 'I will give her to the first suitable man who comes and asks for her hand.' Not long after a suitor appeared, and as he appeared to be very rich and the miller could see nothing in him with which to find fault, he betrothed his daughter to him. But the girl did not care for the man as a girl ought to care for her betrothed husband. She did not feel that she could trust him, and she could not look at him nor think of him without an inward shudder. One day he said to her, 'You have not yet paid me a visit, although we have been betrothed for some time.' 'I do not know where your house is,' she answered. 'My house is out there in the dark forest,' he said. She tried to excuse herself by saying that she would not be able to find the way thither. Her betrothed only replied, 'You must come and see me next Sunday; I have already invited guests for that day, and that you may not mistake the way, I will strew ashes along the path.'

When Sunday came, and it was time for the girl to start, a feeling of dread came over her which she could not explain, and that she might be able to find her path again, she filled her pockets with peas and lentils to sprinkle on the ground as she went along. On reaching the entrance to the forest she found the path strewed with ashes, and these she followed, throwing down some peas on either side of her at every step she took. She walked the whole day until she came to the deepest, darkest part of the forest. There she saw a lonely house, looking so grim and mysterious, that it did not please her at all. She stepped inside, but not a soul was to be seen, and a great silence reigned throughout. Suddenly a voice cried:

> *'Turn back, turn back, young maiden fair,*
> *Linger not in this murderers' lair.'*

The girl looked up and saw that the voice came from a bird hanging in a cage on the wall. Again it cried:

> *'Turn back, turn back, young maiden fair,*
> *Linger not in this murderers' lair.'*

The girl passed on, going from room to room of the house, but they were all empty, and still she saw no one. At last she came to the cellar, and there sat a very, very old woman, who could not keep her head from shaking. 'Can you tell me,' asked the girl, 'if my betrothed husband lives here?'

'Ah, you poor child,' answered the old woman, 'what a place for you to come to! This is a murderers' den. You think yourself a promised bride, and that your marriage will soon take place, but it is with death that you will keep your marriage feast. Look, do you see that large cauldron of water which I am obliged to keep on the fire! As soon as they have you in their power they will kill you without mercy, and cook and eat you, for they are eaters of men. If I did not take pity on you and save you, you would be lost.'

Thereupon the old woman led her behind a large cask, which quite hid her from view. 'Keep as still as a mouse,' she said; 'do not move or speak, or it will be all over with you. Tonight, when the robbers are all asleep, we will flee together. I have long been waiting for an opportunity to escape.'

The words were hardly out of her mouth when the godless crew returned, dragging another young girl along with them. They were all drunk, and paid no heed to her cries and lamentations. They gave her wine to drink, three glasses full, one of white wine, one of red, and one of yellow, and with that her heart gave way and she died. Then they tore off her dainty clothing, laid her on a table, and cut her beautiful body into pieces, and sprinkled salt upon it.

The poor betrothed girl crouched trembling and shuddering behind the cask, for she saw what a terrible fate had been intended for her by the robbers. One of them now noticed a gold ring still remaining on the little finger of the murdered girl, and as he could not draw it off easily, he took a hatchet and cut off the finger; but the finger sprang into the air, and fell behind the cask into the lap of the girl who was hiding there. The robber took a light and began looking for it, but he could not find it. 'Have you looked behind the large cask?' said one of the others. But the old woman called out, 'Come and eat your suppers, and let the thing be till tomorrow; the finger won't run away.'

'The old woman is right,' said the robbers, and they ceased looking for the finger and sat down.

The old woman then mixed a sleeping draught with their wine, and before long they were all lying on the floor of the cellar, fast asleep and snoring. As soon as the girl was assured of this, she came from behind the cask. She was obliged to step over the bodies of the sleepers, who were lying close together, and every moment she was filled with renewed dread lest she should awaken them. But God helped her, so that she passed safely over them, and then she and the old woman went upstairs, opened the door, and hastened as fast as they could from the murderers' den. They found the ashes scattered by the wind, but the peas and lentils had sprouted, and grown sufficiently above the ground, to guide them in the moonlight along the path. All night long they walked, and it was morning before they reached the mill. Then the girl told her father all that had happened.

The day came that had been fixed for the marriage. The bridegroom arrived and also a large company of guests, for the miller had taken care to invite all his friends and relations. As they sat at the feast, each guest in turn was asked to tell a tale; the bride sat still and did not say a word.

'And you, my love,' said the bridegroom, turning to her, 'is there no tale you know? Tell us something.'

'I will tell you a dream, then,' said the bride. 'I went alone through a forest and came at last to a house; not a soul could I find within, but a bird that was hanging in a cage on the wall cried:

> *'Turn back, turn back, young maiden fair,*
> *Linger not in this murderers' lair.'*

and again a second time it said these words.'

'My darling, this is only a dream.'

'I went on through the house from room to room, but they were all empty, and everything was so grim and mysterious. At last I went down to the cellar, and there sat a very, very old woman, who could not keep her head still. I asked her if my betrothed lived here, and she answered, "Ah, you poor child, you are come to a murderers' den; your betrothed does indeed live here, but he will kill you without mercy and afterwards cook and eat you."'

'My darling, this is only a dream.'

'The old woman hid me behind a large cask, and scarcely had she done this when the robbers returned home, dragging a young girl along with them. They gave her three kinds of wine to drink, white, red, and yellow, and with that she died.'

'My darling, this is only a dream.'

'Then they tore off her dainty clothing, and cut her beautiful body into pieces and sprinkled salt upon it.'

'My darling, this is only a dream.'

'And one of the robbers saw that there was a gold ring still left on her finger, and as it was difficult to draw off, he took a hatchet and cut off her finger; but the finger sprang into the air and fell behind the great cask into my lap. And here is the finger with the ring.' And with these words the bride drew forth the finger and shewed it to the assembled guests.

The bridegroom, who during this recital had grown deadly pale, up and tried to escape, but the guests seized him and held him fast. They delivered him up to justice, and he and all his murderous band were condemned to death for their wicked deeds.

TOM THUMB

A poor woodman sat in his cottage one night, smoking his pipe by the fireside, while his wife sat by his side spinning. 'How lonely it is, wife,' said he, as he puffed out a long curl of smoke, 'for you and me to sit here by ourselves, without any children to play about and amuse us while other people seem so happy and merry with their children!' 'What you say is very true,' said the wife, sighing, and turning round her wheel; 'how happy should I be if I had but one child! If it were ever so small—nay, if it were no bigger than my thumb—I should be very happy, and love it dearly.' Now—odd as you may think it—it came to pass that this good woman's wish was fulfilled, just in the very way she had wished it; for, not long afterwards, she had a little boy, who was quite healthy and strong, but was not much bigger than my thumb. So they said, 'Well, we cannot say we have not got what we wished for, and, little as he is, we will love him dearly.' And they called him Thomas Thumb.

They gave him plenty of food, yet for all they could do he never grew bigger, but kept just the same size as he had been when he was born. Still, his eyes were sharp and sparkling, and he soon showed himself to be a clever little fellow, who always knew well what he was about.

One day, as the woodman was getting ready to go into the wood to cut fuel, he said, 'I wish I had someone to bring the cart after me, for I want to make haste.' 'Oh, father,' cried Tom, 'I will take care of that; the cart shall be in the wood by the time you want it.' Then the woodman laughed, and said, 'How can that be? you cannot reach up to the horse's bridle.' 'Never mind that, father,' said Tom; 'if my mother will only harness the horse, I will get into his ear and tell him which way to go.' 'Well,' said the father, 'we will try for once.'

When the time came the mother harnessed the horse to the cart, and put Tom into his ear; and as he sat there the little man told the beast how to go, crying out, 'Go on!' and 'Stop!' as he wanted: and thus the horse went on just as well as if the woodman had driven it himself into the wood. It happened that as the horse was going a little too fast, and Tom was calling out, 'Gently! gently!' two strangers came up. 'What an odd thing that is!' said one: 'there is a cart going along, and I hear a carter talking to the horse, but yet I can see no one.' 'That is queer, indeed,' said the other; 'let us follow the cart, and see where it goes.' So they went on into the wood, till at last they came to the place where the woodman was. Then Tom Thumb, seeing his father, cried out, 'See, father, here I am with the cart, all right and safe! now take me down!' So his father took hold of the horse with one hand, and with the other took his son out of the horse's ear, and put him down upon a straw, where he sat as merry as you please.

The two strangers were all this time looking on, and did not know what to say for wonder. At last one took the other aside, and said, 'That little urchin will make our fortune, if we can get him, and carry him about from town to town as a show; we must buy him.' So they went up to the woodman, and asked him what he would take for the little man. 'He will be better off,' said they, 'with us than with you.' 'I won't sell him at all,' said the father; 'my own flesh and blood is dearer to me than all the silver and gold in the world.' But Tom, hearing of the bargain they wanted to make, crept up his father's coat to his shoulder and whispered in his ear, 'Take the money, father, and let them have me; I'll soon come back to you.'

So the woodman at last said he would sell Tom to the strangers for a large piece of gold, and they paid the price. 'Where would you like to sit?' said one of them. 'Oh, put me on the rim of your hat; that will be a nice gallery for me; I can walk about there and see the country as we go along.' So they did as he wished; and when Tom had taken leave of his father they took him away with them. They journeyed on till it began to be dusky, and then the little man said, 'Let me get down, I'm tired.' So the man took off his hat, and put him down on a clod of earth, in a ploughed field by the side of the road. But Tom ran about amongst the furrows, and at last slipped into an old mouse-hole. 'Good night, my masters!' said he, 'I'm off! mind and look sharp after me the next time.' Then they ran at once to the place, and poked the ends of their sticks into the mouse-hole, but all in vain; Tom only crawled farther and farther in; and at last it became quite dark, so that they were forced to go their way without their prize, as sulky as could be.

When Tom found they were gone, he came out of his hiding-place. 'What dangerous walking it is,' said he, 'in this ploughed field! If I were to fall from one of these great clods, I should undoubtedly break my neck.' At last, by good luck, he found a large empty snail-shell. 'This is lucky,' said he, 'I can sleep here very well'; and in he crept.

Just as he was falling asleep, he heard two men passing by, chatting together; and one said to the other, 'How can we rob that rich parson's house of his silver and gold?' 'I'll tell you!' cried Tom. 'What noise was that?' said the thief, frightened; 'I'm sure I heard someone speak.' They stood still listening, and Tom said, 'Take me with you, and I'll soon show you how to get the parson's money.' 'But where are you?' said they. 'Look about on the ground,' answered he, 'and listen where the sound comes from.' At last the thieves found him out, and lifted him up in their hands. 'You little urchin!' they said, 'what can you do for us?' 'Why, I can get between the iron window-bars of the parson's house, and throw you out whatever you want.' 'That's a good thought,' said the thieves; 'come along, we shall see what you can do.'

When they came to the parson's house, Tom slipped through the window-bars into the room, and then called out as loud as he could bawl, 'Will you have all that is here?' At this the thieves were frightened, and said, 'Softly, softly! Speak low, that you may not awaken anybody.' But Tom seemed as if he did not understand them, and bawled out again, 'How much will you have? Shall I throw it all out?' Now the cook lay in the next room; and hearing a noise she raised herself up in her bed and listened. Meantime the thieves were frightened, and ran off a little way; but at last they plucked up their hearts, and said, 'The little urchin is only trying to make fools of us.' So they came back and whispered softly to him, saying, 'Now let us have no more of your roguish jokes; but throw us out some of the money.' Then Tom called out as loud as he could, 'Very well! hold your hands! here it comes.'

The cook heard this quite plain, so she sprang out of bed, and ran to open the door. The thieves ran off as if a wolf was at their tails: and the maid, having groped about and found nothing, went away for a light. By the time she came back, Tom had slipped off into the barn; and when she had looked about and searched every hole and corner, and found nobody, she went to bed, thinking she must have been dreaming with her eyes open.

The little man crawled about in the hay-loft, and at last found a snug place to finish his night's rest in; so he laid himself down, meaning to sleep till daylight, and then find his way home to his father and mother. But alas! how woefully he was undone! what crosses and sorrows happen to us all in this world! The cook got up early, before daybreak, to feed the cows; and going straight to the hay-loft, carried away a large bundle of hay, with the little man in the middle of it, fast asleep. He still, however, slept on, and did not awake till he found himself in the mouth of the cow; for the cook had put the hay into the cow's rick, and the cow had taken Tom up in a mouthful of it. 'Good lack-a-day!' said he, 'how came I to tumble into the mill?' But he soon found out where he really was; and was forced to have all his wits about him, that he might not get between the cow's teeth, and so be crushed to death. At last down he went into her stomach. 'It is rather dark,' said he; 'they forgot to build windows in this room to let the sun in; a candle would be no bad thing.'

Though he made the best of his bad luck, he did not like his quarters at all; and the worst of it was, that more and more hay was always coming down, and the space left for him became smaller and smaller. At last he cried out as loud as he could, 'Don't bring me any more hay! Don't bring me any more hay!'

The maid happened to be just then milking the cow; and hearing someone speak, but seeing nobody, and yet being quite sure it was the same voice that she had heard in the night, she was so frightened that she fell off her stool, and overset the milk-pail. As soon as she could pick herself up out of the dirt, she ran off as fast as she could to her master the parson, and said, 'Sir, sir, the cow is talking!' But the parson said, 'Woman, thou art surely mad!' However, he went with her into the cow-house, to try and see what was the matter.

Scarcely had they set foot on the threshold, when Tom called out, 'Don't bring me any more hay!' Then the parson himself was frightened; and thinking the cow was surely bewitched, told his man to kill her on the spot. So the cow was killed, and cut up; and the stomach, in which Tom lay, was thrown out upon a dunghill.

Tom soon set himself to work to get out, which was not a very easy task; but at last, just as he had made room to get his head out, fresh ill-luck befell him. A hungry wolf sprang out, and swallowed up the whole stomach, with Tom in it, at one gulp, and ran away.

Tom, however, was still not disheartened; and thinking the wolf would not dislike having some chat with him as he was going along, he called out, 'My good friend, I can show you a famous treat.' 'Where's that?' said the wolf. 'In such and such a house,' said Tom, describing his own father's house. 'You can crawl through the drain into the kitchen and then into the pantry, and there you will find cakes, ham, beef, cold chicken, roast pig, apple-dumplings, and everything that your heart can wish.'

The wolf did not want to be asked twice; so that very night he went to the house and crawled through the drain into the kitchen, and then into the pantry, and ate and drank there to his heart's content. As soon as he had had enough he wanted to get away; but he had eaten so much that he could not go out by the same way he came in.

This was just what Tom had reckoned upon; and now he began to set up a great shout, making all the noise he could. 'Will you be easy?' said the wolf; 'you'll awaken everybody in the house if you make such a clatter.' 'What's that to me?' said the little man; 'you have had your frolic, now I've a mind to be merry myself'; and he began, singing and shouting as loud as he could.

The woodman and his wife, being awakened by the noise, peeped through a crack in the door; but when they saw a wolf was there, you may well suppose that they were sadly frightened; and the woodman ran for his axe, and gave his wife a scythe. 'Do you stay behind,' said the woodman, 'and when I have knocked him on the head you must rip him up with the scythe.' Tom heard all this, and cried out, 'Father, father! I am here, the wolf has swallowed me.' And his father said,

'Heaven be praised! we have found our dear child again'; and he told his wife not to use the scythe for fear she should hurt him. Then he aimed a great blow, and struck the wolf on the head, and killed him on the spot! and when he was dead they cut open his body, and set Tommy free. 'Ah!' said the father, 'what fears we have had for you!' 'Yes, father,' answered he; 'I have travelled all over the world, I think, in one way or other, since we parted; and now I am very glad to come home and get fresh air again.' 'Why, where have you been?' said his father. 'I have been in a mouse-hole—and in a snail-shell—and down a cow's throat—and in the wolf's belly; and yet here I am again, safe and sound.'

'Well,' said they, 'you are come back, and we will not sell you again for all the riches in the world.'

Then they hugged and kissed their dear little son, and gave him plenty to eat and drink, for he was very hungry; and then they fetched new clothes for him, for his old ones had been quite spoiled on his journey. So Master Thumb stayed at home with his father and mother, in peace; for though he had been so great a traveller, and had done and seen so many fine things, and was fond enough of telling the whole story, he always agreed that, after all, there's no place like HOME!

RUMPELSTILTSKIN

By the side of a wood, in a country a long way off, ran a fine
stream of water; and upon the stream there stood a mill. The
miller's house was close by, and the miller, you must know,
had a very beautiful daughter. She was, moreover, very shrewd
and clever; and the miller was so proud of her, that he one
day told the king of the land, who used to come and hunt in
the wood, that his daughter could spin gold out of straw. Now
this king was very fond of money; and when he heard the
miller's boast his greediness was raised, and he sent for the
girl to be brought before him. Then he led her to a chamber
in his palace where there was a great heap of straw, and gave
her a spinning-wheel, and said, 'All this must be spun into
gold before morning, as you love your life.' It was in vain that
the poor maiden said that it was only a silly boast of her father,
for that she could do no such thing as spin straw into gold:
the chamber door was locked, and she was left alone.

She sat down in one corner of the room, and began to
bewail her hard fate; when on a sudden the door opened, and
a droll-looking little man hobbled in, and said, 'Good morrow
to you, my good lass; what are you weeping for?' 'Alas!' said
she, 'I must spin this straw into gold, and I know not how.'
'What will you give me,' said the hobgoblin, 'to do it for you?'

'My necklace,' replied the maiden. He took her at her word, and sat himself down to the wheel, and whistled and sang:

> *'Round about, round about,*
> *Lo and behold!*
> *Reel away, reel away,*
> *Straw into gold!'*

And round about the wheel went merrily; the work was quickly done, and the straw was all spun into gold.

When the king came and saw this, he was greatly astonished and pleased; but his heart grew still more greedy of gain, and he shut up the poor miller's daughter again with a fresh task. Then she knew not what to do, and sat down once more to weep; but the dwarf soon opened the door, and said, 'What will you give me to do your task?' 'The ring on my finger,' said she. So her little friend took the ring, and began to work at the wheel again, and whistled and sang:

> *'Round about, round about,*
> *Lo and behold!*
> *Reel away, reel away,*
> *Straw into gold!'*

till, long before morning, all was done again.

The king was greatly delighted to see all this glittering treasure; but still he had not enough: so he took the miller's daughter to a yet larger heap, and said, 'All this must be spun tonight; and if it is, you shall be my queen.' As soon as she was alone that dwarf came in, and said, 'What will you give me to spin gold for you this third time?' 'I have nothing left,' said she. 'Then say you will give me,' said the little man, 'the first little child that you may have when you are queen.' 'That may never be,' thought the miller's daughter: and as she knew no other way to get her task done, she said she would do what he asked.

Round went the wheel again to the old song, and the manikin once more spun the heap into gold. The king came in the morning, and, finding all he wanted, was forced to keep his word; so he married the miller's daughter, and she really became queen.

At the birth of her first little child she was very glad, and forgot the dwarf, and what she had said. But one day he came into her room, where she was sitting playing with her baby, and put her in mind of it. Then she grieved sorely at her misfortune, and said she would give him all the wealth of the kingdom if he would let her off, but in vain; till at last her tears softened him, and he said, 'I will give you three days' grace, and if during that time you tell me my name, you shall keep your child.'

Now the queen lay awake all night, thinking of all the odd names that she had ever heard; and she sent messengers all over the land to find out new ones. The next day the little man came, and she began with TIMOTHY, ICHABOD, BENJAMIN, JEREMIAH, and all the names she could remember; but to all and each of them he said, 'Madam, that is not my name.'

The second day she began with all the comical names she could hear of, BANDY-LEGS, HUNCHBACK, CROOK-SHANKS, and so on; but the little gentleman still said to every one of them, 'Madam, that is not my name.'

The third day one of the messengers came back, and said, 'I have travelled two days without hearing of any other names; but yesterday, as I was climbing a high hill, among the trees of the forest where the fox and the hare bid each other good night, I saw a little hut; and before the hut burnt a fire; and round about the fire a funny little dwarf was dancing upon one leg, and singing:

> '"Merrily the feast I'll make.
> Today I'll brew, tomorrow bake;
> Merrily I'll dance and sing,

For next day will a stranger bring.
Little does my lady dream
Rumpelstiltskin is my name!"'

When the queen heard this she jumped for joy, and as soon as her little friend came she sat down upon her throne, and called all her court round to enjoy the fun; and the nurse stood by her side with the baby in her arms, as if it was quite ready to be given up. Then the little man began to chuckle at the thought of having the poor child, to take home with him to his hut in the woods; and he cried out, 'Now, lady, what is my name?' 'Is it JOHN?' asked she. 'No, madam!' 'Is it TOM?' 'No, madam!' 'Is it JEMMY?' 'It is not.' 'Can your name be RUMPELSTILTSKIN?' said the lady slyly. 'Some witch told you that!—some witch told you that!' cried the little man, and dashed his right foot in a rage so deep into the floor, that he was forced to lay hold of it with both hands to pull it out.

Then he made the best of his way off, while the nurse laughed and the baby crowed; and all the court jeered at him for having had so much trouble for nothing, and said, 'We wish you a very good morning, and a merry feast, Mr RUMPELSTILTSKIN!'

CLEVER GRETEL

There was once a cook named Gretel, who wore shoes with red heels, and when she walked out with them on, she turned herself this way and that, was quite happy and thought: 'You certainly are a pretty girl!' And when she came home she drank, in her gladness of heart, a draught of wine, and as wine excites a desire to eat, she tasted the best of whatever she was cooking until she was satisfied, and said: 'The cook must know what the food is like.'

It came to pass that the master one day said to her: 'Gretel, there is a guest coming this evening; prepare me two fowls very daintily.' 'I will see to it, master,' answered Gretel. She killed two fowls, scalded them, plucked them, put them on the spit, and towards evening set them before the fire, that they might roast. The fowls began to turn brown, and were nearly ready, but the guest had not yet arrived. Then Gretel called out to her master: 'If the guest does not come, I must take the fowls away from the fire, but it will be a sin and a shame if they are not eaten the moment they are at their juiciest.' The master said: 'I will run myself, and fetch the guest.' When the master had turned his back, Gretel laid the spit with the fowls on one side, and thought: 'Standing so long by the fire there, makes one sweat and thirsty; who knows when they will come? Meanwhile, I will run into the cellar, and take a drink.' She ran down, set a jug, said: 'God bless it for you, Gretel,' and took a good drink, and thought that wine should flow on, and should not be interrupted, and took yet another hearty draught.

Then she went and put the fowls down again to the fire, basted them, and drove the spit merrily round. But as the roast meat smelt so good, Gretel thought: 'Something might be wrong, it ought to be tasted!' She touched it with her finger, and said: 'Ah! how good fowls are! It certainly is a sin and a shame that they are not eaten at the right time!' She ran to the window, to see if the master was not coming with his guest, but she saw no one, and went back to the fowls and thought: 'One of the wings is burning! I had better take it off and eat it.' So she cut it off, ate it, and enjoyed it, and when she had done, she thought: 'The other must go down too, or else master will observe that something is missing.' When the two wings were eaten, she went and looked for her master, and did not see him. It suddenly occurred to her: 'Who knows? They are perhaps not coming at all, and have turned in somewhere.' Then she said: 'Well, Gretel, enjoy yourself, one fowl has been cut into, take another drink, and eat it up entirely; when it is eaten you will have some peace, why should God's good gifts be spoilt?' So she ran into the cellar again, took an enormous drink and ate up the one chicken in great glee. When one of the chickens was swallowed down, and still her master did not come, Gretel looked at the other and said: 'What one is, the other should be likewise, the two go together; what's right for the one is right for the other; I think if I were to take another draught it would do me no harm.' So she took another hearty drink, and let the second chicken follow the first.

While she was making the most of it, her master came and cried: 'Hurry up, Gretel, the guest is coming directly after me!' 'Yes, sir, I will soon serve up,' answered Gretel. Meantime the master looked to see what the table was properly laid, and took the great knife, wherewith he was going to carve the chickens, and sharpened it on the steps. Presently the guest came, and knocked politely and courteously at the house-door. Gretel ran, and looked to see who was there, and when she saw the guest, she put her finger to her lips and said: 'Hush! hush! go away as quickly as you can, if my master catches you it will be the worse for you; he certainly did ask you to supper, but his intention is to cut off your two ears. Just listen how he is sharpening the knife for it!' The guest heard the sharpening, and hurried down the steps again as fast as he could. Gretel was not idle; she ran screaming to her master, and cried: 'You have invited a fine guest!' 'Why, Gretel? What do you mean by that?' 'Yes,' said she, 'he has taken the chickens which I was just going to serve up, off the dish, and has run away with them!' 'That's a nice trick!' said her master, and lamented the fine chickens. 'If he had but left me one, so that something remained for me to eat.' He called to him to stop, but the guest pretended not to hear. Then he ran after him with the knife still in his hand, crying: 'Just one, just one,' meaning that the guest should leave him just one chicken, and not take both. The guest, however, thought no otherwise than that he was to give up one of his ears, and ran as if fire were burning under him, in order to take them both with him.

THE OLD MAN AND HIS GRANDSON

There was once a very old man, whose eyes had become dim, his ears dull of hearing, his knees trembled, and when he sat at table he could hardly hold the spoon, and spilt the broth upon the table-cloth or let it run out of his mouth. His son and his son's wife were disgusted at this, so the old grandfather at last had to sit in the corner behind the stove, and they gave him his food in an earthenware bowl, and not even enough of it. And he used to look towards the table with his eyes full of tears. Once, too, his trembling hands could not hold the bowl, and it fell to the ground and broke. The young wife scolded him, but he said nothing and only sighed. Then they brought him a wooden bowl for a few half-pence, out of which he had to eat.

They were once sitting thus when the little grandson of four years old began to gather together some bits of wood upon the ground. 'What are you doing there?' asked the father. 'I am making a little trough,' answered the child, 'for father and mother to eat out of when I am big. The man and his wife looked at each other for a while, and presently began to cry. Then they took the old grandfather to the table, and henceforth always let him eat with them, and likewise said nothing if he did spill a little of anything.

THE LITTLE PEASANT

There was a certain village wherein no one lived but really rich peasants, and just one poor one, whom they called the little peasant. He had not even so much as a cow, and still less money to buy one, and yet he and his wife did so wish to have one. One day he said to her: 'Listen, I have a good idea, there is our gossip the carpenter, he shall make us a wooden calf, and paint it brown, so that it looks like any other, and in time it will certainly get big and be a cow.' The woman also liked the idea, and their gossip the carpenter cut and planed the calf, and painted it as it ought to be, and made it with its head hanging down as if it were eating.

Next morning when the cows were being driven out, the little peasant called the cow-herd in and said: 'Look, I have a little calf there, but it is still small and has to be carried.' The cow-herd said: 'All right,' and took it in his arms and carried it to the pasture, and set it among the grass. The little calf always remained standing like one which was eating, and the cow-herd said: 'It will soon run by itself, just look how it eats already!' At night when he was going to drive the herd home again, he said to the calf: 'If you can stand there and eat your fill, you can also go on your four legs; I don't care to drag you home again in my arms.' But the little peasant stood at his door, and waited for his little calf, and when the cow-herd drove the cows through the village, and the calf was missing, he inquired where it was. The cow-herd answered: 'It is still standing out there eating. It would not stop and come with us.' But the little peasant said: 'Oh, but I must have my beast back again.' Then they went back to the meadow together, but someone had stolen the calf, and it was gone. The cow-herd said: 'It must have run away.' The peasant, however, said: 'Don't tell me that,' and led the cow-herd before the mayor, who for his carelessness condemned him to give the peasant a cow for the calf which had run away.

And now the little peasant and his wife had the cow for which they had so long wished, and they were heartily glad, but they had no food for it, and could give it nothing to eat, so it soon had to be killed. They salted the flesh, and the peasant went into the town and wanted to sell the skin there, so that he might buy a new calf with the proceeds. On the way he passed by a mill, and there sat a raven with broken wings, and out of pity he took him and wrapped him in the skin. But as the weather grew so bad and there was a storm of rain and wind, he could go no farther, and turned back to the mill and begged for shelter. The miller's wife was alone in the house, and said to the peasant: 'Lay yourself on the straw there,' and gave him a slice of bread and cheese. The peasant ate it, and lay down with his skin beside him, and the woman thought: 'He is tired and has gone to sleep.' In the meantime came the parson; the miller's wife received him well, and said: 'My husband is out, so we will have a feast.' The peasant listened, and when he heard them talk about feasting he was vexed that he had been forced to make shift with a slice of bread and cheese. Then the woman served up four different things, roast meat, salad, cakes, and wine.

Just as they were about to sit down and eat, there was a knocking outside. The woman said: 'Oh, heavens! It is my husband!' she quickly hid the roast meat inside the tiled stove, the wine under the pillow, the salad on the bed, the cakes under it, and the parson in the closet on the porch. Then she opened the door for her husband, and said: 'Thank heaven, you are back again! There is such a storm, it looks as if the world were coming to an end.' The miller saw the peasant lying on the straw, and asked, 'What is that fellow doing there?' 'Ah,' said the wife, 'the poor knave came in the storm and rain, and begged for shelter, so I gave him a bit of bread and cheese, and showed him where the straw was.' The man said: 'I have no objection, but be quick and get me something to eat.' The woman said: 'But I have nothing but bread and cheese.' 'I am contented with anything,' replied the husband, 'so far as I am concerned, bread and cheese will do,' and looked at the peasant and said: 'Come and eat some more with me.' The peasant did not require to be invited twice, but got up and ate. After this the miller saw the skin in which the raven was, lying on the ground, and asked: 'What have you there?' The peasant answered: 'I have a soothsayer inside it.' 'Can he foretell anything to me?' said the miller. 'Why not?' answered the peasant: 'but he only says four things, and the fifth he keeps to himself.' The miller was curious, and said: 'Let him foretell something for once.' Then the peasant pinched the raven's head, so that he croaked and made a noise like *krr*, *krr*. The miller said: 'What did he say?' The peasant answered: 'In the first place, he says that there is some wine hidden under the pillow.' 'Bless me!' cried the miller, and went there and found the wine. 'Now go on,' said he. The peasant made the raven croak again, and said: 'In the second place, he says that there is some roast meat in the tiled stove.' 'Upon my word!' cried the miller, and went thither, and found the roast meat. The peasant made the raven prophesy still more, and said: 'Thirdly, he says that there is some salad on the bed.' 'That would be a fine thing!' cried the miller, and went there and found the salad. At last the peasant pinched the raven once more till he croaked, and said: 'Fourthly, he says that there are some cakes under the bed.' 'That would be a fine thing!' cried the miller, and looked there, and found the cakes.

And now the two sat down to the table together, but the miller's wife was frightened to death, and went to bed and took all the keys with her. The miller would have liked much to know the fifth, but the little peasant said: 'First, we will quickly eat the four things, for the fifth is something bad.' So they ate, and after that they bargained how much the miller was to give for the fifth prophecy, until they agreed on three hundred talers. Then the peasant once more pinched the raven's head till he croaked loudly. The miller asked: 'What did he say?' The peasant replied: 'He says that the Devil is hiding outside there in the closet on the porch.' The miller said: 'The Devil must go out,' and opened the house-door; then the woman was forced to give up the keys, and the peasant unlocked the closet. The parson ran out as fast as he could, and the miller said: 'It was true; I saw the black rascal with my own eyes.' The peasant, however, made off next morning by daybreak with the three hundred talers.

At home the small peasant gradually launched out; he built a beautiful house, and the peasants said: 'The small peasant has certainly been to the place where golden snow falls, and people carry the gold home in shovels.' Then the small peasant was brought before the mayor, and bidden to say from whence his wealth came. He answered: 'I sold my cow's skin in the town, for three hundred talers.' When the peasants heard that, they too wished to enjoy this great profit, and ran home, killed all their cows, and stripped off their skins in order to sell them in the town to the greatest advantage. The mayor, however, said: 'But my servant must go first.' When she came to the merchant in the town, he did not give her more than two talers for a skin, and when the others came, he did not give them so much, and said: 'What can I do with all these skins?'

Then the peasants were vexed that the small peasant should have thus outwitted them, wanted to take vengeance on him, and accused him of this treachery before the major. The innocent little peasant was unanimously sentenced to death, and was to be rolled into the water, in a barrel pierced full of holes. He was led forth, and a priest was brought who was to say a mass for his soul. The others were all obliged to retire to a distance, and when the peasant looked at the priest, he recognized the man who had been with the miller's wife. He said to him: 'I set you free from the closet, set me free from the barrel.' At this same moment up came, with a flock of sheep, the very shepherd whom the peasant knew had long been wishing to be mayor, so he cried with all his might: 'No, I will not do it; if the whole world insists on it, I will not do it!' The shepherd hearing that, came up to him, and asked: 'What are you about? What is it that you will not do?' The peasant said: 'They want to make me mayor, if I will but put myself in the barrel, but I will not do it.' The shepherd said: 'If nothing more than that is needful in order to be mayor, I would get into the barrel at once.' The peasant said: 'If you will get in, you will be mayor.' The shepherd was willing, and got in, and the peasant shut the top down on him; then he took the shepherd's flock for himself, and drove it away. The parson went to the crowd, and declared that the mass had been said. Then they came and rolled the barrel towards the water. When the barrel began to roll, the shepherd cried: 'I am quite willing to be mayor.' They believed no otherwise than that it was the peasant who was saying this, and answered: 'That is what we intend, but first you shall look about you a little down below there,' and they rolled the barrel down into the water.

After that the peasants went home, and as they were entering the village, the small peasant also came quietly in, driving a flock of sheep and looking quite contented. Then the peasants were astonished, and said: 'Peasant, from whence do you come? Have you come out of the water?' 'Yes, truly,' replied the peasant, 'I sank deep, deep down, until at last I got to the bottom; I pushed the bottom out of the barrel, and crept out, and there were pretty meadows on which a number of lambs were feeding, and from thence I brought this flock away with me.' Said the peasants: 'Are there any more there?' 'Oh, yes,' said he, 'more than I could want.' Then the peasants made up their minds that they too would fetch some sheep for themselves, a flock apiece, but the mayor said: 'I come first.' So they went to the water together, and just then there were some of the small fleecy clouds in the blue sky, which are called little lambs, and they were reflected in the water, whereupon the peasants cried: 'We already see the sheep down below!' The mayor pressed forward and said: 'I will go down first, and look about me, and if things promise well I'll call you.' So he jumped in; splash! went the water; it sounded as if he were calling them, and the whole crowd plunged in after him as one man. Then the entire village was dead, and the small peasant, as sole heir, became a rich man.

FREDERICK AND CATHERINE

There was once a man called Frederick: he had a wife whose name was Catherine, and they had not long been married. One day Frederick said. 'Kate! I am going to work in the fields; when I come back I shall be hungry so let me have something nice cooked, and a good draught of ale.' 'Very well,' said she, 'it shall all be ready.' When dinner-time drew nigh, Catherine took a nice steak, which was all the meat she had, and put it on the fire to fry. The steak soon began to look brown, and to crackle in the pan; and Catherine stood by with a fork and turned it: then she said to herself, 'The steak is almost ready, I may as well go to the cellar for the ale.' So she left the pan on the fire and took a large jug and went into the cellar and tapped the ale cask. The beer ran into the jug and Catherine stood looking on. At last it popped into her head, 'The dog is not shut up—he may be running away with the steak; that's well thought of.' So up she ran from the cellar; and sure enough the rascally cur had got the steak in his mouth, and was making off with it.

Away ran Catherine, and away ran the dog across the field: but he ran faster than she, and stuck close to the steak. 'It's all gone, and "what can't be cured must be endured",' said Catherine. So she turned round; and as she had run a good way and was tired, she walked home leisurely to cool herself.

Now all this time the ale was running too, for Catherine had not turned the cock; and when the jug was full the liquor ran upon the floor till the cask was empty. When she got to the cellar stairs she saw what had happened. 'My stars!' said she, 'what shall I do to keep Frederick from seeing all this slopping about?' So she thought a while; and at last remembered that there was a sack of fine meal bought at the last fair, and that if she sprinkled this over the floor it would suck up the ale nicely. 'What a lucky thing,' said she, 'that we kept that meal! we have now a good use for it.' So away she went for it: but she managed to set it down just upon the great jug full of beer, and upset it; and thus all the ale that had been saved was set swimming on the floor also. 'Ah! well,' said she, 'when one goes another may as well follow.' Then she strewed the meal all about the cellar, and was quite pleased with her cleverness, and said, 'How very neat and clean it looks!'

At noon Frederick came home. 'Now, wife,' cried he, 'what have you for dinner?' 'O Frederick!' answered she, 'I was cooking you a steak; but while I went down to draw the ale, the dog ran away with it; and while I ran after him, the ale ran out; and when I went to dry up the ale with the sack of meal that we got at the fair, I upset the jug: but the cellar is now quite dry, and looks so clean!' 'Kate, Kate,' said he, 'how could you do all this?' Why did you leave the steak to fry, and the ale to run, and then spoil all the meal?' 'Why, Frederick,' said she, 'I did not know I was doing wrong; you should have told me before.'

The husband thought to himself, 'If my wife manages matters thus, I must look sharp myself.' Now he had a good deal of gold in the house: so he said to Catherine, 'What pretty yellow buttons these are! I shall put them into a box and bury them in the garden; but take care that you never go near or meddle with them.' 'No, Frederick,' said she, 'that I never will.' As soon as he was gone, there came by some pedlars with earthenware plates and dishes, and they asked her whether she would buy. 'Oh dear me, I should like to buy very much, but I have no money: if you had any use for yellow buttons, I might deal with you.' 'Yellow buttons!' said they: 'let us have a look at them.' 'Go into the garden and dig where I tell you, and you will find the yellow buttons: I dare not go myself.' So the rogues went: and when they found what these yellow buttons were, they took them all away, and left her plenty of plates and dishes. Then she set them all about the house for a show: and when Frederick came back, he cried out, 'Kate, what have you been doing?' 'See,' said she, 'I have bought all these with your yellow buttons: but I did not touch them myself; the pedlars went themselves and dug them up.' 'Wife, wife,' said Frederick, 'what a pretty piece of work you have made! those yellow buttons were all my money: how came you to do such a thing?' 'Why,' answered she, 'I did not know there was any harm in it; you should have told me.'

Catherine stood musing for a while, and at last said to her husband, 'Hark ye, Frederick, we will soon get the gold back: let us run after the thieves.' 'Well, we will try,' answered he; 'but take some butter and cheese with you, that we may have something to eat by the way.' 'Very well,' said she; and they set out: and as Frederick walked the fastest, he left his wife some way behind. 'It does not matter,' thought she: 'when we turn back, I shall be so much nearer home than he.'

Presently she came to the top of a hill, down the side of which there was a road so narrow that the cart wheels always chafed the trees on each side as they passed. 'Ah, see now,' said she, 'how they have bruised and wounded those poor trees; they will never get well.' So she took pity on them, and made use of the butter to grease them all, so that the wheels might not hurt them so much. While she was doing this kind office one of her cheeses fell out of the basket, and rolled down the hill. Catherine looked, but could not see where it had gone; so she said, 'Well, I suppose the other will go the same way and find you; he has younger legs than I have.' Then she rolled the other cheese after it; and away it went, nobody knows where, down the hill. But she said she supposed that they knew the road, and would follow her, and she could not stay there all day waiting for them.

At last she overtook Frederick, who desired her to give him something to eat. Then she gave him the dry bread. 'Where are the butter and cheese?' said he. 'Oh!' answered she, 'I used the butter to grease those poor trees that the wheels chafed so: and one of the cheeses ran away so I sent the other after it to find it, and I suppose they are both on the road together somewhere.' 'What a goose you are to do such silly things!' said the husband. 'How can you say so?' said she; 'I am sure you never told me not.'

They ate the dry bread together; and Frederick said, 'Kate, I hope you locked the door safe when you came away.' 'No,' answered she, 'you did not tell me.' 'Then go home, and do it now before we go any farther,' said Frederick, 'and bring with you something to eat.'

Catherine did as he told her, and thought to herself by the way, 'Frederick wants something to eat; but I don't think he is very fond of butter and cheese: I'll bring him a bag of fine nuts, and the vinegar, for I have often seen him take some.'

When she reached home, she bolted the back door, but the front door she took off the hinges, and said, 'Frederick told me to lock the door, but surely it can nowhere be so safe if I take it with me.' So she took her time by the way; and when she overtook her husband she cried out, 'There, Frederick, there is the door itself, you may watch it as carefully as you please.' 'Alas! alas!' said he, 'what a clever wife I have! I sent you to make the house fast, and you take the door away, so that everybody may go in and out as they please—however, as you have brought the door, you shall carry it about with you for your pains.' 'Very well,' answered she, 'I'll carry the door; but I'll not carry the nuts and vinegar bottle also—that would be too much of a load; so if you please, I'll fasten them to the door.'

Frederick of course made no objection to that plan, and

they set off into the wood to look for the thieves; but they could not find them: and when it grew dark, they climbed up into a tree to spend the night there. Scarcely were they up, than who should come by but the very rogues they were looking for. They were in truth great rascals, and belonged to that class of people who find things before they are lost; they were tired; so they sat down and made a fire under the very tree where Frederick and Catherine were. Frederick slipped down on the other side, and picked up some stones. Then he climbed up again, and tried to hit the thieves on the head with them: but they only said, 'It must be near morning, for the wind shakes the fir-apples down.'

Catherine, who had the door on her shoulder, began to be very tired; but she thought it was the nuts upon it that were so heavy: so she said softly, 'Frederick, I must let the nuts go.' 'No,' answered he, 'not now, they will discover us.' 'I can't help that: they must go.' 'Well, then, make haste and throw them down, if you will.' Then away rattled the nuts down among the boughs and one of the thieves cried, 'Bless me, it is hailing.'

A little while after, Catherine thought the door was still very heavy: so she whispered to Frederick, 'I must throw the vinegar down.' 'Pray don't,' answered he, 'it will discover us.' 'I can't help that,' said she, 'go it must.' So she poured all the vinegar down; and the thieves said, 'What a heavy dew there is!'

At last it popped into Catherine's head that it was the door itself that was so heavy all the time: so she whispered, 'Frederick, I must throw the door down soon.' But he begged and prayed her not to do so, for he was sure it would betray them. 'Here goes, however,' said she: and down went the door with such a clatter upon the thieves, that they cried out 'Murder!' and not knowing what was coming, ran away as fast as they could, and left all the gold. So when Frederick and Catherine came down, there they found all their money safe and sound.

SWEETHEART ROLAND

There was once upon a time a woman who was a real witch and had two daughters, one ugly and wicked, and this one she loved because she was her own daughter, and one beautiful and good, and this one she hated, because she was her stepdaughter. The stepdaughter once had a pretty apron, which the other fancied so much that she became envious, and told her mother that she must and would have that apron. 'Be quiet, my child,' said the old woman, 'and you shall have it. Your stepsister has long deserved death; tonight when she is asleep I will come and cut her head off. Only be careful that you are at the far side of the bed, and push her well to the front.' It would have been all over with the poor girl if she had not just then been standing in a corner, and heard everything. All day long she dared not go out of doors, and when bedtime had come, the witch's daughter got into bed first, so as to lie at the far side, but when she was asleep, the other pushed her gently to the front, and took for herself the place at the back, close by the wall. In the night, the old woman came creeping in, she held an axe in her right hand, and felt with her left to see if anyone were lying at the outside, and then she grasped the axe with both hands, and cut her own child's head off.

When she had gone away, the girl got up and went to

her sweetheart, who was called Roland, and knocked at his door. When he came out, she said to him: 'Listen, dearest Roland, we must fly in all haste; my stepmother wanted to kill me, but has struck her own child. When daylight comes, and she sees what she has done, we shall be lost.' 'But,' said Roland, 'I counsel you first to take away her magic wand, or we cannot escape if she pursues us.' The maiden fetched the magic wand, and she took the dead girl's head and dropped three drops of blood on the ground, one in front of the bed, one in the kitchen, and one on the stairs. Then she hurried away with her lover.

When the old witch got up next morning, she called her daughter, and wanted to give her the apron, but she did not come. Then the witch cried: 'Where are you?' 'Here, on the stairs, I am sweeping,' answered the first drop of blood. The old woman went out, but saw no one on the stairs, and cried again: 'Where are you?' 'Here in the kitchen, I am warming myself,' cried the second drop of blood. She went into the kitchen, but found no one. Then she cried again: 'Where are you?' 'Ah, here in the bed, I am sleeping,' cried the third drop of blood. She went into the room to the bed. What did she see there? Her own child, whose head she had cut off, bathed in her blood. The witch fell into a passion, sprang to the window, and as she could look forth quite far into the world, she perceived her stepdaughter hurrying away with her sweetheart Roland. 'That shall not help you,' cried she, 'even if you have got a long way off, you shall still not escape me.' She put on her many-league boots, in which she covered an hour's walk at every step, and it was not long before she overtook them. The girl, however, when she saw the old woman striding towards her, changed, with her magic wand, her sweetheart Roland into a lake, and herself into a duck swimming in the middle of it. The witch placed herself on the shore, threw breadcrumbs in, and went to endless trouble to entice the duck; but the duck did not let herself be enticed, and the old woman had to go home at night as she had come. At this the girl and her sweetheart Roland resumed their natural shapes again, and they walked on the whole night until daybreak. Then the maiden changed herself into a beautiful flower which stood in the midst of a briar hedge, and her sweetheart Roland into a fiddler. It was not long before the witch came striding up towards them, and said to the musician: 'Dear musician, may I pluck that beautiful flower for myself?' 'Oh, yes,' he replied, 'I will play to you while you do it.' As she was hastily creeping into the hedge and was just going to pluck the flower, knowing perfectly well who the flower was, he began to play, and whether she would or not, she was forced to dance, for it was a magical dance. The faster he played, the more violent springs was she forced to make, and the thorns tore her clothes from her body, and pricked her and wounded her till she bled, and as he did not stop, she had to dance till she lay dead on the ground.

As they were now set free, Roland said: 'Now I will go to my father and arrange for the wedding.' 'Then in the meantime I will stay here and wait for you,' said the girl, 'and that no one may recognize me, I will change myself into a red stone landmark.' Then Roland went away, and the girl stood like a red landmark in the field and waited for her beloved. But when Roland got home, he fell into the snares of another, who so fascinated him that he forgot the maiden. The poor girl remained there a long time, but at length, as he did not return at all, she was sad, and changed herself into a flower, and thought: 'Someone will surely come this way, and trample me down.'

It befell, however, that a shepherd kept his sheep in the field and saw the flower, and as it was so pretty, plucked it, took it with him, and laid it away in his chest. From that time forth, strange things happened in the shepherd's house. When he arose in the morning, all the work was already done, the room was swept, the table and benches cleaned, the fire in the hearth was lighted, and the water was fetched, and at noon, when he came home, the table was laid, and a good dinner served. He could not conceive how this came to pass, for he never saw a human being in his house, and no one could have concealed himself in it. He was certainly pleased with this good attendance, but still at last he was so afraid that he went to a wise woman and asked for her advice. The wise woman said: 'There is some enchantment behind it, listen very early some morning if anything is moving in the room, and if you see anything, no matter what it is, throw a white cloth over it, and then the magic will be stopped.'

The shepherd did as she bade him, and next morning just as day dawned, he saw the chest open, and the flower come out. Swiftly he sprang towards it, and threw a white cloth over it. Instantly the transformation came to an end, and a beautiful girl stood before him, who admitted to him that she had been the flower, and that up to this time she had attended to his house-keeping. She told him her story, and as she pleased him he asked her if she would marry him, but she answered: 'No,' for she wanted to remain faithful to her sweetheart Roland, although he had deserted her. Nevertheless, she promised not to go away, but to continue keeping house for the shepherd.

And now the time drew near when Roland's wedding was to be celebrated, and then, according to an old custom in the country, it was announced that all the girls were to be present at it, and sing in honour of the bridal pair. When the faithful maiden heard of this, she grew so sad that she thought her heart would break, and she would not go thither, but the other girls came and took her. When it came to her turn to sing, she stepped back, until at last she was the only one left, and then she could not refuse. But when she began her song, and it reached Roland's ears, he sprang up and cried: 'I know the voice, that is the true bride, I will have no other!' Everything he had forgotten, and which had vanished from his mind, had suddenly come home again to his heart. Then the faithful maiden held her wedding with her sweetheart Roland, and grief came to an end and joy began.

SNOWDROP

It was the middle of winter, when the broad flakes of snow were falling around, that the queen of a country many thousand miles off sat working at her window. The frame of the window was made of fine black ebony, and as she sat looking out upon the snow, she pricked her finger, and three drops of blood fell upon it. Then she gazed thoughtfully upon the red drops that sprinkled the white snow, and said, 'Would that my little daughter may be as white as that snow, as red as that blood, and as black as this ebony window-frame!' And so the little girl really did grow up; her skin was as white as snow, her cheeks as rosy as the blood, and her hair as black as ebony; and she was called Snowdrop.

But this queen died; and the king soon married another wife, who became queen, and was very beautiful, but so vain that she could not bear to think that anyone could be handsomer than she was. She had a fairy looking-glass, to which she used to go, and then she would gaze upon herself in it, and say:

> 'Tell me, glass, tell me true!
> Of all the ladies in the land,
> Who is fairest, tell me, who?'

And the glass had always answered:

'Thou, queen, art the fairest in all the land.'

But Snowdrop grew more and more beautiful; and when she was seven years old she was as bright as the day, and fairer than the queen herself. Then the glass one day answered the queen, when she went to look in it as usual:

'Thou, queen, art fair, and beauteous to see,
But Snowdrop is lovelier far than thee!'

When she heard this she turned pale with rage and envy, and called to one of her servants, and said, 'Take Snowdrop away into the wide wood, that I may never see her any more.' Then the servant led her away; but his heart melted when Snowdrop begged him to spare her life, and he said, 'I will not hurt you, thou pretty child.' So he left her by herself; and though he thought it most likely that the wild beasts would tear her in pieces, he felt as if a great weight were taken off his heart when he had made up his mind not to kill her but to leave her to her fate, with the chance of someone finding and saving her.

Then poor Snowdrop wandered along through the wood in great fear; and the wild beasts roared about her, but none did her any harm. In the evening she came to a cottage among the hills, and went in to rest, for her little feet would carry her no further. Everything was spruce and neat in the cottage: on the table was spread a white cloth, and there were seven little plates, seven little loaves, and seven little glasses with wine in them; and seven knives and forks laid in order; and by the wall stood seven little beds. As she was very hungry, she picked a little piece of each loaf and drank a very little wine out of each glass; and after that she thought she would lie down and rest. So she tried all the little beds; but one was too long, and another was too short, till at last the seventh suited her: and there she laid herself down and went to sleep.

By and by in came the masters of the cottage. Now they were seven little dwarfs, that lived among the mountains, and dug and searched for gold. They lighted up their seven lamps, and saw at once that all was not right. The first said, 'Who has been sitting on my stool?' The second, 'Who has been eating off my plate?' The third, 'Who has been picking my bread?' The fourth, 'Who has been meddling with my spoon?' The fifth, 'Who has been handling my fork?' The sixth, 'Who has been cutting with my knife?' The seventh, 'Who has been drinking my wine?' Then the first looked round and said, 'Who has been lying on my bed?' And the rest came running to him, and everyone cried out that somebody had been upon his bed. But the seventh saw Snowdrop, and called all his brethren to come and see her; and they cried out with wonder and astonishment and brought their lamps to look at her, and said, 'Good heavens! what a lovely child she is!' And they were very glad to see her, and took care not to wake her; and the seventh dwarf slept an hour with each of the other dwarfs in turn, till the night was gone.

In the morning Snowdrop told them all her story; and they pitied her, and said if she would keep all things in order, and cook and wash and knit and spin for them, she might stay where she was, and they would take good care of her. Then they went out all day long to their work, seeking for gold and silver in the mountains: but Snowdrop was left at home; and they warned her, and said, 'The queen will soon find out where you are, so take care and let no one in.'

But the queen, now that she thought Snowdrop was dead, believed that she must be the handsomest lady in the land; and she went to her glass and said:

> *'Tell me, glass, tell me true!*
> *Of all the ladies in the land,*
> *Who is fairest, tell me, who?'*

And the glass answered:

> *'Thou, queen, art the fairest in all this land:*
> *But over the hills, in the greenwood shade,*
> *Where the seven dwarfs their dwelling have made,*
> *There Snowdrop is hiding her head; and she*
> *Is lovelier far, O queen! than thee.'*

Then the queen was very much frightened; for she knew that the glass always spoke the truth, and was sure that the servant had betrayed her. And she could not bear to think that anyone lived who was more beautiful than she was; so she dressed herself up as an old pedlar, and went her way over the hills, to the place where the dwarfs dwelt. Then she knocked at the door, and cried, 'Fine wares to sell!' Snowdrop looked out at the window, and said, 'Good day, good woman! what have you to sell?' 'Good wares, fine wares,' said she; 'laces and bobbins of all colours.' 'I will let the old lady in; she seems to be a very good sort of body,' thought Snowdrop, as she ran down and unbolted the door. 'Bless me!' said the old woman, 'how badly your stays are laced! Let me lace them up with one of my nice new laces.' Snowdrop did not dream of any mischief; so she stood before the old woman; but she set to work so nimbly, and pulled the lace so tight, that Snowdrop's breath was stopped, and she fell down as if she were dead. 'There's an end to all thy beauty,' said the spiteful queen, and went away home.

In the evening the seven dwarfs came home; and I need not say how grieved they were to see their faithful Snowdrop stretched out upon the ground, as if she was quite dead. However, they lifted her up, and when they found what ailed her, they cut the lace; and in a little time she began to breathe, and very soon came to life again. Then they said, 'The old woman was the queen herself; take care another time, and let no one in when we are away.'

When the queen got home, she went straight to her glass, and spoke to it as before; but to her great grief it still said:

'Thou, queen, art the fairest in all this land:
But over the hills, in the greenwood shade,
Where the seven dwarfs their dwelling have made,
There Snowdrop is hiding her head; and she
Is lovelier far, O queen! than thee.'

Then the blood ran cold in her heart with spite and malice, to see that Snowdrop still lived; and she dressed herself up again, but in quite another dress from the one she wore before, and took with her a poisoned comb. When she reached the dwarfs' cottage, she knocked at the door, and cried, 'Fine wares to sell!' But Snowdrop said, 'I dare not let anyone in.' Then the queen said, 'Only look at my beautiful combs!' and gave her the poisoned one. And it looked so pretty, that she took it up and put it into her hair to try it; but the moment it touched her head, the poison was so powerful that she fell down senseless. 'There you may lie,' said the queen, and went her way. But by good luck the dwarfs came in very early that evening; and when they saw Snowdrop lying on the ground, they thought what had happened, and soon found the poisoned comb. And when they took it away she got well, and told them all that had passed; and they warned her once more not to open the door to anyone.

Meantime the queen went home to her glass, and shook with rage when she read the very same answer as before; and she said, 'Snowdrop shall die, if it cost me my life.' So she went by herself into her chamber, and got ready a poisoned apple: the outside looked very rosy and tempting, but whoever tasted it was sure to die. Then she dressed herself up as a peasant's wife, and travelled over the hills to the dwarfs' cottage, and knocked at the door; but Snowdrop put her head out of the window and said, 'I dare not let anyone in, for the dwarfs have told me not.' 'Do as you please,' said the old woman, 'but at any rate take this pretty apple; I will give it you.' 'No,' said Snowdrop, 'I dare not take it.' 'You silly girl!' answered the other, 'what are you afraid of? Do you think it is poisoned? Come! do you eat one part, and I will eat the other.' Now the apple was so made up that one side was good, though the other side was poisoned. Then Snowdrop was much tempted to taste, for the apple looked so very nice; and when she saw the old woman eat, she could wait no longer. But she had scarcely put the piece into her mouth, when she fell down dead upon the ground. 'This time nothing will save thee,' said the queen; and she went home to her glass, and at last it said:

> *'Thou, queen, art the fairest of all the fair.'*

And then her wicked heart was glad, and as happy as such a heart could be.

When evening came, and the dwarfs had gone home, they found Snowdrop lying on the ground: no breath came from her lips, and they were afraid that she was quite dead. They lifted her up, and combed her hair, and washed her face with wine and water; but all was in vain, for the little girl seemed quite dead. So they laid her down upon a bier, and all seven watched and bewailed her three whole days; and then they thought they would bury her: but her cheeks were still rosy; and her face looked just as it did while she was alive; so they said, 'We will never bury her in the cold ground.' And they made a coffin of glass, so that they might still look at her, and wrote upon it in golden letters what her name was, and that she was a king's daughter. And the coffin was set among the hills, and one of the dwarfs always sat by it and watched. And the birds of the air came too, and bemoaned Snowdrop; and first of all came an owl, and then a raven, and at last a dove, and sat by her side.

And thus Snowdrop lay for a long, long time, and still only looked as though she was asleep; for she was even now as white as snow, and as red as blood, and as black as ebony. At last a prince came and called at the dwarfs' house; and he saw Snowdrop, and read what was written in golden letters. Then he offered the dwarfs money, and prayed and besought them to let him take her away; but they said, 'We will not part with her for all the gold in the world.' At last, however, they had pity on him, and gave him the coffin; but the moment he lifted it up to carry it home with him, the piece of apple fell from between her lips, and Snowdrop awoke, and said, 'Where am I?' And the prince said, 'Thou art quite safe with me.'

Then he told her all that had happened, and said, 'I love you far better than all the world; so come with me to my father's palace, and you shall be my wife.' And Snowdrop consented, and went home with the prince; and everything was got ready with great pomp and splendour for their wedding.

To the feast was asked, among the rest, Snowdrop's old enemy the queen; and as she was dressing herself in fine rich clothes, she looked in the glass and said:

> 'Tell me, glass, tell me true!
> Of all the ladies in the land,
> Who is fairest, tell me, who?'

And the glass answered:

> 'Thou, lady, art loveliest here, I ween;
> But lovelier far is the new-made queen.'

When she heard this she started with rage; but her envy and curiosity were so great, that she could not help setting out to see the bride. And when she got there, and saw that it was no other than Snowdrop, who, as she thought, had been dead a long while, she choked with rage, and fell down and died: but Snowdrop and the prince lived and reigned happily over that land many, many years; and sometimes they went up into the mountains, and paid a visit to the little dwarfs, who had been so kind to Snowdrop in her time of need.

THE PINK

There was once upon a time a queen to whom God had given no children. Every morning she went into the garden and prayed to God in heaven to bestow on her a son or a daughter. Then an angel from heaven came to her and said: 'Be at rest, you shall have a son with the power of wishing, so that what-soever in the world he wishes for, that shall he have.' Then she went to the king, and told him the joyful tidings, and when the time was come she gave birth to a son, and the king was filled with gladness.

Every morning she went with the child to the garden where the wild beasts were kept, and washed herself there in a clear stream. It happened once when the child was a little older, that it was lying in her arms and she fell asleep. Then came the old cook, who knew that the child had the power of wishing, and stole it away, and he took a hen, and cut it in pieces, and dropped some of its blood on the queen's apron and on her dress. Then he carried the child away to a secret place, where a nurse was obliged to suckle it, and he ran to the king and accused the queen of having allowed her child to be taken from her by the wild beasts. When the king saw the blood on her apron, he believed this, fell into such a passion that he ordered a high tower to be built, in which neither sun nor moon could be seen and had his wife put into it, and walled up. Here she was to stay for seven years without meat or drink, and die of hunger. But God sent two angels from heaven in the shape of white doves, which flew to her twice a day, and carried her food until the seven years were over. The cook, however, thought to himself: 'If the child has the power of wishing, and I am here, he might very easily get me into trouble.' So he left the palace and went to the boy, who was already big enough to speak, and said to him: 'Wish for a beautiful palace for yourself with a garden, and all else that pertains to it.' Scarcely were the words out of the boy's mouth, when everything was there that he had wished for. After a while the cook said to him: 'It is not well for you to be so alone, wish for a pretty girl as a companion.' Then the king's son wished for one, and she immediately stood before him, and was more beautiful than any painter could have painted her. The two played together, and loved each other with all their hearts, and the old cook went out hunting like a nobleman. The thought occurred to him, however, that the king's son might some day wish to be with his father, and thus bring him into great peril. So he went out and took the maiden aside, and said: 'Tonight when the boy is asleep, go to his bed and plunge this knife into his heart, and bring me his heart and tongue, and if you do not do it, you shall lose your life.' Thereupon he went away, and when he returned next day she had not done it, and said: 'Why should I shed the blood of an innocent boy who has never harmed anyone?' The cook once more said: 'If you do not do it, it shall cost you your own life.' When he had gone away, she had a little hind brought to her, and ordered her to be killed, and took her heart and tongue, and laid them on a plate, and when she saw the old man coming, she said to the boy: 'Lie down in your bed, and draw the clothes over you.' Then the wicked wretch came in and said: 'Where are the boy's heart and tongue?' The girl reached the plate to him, but the king's son threw off the quilt, and said: 'You old sinner, why did you want to kill me? Now will I pronounce thy sentence. You shall become a black poodle and have a gold collar round your neck, and shall eat burning coals, till the flames burst forth from your throat.' And when he had spoken these words, the old man was changed into a poodle dog, and had a gold collar round his neck, and the cooks were ordered to bring up some live coals, and these he ate, until the flames broke forth from his throat. The king's son remained there a short while longer, and he thought of his mother, and wondered if she were still alive. At length he said to the maiden: 'I will go home to my own country; if you will go with me, I will provide for you.' 'Ah,' she replied, 'the way is so long, and what shall I do in a strange land where I am unknown?' As she did not seem quite willing, and as they could not be parted from each other, he wished that she might be changed into a beautiful pink, and took her with him. Then he went away to his own country, and the poodle had to run after him. He went to the tower in which his mother was confined, and as it was so high, he wished for a ladder which would reach up to the very top. Then he mounted up and looked inside, and cried: 'Beloved mother, Lady Queen, are you still alive, or are you dead?' She answered: 'I have just eaten, and am still satisfied,' for she thought the angels were there. Said he: 'I am your dear son, whom the wild beasts were said to have torn from your arms; but I am alive still, and will soon set you free.' Then he descended again, and went to his father, and caused himself to be announced as a strange huntsman, and asked if he could offer him service. The king said yes, if he was skilful and could get game for him, he should come to him, but that deer had never taken up their quarters in any part of the district or country. Then the huntsman promised to procure as much game for him as he could possibly use at the royal table. So he summoned all the huntsmen together, and bade them go out into the forest with him. And he went with them and made them form a great circle, open at one end where he stationed himself, and began to wish. Two hundred deer and more came running inside the circle at once, and the huntsmen shot them. Then they were all placed on sixty country carts, and driven home to the king, and for once he was able to deck his table with game, after having had none at all for years.

Now the king felt great joy at this, and commanded that his entire household should eat with him next day, and made a great feast. When they were all assembled together, he said to the huntsman: 'As you are so clever, you shall sit by me.' He replied: 'Lord King, your majesty must excuse me, I am a poor huntsman.' But the king insisted on it, and said: 'You shall sit by me,' until he did it. Whilst he was sitting there, he thought of his dearest mother, and wished that one of the king's principal servants would begin to speak of her, and would ask how it was faring with the queen in the tower, and if she were alive still, or had perished. Hardly had he formed the wish than the marshal began, and said: 'Your majesty, we live joyously here, but how is the queen living in the tower? Is she still alive, or has she died?' But the king replied: 'She let my dear son be torn to pieces by wild beasts; I will not have her named.' Then the huntsman arose and said: 'Gracious lord father she is alive still, and I am her son, and I was not carried away by wild beasts, but by that wretch the old cook, who tore me from her arms when she was asleep, and sprinkled her apron with the blood of a chicken.' Thereupon he took the dog with the golden collar, and said: 'That is the wretch!' and caused live coals to be brought, and these the dog was compelled to devour before the sight of all, until flames burst forth from its throat. On this the huntsman asked the king if he would like to see the dog in his true shape, and wished him back into the form of the cook, in the which he stood immediately, with his white apron, and his knife by his side. When the king saw him he fell into a passion, and ordered him to be cast into the deepest dungeon. Then the huntsman spoke further and said: 'Father, will you see the maiden who brought me up so tenderly and who was afterwards to murder me, but did not do it, though her own life depended on it?' The king replied: 'Yes, I would like to see her.' The son said: 'Most gracious father, I will show her to you in the form of a beautiful flower,' and he thrust his hand into his pocket and brought forth the pink, and placed it on the royal table, and it was so beautiful that the king had never seen one to equal it. Then the son said: 'Now will I show her to you in her own form,' and wished that she might become a maiden, and she stood there looking so beautiful that no painter could have made her look more so.

And the king sent two waiting-maids and two attendants into the tower, to fetch the queen and bring her to the royal table. But when she was led in she ate nothing, and said: 'The gracious and merciful God who has supported me in the tower, will soon set me free.' She lived three days more, and then died happily, and when she was buried, the two white doves which had brought her food to the tower, and were angels of heaven, followed her body and seated themselves on her grave. The aged king ordered the cook to be torn in four pieces, but grief consumed the king's own heart, and he soon died. His son married the beautiful maiden whom he had brought with him as a flower in his pocket, and whether they are still alive or not, is known to God.

CLEVER ELSIE

There was once a man who had a daughter who was called Clever Elsie. And when she had grown up her father said: 'We will get her married.' 'Yes,' said the mother, 'if only someone would come who would have her.' At length a man came from a distance and wooed her, who was called Hans; but he stipulated that Clever Elsie should be really smart. 'Oh,' said the father, 'she has plenty of good sense'; and the mother said: 'Oh, she can see the wind coming up the street, and hear the flies coughing.' 'Well,' said Hans, 'if she is not really smart, I won't have her.' When they were sitting at dinner and had eaten, the mother said: 'Elsie, go into the cellar and fetch some beer.' Then Clever Elsie took the pitcher from the wall, went into the cellar, and tapped the lid briskly as she went, so that the time might not appear long. When she was below she fetched herself a chair, and set it before the barrel so that she had no need to stoop, and did not hurt her back or do herself any unexpected injury. Then she placed the can before her, and turned the tap, and while the beer was running she would not let her eyes be idle, but looked up at the wall, and after much peering here and there, saw a pick-axe exactly above her, which the masons had accidentally left there.

Then Clever Elsie began to weep and said: 'If I get Hans, and we have a child, and he grows big, and we send him into the cellar here to draw beer, then the pick-axe will fall on his head and kill him.' Then she sat and wept and screamed with all the strength of her body, over the misfortune which lay before her. Those upstairs waited for the drink, but Clever Elsie still did not come. Then the woman said to the servant: 'Just go down into the cellar and see where Elsie is.' The maid went and found her sitting in front of the barrel, screaming loudly. 'Elsie why do you weep?' asked the maid. 'Ah,' she answered, 'have I not reason to weep? If I get Hans, and we have a child, and he grows big, and has to draw beer here, the pick-axe will perhaps fall on his head, and kill him.' Then said the maid: 'What a clever Elsie we have!' and sat down beside her and began loudly to weep over the misfortune. After a while, as the maid did not come back, and those upstairs were thirsty for the beer, the man said to the boy: 'Just go down into the cellar and see where Elsie and the girl are.' The boy went down, and there sat Clever Elsie and the girl both weeping together. Then he asked: 'Why are you weeping?' 'Ah,' said Elsie, 'have I not reason to weep? If I get Hans, and we have a child, and he grows big, and has to draw beer here, the pick-axe will fall on his head and kill him.' Then said the boy: 'What a clever Elsie we have!' and sat down by her, and likewise began to howl loudly. Upstairs they waited for the boy, but as he still did not return, the man said to the woman: 'Just go down into the cellar and see where Elsie is!' The woman went down, and found all three in the midst of their lamentations, and inquired what was the cause; then Elsie told her also that her future child was to be killed by the pick-axe, when it grew big and had to draw beer, and the pick-axe fell down. Then said the mother likewise: 'What a clever Elsie we have!' and sat down and wept with them. The man upstairs waited a short time, but as his wife did not come back and his thirst grew ever greater, he said: 'I must go into the cellar myself and see where Elsie is.' But when he got into the cellar, and they were all sitting together crying, and he heard the reason, and that Elsie's child was the cause, and the Elsie might perhaps bring one into the world some day, and that he might be killed by the pick-axe, if he should happen to be sitting beneath it, drawing beer just at the very time when it fell down, he cried: 'Oh, what a clever Elsie!' and sat down, and likewise wept with them. The bridegroom stayed upstairs alone for a long time; then as no one would come back he thought: 'They must be waiting for me below: I too must go there and see what they are about.' When he got down, the five of them were sitting screaming and lamenting quite piteously, each out-doing the other. 'What misfortune has happened then?' asked he. 'Ah, dear Hans,' said Elsie, 'if we marry each other and have a child, and he is big, and we perhaps send him here to draw something to drink, then the pick-axe which has been left up there might dash his brains out if it were to fall down, so have we not reason to weep?' 'Come,' said Hans, 'more understanding than that is not needed for my household, as you are such a clever Elsie, I will have you,' and seized her hand, took her upstairs with him, and married her.

After Hans had had her some time, he said: 'Wife, I am going out to work and earn some money for us; go into the field and cut the corn that we may have some bread.' 'Yes, dear Hans, I will do that.' After Hans had gone away, she cooked herself some good broth and took it into the field with her. When she came to the field she said to herself: 'What shall I do; shall I cut first, or shall I eat first? Oh, I will eat first.' Then she drank her cup of broth and when she was fully satisfied, she once more said: 'What shall I do? Shall I cut first, or shall I sleep first? I will sleep first.' Then she lay down among the corn and fell asleep. Hans had been at home for a long time, but Elsie did not come; then said he: 'What a clever Elsie I have; she is so industrious that she does not even come home to eat.' But when evening came and she still stayed away, Hans went out to see what she had cut, but nothing was cut, and she was lying among the corn asleep. Then Hans hastened home and brought a fowler's net with little bells and hung it round about her, and she still went on sleeping. Then he ran home, shut the house-door, and sat down in his chair and worked. At length, when it was quite dark, Clever Elsie awoke and when she got up there was a jingling all round about her, and the bells rang at each step which she took. Then she was alarmed, and became uncertain whether she really was Clever Elsie or not, and said: 'Is it I, or is it not I?' But she knew not what answer to make to this, and stood for a time in doubt; at length she thought: 'I will go home and ask if it be I, or if it be not I, they will be sure to know.' She ran to the door of her own house, but it was shut; then she knocked at the window and cried: 'Hans, is Elsie within?' 'Yes,' answered Hans, 'she is within.' Hereupon she was terrified, and said: 'Ah, heavens! Then it is not I,' and went to another door; but when the people heard the jingling of the bells they would not open it, and she could get in nowhere. Then she ran out of the village, and no one has seen her since.

THE MISER IN THE BUSH

A farmer had a faithful and diligent servant, who had worked hard for him three years, without having been paid any wages. At last it came into the man's head that he would not go on thus without pay any longer; so he went to his master, and said, 'I have worked hard for you a long time, I will trust to you to give me what I deserve to have for my trouble.' The farmer was a sad miser, and knew that his man was very simple-hearted; so he took out threepence, and gave him for every year's service a penny. The poor fellow thought it was a great deal of money to have, and said to himself, 'Why should I work hard, and live here on bad fare any longer? I can now travel into the wide world, and make myself merry.' With that he put his money into his purse, and set out, roaming over hill and valley.

As he jogged along over the fields, singing and dancing, a little dwarf met him, and asked him what made him so merry. 'Why, what should make me down-hearted?' said he; 'I am sound in health and rich in purse, what should I care for? I have saved up my three years' earnings and have it all safe in my pocket.' 'How much may it come to?' said the little man. 'Full threepence,' replied the countryman. 'I wish you would give them to me,' said the other; 'I am very poor.'

Then the man pitied him, and gave him all he had; and the little dwarf said in return, 'As you have such a kind honest heart, I will grant you three wishes—one for every penny; so choose whatever you like.' Then the countryman rejoiced at his good luck, and said, 'I like many things better than money: first, I will have a bow that will bring down everything I shoot at; secondly, a fiddle that will set everyone dancing that hears me play upon it; and thirdly, I should like that everyone should grant what I ask.' The dwarf said he should have his three wishes; so he gave him the bow and fiddle, and went his way.

Our honest friend journeyed on his way too; and if he was merry before, he was now ten times more so. He had not gone far before he met an old miser: close by them stood a tree, and on the topmost twig sat a thrush singing away most joyfully. 'Oh, what a pretty bird!' said the miser; 'I would give a great deal of money to have such a one.' 'If that's all,' said the countryman, 'I will soon bring it down.' Then he took up his bow, and down fell the thrush into the bushes at the foot of the tree. The miser crept into the bush to find it; but directly he had got into the middle, his companion took up his fiddle and played away, and the miser began to dance and spring about, capering higher and higher in the air. The thorns soon began to tear his clothes till they all hung in rags about him, and he himself was all scratched and wounded, so that the blood ran down. 'Oh, for heaven's sake!' cried the miser, 'Master! master! pray let the fiddle alone. What have I done to deserve this?' 'Thou hast shaved many a poor soul close enough,' said the other; 'thou art only meeting thy reward': so he played up another tune. Then the miser began to beg and promise, and offered money for his liberty; but he did not come up to the musician's price for some time, and he danced him along brisker and brisker, and the miser bid higher and higher, till at last he offered a round hundred of florins that he had in his purse, and had just gained by cheating some poor fellow. When the countryman saw so much money, he said, 'I will agree to your proposal.' So he took the purse, put up his fiddle, and travelled on very pleased with his bargain.

Meanwhile the miser crept out of the bush half-naked and in a piteous plight, and began to ponder how he should take his revenge, and serve his late companion some trick. At last he went to the judge, and complained that a rascal had robbed him of his money, and beaten him into the bargain; and that the fellow who did it carried a bow at his back and a fiddle hung round his neck. Then the judge sent out his officers to bring up the accused wherever they should find him; and he was soon caught and brought up to be tried.

The miser began to tell his tale, and said he had been robbed of his money. 'No, you gave it me for playing a tune to you.' said the countryman; but the judge told him that was not likely, and cut the matter short by ordering him off to the gallows.

So away he was taken; but as he stood on the steps he said, 'My Lord Judge, grant me one last request.' 'Anything but thy life,' replied the other. 'No,' said he, 'I do not ask my life; only to let me play upon my fiddle for the last time.' The miser cried out, 'Oh, no! no! for heaven's sake don't listen to him! don't listen to him!' But the judge said, 'It is only this once, he will soon have done.' The fact was, he could not refuse the request, on account of the dwarf's third gift.

Then the miser said, 'Bind me fast, bind me fast, for pity's sake.' But the countryman seized his fiddle, and struck up a tune, and at the first note judge, clerks, and jailer were in motion; all began capering, and no one could hold the miser. At the second note the hangman let his prisoner go, and danced also, and by the time he had played the first bar of the tune, all were dancing together—judge, court, and miser, and all the people who had followed to look on. At first the thing was merry and pleasant enough; but when it had gone on a while, and there seemed to be no end of playing or dancing, they began to cry out, and beg him to leave off; but he stopped not a whit the more for their entreaties, till the judge not only gave him his life, but promised to return him the hundred florins.

Then he called to the miser, and said, 'Tell us now, you vagabond, where you got that gold, or I shall play on for your amusement only,' 'I stole it,' said the miser in the presence of all the people; 'I acknowledge that I stole it, and that you earned it fairly.' Then the countryman stopped his fiddle, and left the miser to take his place at the gallows.

ASHPUTTEL

The wife of a rich man fell sick; and when she felt that her end drew nigh, she called her only daughter to her bed-side, and said, 'Always be a good girl, and I will look down from heaven and watch over you.' Soon afterwards she shut her eyes and died, and was buried in the garden; and the little girl went every day to her grave and wept, and was always good and kind to all about her. And the snow fell and spread a beautiful white covering over the grave; but by the time the spring came, and the sun had melted it away again, her father had married another wife. This new wife had two daughters of her own, that she brought home with her; they were fair in face but foul at heart, and it was now a sorry time for the poor little girl. 'What does the good-for-nothing want in the parlour?' said they; 'they who would eat bread should first earn it; away with the kitchen-maid!' Then they took away her fine clothes, and gave her an old grey frock to put on, and laughed at her, and turned her into the kitchen.

There she was forced to do hard work; to rise early before daylight, to bring the water, to make the fire, to cook and to wash. Besides that, the sisters plagued her in all sorts of ways, and laughed at her. In the evening when she was tired, she had no bed to lie down on, but was made to lie by the hearth among the ashes; and as this, of course, made her always dusty and dirty, they called her Ashputtel.

It happened once that the father was going to the fair, and asked his wife's daughters what he should bring them. 'Fine clothes,' said the first; 'Pearls and diamonds,' cried the second. 'Now, child,' said he to his own daughter, 'what will you have?' 'The first twig, dear father, that brushes against your hat when you turn your face to come homewards,' said she. Then he bought for the first two the fine clothes and pearls and diamonds they had asked for: and on his way home, as he rode through a green copse, a hazel twig brushed against him, and almost pushed off his hat: so he broke it off and brought it away; and when he got home he gave it to his daughter. Then she took it, and went to her mother's grave and planted it there; and cried so much that it was watered with her tears; and there it grew and became a fine tree. Three times every day she went to it and cried; and soon a little bird came and built its nest upon the tree, and talked with her, and watched over her, and brought her whatever she wished for.

Now it happened that the king of that land held a feast, which was to last three days; and out of those who came to it his son was to choose a bride for himself. Ashputtel's two sisters were asked to come; so they called her up, and said, 'Now, comb our hair, brush our shoes, and tie our sashes for us, for we are going to dance at the king's feast.' Then she did as she was told; but when all was done she could not help crying, for she thought to herself, she should so have liked to have gone with them to the ball; and at last she begged her mother very hard to let her go. 'You, Ashputtel!' said she; 'you who have nothing to wear, no clothes at all, and who cannot even dance—you want to go to the ball? And when she kept on begging, she said at last, to get rid of her, 'I will throw this dishful of peas into the ash-heap, and if in two hours' time you have picked them all out, you shall go to the feast too.'

Then she threw the peas down among the ashes, but the little maiden ran out at the back door into the garden, and cried out:

> 'Hither, hither, through the sky,
> Turtle-doves and linnets, fly!
> Blackbird, thrush, and chaffinch gay,
> Hither, hither, haste away!
> One and all come help me, quick!
> Haste ye, haste ye!—pick, pick, pick!'

Then first came two white doves, flying in at the kitchen window; next came two turtle-doves; and after them came all the little birds under heaven, chirping and fluttering in: and they flew down into the ashes. And the little doves stooped their heads down and set to work, pick, pick, pick; and then the others began to pick, pick, pick: and among them all they soon picked out all the good grain, and put it into a dish but left the ashes. Long before the end of the hour the work was quite done, and all flew out again at the windows.

Then Ashputtel brought the dish to her mother, over-joyed at the thought that now she should go to the ball. But the mother said, 'No, no! you slut, you have no clothes, and cannot dance; you shall not go.' And when Ashputtel begged very hard to go, she said, 'If you can in one hour's time pick two of those dishes of peas out of the ashes, you shall go too.' And thus she thought she should at least get rid of her. So she shook two dishes of peas into the ashes.

But the little maiden went out into the garden at the back of the house, and cried out as before:

> 'Hither, hither, through the sky,
> Turtle-doves and linnets, fly!
> Blackbird, thrush, and chaffinch gay,
> Hither, hither, haste away!

One and all come help me, quick!
Haste ye, haste ye!—pick, pick, pick!'

Then first came two white doves in at the kitchen window; next came two turtle-doves; and after them came all the little birds under heaven, chirping and hopping about. And they flew down into the ashes; and the little doves put their heads down and set to work, pick, pick, pick; and then the others began pick, pick, pick; and they put all the good grain into the dishes, and left all the ashes. Before half an hour's time all was done, and out they flew again. And then Ashputtel took the dishes to her mother, rejoicing to think that she should now go to the ball. But her mother said, 'It is all of no use, you cannot go; you have no clothes, and cannot dance, and you would only put us to shame': and off she went with her two daughters to the ball.

Now when all were gone, and nobody left at home, Ashputtel went sorrowfully and sat down under the hazel-tree, and cried out:

'Shake, shake, hazel-tree,
Gold and silver over me!'

Then her friend the bird flew out of the tree, and brought a gold and silver dress for her, and slippers of spangled silk; and she put them on, and followed her sisters to the feast. But they did not know her, and thought it must be some strange princess, she looked so fine and beautiful in her rich clothes; and they never once thought of Ashputtel, taking it for granted that she was safe at home in the dirt.

The king's son soon came up to her, and took her by the hand and danced with her, and no one else: and he never left her hand; but when anyone else came to ask her to dance, he said, 'This lady is dancing with me.'

Thus they danced till a late hour of the night; and then

she wanted to go home: and the king's son said, 'I shall go and take care of you to your home'; for he wanted to see where the beautiful maiden lived. But she slipped away from him, unawares, and ran off towards home; and as the prince followed her, she jumped up into the pigeon-house and shut the door. Then he waited till her father came home, and told him that the unknown maiden, who had been at the feast, had hid herself in the pigeon-house. But when they had broken open the door they found no one within; and as they came back into the house, Ashputtel was lying, as she always did, in her dirty frock by the ashes, and her dim little lamp was burning in the chimney. For she had run as quickly as she could through the pigeon-house and on to the hazel-tree, and had there taken off her beautiful clothes, and put them beneath the tree, that the bird might carry them away, and had lain down again amid the ashes in her little grey frock.

The next day when the feast was again held, and her father, mother, and sisters were gone, Ashputtel went to the hazel-tree, and said:

> 'Shake, shake, hazel-tree,
> Gold and silver over me!'

And the bird came and brought a still finer dress than the one she had worn the day before. And when she came in it to the ball, everyone wondered at her beauty: but the king's son, who was waiting for her, took her by the hand, and danced with her; and when anyone asked her to dance, he said as before, 'This lady is dancing with me.'

When night came she wanted to go home; and the king's son followed here as before, that he might see into what house she went: but she sprang away from him all at once into the garden behind her father's house. In this garden stood a fine large pear-tree full of ripe fruit; and Ashputtel, not knowing where to hide herself, jumped up into it without being seen.

Then the king's son lost sight of her, and could not find out where she was gone, but waited till her father came home, and said to him, 'The unknown lady who danced with me has slipped away, and I think she must have sprung into the pear-tree.' The father thought to himself, 'Can it be Ashputtel?' So he had an axe brought; and they cut down the tree, but found no one upon it. And when they came back into the kitchen, there lay Ashputtel among the ashes; for she had slipped down on the other side of the tree, and carried her beautiful clothes back to the bird at the hazel-tree, and then put on her little grey frock.

The third day, when her father and mother and sisters were gone, she went again into the garden, and said:

> *'Shake, shake, hazel-tree,*
> *Gold and silver over me!'*

Then her kind friend the bird brought a dress still finer than the former one, and slippers which were all of gold: so that when she came to the feast no one knew what to say, for wonder at her beauty: and the king's son danced with nobody but her; and when anyone else asked her to dance, he said, 'This lady is *my* partner, sir.'

When night came she wanted to go home; and the king's son would go with her, and said to himself, 'I will not lose her this time'; but, however, she again slipped away from him, though in such a hurry that she dropped her left golden slipper upon the stairs.

The prince took the shoe, and went the next day to the king his father, and said, 'I will take for my wife the lady that this golden slipper fits.' Then both the sisters were overjoyed to hear it; for they had beautiful feet, and had no doubt that they could wear the golden slipper. The eldest went first into the room where the slipper was, and wanted to try it on, and the mother stood by. But her great toe could not go into it, and the shoe was altogether much too small for her. Then the mother gave her a knife, and said, 'Never mind, cut it off; when you are queen you will not care about toes; you will not want to walk.' So the silly girl cut off her great toe, and thus squeezed on the shoe, and went to the king's son. Then he took her for his bride, and set her beside him on his horse, and rode away with her homewards.

But on their way home they had to pass by the hazel-tree that Ashputtel had planted; and on the branch sat a little dove singing:

> 'Back again! back again! look to the shoe!
> The shoe is too small, and not made for you!
> Prince! prince! look again for thy bride,
> For she's not the true one that sits by thy side.'

Then the prince got down and looked at her foot; and he saw, by the blood that streamed from it, what a trick she had played him. So he turned his horse round, and brought the false bride back to her home, and said, 'This is not the right bride; let the other sister try and put on the slipper.' Then she went into the room and got her foot into the shoe, all but the heel, which was too large. But her mother squeezed it in till the blood came, and took her to the king's son: and he set her as his bride by his side on his horse, and rode away with her.

But when they came to the hazel-tree the little dove sat there still, and sang:

> 'Back again! back again! look to the shoe!
> The shoe is too small, and not made for you!
> Prince! prince! look again for thy bride,
> For she's not the true one that sits by thy side.'

Then he looked down, and saw that the blood streamed so much from the shoe, that her white stockings were quite red. So he turned his horse and brought her also back again. 'This is not the true bride,' said he to the father; 'have you no other daughters?' 'No,' said he; 'there is only a little dirty Ashputtel here, the child of my first wife; I am sure she cannot be the bride.' The prince told him to send her. But the mother said, 'No, no, she is much too dirty; she will not dare to show herself.' However, the prince would have her come; and she first washed her face and hands, and then went in and curtsied to him, and he reached her the golden slipper. Then she took her clumsy shoe off her left foot, and put on the golden slipper; and it fitted her as if it had been made for her. And when he drew near and looked at her face he knew her, and said, 'This is the right bride.' But the mother and both the sisters were frightened, and turned pale with anger as he took Ashputtel on his horse, and rode away with her. And when they came to the hazel-tree, the white dove sang:

> 'Home! home! look at the shoe!
> Princess! the shoe was made for you!
> Prince! prince! take home thy bride,
> For she is the true one that sits by thy side!'

And when the dove had done its song, it came flying, and perched upon her right shoulder, and so went home with her.

THE WHITE SNAKE

A long time ago there lived a king who was famed for his wisdom through all the land. Nothing was hidden from him, and it seemed as if news of the most secret things was brought to him through the air. But he had a strange custom; every day after dinner, when the table was cleared, and no one else was present, a trusty servant had to bring him one more dish. It was covered, however, and even the servant did not know what was in it, neither did anyone know, for the king never took off the cover to eat of it until he was quite alone.

This had gone on for a long time, when one day the servant, who took away the dish, was overcome with such curiosity that he could not help carrying the dish into his room. When he had carefully locked the door, he lifted up the cover, and saw a white snake lying on the dish. But when he saw it he could not deny himself the pleasure of tasting it, so he cut off a little bit and put it into his mouth. No sooner had it touched his tongue than he heard a strange whispering of little voices outside his window. He went and listened, and then noticed that it was the sparrows who were chattering together, and telling one another of all kinds of things which they had seen in the fields and woods. Eating the snake had given him power of understanding the language of animals.

Now it so happened that on this very day the queen lost her most beautiful ring, and suspicion of having stolen it fell upon this trusty servant, who was allowed to go everywhere. The king ordered the man to be brought before him, and threatened with angry words that unless he could before the morrow point out the thief, he himself should be looked upon as guilty and executed. In vain he declared his innocence; he was dismissed with no better answer.

In his trouble and fear he went down into the courtyard and took thought how to help himself out of his trouble. Now some ducks were sitting together quietly by a brook and taking their rest; and, whilst they were making their feathers smooth with their bills, they were having a confidential conversation together. The servant stood by and listened. They were telling one another of all the places where they had been waddling about all the morning, and what good food they had found; and one said in a pitiful tone: 'Something lies heavy on my stomach; as I was eating in haste I swallowed a ring which lay under the queen's window.' The servant at once seized her by the neck, carried her to the kitchen, and said to the cook: 'Here is a fine duck; pray, kill her.' 'Yes,' said the cook, and weighed her in his hand; 'she has spared no trouble to fatten herself, and has been waiting to be roasted long enough.' So he cut off her head, and as she was being dressed for the spit, the queen's ring was found inside her.

The servant could now easily prove his innocence; and the king, to make amends for the wrong, allowed him to ask a favour, and promised him the best place in the court that he could wish for. The servant refused everything, and only asked for a horse and some money for travelling, as he had a mind to see the world and go about a little. When his request was granted he set out on his way, and one day came to a pond, where he saw three fishes caught in the reeds and gasping for water. Now, though it is said that fishes are dumb, he heard them lamenting that they must perish so miserably, and, as he had a kind heart, he got off his horse and put the three prisoners back into the water. They leapt with delight, put out their heads, and cried to him: 'We will remember you and repay you for saving us!'

He rode on, and after a while it seemed to him that he heard a voice in the sand at his feet. He listened, and heard an ant-king complain: 'Why cannot folks, with their clumsy beasts, keep off our bodies? That stupid horse, with his heavy hoofs, has been treading down my people without mercy!' So he turned on to a side path and the ant-king cried out to him: 'We will remember you—one good turn deserves another!'

The path led him into a wood, and there he saw two old ravens standing by their nest, and throwing out their young ones. 'Out with you, you idle, good-for-nothing creatures!' cried they; 'we cannot find food for you any longer; you are big enough, and can provide for yourselves.' But the poor young ravens lay upon the ground, flapping their wings, and crying: 'Oh, what helpless chicks we are! We must shift for ourselves, and yet we cannot fly! What can we do, but lie here and starve?' So the good young fellow alighted and killed his horse with his sword, and gave it to them for food. Then they came hopping up to it, satisfied their hunger, and cried: 'We will remember you—one good turn deserves another!'

And now he had to use his own legs, and when he had walked a long way, he came to a large city. There was a great noise and crowd in the streets, and a man rode up on horseback, crying aloud: 'The king's daughter wants a husband; but whoever seeks her hand must perform a hard task, and if he does not succeed he will forfeit his life.' Many had already made the attempt, but in vain; nevertheless when the youth saw the king's daughter he was so overcome by her great beauty that he forgot all danger, went before the king, and declared himself a suitor.

So he was led out to the sea, and a gold ring was thrown into it, before his eyes; then the king ordered him to fetch this ring up from the bottom of the sea, and added: 'If you come up again without it you will be thrown in again and again until you perish amid the waves.' All the people grieved for the handsome youth; then they went away, leaving him alone by the sea.

He stood on the shore and considered what he should do, when suddenly he saw three fishes come swimming towards him, and they were the very fishes whose lives he had saved. The one in the middle held a mussel in its mouth, which it laid on the shore at the youth's feet, and when he had taken it up and opened it, there lay the gold ring in the shell. Full of joy he took it to the king and expected that he would grant him the promised reward.

But when the proud princess perceived that he was not her equal in birth, she scorned him, and required him first to perform another task. She went down into the garden and strewed with her own hands ten sacksful of millet-seed on the grass; then she said: 'Tomorrow morning before sunrise these must be picked up, and not a single grain be wanting.'

The youth sat down in the garden and considered how it might be possible to perform this task, but he could think of nothing, and there he sat sorrowfully awaiting the break of day, when he should be led to death. But as soon as the first rays of the sun shone into the garden he saw all the ten sacks standing side by side, quite full, and not a single grain was missing. The ant-king had come in the night with thousands and thousands of ants, and the grateful creatures had by great industry picked up all the millet-seed and gathered them into the sacks.

Presently the king's daughter herself came down into the garden, and was amazed to see that the young man had done the task she had given him. But she could not yet conquer her proud heart, and said: 'Although he has performed both the tasks, he shall not be my husband until he had brought me an apple from the Tree of Life.' The youth did not know where the Tree of Life stood, but he set out, and would have gone on for ever, as long as his legs would carry him, though he had no hope of finding it. After he had wandered through three kingdoms, he came one evening to a wood, and lay down under a tree to sleep. But he heard a rustling in the branches, and a golden apple fell into his hand. At the same time three ravens flew down to him, perched themselves upon his knee, and said: 'We are the three young ravens whom you saved from starving; when we had grown big, and heard that you were seeking the Golden Apple, we flew over the sea to the end of the world, where the Tree of Life stands, and have brought you the apple.' The youth, full of joy, set out homewards, and took the Golden Apple to the king's beautiful daughter, who had now no more excuses left to make. They cut the Apple of Life in two and ate it together; and then her heart became full of love for him, and they lived in undisturbed happiness to a great age.

THE WOLF AND THE SEVEN
LITTLE KIDS

There was once upon a time an old goat who had seven little kids, and loved them with all the love of a mother for her children. One day she wanted to go into the forest and fetch some food. So she called all seven to her and said: 'Dear children, I have to go into the forest, be on your guard against the wolf; if he comes in, he will devour you all—skin, hair, and everything. The wretch often disguises himself, but you will know him at once by his rough voice and his black feet.' The kids said: 'Dear mother, we will take good care of ourselves; you may go away without any anxiety.' Then the old one bleated, and went on her way with an easy mind.

It was not long before someone knocked at the house-door and called: 'Open the door, dear children; your mother is here, and has brought something back with her for each of you.' But the little kids knew that it was the wolf, by the rough voice. 'We will not open the door,' cried they, 'you are not our mother. She has a soft, pleasant voice, but your voice is rough; you are the wolf!' Then the wolf went away to a shopkeeper and bought himself a great lump of chalk, ate this and made his voice soft with it. Then he came back, knocked at the door of the house, and called: 'Open the door, dear children, your mother is here and has brought something back with her for each of you.' But the wolf had laid his black paws against the window, and the children saw them and cried: 'We will not open the door, our mother has not black feet like you: you are the wolf!' Then the wolf ran to a baker and said: 'I have hurt my feet, rub some dough over them for me.' And when the baker had rubbed his feet over, he ran to the miller and said: 'Strew some white meal over my feet for me.' The miller thought to himself: 'The wolf wants to deceive someone,' and refused; but the wolf said: 'If you will not do it, I will devour you.' Then the miller was afraid, and made his paws white for him. Truly, this is the way of mankind.

So now the wretch went for the third time to the house-door, knocked at it and said: 'Open the door for me, children, your dear little mother has come home, and has brought every one of you something back from the forest with her.' The little kids cried: 'First show us your paws that we may know if you are our dear little mother.' Then he put his paws in through the window and when the kids saw that they were white, they believed that all he said was true, and opened the door. But who should come in but the wolf! They were terrified and wanted to hide themselves. One sprang under the table, the second into the bed, the third into the stove, the fourth into the kitchen, the fifth into the cupboard, the sixth under the washing-bowl, and the seventh into the clock-case. But the wolf found them all, and used no great ceremony; one after the other he swallowed them down his throat. The youngest, who was in the clock-case, was the only one he did not find. When the wolf had satisfied his appetite he took himself off, laid himself down under a tree in the green meadow outside, and began to sleep. Soon afterwards the old goat came home again from the forest. Ah! what a sight she saw there! The house-door stood wide open. The table, chairs, and benches were thrown down, the washing-bowl lay broken to pieces, and the quilts and pillows were pulled off the bed.

She sought her children, but they were nowhere to be found. She called them one after another by name, but no one answered. At last, when she came to the youngest, a soft voice cried: 'Dear mother, I am in the clock-case.' She took the kid out, and it told her that the wolf had come and had eaten all the others. Then you may imagine how she wept over her poor children.

At length in her grief she went out, and the youngest kid ran with her. When they came to the meadow, there lay the wolf by the tree and snored so loud that the branches shook. She looked at him on every side and saw that something was moving and struggling in his gorged belly. 'Ah, heavens,' she said, 'is it possible that my poor children whom he has swallowed down for his supper, can be still alive?' Then the kid had to run home and fetch scissors, and a needle and thread, and the goat cut open the monster's stomach, and hardly had she made one cut, than one little kid thrust its head out, and when she had cut farther, all six sprang out one after another, and were all still alive, and had suffered no injury whatever, for in his greediness the monster had swallowed them down whole. What rejoicing there was! They embraced their dear mother, and jumped like a tailor at his wedding. The mother, however, said: 'Now go and look for some big stones, and we will fill the wicked beast's stomach with them while he is still asleep.' Then the seven kids dragged the stones thither with all speed, and put as many of them into this stomach as they could get in; and the mother sewed him up again in the greatest haste, so that he was not aware of anything and never once stirred.

When the wolf at length had had his fill of sleep, he got on his legs, and as the stones in his stomach made him very thirsty, he wanted to go to a well to drink. But when he began to walk and to move about, the stones in his stomach knocked against each other and rattled. Then cried he:

> '*What rumbles and tumbles*
> *Against my poor bones?*
> *I thought 'twas six kids,*
> *But it feels like big stones.*'

And when he got to the well and stooped over the water to drink, the heavy stones made him fall in, and he drowned miserably. When the seven kids saw that, they came running to the spot and cried aloud: 'The wolf is dead! The wolf is dead!' and danced for joy round about the well with their mother.

THE QUEEN BEE

Two kings' sons once upon a time went into the world to seek their fortunes; but they soon fell into a wasteful foolish way of living, so that they could not return home again. Then their brother, who was a little insignificant dwarf, went out to seek for his brothers: but when he had found them they only laughed at him, to think that he, who was so young and simple, should try to travel through the world, when they, who were so much wiser, had been unable to get on. However, they all set out on their journey together, and came at last to an ant-hill. The two elder brothers would have pulled it down, in order to see how the poor ants in their fright would run about and carry off their eggs. But the little dwarf said, 'Let the poor things enjoy themselves, I will not suffer you to trouble them.'

So on they went, and came to a lake where many many ducks were swimming about. The two brothers wanted to catch two, and roast them. But the dwarf said, 'Let the poor things enjoy themselves, you shall not kill them.' Next they came to a bees'-nest in a hollow tree, and there was so much honey that it ran down the trunk; and the two brothers wanted to light a fire under the tree and kill the bees, so as to get their honey. But the dwarf held them back, and said, 'Let the pretty insects enjoy themselves, I cannot let you burn them.'

At length the three brothers came to a castle: and as they passed by the stables they saw fine horses standing there, but all were of marble, and no man was to be seen. Then they went through all the rooms, till they came to a door on which were three locks: but in the middle of the door was a wicket, so that they could look into the next room. There they saw a little grey old man sitting at a table; and they called to him once or twice, but he did not hear: however, they called a third time, and then he rose and came out to them.

He said nothing, but took hold of them and led them to a beautiful table covered with all sorts of good things: and when they had eaten and drunk, he showed each of them to a bed-chamber.

The next morning he came to the eldest and took him to a marble table, where there were three tablets, containing an account of the means by which the castle might be disenchanted. The first tablet said: 'In the wood, under the moss, lie the thousand pearls belonging to the king's daughter; they must all be found: and if one be missing by set of sun, he who seeks them will be turned into marble.'

The eldest brother set out, and sought for the pearls the whole day: but the evening came, and he had not found the first hundred: so he was turned into stone as the tablet had foretold.

The next day the second brother undertook the task; but he succeeded no better than the first; for he could only find the second hundred of the pearls; and therefore he too was turned into stone.

At last came the little dwarf's turn; and he looked in the moss; but it was so hard to find the pearls, and the job was so tiresome!—so he sat down upon a stone and cried. And as he sat there, the king of the ants (whose life he had saved) came to help him, with five thousand ants; and it was not long before they had found all the pearls and laid them in a heap.

The second tablet said: 'The key of the princess's bed-chamber must be fished up out of the lake.' And as the dwarf came to the brink of it, he saw the two ducks whose lives he had saved swimming about; and they dived down and soon brought in the key from the bottom.

The third task was the hardest. It was to choose out the youngest and the best of the king's three daughters. Now they were all beautiful, and all exactly alike: but he was told that the eldest had eaten a piece of sugar, the next some sweet syrup, and the youngest a spoonful of honey; so he was to guess which it was that had eaten the honey.

Then came the queen of the bees, who had been saved by the little dwarf from the fire, and she tried the lips of all three; but at last she sat upon the lips of the one that had eaten the honey: and so the dwarf knew which was the youngest. Thus the spell was broken, and all who had been turned into stones awoke, and took their proper forms. And the dwarf married the youngest and the best of the princesses, and was king after her father's death; but his two brothers married the other two sisters.

THE ELVES AND THE
SHOEMAKER

There was once a shoemaker, who worked very hard and was very honest: but still he could not earn enough to live upon; and at last all he had in the world was gone, save just leather enough to make one pair of shoes.

Then he cut his leather out, all ready to make up the next day, meaning to rise early in the morning to his work. His conscience was clear and his heart light amidst all his troubles; so he went peaceably to bed, left all his cares to Heaven, and soon fell asleep. In the morning after he had said his prayers, he sat himself down to his work; when, to his great wonder, there stood the shoes all ready made, upon the table. The good man knew not what to say or think at such an odd thing happening. He looked at the workmanship; there was not one false stitch in the whole job; all was so neat and true, that it was quite a masterpiece.

The same day a customer came in, and the shoes suited him so well that he willingly paid a price higher than usual for them; and the poor shoemaker, with the money, bought leather enough to make two pairs more. In the evening he cut out the work, and went to bed early, that he might get up and begin betimes next day; but he was saved all the trouble, for when he got up in the morning the work was done ready to his hand. Soon in came buyers, who paid him handsomely for his goods, so that he bought leather enough for four pair more. He cut out the work again overnight and found it done in the morning, as before; and so it went on for some time: what was got ready in the evening was always done by daybreak, and the good man soon became thriving and well off again.

One evening, about Christmas-time, as he and his wife were sitting over the fire chatting together, he said to her, 'I should like to sit up and watch tonight, that we may see who it is that comes and does my work for me.' The wife liked the thought; so they left a light burning, and hid themselves in a corner of the room, behind a curtain that was hung up there, and watched what would happen.

As soon as it was midnight, there came in two little naked dwarfs; and they sat themselves upon the shoemaker's bench, took up all the work that was cut out, and began to ply with their little fingers, stitching and rapping and tapping away at such a rate, that the shoemaker was all wonder, and could not take his eyes off them. And on they went, till the job was quite done, and the shoes stood ready for use upon the table. This was long before daybreak; and then they bustled away as quick as lightning.

The next day the wife said to the shoemaker. 'These little wights have made us rich, and we ought to be thankful to them, and do them a good turn if we can. I am quite sorry to see them run about as they do; and indeed it is not very decent, for they have nothing upon their backs to keep off the cold. I'll tell you what, I will make each of them a shirt, and a coat and waistcoat, and a pair of pantaloons into the bargain; and do you make each of them a little pair of shoes.'

The thought pleased the good cobbler very much; and one evening, when all the things were ready, they laid them on the table, instead of the work that they used to cut out, and then went and hid themselves, to watch what the little elves would do.

About midnight in they came, dancing and skipping, hopped round the room, and then went to sit down to their work as usual; but when they saw the clothes lying for them, they laughed and chuckled, and seemed mightily delighted.

Then they dressed themselves in the twinkling of an eye, and danced and capered and sprang about, as merry as could be; till at last they danced out at the door, and away over the green.

The good couple saw them no more; but everything went well with them from that time forward, as long as they lived.

THE JUNIPER-TREE

Long, long ago, some two thousand years or so, there lived a rich man with a good and beautiful wife. They loved each other dearly, but sorrowed much that they had no children. So greatly did they desire to have one, that the wife prayed for it day and night, but still they remained childless.

In front of the house there was a court, in which grew a juniper-tree. One winter's day the wife stood under the tree to peel some apples, and as she was peeling them, she cut her finger, and the blood fell on the snow. 'Ah,' sighed the woman heavily, 'if I had but a child, as red as blood and as white as snow,' and as she spoke the words, her heart grew light within her, and it seemed to her that her wish was granted, and she returned to the house feeling glad and comforted. A month passed, and the snow had all disappeared; then another month went by, and all the earth was green. So the months followed one another, and first the trees budded in the woods, and soon the green branches grew thickly intertwined, and then the blossoms began to fall. Once again the wife stood under the juniper-tree, and it was so full of sweet scent that her heart leaped for joy, and she was so overcome with her happiness, that she fell on her knees. Presently the fruit became round and firm, and she was glad and at peace; but when they were fully ripe she picked the berries and ate eagerly of them, and then she grew sad and ill. A little while later she called her husband, and said to him, weeping. 'If I die, bury me under the juniper-tree.' Then she felt comforted and happy again, and before another month had passed she had a little child, and when she saw that it was as white as snow and as red as blood, her joy was so great that she died.

Her husband buried her under the juniper-tree, and wept bitterly for her. By degrees, however, his sorrow grew less, and although at times he still grieved over his loss, he was able to go about as usual, and later on he married again.

He now had a little daughter born to him; the child of his first wife was a boy, who was as red as blood and as white as snow. The mother loved her daughter very much, and when she looked at her and then looked at the boy, it pierced her heart to think that he would always stand in the way of her own child, and she was continually thinking how she could get the whole of the property for her. This evil thought took possession of her more and more, and made her behave very unkindly to the boy. She drove him from place to place with cuffings and buffetings, so that the poor child went about in fear, and had no peace from the time he left school to the time he went back.

One day the little daughter came running to her mother in the store-room, and said, 'Mother, give me an apple.' 'Yes, my child,' said the wife, and she gave her a beautiful apple out of the chest; the chest had a very heavy lid and a large iron lock.

'Mother,' said the little daughter again, 'may not brother have one too?' The mother was angry at this, but she answered, 'Yes, when he comes out of school.'

Just then she looked out of the window and saw him coming, and it seemed as if an evil spirit entered into her, for she snatched the apple out of her little daughter's hand, and said, 'You shall not have one before your brother.' She threw the apple into the chest and shut it to. The little boy now came in, and the evil spirit in the wife made her say kindly to him, 'My son, will you have an apple?' but she gave him a wicked look. 'Mother,' said the boy, 'how dreadful you look! Yes, give me an apple.' The thought came to her that she would kill him. 'Come with me,' she said, and she lifted up the lid of the chest; 'take one out for yourself.' And as he bent over to do so, the evil spirit urged her, and crash! down went the lid, and off went the little boy's head. Then she was overwhelmed with fear at the thought of what she had done. 'If only I can prevent anyone knowing that I did it,' she thought. So she went upstairs to her room, and took a white handkerchief out of her top drawer; then she set the boy's head again on his shoulders, and bound it with the handkerchief so that nothing could be seen, and placed him on a chair by the door with an apple in his hand.

Soon after this, little Marleen came up to her mother who was stirring a pot of boiling water over the fire, and said, 'Mother, brother is sitting by the door with an apple in his hand, and he looks so pale; and when I asked him to give me the apple, he did not answer, and that frightened me.'

'Go to him again,' said her mother, 'and if he does not answer, give him a box on the ear.' So little Marleen went, and said, 'Brother, give me that apple,' but he did not say a word; then she gave him a box on the ear, and his head rolled off. She was so terrified at this, that she ran crying and screaming to her mother. 'Oh!' she said, 'I have knocked off brother's head,' and then she wept and wept, and nothing would stop her.

'What have you done!' said her mother, 'but no one must know about it, so you must keep silence; what is done can't be undone; we will make him into puddings.' And she took the little boy and cut him up, made him into puddings, and put him in the pot. But Marleen stood looking on, and wept and wept, and her tears fell into the pot, so that there was no need of salt.

Presently the father came home and sat down to his

dinner; he asked, 'Where is my son?' The mother said nothing, but gave him a large dish of black pudding, and Marleen still wept without ceasing.

The father again asked, 'Where is my son?'

'Oh,' answered the wife, 'he is gone into the country to his mother's great uncle; he is going to stay there some time.'

'What has he gone there for, and he never even said goodbye to me!'

'Well, he likes being there, and he told me he should be away quite six weeks; he is well looked after there.'

'I feel very unhappy about it,' said the husband, 'in case it should not be all right, and he ought to have said goodbye to me.'

With this he went on with his dinner, and said, 'Little Marleen, why do you weep? Brother will soon be back.' Then he asked his wife for more pudding, and as he ate, he threw the bones under the table. Little Marleen went upstairs and took her best silk handkerchief out of her bottom drawer, and in it she wrapped all the bones from under the table and carried them outside, and all the time she did nothing but weep. Then she laid them in the green grass under the juniper-tree, and she had no sooner done so, then all her sadness seemed to leave her, and she wept no more. And now the juniper-tree began to move, and the branches waved backwards and forwards, first away from one another, and then together again, as it might be someone clapping their hands for joy. After this a mist came round the tree, and in the midst of it there was a burning as of fire, and out of the fire there flew a beautiful bird, that rose high into the air, singing magnificently, and when it could no more be seen, the juniper-tree stood there as before, and the silk handkerchief and the bones were gone.

Little Marleen now felt as lighthearted and happy as if her brother were still alive, and she went back to the house and sat down cheerfully to the table and ate.

The bird flew away and alighted on the house of a gold-smith and began to sing:

> '*My mother killed her little son;*
> *My father grieved when I was gone;*
> *My sister loved me best of all;*
> *She laid her kerchief over me,*
> *And took my bones that they might lie*
> *Underneath the juniper-tree*
> *Kywitt, Kywitt, what a beautiful bird am I!'*

The goldsmith was in his workshop making a gold chain, when he heard the song of the bird on his roof. He thought it so beautiful that he got up and ran out, and as he crossed the threshold he lost one of his slippers. But he ran on into the middle of the street, with a slipper on one foot and a sock on the other; he still had on his apron, and still held the gold chain and the pincers in his hands, and so he stood gazing up at the bird, while the sun came shining brightly down on the street.

'Bird,' he said, 'how beautifully you sing! Sing me that song again.'

'Nay,' said the bird, 'I do not sing twice for nothing. Give that gold chain, and I will sing it you again.'

'Here is the chain, take it,' said the goldsmith. 'Only sing me that again.'

The bird flew down and took the gold chain in his right claw, and then he alighted again in front of the goldsmith and sang:

> '*My mother killed her little son;*
> *My father grieved when I was gone;*
> *My sister loved me best of all;*
> *She laid her kerchief over me,*
> *And took my bones that they might lie*

> *Underneath the juniper-tree*
> *Kywitt, Kywitt, what a beautiful bird am I!'*

Then he flew away, and settled on the roof of a shoe-maker's house and sang:

> *'My mother killed her little son;*
> *My father grieved when I was gone;*
> *My sister loved me best of all;*
> *She laid her kerchief over me,*
> *And took my bones that they might lie*
> *Underneath the juniper-tree*
> *Kywitt, Kywitt, what a beautiful bird am I!'*

The shoemaker heard him, and he jumped up and ran out in his shirt-sleeves, and stood looking up at the bird on the roof with his hand over his eyes to keep himself from being blinded by the sun.

'Bird,' he said, 'how beautifully you sing!' Then he called through the door to his wife: 'Wife, come out; here is a bird, come and look at it and hear how beautifully it sings.' Then he called his daughter and the children, then the apprentices, girls and boys, and they all ran up the street to look at the bird, and saw how splendid it was with its red and green feathers, and its neck like burnished gold, and eyes like two bright stars in its head.

'Bird,' said the shoemaker, 'sing me that song again.'

'Nay,' answered the bird, 'I do not sing twice for nothing; you must give me something.'

'Wife,' said the man, 'go into the garret; on the upper shelf you will see a pair of red shoes; bring them to me.' The wife went in and fetched the shoes.

'There, bird,' said the shoemaker, 'now sing me that song again.'

The bird flew down and took the red shoes in his left claw, and then he went back to the roof and sang:

> *'My mother killed her little son;*
> *My father grieved when I was gone;*
> *My sister loved me best of all;*
> *She laid her kerchief over me,*
> *And took my bones that they might lie*
> *Underneath the juniper-tree*
> *Kywitt, Kywitt, what a beautiful bird am I!'*

When he had finished, he flew away. He had the chain in his right claw and the shoes in his left, and he flew right away to a mill, and the mill went 'Click clack, click clack, click clack.' Inside the mill were twenty of the miller's men hewing a stone, and as they went 'Hick hack, hick hack, hick hack,' the mill went 'Click clack, click clack, click clack.'

The bird settled on a lime-tree in front of the mill and sang:

> *'My mother killed her little son;*

then one of the men left off,

> *My father grieved when I was gone;*

two more men left off and listened,

> *My sister loved me best of all;*

then four more left off,

> *She laid her kerchief over me,*
> *And took my bones that they might lie*

now there were only eight at work,

> *Underneath*

And now only five,

> *the juniper-tree*

and now only one,

> *Kywitt, Kywitt, what a beautiful bird am I!'*

then he looked up and the last one had left off work.

'Bird,' he said, 'what a beautiful song that is you sing! Let me hear it too; sing it again.'

'Nay,' answered the bird, 'I do not sing twice for nothing; give me that millstone, and I will sing it again.'

'If it belonged to me alone,' said the man, 'you should have it.'

'Yes, yes,' said the others: 'if he will sing again, he can have it.'

The bird came down, and all the twenty millers set to and lifted up the stone with a beam; then the bird put his head through the hole and took the stone round his neck like a collar, and flew back with it to the tree and sang—

> *'My mother killed her little son;*
> *My father grieved when I was gone;*
> *My sister loved me best of all;*
> *She laid her kerchief over me,*
> *And took my bones that they might lie*
> *Underneath the juniper-tree*
> *Kywitt, Kywitt, what a beautiful bird am I!'*

And when he had finished his song, he spread his wings, and with the chain in his right claw, the shoes in his left, and the millstone round his neck, he flew right away to his father's house.

The father, the mother, and little Marleen were having their dinner.

'How lighthearted I feel,' said the father, 'so pleased and cheerful.'

'And I,' said the mother, 'I feel so uneasy, as if a heavy thunderstorm were coming.'

But little Marleen sat and wept and wept.

Then the bird came flying towards the house and settled on the roof.

'I do feel so happy,' said the father, 'and how beautifully the sun shines; I feel just as if I were going to see an old friend again.'

'Ah!' said the wife, 'and I am so full of distress and uneasiness that my teeth chatter, and I feel as if there were a fire in my veins,' and she tore open her dress; and all the while little Marleen sat in the corner and wept, and the plate on her knees was wet with her tears.

The bird now flew to the juniper-tree and began singing:

'My mother killed her little son;

the mother shut her eyes and her ears, that she might see and hear nothing, but there was a roaring sound in her ears like that of a violent storm, and in her eyes a burning and flashing like lightning:

My father grieved when I was gone;

'Look, mother,' said the man, 'at the beautiful bird that is singing so magnificently; and how warm and bright the sun is, and what a delicious scent of spice in the air!'

> *My sister loved me best of all;*

then little Marleen laid her head down on her knees and sobbed.

'I must go outside and see the bird nearer,' said the man.

'Ah, do not go!' cried the wife. 'I feel as if the whole house were in flames!'

But the man went out and looked at the bird.

> *She laid her kerchief over me,*
> *And took my bones that they might lie*
> *Underneath the juniper-tree*
> *Kywitt, Kywitt, what a beautiful bird am I!'*

With that the bird let fall the gold chain, and it fell just round the man's neck, so that it fitted him exactly.

He went inside, and said, 'See, what a splendid bird that is; he has given me this beautiful gold chain, and looks so beautiful himself.'

But the wife was in such fear and trouble, that she fell on the floor, and her cap fell from her head.

Then the bird began again:

> *'My mother killed her little son;*

'Ah me!' cried the wife, 'if I were but a thousand feet beneath the earth, that I might not hear that song.'

> *My father grieved when I was gone;*

then the woman fell down again as if dead.

> *My sister loved me best of all;*

'Well,' said little Marleen, 'I will go out too and see if the bird will give me anything.'

So she went out.

> *She laid her kerchief over me,*
> *And took my bones that they might lie*

and he threw down the shoes to her,

> *Underneath the juniper-tree*
> *Kywitt, Kywitt, what a beautiful bird am I!'*

And she now felt quite happy and lighthearted; she put on the shoes and danced and jumped about in them. 'I was so miserable,' she said, 'when I came out, but that has all passed away; that is indeed a splendid bird, and he has given me a pair of red shoes.'

The wife sprang up, with her hair standing out from her head like flames of fire. 'Then I will go out too,' she said, 'and see if it will lighten my misery, for I feel as if the world were coming to an end.'

But as she crossed the threshold, crash! the bird threw the millstone down on her head, and she was crushed to death.

The father and little Marleen heard the sound and ran out, but they only saw mist and flame and fire rising from the spot, and when these had passed, there stood the little brother, and he took the father and little Marleen by the hand; then they all three rejoiced, and went inside together and sat down to their dinners and ate.

THE TURNIP

There were two brothers who were both soldiers; the one was rich and the other poor. The poor man thought he would try to better himself; so, pulling off his red coat, he became a gardener, and dug his ground well, and sowed turnips.

When the seed came up, there was one plant bigger than all the rest; and it kept getting larger and larger, and seemed as if it would never cease growing; so that it might have been called the prince of turnips for there never was such a one seen before, and never will again. At last it was so big that it filled a cart, and two oxen could hardly draw it; and the gardener knew not what in the world to do with it, nor whether it would be a blessing or a curse to him. One day he said to himself, 'What shall I do with it? if I sell it, it will bring no more than another; and for eating, the little turnips are better than this; the best thing perhaps is to carry it and give it to the king as a mark of respect.'

Then he yoked his oxen, and drew the turnip to the court, and gave it to the king. 'What a wonderful thing!' said the king; 'I have seen many strange things, but such a monster as this I never saw. Where did you get the seed? or is it only your good luck? If so, you are a true child of fortune.' 'Ah, no!' answered the gardener, 'I am no child of fortune; I am a poor soldier, who never could get enough to live upon; so I laid aside my red coat, and set to work, tilling the ground. I have a brother, who is rich, and your majesty knows him well, and all the world knows him; but because I am poor, everybody forgets me.'

The king then took pity on him, and said, 'You shall be poor no longer. I will give you so much that you shall be even richer than your brother.' Then he gave him gold and lands and flocks, and made him so rich that his brother's fortune could not at all be compared with his.

When the brother heard of all this, and how a turnip had made the gardener so rich, he envied him sorely, and bethought himself how he could contrive to get the same good fortune for himself. However, he determined to manage more cleverly than his brother, and got together a rich present of gold and fine horses for the king; and thought he must have a much larger gift in return; for if his brother had received so much for only a turnip, what must his present be wroth?

The king took the gift very graciously, and said he knew not what to give in return more valuable and wonderful than the great turnip; so the soldier was forced to put it into a cart, and drag it home with him. When he reached home, he knew not upon whom to vent his rage and spite; and at length wicked thoughts came into his head, and he resolved to kill his brother.

So he hired some villains to murder him; and having shown them where to lie in ambush, he went to his brother, and said, 'Dear brother, I have found a hidden treasure; let us go and dig it up, and share it between us.' The other had no suspicions of his roguery: so they went out together, and as they were travelling along, the murderers rushed out upon him, bound him, and were going to hang him on a tree.

But whilst they were getting all ready, they heard the trampling of a horse at a distance, which so frightened them that they pushed their prisoner neck and shoulders together into a sack, and swung him up by a cord to the tree, where they left him dangling, and ran away. Meantime he worked and worked away, till he made a hole large enough to put out his head.

When the horseman came up, he proved to be a student, a merry fellow, who was journeying along on his nag, and singing as he went. As soon as the man in the sack saw him passing under the tree, he cried out, 'Good morning! good morning to thee, my friend!' The student looked about everywhere; and seeing no one, and not knowing where the voice came from, cried out, 'Who calls me?'

Then the man in the tree answered, 'Lift up thine eyes, for behold here I sit in the sack of wisdom; here have I, in a short time, learned great and wondrous things. Compared to this seat, all the learning of the schools is as empty air. A little longer, and I shall know all that man can know, and shall come forth wiser than the wisest of mankind. Here I discern the signs and motions of the heavens and the stars; the laws that control the winds; the number of the sands on the seashore; the healing of the sick; the virtues of all simples, of birds, and of precious stones. Wert thou but once here, my friend, though wouldst feel and own the power of knowledge.

The student listened to all this and wondered much; at last he said, 'Blessed be the day and hour when I found you; cannot you contrive to let me into the sack for a little while?' Then the other answered, as if very unwillingly, 'A little space I may allow thee to sit here, if thou wilt reward me well and entreat me kindly; but thou must tarry yet an hour below, till I have learnt some little matters that are yet unknown to me.'

So the student sat himself down and waited a while; but the time hung heavy upon him, and he begged earnestly that he might ascend forthwith, for his thirst for knowledge was great. Then the other pretended to give way, and said, 'Thou must let the sack of wisdom descend, by untying yonder cord, and then thou shalt enter.' So the student let him down, opened the sack, and set him free. 'Now then,' cried he, 'let me ascend quickly.' As he began to put himself into the sack heels first, 'Wait a while,' said the gardener, 'that is not the way.' Then he pushed him in head first, tied up the sack, and soon swung up the searcher after wisdom dangling in the air. 'How is it with thee, friend?' said he, 'dost thou not feel that wisdom comes unto thee? Rest there in peace, till thou art a wiser man than thou wert.'

So saying, he trotted off on the student's nag, and left the poor fellow to gather wisdom till somebody should come and let him down.

CLEVER HANS

The mother of Hans said: 'Whither away, Hans?' Hans answered: 'To Gretel.' 'Behave well, Hans.' 'Oh, I'll behave well. Goodbye, mother.' 'Goodbye, Hans.' Hans comes to Gretel. 'Good day, Gretel.' 'Good day, Hans. What do you bring that is good?' 'I bring nothing, I want to have something given me.' Gretel presents Hans with a needle, Hans says: 'Goodbye, Gretel.' 'Goodbye, Hans.'

Hans takes the needle, sticks it into a hay-cart, and follows the cart home. 'Good evening, mother.' 'Good evening, Hans. Where have you been?' 'With Gretel.' 'What did you take her?' 'Took nothing; had something given me.' 'What did Gretel give you?' 'Gave me a needle.' 'Where is the needle, Hans?' 'Stuck in the hay-cart.' 'That was ill done, Hans. You should have stuck the needle in your sleeve.' 'Never mind, I'll do better next time.'

'Whither away, Hans?' 'To Gretel, mother.' 'Behave well, Hans.' 'Oh, I'll behave well. Goodbye, mother.' 'Goodbye, Hans.' Hans comes to Gretel. 'Good day, Gretel.' 'Good day, Hans. What do you bring that is good?' 'I bring nothing. I want to have something given to me.' Gretel presents Hans with a knife. 'Goodbye, Gretel.' 'Goodbye, Hans.' Hans takes the knife, sticks it in his sleeve, and goes home. 'Good evening, mother.' 'Good evening, Hans. Where have you been?' 'With Gretel.' What did you take her?' 'Took her nothing, she gave me something.' 'What did Gretel give you?' 'Gave me a knife.' 'Where is the knife, Hans?' 'Stuck in my sleeve.' 'That's ill done, Hans, you should have put the knife in your pocket.' 'Never mind, will do better next time.'

'Whither away, Hans?' 'To Gretel, mother.' 'Behave well, Hans.' 'Oh, I'll behave well. Goodbye, mother.' 'Goodbye, Hans.' Hans comes to Gretel. 'Good day, Gretel.' 'Good day, Hans. What good thing do you bring?' 'I bring nothing, I want something given me.' Gretel presents Hans with a young goat. 'Goodbye, Gretel.' 'Goodbye, Hans.' Hans takes the goat, ties its legs, and puts it in his pocket. When he gets home it is suffocated. 'Good evening, mother.' 'Good evening, Hans. Where have you been?' 'With Gretel.' 'What did you take her?' 'Took nothing, she gave me something.' 'What did Gretel give you?' 'She gave me a goat.' 'Where is the goat, Hans?' 'Put it in my pocket.' 'That was ill done, Hans, you should have put a rope round the goat's neck.' 'Never mind, will do better next time.'

'Whither away, Hans?' 'To Gretel, mother.' 'Behave well, Hans.' 'Oh, I'll behave well. Goodbye, mother.' 'Goodbye, Hans.' Hans comes to Gretel. 'Good day, Gretel.' 'Good day, Hans. What good thing do you bring?' 'I bring nothing, I want something given me.' Gretel presents Hans with a piece of bacon. 'Goodbye, Gretel.' 'Goodbye, Hans.'

Hans takes the bacon, ties it to a rope, and drags it away behind him. The dogs come and devour the bacon. When he gets home, he has the rope in his hand, and there is no longer anything hanging on to it. 'Good evening, mother.' 'Good evening, Hans. Where have you been?' 'With Gretel.' 'What did you take her?' 'I took her nothing, she gave me something.' 'What did Gretel give you?' 'Gave me a bit of bacon.' 'Where is the bacon, Hans?' 'I tied it to a rope, brought it home, dogs took it.' 'That was ill done, Hans, you should have carried the bacon on your head.' 'Never mind, will do better next time.'

'Whither away, Hans?' 'To Gretel, mother.' 'Behave well, Hans.' 'I'll behave well. Goodbye, mother.' 'Goodbye, Hans.' Hans comes to Gretel. 'Good day, Gretel.' 'Good day, Hans, What good thing do you bring?' 'I bring nothing, but would have something given.' Gretel presents Hans with a calf. 'Goodbye, Gretel.' 'Goodbye, Hans.'

Hans takes the calf, puts it on his head, and the calf kicks his face. 'Good evening, mother.' 'Good evening, Hans. Where have you been?' 'With Gretel.' 'What did you take her?' 'I took nothing, but had something given me.' 'What did Gretel give you?' 'A calf.' 'Where have you the calf, Hans?' 'I set it on my head and it kicked my face.' 'That was ill done, Hans, you should have led the calf, and put it in the stall.' 'Never mind, will do better next time.'

'Whither away, Hans?' 'To Gretel, mother.' 'Behave well, Hans.' 'I'll behave well. Goodbye, mother.' 'Goodbye, Hans.'

Hans comes to Gretel. 'Good day, Gretel.' 'Good day, Hans. What good thing do you bring?' 'I bring nothing, but would have something given.' Gretel says to Hans: 'I will go with you.' Hans takes Gretel, ties her to a rope, leads her to the rack, and binds her fast. Then Hans goes to his mother. 'Good evening, mother.' 'Good evening, Hans. Where have you been?' 'With Gretel.' 'What did you take her?' 'I took her nothing.' 'What did Gretel give you?' 'She gave me nothing, she came with me.' 'Where have you left Gretel?' 'I led her by the rope, tied her to the rack, and scattered some grass for her.' 'That was ill done, Hans, you should have cast friendly eyes on her.' 'Never mind, will do better.'

Hans went into the stable, cut out all the calves' and sheep's eyes, and threw them in Gretel's face. Then Gretel became angry, tore herself loose and ran away, and was no longer the bride of Hans.

THE THREE LANGUAGES

An aged count once lived in Switzerland, who had an only son, but he was stupid, and could learn nothing. Then said the father: 'Hark you, my son, try as I will I can get nothing into your head. You must go from hence, I will give you into the care of a celebrated master, who shall see what he can do with you.' The youth was sent into a strange town, and remained a whole year with the master. At the end of this time, he came home again, and his father asked: 'Now, my son, what have you learnt?' 'Father, I have learnt what the dogs say when they bark.' 'Lord have mercy on us!' cried the father; 'is that all you have learnt? I will send you into another town, to another master.' The youth was taken thither, and stayed a year with this master likewise. When he came back the father again asked: 'My son, what have you learnt?' He answered: 'Father, I have learnt what the birds say.' Then the father fell into a rage and said: 'Oh, you lost man, you have spent the precious time and learnt nothing; are you not ashamed to appear before my eyes? I will send you to a third master, but if you learn nothing this time also, I will no longer be your father.' The youth remained a whole year with the third master also, and when he came home again, and his father inquired: 'My son, what have you learnt?' he answered:

'Dear father, I have this year learnt what the frogs croak.'
Then the father fell into the most furious anger, sprang up,
called his people thither, and said: 'This man is no longer my
son, I drive him forth, and command you to take him out into
the forest, and kill him.' They took him forth, but when they
should have killed him, they could not do it for pity, and let
him go, and they cut the eyes and tongue out of a deer that
they might carry them to the old man as a token.

The youth wandered on, and after some time came to a
fortress where he begged for a night's lodging. 'Yes,' said the
lord of the castle, 'if you will pass the night down there in
the old tower, go thither; but I warn you, it is at the peril of
your life, for it is full of wild dogs, which bark and howl
without stopping, and at certain hours a man has to be given
to them, whom they at once devour.' The whole district was
in sorrow and dismay because of them, and yet no one could
do anything to stop this. The youth, however, was without
fear, and said: 'Just let me go down to the barking dogs, and
give me something that I can throw to them; they will do
nothing to harm me.' As he himself would have it so, they
gave him some food for the wild animals, and led him down
to the tower. When he went inside, the dogs did not bark at
him, but wagged their tails quite amicably around him, ate
what he set before them, and did not hurt one hair of his
head. Next morning, to the astonishment of everyone, he
came out again safe and unharmed, and said to the lord of
the castle: 'The dogs have revealed to me, in their own
language, why they dwell there, and bring evil on the land.
They are bewitched, and are obliged to watch over a great
treasure which is below in the tower, and they can have no
rest until it is taken away, and I have likewise learnt, from
their discourse, how that is to be done.' Then all who heard
this rejoiced, and the lord of the castle said he would adopt
him as a son if he accomplished it successfully. He went down
again, and as he knew what he had to do, he did it thoroughly,

and brought a chest full of gold out with him. The howling of the wild dogs was henceforth heard no more; they had disappeared, and the country was freed from the trouble.

After some time he took it in his head that he would travel to Rome. On the way he passed by a marsh, in which a number of frogs were sitting croaking. He listened to them, and when he became aware of what they were saying, he grew very thoughtful and sad. At last he arrived in Rome, where the Pope had just died, and there was great doubt among the cardinals as to whom they should appoint as his successor. They at length agreed that the person should be chosen as pope who should be distinguished by some divine and miraculous token. And just as that was decided on, the young count entered into the church, and suddenly two snow-white doves flew on his shoulders and remained sitting there. The ecclesiastics recognized therein the token from above, and asked him on the spot if he would be pope. He was undecided, and knew not if he were worthy of this, but the doves counselled him to do it, and at length he said yes. Then was he anointed and consecrated, and thus was fulfilled what he had heard from the frogs on his way, which had so affected him, that he was to be his Holiness the Pope. Then he had to sing a mass, and did not know one word of it, but the two doves sat continually on his shoulders, and said it all in his ear.

THE FOX AND THE CAT

It happened that the cat met the fox in a forest, and as she thought to herself: 'He is clever and full of experience, and much esteemed in the world,' she spoke to him in a friendly way. 'Good day, dear Mr Fox, how are you? How is all with you? How are you getting on in these hard times?' The fox, full of all kinds of arrogance, looked at the cat from head to foot, and for a long time did not know whether he would give any answer or not. At last he said: 'Oh, you wretched beard-cleaner, you piebald fool, you hungry mouse-hunter, what can you be thinking of? Have you the cheek to ask how I am getting on? What have you learnt? How many arts do you understand?' 'I understand but one,' replied the cat, modestly. 'What art is that?' asked the fox. 'When the hounds are following me, I can spring into a tree and save myself.' 'Is that all?' said the fox. 'I am master of a hundred arts, and have into the bargain a sackful of cunning. You make me sorry for you; come with me, I will teach you how people get away from the hounds.' Just then came a hunter with four dogs. The cat sprang nimbly up a tree, and sat down at the top of it, where the branches and foliage quite concealed her. 'Open your sack, Mr Fox, open your sack,' cried the cat to him, but the dogs had already seized him, and were holding him fast. 'Ah, Mr Fox,' cried the cat. 'You with your hundred arts are left in the lurch! Had you been able to climb like me, you would not have lost your life.'

THE FOUR CLEVER
BROTHERS

'Dear children,' said a poor man to his four sons, 'I have nothing to give you; you must go out into the wide world and try your luck. Begin by learning some craft or another, and see how you can get on.' So the four brothers took their walking-sticks in their hands, and their little bundles on their shoulders, and after bidding their father goodbye, went all out at the gate together. When they had got on some way they came to four crossways, each leading to a different country. Then the eldest said, 'Here we must part; but this day four years we will come back to this spot, and in the meantime each must try what he can do for himself.'

So each brother went his way; and as the eldest was hastening on a man met him, and asked him where he was going, and what he wanted. 'I am going to try my luck in the world, and should like to begin by learning some art or trade,' answered he. 'Then,' said the man, 'go with me, and I will teach you to become the cunningest thief that ever was.' 'No,' said the other, 'that is not an honest calling, and what can one look to earn by it in the end but the gallows?' 'Oh!' said the man, 'you need not fear the gallows; for I will only teach you to steal what will be fair game: I meddle with nothing but what no one else can get or care anything about, and where no one can find you out.' So the young man agreed to follow his trade, and he soon showed himself so clever, that nothing could escape him that he had once set his mind upon.

The second brother also met a man, who, when he found out what he was setting out upon, asked him what craft he meant to follow. 'I do not know yet,' said he. 'Then come with me, and be a star-gazer. It is a noble art, for nothing can be hidden from you, when once you understand the stars.' The plan pleased him much, and he soon became such a skilful star-gazer, that when he had served out his time, and wanted to leave his master, he gave him a glass, and said, 'With this you can see all that is passing in the sky and on earth, and nothing can be hidden from you.'

The third brother met a huntsman, who took him with him, and taught him so well all that belonged to hunting, that he became very clever in the craft of the woods; and when he left his master he gave him a bow, and said, 'Whatever you shoot at with this bow you will be sure to hit.'

The youngest brother likewise met a man who asked him what he wished to do. 'Would not you like,' said he, 'to be a tailor?' 'Oh, no!' said the young man; 'sitting cross-legged from morning to night, working backwards and forwards with a needle and goose, will never suit me.' 'Oh!' answered the man, 'that is not my sort of tailoring; come with me, and you will learn quite another kind of craft from that.' Not knowing what better to do, he came into the plan, and learnt tailoring from the beginning; and when he left his master, he gave him a needle, and said, 'You can sew anything with this, be it as soft as an egg or as hard as steel; and the joint will be so fine that no seam will be seen.'

After the space of four years, at the time agreed upon, the four brothers met at the four cross-roads; and having welcomed each other, set off towards their father's home, where they told him all that had happened to them, and how each had learned some craft.

Then, one day, as they were sitting before the house under a very high tree, the father said, 'I should like to try what each of you can do in this way.' So he looked up, and said to the second son, 'At the top of this tree there is a chaffinch's nest; tell me how many eggs there are in it.' The star-gazer took his glass, looked up, and said, 'Five.' 'Now,' said the father to the eldest son, 'take away the eggs without letting the bird that is sitting upon them and hatching them know anything of what you are doing.' So the cunning thief climbed up the tree, and brought away to his father the five eggs from under the bird; and it never saw or felt what he was doing, but kept sitting on at its ease. Then the father took the eggs, and put one on each corner of the table, and the fifth in the middle, and said to the huntsman, 'Cut all the eggs in two pieces at one shot.' The huntsman took up his bow, and at one shot struck all the five eggs as his father wished.

'Now comes your turn,' said he to the young tailor; 'sew the eggs and the young birds in them together again, so neatly that the shot shall have done them no harm.' Then the tailor took his needle, and sewed the eggs as he was told; and when he had done, the thief was sent to take them back to the nest, and put them under the bird without its knowing it. Then she went on sitting, and hatched them: and in a few days they crawled out, and had only a little red streak across their necks, where the tailor had sewn them together.

'Well done, sons!' said the old man; 'you have made good use of your time, and learnt something worth the knowing; but I am sure I do not know which ought to have the prize. Oh, that a time might soon come for you to turn your skill to some account!'

Not long after this there was a great bustle in the country; for the king's daughter had been carried off by a mighty dragon, and the king mourned over his loss day and night, and made it known that whoever brought her back to him should have her for a wife. Then the four brothers said to each other, 'Here is a chance for us; let us try what we can do.' And they agreed to see whether they could not set the princess free. 'I will soon find out where she is, however,' said the star-gazer, as he looked through his glass; and he soon cried out, 'I see her afar off, sitting upon a rock in the sea, and I can spy the dragon close by, guarding her.' Then he went to the king, and asked for a ship for himself and his brothers; and they sailed together over the sea, till they came to the right place. There they found the princess sitting, as the star-gazer had said, on the rock; and the dragon was lying asleep, with his head upon her lap. 'I dare not shoot at him,' said the huntsman, 'for I should kill the beautiful young lady also.' 'Then I will try my skill,' said the thief, and went and stole her away from under the dragon, so quietly and gently that the beast did not know it, but went on snoring.

Then away they hastened with her full of joy in their boat towards the ship; but soon came the dragon roaring behind them through the air; for he awoke and missed the princess. But when he got over the boat, and wanted to pounce upon them and carry off the princess, the huntsman took up his bow and shot him straight through the heart so that he fell down dead. They were still not safe; for he was such a great beast that in his fall he overset the boat, and they had to swim in the open sea upon a few planks. So the tailor took his needle, and with a few large stitches put some of the planks together; and he sat down upon these, and sailed about and gathered up all pieces of the boat; and then tacked them together so quickly that the boat was soon ready, and they then reached the ship and got home safe.

When they had brought home the princess to her father, there was great rejoicing; and he said to the four brothers, 'One of you shall marry her, but you must settle amongst yourselves which it is to be.' Then there arose a quarrel between them; and the star-gazer said, 'If I had not found the princess out, all your skill would have been of no use; therefore she ought to be mine.' 'Your seeing her would have been of no use,' said the thief, 'if I had not taken her away from the dragon; therefore she ought to be mine.' 'No, she is mine,' said the huntsman; 'for if I had not killed the dragon, he would, after all, have torn you and the princess into pieces.' 'And if I had not sewn the boat together again,' said the tailor, 'you would all have been drowned, therefore she is mine.' Then the king put in a word, and said, 'Each of you is right; and as all cannot have the young lady, the best way is for neither of you to have her: for the truth is, there is somebody she likes a great deal better. But to make up for your loss, I will give each of you, as a reward for his skill, half a kingdom.' So the brothers agreed that this plan would be much better than either quarrelling or marrying a lady who had no mind to have them. And the king then gave to each half a kingdom, as he had said; and they lived very happily the rest of their days, and took good care of their father; and somebody took better care of the young lady, than to let either the dragon or one of the craftsmen have her again.

LILY AND THE LION

A merchant, who had three daughters, was once setting out upon a journey, but before he went he asked each daughter what gift he should bring back for her. The eldest wished for pearls; the second for jewels; but the third, who was called Lily, said, 'Dear father, bring me a rose.' Now it was no easy task to find a rose, for it was the middle of winter; yet as she was his prettiest daughter, and was very fond of flowers, her father said he would try what he could do. So he kissed all three, and bid them goodbye.

And when the time came for him to go home, he had bought pearls and jewels for the two eldest, but he had sought everywhere in vain for the rose; and when he went into any garden and asked for such a thing, the people laughed at him, and asked him whether he thought roses grew in snow. This grieved him very much, for Lily was his dearest child; and as he was journeying home, thinking what he should bring her, he came to a fine castle; and around the castle was a garden, in one half of which it seemed to be summer-time and in the other half winter. On one side the finest flowers were in full bloom, and on the other everything looked dreary and buried in the snow. 'A lucky hit!' said he, as he called to his servant, and told him to go to a beautiful bed of roses that was there, and bring him away one of the finest flowers.

This done, they were riding away well pleased, when up sprang a fierce lion, and roared out, 'Whoever has stolen my roses shall be eaten up alive!' Then the man said, 'I knew not that the garden belonged to you; can nothing save my life?' 'No!' said the lion, 'nothing, unless you undertake to give me whatever meets you on your return home; if you agree to this, I will give you your life, and the rose too for your daughter.' But the man was unwilling to do so and said, 'It may be my youngest daughter, who loves me most, and always runs to meet me when I go home.' Then the servant was greatly frightened, and said, 'It may perhaps be only a cat or a dog.' And at last the man yielded with a heavy heart, and took the rose; and said he would give the lion whatever should meet him first on his return.

And as he came near home, it was Lily, his youngest and dearest daughter, that met him; she came running, and kissed him, and welcomed him home; and when she saw that he had brought her the rose, she was still more glad. But her father began to be very sorrowful, and to weep, saying, 'Alas, my dearest child! I have bought this flower at a high price, for I have said I would give you to a wild lion; and when he has you, he will tear you in pieces, and eat you.' Then he told her all that had happened, and said she should not go, let what would happen.

But she comforted him, and said, 'Dear father, the word you have given must be kept; I will go to the lion, and soothe him: perhaps he will let me come safe home again.'

The next morning she asked the way she was to go, and took leave of her father, and went forth with a bold heart into the wood. But the lion was an enchanted prince. By day he and all his court were lions, but in the evening they took their right forms again. And when Lily came to the castle, he welcomed her so courteously that she agreed to marry him. The wedding-feast was held, and they lived happily together a long time. The prince was only to be seen as soon as evening came, and then he held his court; but every morning he left his bride, and went away by himself, she knew not whither, till the night came again.

After some time he said to her, 'Tomorrow there will be a great feast in your father's house, for your eldest sister is to be married; and if you wish to go and visit her my lions shall lead you thither.' Then she rejoiced much at the thoughts of seeing her father once more, and set out with the lions; and everyone was overjoyed to see her, for they had thought her dead long since. But she told them how happy she was, and stayed till the feast was over, and then went back to the wood.

Her second sister was soon after married, and when Lily was asked to go to the wedding, she said to the prince, 'I will not go alone this time—you must go with me.' But he would not, and said that it would be a very hazardous thing; for if the least ray of the torch-light should fall upon him his enchantment would become still worse, for he should be changed into a dove, and be forced to wander about the world for seven long years. However, she gave him no rest, and said she would take care no light should fall upon him. So at last they set out together, and took with them their little child; and she chose a large hall with thick walls for him to sit in while the wedding-torches were lighted; but, unluckily, no one saw that there was a crack in the door. Then the wedding was held with great pomp, but as the train came from the church, and passed with the torches before the hall, a very small ray of light fell upon the prince. In a moment he disappeared, and when his wife came in and looked for him, she found only a white dove; and it said to her, 'Seven years must I fly up and down over the face of the earth, but every now and then I will let fall a white feather, that will show you the way I am going; follow it, and at last you may overtake and set me free.'

This said, he flew out at the door, and poor Lily followed; and every now and then a white feather fell, and showed her the way she was to journey. Thus she went roving on through the wide world, and looked neither to the right hand nor to the left, nor took any rest, for seven years. Then she began to be glad, and thought to herself that the time was fast coming when all her troubles should end; yet repose was still far off, for one day as she was travelling on she missed the white feather, and when she lifted up her eyes she could nowhere see the dove. 'Now,' thought she to herself, 'no aid of man can be of use to me.' So she went to the sun and said, 'Thou shinest everywhere, on the hill's top and the valley's depth—hast thou anywhere seen my white dove?' 'No,' said the sun, 'I have not seen it; but I will give thee a casket—open it when thy hour of need comes.' So she thanked the sun, and went on her way till eventide; and when the moon arose, she cried unto it, and said, 'Thou shinest through the night, over field and grove—hast thou nowhere seen my white dove?' 'No,' said the moon, 'I cannot help thee but I will give thee an egg—break it when need comes.'

Then she thanked the moon, and went on till the night-wind blew; and she raised up her voice to it, and said, 'Thou blowest through every tree and under every leaf—hast thou not seen my white dove?' 'No,' said the night-wind, 'but I will ask three other winds; perhaps they have seen it.' Then the east wind and the west wind came, and said they too had not seen it, but the south wind said, 'I have seen the white dove—he has fled to the Red Sea, and is changed once more into a lion, for the seven years are passed away, and there he is fighting with a dragon; and the dragon is an enchanted princess, who seeks to separate him from you.' Then the night-wind said, 'I will give thee counsel. Go to the Red Sea; on the right shore stand many rods—count them, and when thou comest to the eleventh, break it off, and smite the dragon with it; and so the lion will have the victory, and both of them will appear to you in their own forms. Then look round and thou wilt see a griffin, winged like bird, sitting by the Red Sea; jump on to his back with thy beloved one as quickly as possible, and he will carry you over the waters to your home. I will also give thee this nut,' continued the night-wind. 'When you are half-way over, throw it down, and out of the waters will immediately spring up a high nut-tree on which the griffin will be able to rest, otherwise he would not have the strength to bear you the whole way; if, therefore, thou dost forget to throw down the nut, he will let you both fall into the sea.'

So our poor wanderer went forth, and found all as the night-wind had said; and she plucked the eleventh rod, and smote the dragon, and the lion forthwith became a prince, and the dragon a princess again. But no sooner was the princess released from the spell, than she seized the prince by the arm and sprang on to the griffin's back, and went off carrying the prince away with her.

Thus the unhappy traveller was again forsaken and forlorn; but she took heart and said, 'As far as the wind blows, and so long as the cock crows, I will journey on, till I find him once again.' She went on for a long, long way, till at length she came to the castle whither the princess had carried the prince; and there was a feast got ready, and she heard that the wedding was about to be held. 'Heaven aid me now!' said she; and she took the casket that the sun had given her, and found that within it lay a dress as dazzling as the sun itself. So she put it on, and went into the palace, and all the people gazed upon her; and the dress pleased the bride so much that she asked whether it was to be sold. 'Not for gold and silver.' said she, 'but for flesh and blood.' The princess asked what she meant, and she said, 'Let me speak with the bridegroom this night in his chamber, and I will give thee the dress.' At last the princess agreed, but she told her chamberlain to give the prince a sleeping draught, that he might not hear or see her. When evening came, and the prince had fallen asleep, she was led into his chamber, and she sat herself down at his feet, and said: 'I have followed thee seven years. I have been to the sun, the moon, and the night-wind, to seek thee, and at last I have helped thee to overcome the dragon. Wilt thou then forget me quite?' But the prince all the time slept so soundly, that her voice only passed over him, and seemed like the whistling of the wind among the fir-trees.

Then poor Lily was led away, and forced to give up the golden dress; and when she saw that there was no help for her, she went out into a meadow, and sat herself down and wept. But as she sat she bethought herself of the egg that the moon had given her; and when she broke it, there ran out a hen and twelve chickens of pure gold, that played about, and then nestled under the old one's wings, so as to form the most beautiful sight in the world. And she rose up and drove them before her, till the bride saw them from her window, and was so pleased that she came forth and asked her if she would sell the brood. 'Not for gold or silver, but for flesh and blood: let me again this evening speak with the bridegroom in his chamber, and I will give thee the whole brood.'

Then the princess thought to betray her as before, and agreed to what she asked: but when the prince went to his chamber he asked the chamberlain why the wind had whistled so in the night. And the chamberlain told him all—how he had given him a sleeping draught, and how a poor maiden had come and spoken to him in his chamber, and was to come again that night. Then the prince took care to throw away the sleeping draught; and when Lily came and began again to tell him what woes had befallen her, and how faithful and true to him she had been, he knew his beloved wife's voice, and sprang up, and said, 'You have awakened me as from a dream, for the strange princess had thrown a spell around me, so that I had altogether forgotten you; but Heaven hath sent you to me in a lucky hour.'

And they stole away out of the palace by night unawares, and seated themselves on the griffin, who flew back with them over the Red Sea. When they were half-way across Lily let the nut fall into the water, and immediately a large nut-tree arose from the sea, whereon the griffin rested for a while, and then carried them safely home. There they found their child, now grown up to be comely and fair; and after all their troubles they lived happily together to the end of their days.

THE FOX AND THE HORSE

A farmer had a horse that had been an excellent faithful servant to him: but he was now grown too old to work; so the farmer would give him nothing more to eat, and said, 'I want you no longer, so take yourself off out of my stable; I shall not take you back again until you are stronger than a lion.' Then he opened the door and turned him adrift.

The poor horse was very melancholy, and wandered up and down in the wood, seeking some little shelter from the cold wind and rain. Presently a fox met him: 'What's the matter, my friend?' said he, 'why do you hang down your head and look so lonely and woe-begone?' 'Ah!' replied the horse, 'justice and avarice never dwell in one house; my master has forgotten all that I have done for him so many years, and because I can no longer work he has turned me adrift, and says unless I become stronger than a lion he will not take me back again; what chance can I have of that? he knows I have none, or he would not talk so.'

However, the fox bid him be of good cheer, and said, 'I will help you; lie down there, stretch yourself out quite stiff, and pretend to be dead.' The horse did as he was told, and the fox went straight to the lion who lived in a cave close by, and said to him, 'A little way off lies a dead horse; come with me and you may make an excellent meal of his carcase.' The lion was greatly pleased, and set off immediately; and when they came to the horse, the fox said, 'You will not be able to eat him comfortably here; I'll tell you what—I will tie you fast to his tail, and then you can draw him to your den, and eat him at your leisure.'

This advice pleased the lion, so he laid himself down quietly for the fox to make him fast to the horse. But the fox managed to tie his legs together and bound all so hard and fast that with all his strength he could not set himself free. When the work was done, the fox clapped the horse on the shoulder, and said, 'Jip! Dobbin! Jip!' Then up he sprang, and moved off, dragging the lion behind him. The beast began to roar and bellow, till all the birds of the wood flew away for fright; but the horse let him sing on, and made his way quietly over the fields to his master's house.

'Here he is, master,' said he, 'I have got the better of him': and when the farmer saw his old servant, his heart relented, and he said. 'Thou shalt stay in thy stable and be well taken care of.' And so the poor old horse had plenty to eat, and lived—till he died.

THE BLUE LIGHT

There was once upon a time a soldier who for many years had served the king faithfully, but when the war came to an end could serve no longer because of the many wounds which he had received. The king said to him: 'You may return to your home, I need you no longer, and you will not receive any more money, for he only receives wages who renders me service for them.' Then the soldier did not know how to earn a living, went away greatly troubled, and walked the whole day, until in the evening he entered a forest. When darkness came on, he saw a light, which he went up to, and came to a house wherein lived a witch. 'Do give me one night's lodging, and a little to eat and drink,' said he to her, 'or I shall starve.' 'Oho!' she answered, 'who gives anything to a run-away soldier? Yet will I be compassionate, and take you in, if you will do what I wish.' 'What do you wish?' said the soldier. 'That you should dig all round my garden for me, tomorrow.' The soldier consented, and next day laboured with all his strength, but could not finish it by the evening. 'I see well enough,' said the witch, 'that you can do no more today, but I will keep you yet another night, in payment for which you must tomorrow chop me a load of wood, and chop it small.' The soldier spent the whole day in doing it, and in the evening the witch proposed that he should stay one night more. 'Tomorrow, you shall only do me a very trifling piece of work. Behind my house, there is an old dry well, into which my light has fallen, it burns blue, and never goes out, and you shall bring it up again.' Next day the old woman took him to the well, and let him down in a basket. He found the blue light, and made her a signal to draw him up again. She did draw him up, but when he came near the edge, she stretched down her hand and wanted to take the blue light away from him. 'No,' said he, perceiving her evil intention, 'I will not give you the light until I am standing with both feet upon the ground.' The witch fell into a passion, let him fall again into the well, and went away.

The poor soldier fell without injury on the moist ground, and the blue light went on burning, but of what use was that to him? He saw very well that he could not escape death. He sat for a while very sorrowfully, then suddenly he felt in his pocket and found his tobacco pipe, which was still half full. 'This shall be my last pleasure,' thought he, pulled it out, lit it at the blue light and began to smoke. When the smoke had circled about the cavern, suddenly a little black dwarf stood before him, and said: 'Lord, what are your commands?' 'What my commands are?' replied the soldier, quite astonished. 'I must do everything you bid me,' said the little man. 'Good,' said the soldier; 'then in the first place help me out of this well.' The little man took him by the hand, and led him through an underground passage, but he did not forget to take the blue light with him. On the way the dwarf showed him the treasures which the witch had collected and hidden there, and the soldier took as much gold as he could carry. When he was above, he said to the little man: 'Now go and bind the old witch, and carry her before the judge.' In a short time she came by like the wind, riding on a wild tom-cat and screaming frightfully. Nor was it long before the little man reappeared. 'It is all done,' said he, 'and the witch is already hanging on the gallows. What further commands has my lord?' inquired the dwarf. 'At this moment, none,' answered the soldier; 'you can return home, only be at hand immediately, if I summon you.' 'Nothing more is needed than that you should light your pipe at the blue light, and I will appear before you at once.' Thereupon he vanished from his sight.

The soldier returned to the town from which he came. He went to the best inn, ordered himself handsome clothes, and then bade the landlord furnish him a room as handsome as possible. When it was ready and the soldier had taken possession of it, he summoned the little black manikin and said: 'I have served the king faithfully, but he has dismissed me, and left me to hunger, and now I want to take my revenge.' 'What am I to do?' asked the little man. 'Late at night, when the king's daughter is in bed, bring her here in her sleep, she shall do servant's work for me.' The manikin said: 'That is an easy thing for me to do, but a very dangerous thing for you, for if it is discovered, you will fare ill.' When twelve o'clock had struck, the door sprang open, and the manikin carried in the princess. 'Aha! are you there?' cried the soldier, 'get to your work at once! Fetch the broom and sweep the chamber.' When she had done this, he ordered her to come to his chair, and then he stretched out his feet and said: 'Pull off my boots,' and then he threw them in her face, and made her pick them up again, and clean and brighten them. She, however, did everything he bade her, without opposition, silently and with half-shut eyes. When the first cock crowed, the manikin carried her back to the royal palace, and laid her in her bed.

Next morning when the princess arose she went to her father, and told him that she had had a very strange dream. 'I was carried through the streets with the rapidity of lightning,' said she, 'and taken into a soldier's room, and I had to wait upon him like a servant, sweep his room, clean his boots, and do all kinds of menial work. It was only a dream, and yet

I am just as tired as if I really had done everything.' 'The dream may have been true,' said the king. 'I will give you a piece of advice. Fill your pocket full of peas, and make a small hole in the pocket, and then if you are carried away again, they will fall out and leave a track in the streets.' But unseen by the king, the manikin was standing beside him when he said that, and heard all. At night when the sleeping princess was again carried through the streets, some peas certainly did fall out of her pocket, but they made no track, for the crafty manikin had just before scattered peas in every street there was. And again the princess was compelled to do servant's work until cock-crow.

Next morning the king sent his people out to seek the track, but it was all in vain, for in every street poor children were sitting, picking up peas, and saying: 'It must have rained peas, last night.' 'We must think of something else,' said the king; 'keep your shoes on when you go to bed, and before you come back from the place where you are taken, hide one of them there, I will soon contrive to find it.' The black manikin heard this plot, and at night when the soldier again ordered him to bring the princess, revealed it to him, and told him that he knew of no expedient to counteract this stratagem, and that if the shoe were found in the soldier's house it would go badly with him. 'Do what I bid you,' replied the soldier, and again this third night the princess was obliged to work like a servant, but before she went away, she hid her shoe under the bed.

Next morning the king had the entire town searched for his daughter's shoe. It was found at the soldier's, and the soldier himself, who at the entreaty of the dwarf had gone outside the gate, was soon brought back, and thrown into prison. In his flight he had forgotten the most valuable things he had, the blue light and the gold, and had only one ducat in his pocket. And now loaded with chains, he was standing at the window of his dungeon, when he chanced to see one of his comrades passing by. The soldier tapped at the pane of glass, and when this man came up, said to him: 'Be so kind as to fetch me the small bundle I have left lying in the inn, and I will give you a ducat for doing it.' His comrade ran thither and brought him what he wanted. As soon as the soldier was alone again, he lighted his pipe and summoned the black manikin. 'Have no fear,' said the latter to his master. 'Go wheresoever they take you, and let them do what they will, only take the blue light with you.' Next day the soldier was tried, and though he had done nothing wicked, the judge condemned him to death. When he was led forth to die, he begged a last favour of the king. 'What is it?' asked the king. 'That I may smoke one more pipe on my way.' 'You may smoke three,' answered the king, 'but do not imagine that I will spare your life.' Then the soldier pulled out his pipe and lighted it at the blue light, and as soon as a few wreaths of smoke had ascended, the manikin was there with a small cudgel in his hand, and said: 'What does my lord command?' 'Strike down to earth that false judge there, and his constable, and spare not the king who has treated me so ill.' Then the manikin fell on them like lightning, darting this way and that way, and whosoever was so much as touched by his cudgel fell to earth, and did not venture to stir again. The king was terrified; he threw himself on the soldier's mercy, and merely to be allowed to live at all, gave him his kingdom for his own, and his daughter to wife.

THE RAVEN

There was once a queen who had a little daughter, still too young to run alone. One day the child was very troublesome, and the mother could not quiet it, do what she would. She grew impatient, and seeing the ravens flying round the castle, she opened the window, and said: 'I wish you were a raven and would fly away, then I should have a little peace.' Scarcely were the words out of her mouth, when the child in her arms was turned into a raven, and flew away from her through the open window. The bird took its flight to a dark wood and remained there for a long time, and meanwhile the parents could hear nothing of their child.

Long after this, a man was making his way through the wood when he heard a raven calling, and he followed the sound of the voice. As he drew near, the raven said, 'I am by birth a king's daughter, but am now under the spell of some enchantment; you can, however, set me free.' 'What am I to do?' he asked. She replied, 'Go farther into the wood until you come to a house, wherein lives an old woman; she will offer you food and drink, but you must not take of either; if you do, you will fall into a deep sleep, and will not be able to help me. In the garden behind the house is a large tan-heap, and on that you must stand and watch for me. I shall drive there in my carriage at two o'clock in the afternoon for three successive days; the first day it will be drawn by four white, the second by four chestnut, and the last by four black horses; but if you fail to keep awake and I find you sleeping, I shall not be set free.'

The man promised to do all that she wished, but the raven said, 'Alas! I know even now that you will take something from the woman and be unable to save me.' The man assured her again that he would on no account touch a thing to eat or drink.

When he came to the house and went inside, the old woman met him, and said, 'Poor man! how tired you are! Come in and rest and let me give you something to eat and drink.'

'No,' answered the man, 'I will neither eat not drink.'

But she would not leave him alone, and urged him saying, 'If you will not eat anything, at least you might take a draught of wine; one drink counts for nothing,' and at last he allowed himself to be persuaded, and drank.

As it drew towards the appointed hour, he went outside into the garden and mounted the tan-heap to await the raven. Suddenly a feeling of fatigue came over him, and unable to resist it, he lay down for a little while, fully determined, however, to keep awake; but in another minute his eyes closed of their own accord, and he fell into such a deep sleep, that all the noises in the world would not have awakened him. At two o'clock the raven came driving along, drawn by her four white horses; but even before she reached the spot, she said to herself, sighing, 'I know he has fallen asleep.' When she entered the garden, there she found him as she had feared, lying on the tan-heap, fast asleep. She got out of her carriage and went to him; she called him and shook him, but it was all in vain, he still continued sleeping.

The next day at noon, the old woman came to him again with food and drink which he at first refused. At last, overcome by her persistent entreaties that he would take something, he lifted the glass and drank againTowards two o'clock he went into the garden and on to the tan-heap to watch for the raven. He had not been there long before he began to feel so tired that his limbs seemed hardly able to support him, and he could not stand upright any longer; so again he lay down and fell fast asleep. As the raven drove along her four chestnut horses, she said sorrowfully to herself, 'I know he has fallen asleep.' She went as before to look for him, but he slept, and it was impossible to awaken him.

The following day the old woman said to him, 'What is this? You are not eating or drinking anything, do you want to kill yourself?'

He answered, 'I may not and will not either eat or drink.'

But she put down the dish of food and the glass of wine in front of him, and when he smelt the wine, he was unable to resist the temptation, and took a deep draught.

When the hour came round again he went as usual on to the tan-heap in the garden to await the king's daughter, but he felt even more overcome with weariness than on the two previous days, and throwing himself down, he slept like a log. At two o'clock the raven could be seen approaching, and this time her coachman and everything about her, as well as her horses, were black.

She was sadder than ever as she drove along, and said mournfully, 'I know he has fallen asleep, and will not be able to set me free.' She found him sleeping heavily, and all her efforts to awaken him were of no avail. Then she placed beside him a loaf, and some meat, and a flask of wine, of such a kind, that however much he took of them, they would never grow less. After that she drew a gold ring, on which her name was engraved, off her finger, and put it upon one of his. Finally, she laid a letter near him, in which, after giving him particulars of the food and drink she had left for him, she finished with the following words: 'I see that as long as you remain here you will never be able to set me free; if, however, you still wish to do so, come to the golden castle of Stromberg; this is well within your power to accomplish.' She then returned to her carriage and drove to the golden castle of Stromberg.

When the man awoke and found that he had been sleeping, he was grieved at heart, and said, 'She has no doubt been here and driven away again, and it is now too late for me to save her.' Then his eyes fell on the things which were lying beside him; he read the letter, and knew from it all that had happened. He rose up without delay, eager to start on his way and to reach the castle of Stromberg, but he had no idea in which direction he ought to go. He travelled about a long time in search of it and came at last to a dark forest, through which he went on walking for fourteen days and still could not find a way out. Once more the night came on, and worn out he lay down under a bush and fell asleep. Again the next day he pursued his way through the forest, and that evening, thinking to rest again, he lay down as before, but he heard such a howling and wailing that he found it impossible to sleep. He waited till it was darker and people had begun to light up their houses, and then seeing a little glimmer ahead of him, he went towards it.

He found that the light came from a house which looked smaller than it really was, from the contrast of its height with that of an immense giant who stood in front of it. He thought to himself, 'If the giant sees me going in, my life will not be worth much.' However, after a while he summoned up courage and went forward. When the giant saw him, he called out, 'It is lucky for that you have come, for I have not had anything to eat for a long time. I can have you now for my supper.' 'I would rather you let that alone,' said the man, 'for I do not willingly give myself up to be eaten; if you are wanting food I have enough to satisfy your hunger.' 'If that is so,' replied the giant, 'I will leave you in peace; I only thought of eating you because I had nothing else.'

So they went indoors together and sat down, and the man brought out the bread, meat, and wine, which although he had eaten and drunk of them, were still unconsumed. The giant was pleased with the good cheer, and ate and drank to his heart's content. When he had finished his supper the man asked him if he could direct him to the castle of Stromberg. The giant said, 'I will look on my map; on it are marked all the towns, villages, and houses.' So he fetched his map, and looked for the castle, but could not find it. 'Never mind,' he said, 'I have larger maps upstairs in the cupboard, we will look on those,' but they searched in vain, for the castle was not marked even on these. The man now thought he should like to continue his journey, but the giant begged him to remain for a day or two longer until the return of his brother, who was away in search of provisions. When the brother came home, they asked him about the castle of Stromberg, and he told them he would look on his own maps as soon as he had eaten and appeased his hunger. Accordingly, when he had finished his supper, they all went up together to his room and looked through his maps, but the castle was not to be found. Then he fetched other older maps, and they went on looking for the castle until at last they found it, but it was many thousand miles away. 'How shall I be able to get there?' asked the man. 'I have two hours to spare,' said the giant, 'and I will carry you into the neighbourhood of the castle; I must then return to look after the child who is in our care.'

The giant, thereupon, carried the man to within about a hundred leagues of the castle, where he left him, saying, 'You will be able to walk the remainder of the way yourself.' The man journeyed on day and night till he reached the golden castle of Stromberg. He found it situated, however, on a glass mountain, and looking up from the foot he saw the enchanted maiden drive round her castle and then go inside. He was overjoyed to see her, and longed to get to the top of the mountain, but the sides were so slippery that every time he attempted to climb he fell back again. When he saw that it was impossible to reach her, he was greatly grieved, and said to himself, 'I will remain here and wait for her,' so he built himself a little hut, and there he sat and watched for a whole year, and every day he saw the king's daughter driving round her castle, but still was unable to get nearer to her.

Looking out from his hut one day he saw three robbers fighting and he called out to them, 'God be with you.' They stopped when they heard the call, but looking round and seeing nobody, they went on again with their fighting, which now became more furious. 'God be with you,' he cried again, and again they paused and looked about, but seeing no one went back to their fighting. A third time he called out, 'God be with you,' and then thinking he should like to know the cause of dispute between the three men, he went out and asked them why they were fighting so angrily with one another. One of them said that he had found a stick, and that he had but to strike it against any door through which he wished to pass, and it immediately flew open. Another told him that he had found a cloak which rendered its wearer invisible; and the third had caught a horse which would carry its rider over any obstacle, and even up the glass mountain. They had been unable to decide whether they would keep together and have the things in common, or whether they would separate. On hearing this, the man said, 'I will give you something in exchange for those three things; not money, for that I have not got, but something that is of far more value. I must first, however, prove whether all you have told me about your three things is true.' The robbers, therefore, made him get on the horse, and handed him the stick and the cloak, and when he had put this round him he was no longer visible. Then he fell upon them with the stick and beat them one after another, crying, 'There, you idle vagabonds, you have got what you deserve; are you satisfied now!'

After this he rode up the glass mountain. When he

reached the gate of the castle, he found it closed, but he gave it a blow with his stick, and it flew wide open at once and he passed through. He mounted the steps and entered the room where the maiden was sitting, with a golden goblet full of wine in front of her. She could not see him for he still wore his cloak. He took the ring which she had given him off his finger, and threw it into the goblet, so that it rang as it touched the bottom. 'That is my own ring,' she exclaimed, 'and if that is so the man must also be here who is coming to set me free.'

She sought for him about the castle, but could find him nowhere. Meanwhile he had gone outside again and mounted his horse and thrown off the cloak. When therefore she came to the castle gate she saw him, and cried aloud for joy. Then he dismounted and took her in his arms; and she kissed him, and said, 'Now you have indeed set me free, and tomorrow we will celebrate our marriage.'

THE GOLDEN GOOSE

There was a man who had three sons, the youngest of whom was called Dummling*, and was despised, mocked, and sneered at on every occasion.

It happened that the eldest wanted to go into the forest to hew wood, and before he went his mother gave him a beautiful sweet cake and a bottle of wine in order that he might not suffer from hunger or thirst.

When he entered the forest he met a little grey-haired old man who bade him good day, and said: 'Do give me a piece of cake out of your pocket, and let me have a draught of your wine; I am so hungry and thirsty.' But the clever son answered: 'If I give you my cake and wine, I shall have none for myself; be off with you,' and he left the little man standing and went on.

But when he began to hew down a tree, it was not long before he made a false stroke, and the axe cut him in the arm, so that he had to go home and have it bound up. And this was the little grey man's doing.

After this the second son went into the forest, and his mother gave him, like the eldest, a cake and a bottle of wine.

* Simpleton

The little old grey man met him likewise, and asked him for a piece of cake and a drink of wine. But the second son, too, said sensibly enough: 'What I give you will be taken away from myself; be off!' and he left the little man standing and went on. His punishment, however, was not delayed; when he had made a few blows at the tree he struck himself in the leg, so that he had to be carried home.

Then Dummling said: 'Father, do let me go and cut wood.' The father answered: 'Your brothers have hurt themselves with it, leave it alone, you do not understand anything about it.' But Dummling begged so long that at last he said: 'Just go then, you will get wiser by hurting yourself.' His mother gave him a cake made with water and baked in the cinders, and with it a bottle of sour beer.

When he came to the forest the little old grey man met him likewise, and greeting him, said: 'Give me a piece of your cake and a drink out of your bottle; I am so hungry and thirsty.' Dummling answered: 'I have only cinder-cake and sour beer; if that pleases you, we will sit down and eat.' So they sat down, and when Dummling pulled out his cinder-cake, it was a fine sweet cake, and the sour beer had become good wine. So they ate and drank, and after that the little man said: 'Since you have a good heart, and are willing to divide what you have, I will give you good luck. There stands an old tree, cut it down, and you will find something at the roots.' Then the little man took leave of him.

Dummling went and cut down the tree, and when it fell there was a goose sitting in the roots with feathers of pure gold. He lifted her up, and taking her with him, went to an inn where he thought he would stay the night. Now the host had three daughters, who saw the goose and were curious to know what such a wonderful bird might be, and would have liked to have one of its golden feathers.

The eldest thought: 'I shall soon find an opportunity of pulling out a feather,' and as soon as Dummling had gone out she seized the goose by the wing, but her finger and hand remained sticking fast to it.

The second came soon afterwards, thinking only of how she might get a feather for herself, but she had scarcely touched her sister than she was held fast.

At last the third also came with the like intent, and the others screamed out: 'Keep away; for goodness' sake keep away!' But she did not understand why she was to keep away. 'The others are there,' she thought, 'I may as well be there too,' and ran to them; but as soon as she had touched her sister, she remained sticking fast to her. So they had to spend the night with the goose.

The next morning Dummling took the goose under his arm and set out, without troubling himself about the three girls who were hanging on to it. They were obliged to run after him continually, now left, now right, wherever his legs took him.

In the middle of the fields the parson met them, and when he saw the procession he said: 'For shame, you good-for-nothing girls, why are you running across the fields after this young man? Is that seemly?' At the same time he seized the youngest by the hand in order to pull her away, but as soon as he touched her he likewise stuck fast, and was himself obliged to run behind.

Before long the sexton came by and saw his master, the parson, running behind three girls. He was astonished at this and called out: 'Hi! your reverence, whither away so quickly? Do not forget that we have a christening today!' and running after him he took him by the sleeve, but was also held fast to it.

Whilst the five were trotting thus one behind the other, two labourers came with their hoes from the fields; the parson called out to them and begged that they would set him and the sexton free. But they had scarcely touched the sexton when they were held fast, and now there were seven of them running behind Dummling and the goose.

Soon afterwards he came to a city, where a king ruled who had a daughter who was so serious that no one could make her laugh. So he had put forth a decree that whosoever should be able to make her laugh should marry her. When Dummling heard this, he went with his goose and all her train before the king's daughter, and as soon as she saw the seven people running on and on, one behind the other, she began to laugh quite loudly, and as if she would never stop. Thereupon Dummling asked to have her for his wife; but the king did not like the son-in-law, and made all manner of excuses and said he must first produce a man who could drink a cellarful of wine. Dummling thought of the little grey man, who could certainly help him; so he went into the forest, and in the same place where he had felled the tree, he saw a man sitting, who had a very sorrowful face. Dummling asked him what he was taking to heart so sorely, and he answered: 'I have such a great thirst and cannot quench it; cold water I cannot stand, a barrel of wine I have just emptied, but that to me is like a drop on a hot stone!'

'There, I can help you,' said Dummling, 'just come with me and you shall be satisfied.'

He led him into the king's cellar, and the man bent over the huge barrels, and drank and drank till his loins hurt, and before the day was out he had emptied all the barrels. Then Dummling asked once more for his bride, but the king was vexed that such an ugly fellow, whom everyone called Dummling, should take away his daughter, and he made a new condition; he must first find a man who could eat a whole mountain of bread. Dummling did not think long, but went straight into the forest, where in the same place there sat a man who was tying up his body with a strap, and making an awful face, and saying: 'I have eaten a whole ovenful of rolls, but what good is that when one has such a hunger as I? My stomach remains empty, and I must tie myself up if I am not to die of hunger.'

At this Dummling was glad, and said: 'Get up and come with me; you shall eat yourself full.' He led him to the king's palace where all the flour in the whole Kingdom was collected, and from it he caused a huge mountain of bread to be baked. The man from the forest stood before it, began to eat, and by the end of one day the whole mountain had vanished. Then Dummling for the third time asked for his bride; but the king again sought a way out, and ordered a ship which could sail on land and on water. 'As soon as you come sailing back in it,' said he, 'you shall have my daughter for wife.'

Dummling went straight into the forest, and there sat the little grey man to whom he had given his cake. When he heard what Dummling wanted, he said: 'Since you have given me to eat and to drink, I will give you the ship; and I do all this because you once were kind to me.' Then he gave him the ship which could sail on land and water, and when the king saw that, he could no longer prevent him from having his daughter. The wedding was celebrated, and after the king's death, Dummling inherited his kingdom and lived for a long time contentedly with his wife.

THE WATER OF LIFE

Long before you or I were born, there reigned, in a country a great way off, a king who had three sons. This king once fell very ill—so ill that nobody thought he could live. His sons were very much grieved at their father's sickness; and as they were walking together very mournfully in the garden of the palace, a little old man met them and asked what was the matter. They told him that their father was very ill, and that they were afraid nothing could save him. 'I know what would,' said the little old man; 'it is the Water of Life. If he could have a draught of it he would be well again; but it is very hard to get.' Then the eldest son said, 'I will soon find it': and he went to the sick king, and begged that he might go in search of the Water of Life, as it was the only thing that could save him. 'No,' said the king. 'I had rather die than place you in such great danger as you must meet with in your journey.' But he begged so hard that the king let him go; and the prince thought to himself, 'If I bring my father this water, he will make me sole heir to his kingdom.'

Then he set out: and when he had gone on his way some time he came to a deep valley, overhung with rocks and woods; and as he looked around, he saw standing above him on one of the rocks a little ugly dwarf, with a sugarloaf cap and a scarlet cloak; and the dwarf called to him and said, 'Prince, whither so fast?' 'What is that to thee, you ugly imp?' said the prince haughtily, and rode on.

But the dwarf was enraged at his behaviour, and laid a fairy spell of ill-luck upon him; so that as he rode on the mountain pass became narrower and narrower, and at last the way was so straitened that he could not go to step forward: and when he thought to have turned his horse round and go back the way he came, he heard a loud laugh ringing round him, and found that the path was closed behind him, so that he was shut in all round. He next tried to get off his horse and make his way on foot, but again the laugh rang in his ears, and he found himself unable to move a step, and thus he was forced to abide spellbound.

Meantime the old king was lingering on in daily hope of his son's return, till at last the second son said, 'Father, I will go in search of the Water of Life.' For he thought to himself, 'My brother is surely dead, and the kingdom will fall to me if I find the water.' The king was at first very unwilling to let him go, but at last yielded to his wish. So he set out and followed the same road which his brother had done, and met with the same elf, who stopped him at the same spot in the mountains, saying, as before, 'Prince, prince, whither so fast?' 'Mind your own affairs, busybody!' said the prince scornfully, and rode on.

But the dwarf put the same spell upon him as he put on his elder brother, and he, too, was at last obliged to take up his abode in the heart of the mountains. Thus it is with proud silly people, who think themselves above everyone else, and are too proud to ask or take advice.

When the second prince had thus been gone a long time, the youngest son said he would go and search for the Water of Life, and trusted he should soon be able to make his father well again. So he set out, and the dwarf met him too at the same spot in the valley, among the mountains, and said,

'Prince, whither so fast?' And the prince said, 'I am going in search of the Water of Life, because my father is ill, and like to die: can you help me? Pray be kind, and aid me if you can!' 'Do you know where it is to be found?' asked the dwarf. 'No,' said the prince, 'I do not. Pray tell me if you know.' 'Then as you have spoken to me kindly, and are wise enough to seek for advice, I will tell you how and where to go. The water you seek springs from a well in an enchanted castle; and, that you may be able to reach it in safety, I will give you an iron wand and two little loaves of bread; strike the iron door of the castle three times with the wand, and it will open: two hungry lions will be lying down inside gaping for their prey, but if you throw them the bread they will let you pass; then hasten on to the well, and take some of the Water of Life before the clock strikes twelve; for if you tarry longer the door will shut upon you for ever.' Then the prince thanked his little friend with the scarlet cloak for his friendly aid, and took the wand and the bread, and went travelling on and on, over sea and over land, till he came to his journey's end, and found everything to be as the dwarf had told him. The door flew open at the third stroke of the wand, and when the lions were quieted he went on through the castle and came at length to a beautiful hall. Around it he saw several knights sitting in a trance; then he pulled off their rings and put them on his own fingers. In another room he saw on a table a sword and a loaf of bread, which he also took. Further on he came to a room where a beautiful young lady sat upon a couch; and she welcomed him joyfully, and said, if he would set her free from the spell that bound her, the kingdom should be his, if he would come back in a year and marry her. Then she told him that the well that held the Water of Life was in the palace gardens; and bade him make haste, and draw what he wanted before the clock struck twelve.

He walked on; and as he walked through beautiful gardens he came to a delightful shady spot in which stood a couch; and he thought to himself, as he felt tired, that he would rest himself for a while, and gaze on the lovely scenes around him. So he laid himself down, and sleep fell upon him unawares, so that he did not wake up till the clock was striking a quarter to twelve. Then he sprang from the couch dreadfully frightened, ran to the well, filled a cup that was standing by him full of water, and hastened to get away in time. Just as he was going out of the iron door it struck twelve, and the door fell so quickly upon him that it snapped off a piece of his heel.

When he found himself safe, he was overjoyed to think that he had got the Water of Life; and as he was going on his way homewards, he passed by the little dwarf, who, when he saw the sword and the loaf, said, 'You have made a noble prize; with the sword you can at a blow slay whole armies, and the bread will never fail you.' Then the prince thought to himself, 'I cannot go home to my father without my brothers'; so he said, 'My dear friend, cannot you tell me where my two brothers are, who set out in search of the Water of Life before me, and never came back?' 'I have shut them up by a charm between two mountains,' said the dwarf, 'because they were proud and ill-behaved, and scorned to ask advice.' The prince begged so hard for his brothers, that the dwarf at last set them free, though unwillingly, saying, 'Beware of them, for they have bad hearts.' Their brother, however, was greatly rejoiced to see them, and told them all that had happened to him; how he had found the Water of Life, and had taken a cup full of it; and how he had set a beautiful princess free from a spell that bound her; and how she had engaged to wait a whole year, and then to marry him, and to give him the kingdom.

Then they all three rode on together, and on their way home came to a country that was laid waste by war and a dreadful famine, so that it was feared all must die for want. But the prince gave the king of the land the bread, and all his kingdom ate of it. And he lent the king the wonderful sword, and he slew the enemy's army with it; and thus the kingdom was once more in peace and plenty. In the same manner he befriended two other countries through which they passed on their way.

When they came to the sea, they got into a ship and during their voyage the two eldest said to themselves, 'Our brother has got the water which we could not find, therefore our father will forsake us and give him the kingdom, which is our right'; so they were full of envy and revenge, and agreed together how they could ruin him. Then they waited till he was fast asleep, and poured the Water of Life out of the cup, and took it for themselves, giving him bitter sea-water instead.

When they came to their journey's end, the youngest son brought his cup to the sick king, that he might drink and be healed. Scarcely, however, had he tasted the bitter sea-water when he became worse even than he was before; and then both the elder sons came in, and blamed the youngest for what they had done; and said that he wanted to poison their father, but that they had found the Water of Life, and had brought it with them. He no sooner began to drink of what they brought him, than he felt his sickness leave him, and was as strong and well as in his younger days. Then they went to their brother, and laughed at him, and said, 'Well, brother, you found the Water of Life, did you? You have had the trouble and we shall have the reward. Pray, with all your cleverness, why did not you manage to keep your eyes open? Next year one of us will take away your beautiful princess, if you do not take care. You had better say nothing about this to our father, for he does not believe a word you say; and if you tell tales, you shall lose your life into the bargain: but be quiet, and we will let you off.'

The old king was still very angry with his youngest son, and thought that he really meant to have taken away his life; so he called his court together, and asked what should be done, and all agreed that he ought to be put to death. The prince knew nothing of what was going on, till one day, when the king's chief huntsmen went a-hunting with him, and they were alone in the wood together, the huntsman looked so sorrowful that the prince said, 'My friend, what is the matter with you?' 'I cannot and dare not tell you,' said he. But the prince begged very hard, and said, 'Only tell me what it is, and do not think I shall be angry, for I will forgive you.' 'Alas!' said the huntsman; 'the king has ordered me to shoot you.' The prince started at this, and said, 'Let me live, and I will change dresses with you; you shall take my royal coat to show to my father, and do you give me your shabby one.' 'With all my heart,' said the huntsman; 'I am sure I shall be glad to save you, for I could not have shot you.' Then he took the prince's coat, and gave him the shabby one, and went away through the wood.

Some time after, three grand embassies came to the old king's court, with rich gifts of gold and precious stones for his youngest son; now all these were sent from the three kings to whom he had lent his sword and loaf of bread, in order to rid them of their enemy and feed their people. This touched the old king's heart, and he thought his son might still be guiltless, and said to his court, 'O that my son were still alive! how it grieves me that I had him killed!' 'He is still alive,' said the huntsman; 'and I am glad that I had pity on him, but let him go in peace, and brought home his royal coat.' At this the king was overwhelmed with joy, and made it known thoughout all his kingdom, that if his son would come back to his court he would forgive him.

Meanwhile the princess was eagerly waiting till her deliverer should come back; and had a road made leading up to her palace all of shining gold; and told her courtiers that whoever came on horseback, and rode straight up to the gate upon it, was her true lover; and that they must let him in: but whoever rode on one side of it, they must be sure was not the right one; and that they must send him away at once.

The time soon came, when the eldest brother thought that he would make haste to go to the princess, and say that he was the one who had set her free, and that he should have her for his wife, and the kingdom with her. As he came before the palace and saw the golden road, he stopped to look at it, and he thought to himself, 'It is a pity to ride upon this beautiful road'; so he turned aside and rode on the right-hand side of it. But when he came to the gate, the guards, who had seen the road he took, said to him, he could not be what he said he was, and must go about his business.

The second prince set out soon afterwards on the same errand; and when he came to the golden road, and his horse had set one foot upon it, he stopped to look at it, and thought it very beautiful, and said to himself, 'What a pity it is that anything should tread here!' Then he too turned aside and rode on the left side of it. But when he came to the gate the guards said he was not the true prince, and that he too must go away about his business; and away he went.

Now when the full year was come round, the third brother left the forest in which he had lain hid for fear of his father's anger, and set out in search of his betrothed bride. So he journeyed on, thinking of her all the way, and rode so quickly that he did not even see what the road was made of, but went with his horse straight over it; and as he came to the gate it flew open, and the princess welcomed him with joy, and said he was her deliverer, and should now be her husband and lord of the kingdom. When the first joy at their meeting was over, the princess told him she had heard of his father having forgiven him, and of his wish to have him home again: so, before his wedding with the princess, he went to visit his father, taking her with him. Then he told him everything; how his brothers had cheated and robbed him, and yet that he had borne all those wrongs for the love of his father. And the old king was very angry, and wanted to punish his wicked sons; but they made their escape, and got into a ship and sailed away over the wide sea, and where they went to nobody knew and nobody cared.

And now the old king gathered together his court, and asked all his kingdom to come and celebrate the wedding of his son and the princess. And young and old, noble and squire, gentle and simple, came at once on the summons; and among the rest came the friendly dwarf, with the sugarloaf hat, and a new scarlet cloak.

And the wedding was held, and the merry bells run.
And all the good people they danced and they sung,
And feasted and frolick'd I can't tell how long.

THE TWELVE HUNTSMEN

There was once a king's son who had a bride whom he loved very much. And when he was sitting beside her and very happy, news came that his father lay sick unto death, and desired to see him once again before his end. Then he said to his beloved: 'I must now go and leave you, I give you a ring as a remembrance of me. When I am king, I will return and fetch you.' So he rode away, and when he reached his father, the latter was dangerously ill, and near his death. He said to him: 'Dear son, I wished to see you once again before my end, promise me to marry as I wish,' and he named a certain king's daughter who was to be his wife. The son was in such trouble that he did not think what he was doing, and said: 'Yes, dear father, your will shall be done,' and thereupon the king shut his eyes, and died.

When therefore the son had been proclaimed king, and the time of mourning was over, he was forced to keep the promise which he had given his father, and caused the king's daughter to be asked in marriage, and she was promised to him. His first betrothed heard of this, and fretted so much about his faithfulness that she nearly died. Then her father said to her: 'Dearest child, why are you so sad? You shall have whatsoever you will.' She thought for a moment and said:

'Dear father, I wish for eleven girls exactly like myself in face, figure, and size.' The father said: 'If it be possible, your desire shall be fulfilled,' and he caused a search to be made in his whole kingdom, until eleven young maidens were found who exactly resembled his daughter in face, figure, and size.

When they came to the king's daughter, she had twelve suits of huntsmen's clothes made, all alike, and the eleven maidens had to put on the huntsmen's clothes, and she herself put on the twelfth suit. Thereupon she took her leave of her father, and rode away with them, and rode to the court of her former betrothed, whom she loved so dearly. Then she asked if he required any huntsmen, and if he would take all of them into his service. The king looked at her and did not know her, but as they were such handsome fellows, he said: 'Yes,' and that he would willingly take them, and now they were the king's twelve huntsmen.

The king, however, had a lion which was a wondrous animal, for he knew all concealed and secret things. It came to pass that one evening he said to the king: 'You think you have twelve huntsmen?' 'Yes,' said the king, 'they are twelve huntsmen.' The lion continued: 'You are mistaken, they are twelve girls.' The king said: 'That cannot be true! How will you prove that to me?' 'Oh, just let some peas be strewn in the ante-chamber,' answered the lion, 'and then you will soon see. Men have a firm step, and when they walk over peas none of them stir, but girls trip and skip, and drag their feet, and the peas roll about.' The king was well pleased with the counsel, and caused the peas to be strewn.

There was, however, a servant of the king's who favoured the huntsmen, and when he heard that they were going to be put to this test he went to them and repeated everything, and said: 'The lion wants to make the king believe that you are girls.' Then the king's daughter thanked him, and said to her maidens: 'Show some strength, and step firmly on the peas.' So next morning when the king had the twelve huntsmen called before him, and they came into the ante-chamber where the peas were lying, they stepped so firmly on them, and had such a strong, sure walk, that not one of the peas either rolled or stirred. Then they went away again, and the king said to the lion: 'You have lied to me, they walk just like men.' The lion said: 'They have been informed that they were going to be put to the test, and have assumed some strength. Just let twelve spinning-wheels be brought into the ante-chamber, and they will go to them and be pleased with them, and that is what no man would do.' The king liked the advice, and had the spinning-wheels placed in the ante-chamber.

But the servant, who was well disposed to the huntsmen, went to them, and disclosed the project. So when they were alone the king's daughter said to her eleven girls: 'Show some constraint, and do not look round at the spinning-wheels.' And next morning when the king had his twelve huntsmen summoned, they went through the ante-chamber, and never once looked at the spinning-wheels. Then the king again said to the lion: 'You have deceived me, they are men, for they have not looked at the spinning-wheels.' The lion replied: 'They have restrained themselves.' The king, however, would no longer believe the lion.

The twelve huntsmen always followed the king to the chase, and his liking for them continually increased. Now it came to pass that once when they were out hunting, news came that the king's bride was approaching. When the true bride heard that, it hurt her so much that her heart was almost broken, and she fell fainting to the ground. The king thought something had happened to his dear huntsman, ran up to him, wanted to help him, and drew his glove off. Then he saw the ring which he had given to his first bride, and when he looked in her face he recognized her. Then his heart was so touched that he kissed her, and when she opened her eyes he said: 'You are mine, and I am yours, and no one in the world can alter that.' He sent a messenger to the other bride, and entreated her to return to her own kingdom, for he had a wife already, and someone who had just found an old key did not require a new one. Thereupon the wedding was celebrated, and the lion was again taken into favour, because, after all, he had told the truth.

THE KING OF THE GOLDEN MOUNTAIN

There was once a merchant who had only one child, a son, that was very young, and barely able to run alone. He had two richly laden ships then making a voyage upon the seas, in which he had embarked all his wealth, in the hope of making great gains, when the news came that both were lost. Thus from being a rich man he became all at once so very poor that nothing was left to him but one small plot of land; and there he often went in an evening to take his walk, and ease his mind of a little of his trouble.

One day, as he was roaming along in a brown study, thinking with no great comfort on what he had been and what he now was, and was like to be, all on a sudden there stood before him a little, rough-looking, black dwarf. 'Prithee, friend, why so sorrowful?' said he to the merchant; 'what is it you take so deeply to heart?' 'If you would do me any good I would willingly tell you,' said the merchant. 'Who knows but I may?' said the little man: 'tell me what ails you, and perhaps you will find I may be of some use.' Then the merchant told him how all his wealth was gone to the bottom of the sea, and how he had nothing left but that little plot of land. 'Oh, trouble not yourself about that,' said the dwarf; 'only undertake to bring me here, twelve years hence, whatever meets you first on your going home, and I will give you as much as you please.' The merchant thought this was no great thing to ask; that it would most likely be his dog or his cat, or something of that sort, but forgot his little boy Heinel; so he agreed to the bargain, and signed and sealed the bond to do what was asked of him.

But as he drew near home, his little boy was so glad to see him that he crept behind him, and laid fast hold of his legs, and looked up in his face and laughed. Then the father started, trembling with fear and horror, and saw what it was that he had bound himself to do; but as no gold was come, he made himself easy by thinking that it was only a joke that the dwarf was playing him, and that, at any rate, when the money came, he should see the bearer, and would not take it in.

About a month afterwards he went upstairs into a lumber-room to look for some old iron, that he might sell it and raise a little money; and there, instead of his iron, he saw a large pile of gold lying on the floor. At the sight of this he was overjoyed, and forgetting all about his son, went into trade again, and became a richer merchant than before.

Meantime little Heinel grew up, and as the end of the twelve years drew near the merchant began to call to mind his bond, and became very sad and thoughtful; so that care and sorrow were written upon his face. The boy one day asked what was the matter, but his father would not tell for some time; at last, however, he said that he had, without knowing it, sold him for gold to a little, ugly-looking, black dwarf, and that the twelve years were coming round when he must keep his word. Then Heinel said, 'Father, give yourself very little trouble about that; I shall be too much for the little man.'

When the time came, the father and son went out together to the place agreed upon: and the son drew a circle on the ground, and set himself and his father in the middle of it. The little black dwarf soon came, and walked round and round about the circle, but could not find any way to get into it, and he either could not, or dared not, jump over it. At last the boy said to him. 'Have you anything to say to us, my friend, or what do you want?' Now Heinel had found a friend in a good fairy, that was fond of him, and had told him what to do; for this fairy knew what good luck was in store for him. 'Have you brought me what you said you would?' said the dwarf to the merchant. The old man held his tongue, but Heinel said again, 'What do you want here?' The dwarf said, 'I come to talk with your father, not with you.' 'You have cheated and taken in my father,' said the son; 'pray give him up his bond at once.' 'Fair and softly,' said the little old man; 'right is right; I have paid my money, and your father has had it, and spent it; so be so good as to let me have what I paid it for.' 'You must have my consent to that first,' said Heinel, 'so please to step in here, and let us talk it over.' The old man grinned, and showed his teeth, as if he should have been very glad to get into the circle if he could. Then at last, after a long talk, they came to terms. Heinel agreed that his father must give him up, and that so far the dwarf should have his way: but, on the other hand, the fairy had told Heinel what fortune was in store for him, if he followed his own course; and he did not choose to be given up to his hump-backed friend, who seemed so anxious for his company.

So, to make a sort of drawn battle of the matter, it was settled that Heinel should be put into an open boat, that lay on the sea-shore hard by; that the father should push him off with his own hand, and that he should thus be set adrift, and left to the bad or good luck of wind and weather. Then he took leave of his father, and set himself in the boat, but before it got far off a wave struck it, and it fell with one side low in the water, so the merchant thought that poor Heinel was lost, and went home very sorrowful, while the dwarf went his way, thinking that at any rate he had had his revenge.The boat, however, did not sink, for the good fairy took care of her friend, and soon raised the boat up again, and it went safely on. The young man sat safe within, till at length it ran ashore upon an unknown land. As he jumped upon the shore he saw before him a beautiful castle but empty and dreary within, for it was enchanted. 'Here,' said he to himself, 'must I find the prize the good fairy told me of.' So he once more searched the whole palace through, till at last he found a white snake, lying coiled up on a cushion in one of the chambers.

Now the white snake was an enchanted princess; and she was very glad to see him, and said, 'Are you at last come to set me free? Twelve long years have I waited here for the fairy to bring you hither as she promised, for you alone can save me. This night twelve men will come: their faces will be black, and they will be dressed in chain armour. They will ask what you do here, but give no answer; and let them do what they will—beat, whip, pinch, prick, or torment you—bear all; only speak not a word, and at twelve o'clock they must go away. The second night twelve others will come: and the third night twenty-four, who will even cut off your head; but at the twelfth hour of that night their power is gone, and I shall be free, and will come and bring you the Water of Life, and will wash you with it, and bring you back to life and health.' And all came to pass as she had said; Heinel bore all, and spoke not a word; and the third night the princess came, and fell on his neck and kissed him. Joy and gladness burst forth throughout the castle, the wedding was celebrated, and he was crowned king of the Golden Mountain.

They lived together very happily, and the queen had a son. And thus eight years had passed over their heads, when the king thought of his father; and he began to long to see him once again. But the queen was against his going, and said, 'I know well that misfortunes will come upon us if you go.' However, he gave her no rest till she agreed. At his going away she gave him a wishing-ring, and said, 'Take this ring, and put it on your finger; whatever you wish it will bring you; only promise never to make use of it to bring me hence to your father's house.' Then he said he would do what she asked, and put the ring on his finger, and wished himself near the town where his father lived.

Heinel found himself at the gates in a moment; but the guards would not let him go in, because he was so strangely clad. So he went up to a neighbouring hill, where a shepherd dwelt, and borrowed his old frock, and thus passed unknown into the town. When he came to his father's house, he said he was his son; but the merchant would not believe him, and said he had had but one son, his poor Heinel, who he knew was long since dead: and as he was only dressed like a poor shepherd, he would not even give him anything to eat. The king, however, still vowed that he was his son, and said, 'Is there no mark by which you would know me if I am really your son?' 'Yes,' said his mother, 'our Heinel had a mark like a raspberry on his right arm.' Then he showed them the mark, and they knew that what he had said was true.

He next told them how he was king of the Golden Mountain, and was married to a princess, and had a son seven years old. But the merchant said, 'that can never be true; he must be a fine king truly who travels about in a shepherd's frock!' At this the son was vexed; and forgetting his word, turned his ring, and wished for his queen and son. In an instant they stood before him; but the queen wept, and said he had broken his word, and bad luck would follow. He did all he could to soothe her, and she at last seemed to be appeased; but she was not so in truth, and was only thinking how she should punish him.

One day he took her to walk with him out of the town, and showed her the spot where the boat was set adrift upon the wide waters. Then he sat himself down, and said, 'I am very much tired; sit by me, I will rest my head in your lap, and sleep a while.' As soon as he had fallen asleep, however, she drew the ring from his finger, and crept softly away, and wished herself and her son at home in their kingdom. And when he awoke he found himself alone, and saw that the ring was gone from his finger. 'I can never go back to my father's house,' said he; 'they would say I am a sorcerer: I will journey forth into the world, till I come again to my kingdom.'

So saying he set out and travelled till he came to a hill, where three giants were sharing their father's goods; and as they saw him pass they cried out and said, 'Little men have sharp wits; he shall part the goods between us.' Now there was a sword that cut off an enemy's head whenever the wearer gave the words, 'Heads off!'; a cloak that made the owner invisible, or gave him any form he pleased; and a pair of boots that carried the wearer wherever he wished. Heinel said they must first let him try these wonderful things, then he might know how to set a value upon them. Then they gave him the cloak, and he wished himself a fly, and in a moment he was a fly. 'The cloak is very well,' said he: 'now give me the sword.' 'No,' said they; 'not unless you undertake not to say, "Heads off!" for if you do we are all dead men.' So they gave it him, charging him to try it on a tree. He next asked for the boots also; and the moment he had all three in his power, he wished himself at the Golden Mountain; and there he was at once. So the giants were left behind with no goods to share or quarrel about.

As Heinel came near his castle he heard the sound of merry music; and the people around told him that his queen was about to marry another husband. Then he threw his cloak around him, and passed through the castle hall, and placed himself by the side of the queen, where no one saw him. But when anything to eat was put upon her plate, he took it away and ate it himself; and when a glass of wine was handed to her, he took it and drank it; and thus, though they kept on giving her meat and drink, her plate and cup were always empty.

Upon this, fear and remorse came over her, and she went into her chamber alone, and sat there weeping; and he followed her there. 'Alas!' said she to herself, 'was I not once set free? Why then does this enchantment still seem to bind me?'

'False and fickle one!' said he. 'One indeed came who set thee free, and he is now near thee again; but how have you used him? Ought he to have had such treatment from thee?' Then he went out and sent away the company, and said the wedding was at an end, for that he was come back to the kingdom. But the princes, peers, and great men mocked at him. However, he would enter into no parley with them, but only asked them if they would go in peace or not. Then they turned upon him and tried to seize him; but he drew his sword. 'Heads off!' cried he; and with the word the traitors' heads fell before him, and Heinel was once more king of the Golden Mountain.

DOCTOR KNOWALL

There was once upon a time a poor peasant called Crabb, who drove with two oxen a load of wood to the town, and sold it to a doctor for two talers. When the money was being counted out to him, it so happened that the doctor was sitting at table, and when the peasant saw how well he ate and drank, his heart desired what he saw, and would willingly have been a doctor too. So he remained standing a while, and at length inquired if he too could not be a doctor. 'Oh, yes,' said the doctor, 'that is soon managed.' 'What must I do?' asked the peasant. 'In the first place buy yourself an ABC book of the kind which has a cock on the frontispiece; in the second, turn your cart and your two oxen into money, and get yourself some clothes, and whatsoever else pertains to medicine; thirdly, have a sign painted for yourself with the words: "I am Doctor Knowall," and have that nailed up above your house-door.' The peasant did everything that he had been told to do. When he had doctored people awhile, but not long, a rich and great lord had some money stolen. Then he was told about Doctor Knowall who lived in such and such a village, and must know what had become of the money. So the lord had the horses harnessed to his carriage, drove out to the village, and asked Crabb if he were Doctor Knowall.

Yes, he was, he said. Then he was to go with him and bring back the stolen money. 'Oh, yes, but Grete, my wife, must go too.' The lord was willing, and let both of them have a seat in the carriage, and they all drove away together. When they came to the nobleman's castle, the table was spread, and Crabb was told to sit down and eat. 'Yes, but my wife, Grete, too,' said he, and he seated himself with her at the table. And when the first servant came with a dish of delicate fare, the peasant nudged his wife, and said: 'Grete, that was the first,' meaning that was the servant who brought the first dish. The servant, however, thought he intended by that to say: 'That is the first thief,' and as he actually was so, he was terrified, and said to his comrade outside: 'The doctor knows all: we shall fare ill, he said I was the first.' The second did not want to go in at all, but was forced. So when he went in with his dish, the peasant nudged his wife, and said: 'Grete, that is the second.' This servant was equally alarmed, and he got out as fast as he could. The third fared no better, for the peasant again said: 'Grete, that is the third.' The fourth had to carry in a dish that was covered, and the lord told the doctor that he was to show his skill, and guess what was beneath the cover. Actually, there were crabs. The doctor looked at the dish, had no idea what to say, and cried: 'Ah, poor Crabb.' When the lord heard that, he cried: 'There! he knows it; he must also know who has the money!'

On this the servants looked terribly uneasy, and made a sign to the doctor that they wished him to step outside for a moment. When therefore he went out, all four of them confessed to him that they had stolen the money, and said that they would willingly restore it and give him a heavy sum into the bargain, if he would not denounce them, for if he did they would be hanged. They led him to the spot where the money was concealed. With this the doctor was satisfied, and returned to the hall, sat down to the table, and said: 'My lord, now will I search in my book where the gold is hidden.'

The fifth servant, however, crept into the stove to hear if the doctor knew still more. But the doctor sat still and opened his ABC book, turned the pages backwards and forwards, and looked for the cock. As he could not find it immediately he said: 'I know you are there, so you had better come out!' Then the fellow in the stove thought that the doctor meant him, and full of terror, sprang out, crying: 'That man knows everything!' Then Doctor Knowall showed the lord where the money was, but did not say who had stolen it, and received from both sides much money in reward, and became a renowned man.

THE SEVEN RAVENS

There was once a man who had seven sons, and last of all one daughter. Although the little girl was very pretty, she was so weak and small that they thought she could not live; but they said she should at once be christened.

So the father sent one of his sons in haste to the spring to get some water, but the other six ran with him. Each wanted to be first at drawing the water, and so they were in such a hurry that all let their pitchers fall into the well, and they stood very foolishly looking at one another, and did not know what to do, for none dared go home. In the meantime the father was uneasy, and could not tell what made the young men stay so long. 'Surely,' said he, 'the whole seven must have forgotten themselves over some game of play'; and when he had waited still longer and they yet did not come, he flew into a rage and wished them all turned into ravens. Scarcely had he spoken these words when he heard a croaking over his head, and looked up and saw seven ravens as black as coal flying round and round. Sorry as he was to see his wish so fulfilled, he did not know how what was done could be undone, and comforted himself as well as he could for the loss of his seven sons with his dear little daughter, who soon became stronger and every day more beautiful.

For a long time she did not know that she had ever had any brothers; for her father and mother took care not to speak of them before her: but one day by chance she heard the people about her speak of them. 'Yes,' said they, 'she is beautiful indeed, but still 'tis a pity that her brothers should have been lost for her sake.' Then she was much grieved, and went to her father and mother, and asked if she had any brothers, and what had become of them. So they dared no longer hide the truth from her, but said it was the will of Heaven, and that her birth was only the innocent cause of it; but the little girl mourned sadly about it every day, and thought herself bound to do all she could to bring her brothers back; and she had neither rest nor ease, till at length one day she stole away, and set out into the wide world to find her brothers, wherever they might be, and free them, whatever it might cost her.

She took nothing with her but a little ring which her father and mother had given her, a loaf of bread in case she should be hungry, a little pitcher of water in case she should be thirsty, and a little stool to rest upon when she should be weary. Thus she went on and on, and journeyed till she came to the world's end; then she came to the sun, but the sun looked much too hot and fiery; so she ran away quickly to the moon, but the moon was cold and chilly, and said, 'I smell flesh and blood this way!' so she took herself away in a hurry and came to the stars, and the stars were friendly and kind to her, and each star sat upon his own little stool; but the morning star rose up and gave her a little piece of wood, and said, 'If you have not this little piece of wood, you cannot unlock the castle that stands on the glass-mountain, and there your brothers live.' The little girl took the piece of wood, rolled it up in a little cloth, and went on again until she came to the glass-mountain, and found the door shut. Then she felt for the little piece of wood; but when she unwrapped the cloth it was not there, and she saw she had lost the gift of the good stars. What was to be done? She wanted to save her brothers, and had no key of the castle of the glass-mountain; so this faithful little sister took a knife out of her pocket and cut off her little finger, that was just the size of the piece of wood she had lost, and put it in the door and opened it.

As she went in, a little dwarf came up to her, and said, 'What are you seeking for?' 'I seek for my brothers, the seven ravens,' answered she. Then the dwarf said, 'My masters are not at home; but if you will wait till they come, pray step in.' Now the little dwarf was getting their dinner ready, and he brought their food upon seven little plates, and their drink in seven little glasses, and set them upon the table, and out of each little plate their sister ate a small piece, and out of each little glass she drank a small drop; but she let the ring that she had brought with her fall into the last glass.

On a sudden she heard a fluttering and croaking in the air, and the dwarf said, 'Here come my masters.' When they came in, they wanted to eat and drink, and looked for their little plates and glasses. Then said one after the other,

'Who has eaten from my little plate? And who has been drinking out of my little glass?'

> 'Caw! Caw! well I ween
> Mortal lips have this way been.'

When the seventh came to the bottom of his glass, and found there the ring, he looked at it, and knew that it was his father's and mother's, and said, 'O that our little sister would but come! then we should be free.' When the little girl heard this (for she stood behind the door all the time and listened), she ran forward, and in an instant all the ravens took their right form again; and all hugged and kissed each other, and went merrily home.

THE WEDDING OF MRS FOX

FIRST STORY

There was once upon a time an old fox with nine tails, who believed that his wife was not faithful to him, and wished to put her to the test. He stretched himself out under the bench, did not move a limb, and behaved as if he were stone dead. Mrs Fox went up to her room, shut herself in, and her maid, Miss Cat, sat by the fire, and did the cooking. When it became known that the old fox was dead, suitors presented themselves. The maid heard someone standing at the house-door, knocking. She went and opened it, and it was a young fox, who said:

> 'What may you be about, Miss Cat?
> Do you sleep or do you wake?'

She answered:

> 'I am not sleeping, I am waking,
> Would you know what I am making?
> I am boiling warm beer with butter,
> Will you be my guest for supper?'

'No, thank you, miss,' said the fox, 'what is Mrs Fox doing?' The maid replied:

> *She is sitting in her room,*
> *Moaning in her gloom,*
> *Weeping her little eyes quite red,*
> *Because old Mr Fox is dead.'*

'Do just tell her, miss, that a young fox is here, who would like to woo her.' 'Certainly, young sir.'

> *The cat goes up the stairs trip, trap,*
> *The door she knocks at tap, tap, tap,*
> *'Mistress Fox, are you inside?'*
> *'Oh, yes, my little cat,' she cried.*
> *'A wooer he stands at the door out there.'*
> *'What does he look like, my dear?'*

'Has he nine as beautiful tails as the late Mr Fox?' 'Oh, no,' answered the cat, 'he has only one.' 'Then I will not have him.'

Miss Cat went downstairs and sent the wooer away. Soon afterwards there was another knock, and another fox was at the door who wished to woo Mrs Fox. He had two tails, but he did not fare better than the first. After this still more came, each with one tail more than the other, but they were all turned away, until at last one came who had nine tails, like old Mr Fox. When the widow heard that, she said joyfully to the cat:

> *'Now open the gates and doors all wide,*
> *And carry old Mr Fox outside.'*

But just as the wedding was going to be solemnized, old Mr Fox stirred under the bench, and cudgelled all the rabble, and drove them and Mrs Fox out of the house.

SECOND STORY

When old Mr Fox was dead, the wolf came as a suitor, and
knocked at the door, and the cat who was servant to Mrs Fox,
opened it for him. The wolf greeted her, and said:

> '*Good day, Mrs Cat of Kehrewit,*
> *How comes it that alone you sit?*
> *What are you making good?*'

The cat replied:

> '*In milk I'm breaking bread so sweet,*
> *Will you be my guest, and eat?*'

'No, thank you, Mrs Cat,' answered the wolf. 'Is Mrs
Fox not at home?'

The cat said:

> '*She sits upstairs in her room,*
> *Bewailing her sorrowful doom,*
> *Bewailing her trouble so sore,*
> *For old Mr Fox is no more.*'

The wolf answered:

> '*If she's in want of a husband now,*
> *Then will it please her to step below?*'
> *The cat runs quickly up the stair,*
> *And lets her tail fly here and there,*
> *Until she comes to the parlour door.*
> *With her five gold rings at the door she knocks:*
> '*Are you within, good Mistress Fox?*
> *If you're in want of a husband now,*
> *Then will it please you to step below?*'

Mrs Fox asked: 'Has the gentleman red stockings on, and has he a pointed mouth?' 'No,' answered the cat. 'Then he won't do for me.'

When the wolf was gone, came a dog, a stag, a hare, a bear, a lion, and all the beasts of the forest, one after the other. But one of the good qualities which old Mr Fox had possessed, was always lacking, and the cat had continually to send the suitors away. At length came a young fox. Then Mrs Fox said: 'Has the gentleman red stockings on, and has a little pointed mouth?' 'Yes,' said the cat, 'he has.' 'Then let him come upstairs,' said Mrs Fox, and ordered the servant to prepare the wedding feast.

> *'Sweep me the room as clean as you can,*
> *Up with the window, fling out my old ma*
> *For many a fine fat mouse he brought,*
> *Yet of his wife he never thought,*
> *But ate up every one he caught.'*

Then the wedding was solemnized with young Mr Fox, and there was much rejoicing and dancing; and if they have not left off, they are dancing still.

THE SALAD

As a merry young huntsman was once going briskly along through a wood, there came up a little old woman, and said to him, 'Good day, good day; you seem merry enough, but I am hungry and thirsty; do pray give me something to eat.' The huntsman took pity on her, and put his hand in his pocket and gave her what he had. Then he wanted to go his way; but she took hold of him, and said, 'Listen, my friend, to what I am going to tell you; I will reward you for your kindness; go your way, and after a little time you will come to a tree where you will see nine birds sitting on a cloak. Shoot into the midst of them, and one will fall down dead: the cloak will fall too; take it, it is a wishing-cloak, and when you wear it you will find yourself at any place where you may wish to be. Cut open the dead bird, take out its heart and keep it, and you will find a piece of gold under your pillow every morning when you rise. It is the bird's heart that will bring you this good luck.'

The huntsman thanked her, and thought to himself, 'If all this does happen, it will be a fine thing for me.' When he had gone a hundred steps or so, he heard a screaming and chirping in the branches over him, and looked up and saw a flock of birds pulling a cloak with their bills and feet;

screaming, fighting, and tugging at each other as if each wished to have it himself. 'Well,' said the huntsman, 'this is wonderful; this happens just as the old woman said'; then he shot into the midst of them so that their feathers flew all about. Off went the flock chattering away; but one fell down dead, and the cloak with it. Then the huntsman did as the old woman told him, cut open the bird, took out the heart, and carried the cloak home with him.

The next morning when he awoke he lifted up his pillow, and there lay the piece of gold glittering underneath; the same happened next day, and indeed every day when he arose. He heaped up a great deal of gold, and at last thought to himself, 'Of what use is this gold to me whilst I am at home? I will go out into the world and look about me.'

Then he took leave of his friends, and hung his bag and bow about his neck, and went his way. It so happened that his road one day led through a thick wood, at the end of which was a large castle in a green meadow, and at one of the windows stood an old woman with a very beautiful young lady by her side looking about them. Now the old woman was a witch, and said to the young lady, 'There is a young man coming out of the wood who carries a wonderful prize; we must get it away from him, my dear child, for it is more fit for us than for him. He has a bird's heart that brings a piece of gold under his pillow every morning.' Meantime the huntsman came nearer and looked at the lady, and said to himself, 'I have been travelling so long that I should like to go into this castle and rest myself, for I have money enough to pay for anything I want'; but the real reason was, that he wanted to see more of the beautiful lady. Then he went into the house, and was welcomed kindly; and it was not long before he was so much in love that he thought of nothing else but looking at the lady's eyes, and doing everything that she wished. Then the old woman said, 'Now is the time for getting the bird's heart.' So the lady stole it away, and he never found any more gold under his pillow, for it lay now under the young lady's, and the old woman took it away every morning; but he was so much in love that he never missed his prize.

'Well,' said the old witch, 'we have got the bird's heart, but not the wishing-cloak yet, and that we must also get.' 'Let us leave him that,' said the young lady; 'he has already lost his wealth.' Then the witch was very angry, and said, 'Such a cloak is a very rare and wonderful thing, and I must and will have it.' So she did as the old woman told her, and set herself at the window, and looked about the country and seemed very sorrowful; then the huntsman said, 'What makes you so sad?' 'Alas! dear sir,' said she, 'yonder lies the granite rock where all the costly diamonds grow, and I want so much to go there, that whenever I think of it I cannot help being sorrowful, for who can reach it? only the birds and the flies—man cannot.' 'If that's all your grief,' said the huntsman, 'I'll take there with all my heart'; so he drew her under his cloak, and the moment he wished to be on the granite mountain they were both there. The diamonds glittered so on all sides that they were delighted with the sight and picked up the finest. But the old witch made a deep sleep come upon him, and he said to the young lady, 'Let us sit down and rest ourselves a little, I am so tired that I cannot stand any longer.' So they sat down, and he laid his head in her lap and fell asleep; and whilst he was sleeping on she took the cloak from his shoulders, hung it on her own, picked up the diamonds, and wished herself home again.

When he awoke and found that his lady had tricked him, and left him alone on the wild rock, he said, 'Alas! what roguery there is in the world!' and there he sat in great grief and fear, not knowing what to do. Now this rock belonged to fierce giants who lived upon it; and as he saw three of them striding about, he thought to himself, 'I can only save myself by feigning to be asleep'; so he laid himself down as if he were in a sound sleep. When the giants came up to him, the first pushed him with his foot, and said, 'What worm is this that lies here curled up?' 'Tread upon him and kill him,' said the second. 'It's not worth the trouble,' said the third; 'let him live, he'll go climbing higher up the mountain, and some cloud will come rolling and carry him away.' And they passed on. But the huntsman had heard all they said; and as soon as they were gone, he climbed to the top of the mountain, and when he had sat there a short time a cloud came rolling around him, and caught him in a whirlwind and bore him along for some time, till it settled in a garden, and he fell quite gently to the ground amongst the greens and cabbages.

Then he looked around him, and said, 'I wish I had something to eat, if not I shall be worse off than before; for here I see neither apples nor pears, nor any kind of fruits, nothing but vegetables.' At last he thought to himself, 'I can eat salad, it will refresh and strengthen me.' So he picked out a fine head and ate of it; but scarcely had he swallowed two bites when he felt himself quite changed, and saw with horror that he was turned into an ass. However, he still felt very hungry, and the salad tasted very nice; so he ate on till he came to another kind of salad, and scarcely had he tasted it when he felt another change come over him, and soon saw that he was lucky enough to have found his old shape again.

Then he laid himself down and slept off a little of his weariness; and when he awoke the next morning he broke off a head both of the good and the bad salad, and thought to himself, 'This will help me to my fortune again, and enable me to pay off some folks for their treachery.' So he went away to try and find the castle of his friends; and after wandering about a few days he luckily found it. Then he stained his face all over brown, so that even his mother would not have known him, and went into the castle and asked for a lodging; 'I am so tired,' said he, 'that I can go no farther.' 'Countryman,' said the witch, 'who are you? and what is your business?' 'I am,' said he, 'a messenger sent by the king to find the finest salad that grows under the sun. I have been lucky enough to find it, and have brought it with me; but the heat of the sun scorches so that it begins to wither, and I don't know that I can carry it farther.'

When the witch and the young lady heard of his beautiful salad, they longed to taste it, and said, 'Dear countryman, let us just taste it.' 'To be sure,' answered he; 'I have two heads of it with me, and will give you one'; so he opened his bag and gave them the bad. Then the witch herself took it into the kitchen to be dressed; and when it was ready she could not wait till it was carried up, but took a few leaves immediately and put them in her mouth, and scarcely were they swallowed when she lost her own form and ran braying down into the court in the form of an ass. Now the servant-maid came into the kitchen, and seeing the salad ready, was going to carry it up; but on the way she too felt a wish to taste it as the old woman had done, and ate some leaves; so she also was turned into an ass and ran after the other, letting the dish with the salad fall on the ground. The messenger sat all this time with the beautiful young lady, and as nobody came with the salad and she longed to taste it, she said, 'I don't know where the salad can be.' Then he thought something must have happened, and said, 'I will go into the kitchen and see.' And as he went he saw two asses in the court running about, and the salad lying on the ground. 'All right!' said he; 'those two have had their share.' Then he took up the rest of the leaves, laid them on the dish and brought them to the young lady, saying, 'I bring you the dish myself that you may not wait any longer.' So she ate of it, and like the others ran off into the court braying away.

Then the huntsman washed his face and went into the court that they might know him. 'Now you shall be paid for your roguery,' said he; and tied them all three to a rope and took them along with him till he came to a mill and knocked at the window. 'What's the matter?' said the miller. 'I have three tiresome beasts here,' said the other; 'if you will take them, give them food and room, and treat them as I tell you, I will pay you whatever you ask.' 'With all my heart,' said the miller; 'but how shall I treat them?' Then the huntsman said, 'Give the old one stripes three times a day and hay once; give the next (who was the servant-maid) stripes once a day and hay three times; and give the youngest (who was the beautiful lady) hay three times a day and no stripes': for he could not find it in his heart to have her beaten. After this he went back to the castle, where he found everything he wanted.

Some days after, the miller came to him and told him that the old ass was dead; 'The other two,' said he, 'are alive and eat, but are so sorrowful that they cannot last long.' Then the huntsman pitied them, and told the miller to drive them back to him, and when they came, he gave them some of the good salad to eat. And the beautiful young lady fell upon her knees before him, and said, 'O dearest huntsman! forgive me all the ill I have done you; my mother forced me to it, it was against my will, for I always loved you very much. Your wishing-cloak hangs up in the closet, and as for the bird's heart, I will give it you too.' But he said, 'Keep it, it will be just the same thing, for I mean to make you my wife.' So they were married, and lived together very happily till they died.

THE STORY OF THE YOUTH WHO WENT FORTH TO LEARN WHAT FEAR WAS

A certain father had two sons, the elder of who was smart and sensible, and could do everything, but the younger was stupid and could neither learn nor understand anything, and when people saw him they said: 'There's a fellow who will give his father some trouble!' When anything had to be done, it was always the elder who was forced to do it; but if his father bade him fetch anything when it was late, or in the night-time, and the way led through the churchyard, or any other dismal place, he answered: 'Oh, no father, I'll not go there, it makes me shudder!' for he was afraid. Or when stories were told by the fire at night which made the flesh creep, the listeners sometimes said: 'Oh, it makes us shudder!' The younger sat in a corner and listened with the rest of them, and could not imagine what they could mean. 'They are always saying: "It makes me shudder, it makes me shudder!" It does not make me shudder,' thought he. 'That, too, must be an art of which I understand nothing!'

Now it came to pass that his father said to him one day: 'Hearken to me, you fellow in the corner there, you are growing tall and strong, and you too must learn something by which you can earn your bread. Look how your brother works, but you do not even earn your salt.' 'Well, father,' he replied, 'I am quite willing to learn something—indeed, if it could but be managed, I should like to learn how to shudder. I don't understand that at all yet.' The elder brother smiled when he heard that, and thought to himself: 'Goodness, what a blockhead that brother of mine is! He will never be good for anything as long as he lives! He who wants to be a sickle must bend himself betimes.'

The father sighed, and answered him: 'You shall soon learn what it is to shudder, but you will not earn your bread by that.'

Soon after this the sexton came to the house on a visit, and the father bewailed his trouble, and told him how his younger son was so backward in every respect that he knew nothing and learnt nothing. 'Just think,' said he, 'when I asked him how he was going to earn his bread, he actually wanted to learn to shudder.' 'If that be all,' replied the sexton, 'he can learn that with me. Send him to me, and I will soon polish him.' The father was glad to do it, for he thought: 'It will train the boy a little.' The sexton therefore took him into his house, and he had to ring the church bell. After a day or two, the sexton awoke him at midnight, and bade him arise and go up into the church tower and ring the bell. 'You shall soon learn what shuddering is,' thought he, and secretly went there before him; and when the boy was at the top of the tower and turned round, and was just going to take hold of the bell rope, he saw a white figure standing on the stairs opposite the sounding hole. 'Who is there?' cried he, but the figure made no reply, and did not move or stir. 'Give an answer,' cried the boy, 'or take yourself off, you have no business here at night.'

The sexton, however, remained standing motionless that the boy might think he was a ghost. The boy cried a second time: 'What do you want here?—speak if you are an honest fellow, or I will throw you down the steps!' The sexton thought: 'He can't mean to be as bad as his words,' uttered no sound and stood as if he were made of stone. Then the boy called to him for the third time, and as that was also to no purpose, he ran against him and pushed the ghost down the stairs, so that it fell down the ten steps and remained lying there in a corner. Thereupon he rang the bell, went home, and without saying a word went to bed, and fell asleep. The sexton's wife waited a long time for her husband, but he did not come back. At length she became uneasy, and wakened the boy, and asked: 'Do you know where my husband is? He climbed up the tower before you did.' 'No, I don't know,' replied the boy, 'but someone was standing by the sounding hole on the other side of the steps, and as he would neither gave an answer nor go away, I took him for a scoundrel, and threw him downstairs. Just go there and you will see if it was he. I should be sorry if it were.' The woman ran away and found her husband, who was lying moaning in the corner, and had broken his leg.

She carried him down, and then with loud screams she hastened to the boy's father, 'Your boy,' cried she, 'has been the cause of a great misfortune! He has thrown my husband down the steps so that he broke his leg. Take the good-for-nothing fellow out of our house.' The father was terrified, and ran thither and scolded the boy. 'What wicked tricks are these?' said he. 'The devil must have put them into your head.' 'Father,' he replied, 'do listen to me. I am quite innocent. He was standing there by night like one intent on doing evil. I did not know who it was, and I entreated him three times either to speak or to go away.' 'Ah,' said the father, 'I have nothing but unhappiness with you. Go out of my sight. I will see you no more.'

'Yes, father, right willingly, wait only until it is day. Then will I go forth and learn how to shudder, and then I shall, at any rate, understand one art which will support me.' 'Learn what you will,' spoke the father, 'it is all the same to me. Here are fifty talers for you. Take these and go into the wide world, and tell no one from whence you come, and who is your father, for I have reason to be ashamed of you.' 'Yes, father, it shall be as you will. If you desire nothing more than that, I can easily keep it in mind.'

When the day dawned, therefore, the boy put his fifty talers into his pocket, and went forth on the great highway, and continually said to himself: 'If I could but shudder! If I could but shudder!' Then a man approached who heard this conversation which the youth was holding with himself, and when they had walked a little farther to where they could see the gallows, the man said to him: 'Look, there is the tree where seven men have married the ropemaker's daughter, and are now learning how to fly. Sit down beneath it, and wait till night comes, and you will soon learn how to shudder.' 'If that is all that is wanted,' answered the youth, 'it is easily done; but if I learn how to shudder as fast as that, you shall have my fifty talers. Just come back to me early in the morning.' Then the youth went to the gallows, sat down beneath it, and waited till evening came. And as he was cold, he lighted himself a fire, but at midnight the wind blew so sharply that in spite of his fire, he could not get warm. And as the wind knocked the hanged men against each other, and they moved backwards and forwards, he thought to himself: 'If you shiver below by the fire, how those up above must freeze and suffer!' And as he felt pity for them, he raised the ladder, and climbed up, unbound one of them after the other, and brought down all seven. Then he stoked the fire, blew it, and set them all round it to warm themselves. But they sat there and did not stir, and the fire caught their clothes. So he said: 'Take care, or I will hang you up again.' The dead men, however, did not hear, but were quite silent, and let their rags go on burning. At this he grew angry, and said: 'If you will not take care, I cannot help you, I will not be burnt with you,' and he hung them up again each in his turn. Then he sat down by his fire and fell asleep, and the next morning the man came to him and wanted to have the fifty talers, and said: 'Well do you know how to shudder?' 'No,' answered he, 'how should I know? Those fellows up there did not open their mouths, and were so stupid that they let the few old rags which they had on their bodies get burnt.' Then the man saw that he would not get the fifty talers that day, and went away saying: 'Such a youth has never come my way before.'

The youth likewise went his way, and once more began to mutter to himself: 'Ah, if I could but shudder! Ah, if I could but shudder!' A waggoner who was striding behind him heard this and asked: 'Who are you?' 'I don't know,' answered the youth. Then the waggoner asked: 'From whence do you come?' 'I know not.' 'Who is your father?' 'That I may not tell you.' 'What is it that you are always muttering between your teeth?' 'Ah,' replied the youth, 'I do so wish I could shudder, but no one can teach me how.' 'Enough of your foolish chatter,' said the waggoner. 'Come, go with me, I will see about a place for you.' The youth went with the waggoner, and in the evening they arrived at an inn where they wished to pass the night. Then at the entrance of the parlour the youth again said quite loudly: 'If I could but shudder! If I could but shudder!' The host who heard this, laughed and said: 'If that is your desire, there ought to be a good opportunity for you here.' 'Ah, be silent,' said the hostess, 'so many prying persons have already lost their lives, it would be a pity and a shame if such beautiful eyes as these should never see the daylight again.'

But the youth said: 'However difficult it may be, I will learn it. For this purpose indeed have I journeyed forth.' He let the host have no rest, until the latter told him, that not far from thence stood a haunted castle where anyone could very easily learn what shuddering was, if he would but watch in it for three nights. The king had promised that he who would venture should have his daughter to wife, and she was the most beautiful maiden the sun shone on. Likewise in the castle lay great treasures, which were guarded by evil spirits, and these treasures would then be freed, and would make a poor man rich enough. Already many men had gone into the castle, but as yet none had come out again. Then the youth went next morning to the king, and said: 'If it be allowed, I will willingly watch three nights in the haunted castle.' The king looked at him, and as the youth pleased him, he said: 'You may ask for three things to take into the castle with you, but they must be things without life.' Then he answered: 'Then I ask for a fire, a turning lathe, and a cutting-board with the knife.'

The king had these things carried into the castle for him during the day. When night was drawing near, the youth went up and made himself a bright fire in one of the rooms, placed the cutting-board and knife beside it, and seated himself by the turning-lathe. 'Ah, if I could but shudder!' said he, 'but I shall not learn it here either.' Towards midnight he was about to poke his fire, and as he was blowing it, something cried suddenly from one corner: 'Au, miau! how cold we are!' 'You fools!' cried he, 'what are you crying about? If you are cold, come and take a seat by the fire and warm yourselves.' And when he had said that, two great black cats came with one tremendous leap and sat down on each side of him, and looked savagely at him with their fiery eyes. After a short time, when they had warmed themselves, they said: 'Comrade, shall we have a game of cards?' 'Why not?' he replied, 'but just show me your paws.' Then they stretched out their claws. 'Oh,' said he, 'what long nails you have! Wait, I must first cut them for you.' Thereupon he seized them by the throats, put them on the cutting-board and screwed their feet fast. 'I have looked at your fingers,' said he, 'and my fancy for card-playing has gone,' and he struck them dead and threw them out into the water. But when he had made away with these two, and was about to sit down again by his fire, out from every hole and corner came black cats and black dogs with red-hot chains, and more and more of them came until he could no longer move, and they yelled horribly, and got on his fire, pulled it to pieces, and tried to put it out. He watched them for a while quietly, but at last when they were going too far, he seized his cutting-knife, and cried: 'Away with you, vermin,' and began to cut them down. Some of them ran away, the others he killed, and threw out into the fish-pond. When he came back he fanned the embers of his fire again and warmed himself. And as he thus sat, his eyes would keep open no longer, and he felt a desire to sleep. Then he looked round and saw a great bed in the corner. 'That is the very thing for me,' said he, and got into it. When he was just going to shut his eyes, however, the bed began to move of its own accord, and went over the whole of the castle. 'That's right,' said he, 'but go faster.' Then the bed rolled on as if six horses were harnessed to it, up and down, over thresholds and stairs, but suddenly hop, hop, it turned over upside down, and lay on him like a mountain. But he threw quilts and pillows up in the air, got out and said: 'Now anyone who likes, may drive,' and lay down by his fire, and slept till it was day. In the morning the king came, and when he saw him lying there on the ground, he thought the evil spirits had killed him and he was dead. Then said he: 'After all it is a pity—for so handsome a man.' The youth heard it, got up, and said: 'It has not come to that yet.' Then the king was astonished, but very glad, and asked how he had fared. 'Very well indeed,' answered he; 'one night is past, the two others will pass likewise.' Then he went to the innkeeper, who opened his eyes very wide, and said: 'I never expected to see you alive again! Have you learnt how to shudder yet?' 'No,' said he, 'it is all in vain. If someone would but tell me!'

The second night he again went up into the old castle, sat down by the fire, and once more began his old song: 'If I could but shudder!' When midnight came, an uproar and noise of tumbling about was heard; at first it was low, but it grew louder and louder. Then it was quiet for a while, and at length with a loud scream, half a man came down the chimney and fell before him. 'Hullo!' cried he, 'another half belongs to this. This is not enough!' Then the uproar began again, there was a roaring and howling, and the other half fell down likewise. 'Wait,' said he, 'I will just stoke up the fire a little for you.' When he had done that and looked round again, the two pieces were joined together, and a hideous man was sitting in his place. 'That is no part of our bargain,' said the youth, 'the bench is mine.' The man wanted to push him away; the youth, however, would not allow that, but thrust him off with all his strength, and seated himself again in his own place. Then still more men fell down, one after the other; they brought nine dead men's legs and two skulls, and set them up and played at nine-pins with them. The youth also wanted to play and said: 'Listen you, can I join you?' 'Yes, if you have any money.' 'Money enough,' replied he, 'but your balls are not quite round.' Then he took the skulls and put them in the lathe and turned them till they were round. 'There, now they will roll better!' said he. 'Hurrah! now we'll have fun!' He played with them and lost some of his money, but when it struck twelve, everything vanished from his sight. He lay down and quietly fell asleep. Next morning the king came to inquire after him. 'How has it fared with you this time?' asked he. 'I have been playing at nine-pins,' he answered, 'and have lost a couple of farthings.' 'Have you not shuddered then?' 'What?' said he, 'I have had a wonderful time! If I did but know what it was to shudder!'

The third night he sat down again on his bench and said quite sadly: 'If I could but shudder.' When it grew late, six tall men came in and brought a coffin. Then he said: 'Ha, ha, that is certainly my little cousin, who died only a few days ago,' and he beckoned with his finger, and cried: 'Come, little cousin, come.' They placed the coffin on the ground, but he went to it and took the lid off, and a dead man lay therein. He felt his face, but it was cold as ice. 'Wait,' said he, 'I will warm you a little,' and went to the fire and warmed his hand and laid it on the dead man's face, but he remained cold. Then he took him out, and sat down by the fire and laid him on his breast and rubbed his arms that the blood might circulate again. As this also did no good, he thought to himself: 'When two people lie in bed together, they warm each other,' and carried him to the bed, covered him over and lay down by him. After a short time the dead man became warm too, and began to move. Then said the youth, 'See, little cousin, have I not warmed you?' The dead man, however, got up and cried: 'Now will I strangle you.'

'What!' said he, 'is that the way you thank me? You shall at once go into your coffin again,' and he took him up, threw him into it, and shut the lid. Then came the six men and carried him away again. 'I cannot manage to shudder,' said he. 'I shall never learn it here as long as I live.'

Then a man entered who was taller than all others, and looked terrible. He was old, however, and had a long white beard. 'You wretch,' cried he, 'you shall soon learn what it is to shudder, for you shall die.' 'Not so fast,' replied the youth. 'If I am to die, I shall have to have a say in it.' 'I will soon seize you,' said the fiend. 'Softly, softly, do not talk so big. I am as strong as you are, and perhaps even stronger.' 'We shall see,' said the old man. 'If you are stronger, I will let you go—come, we will try.' Then he led him by dark passages to a smith's forge, took an axe, and with one blow struck an anvil into the ground. 'I can do better than that,' said the youth, and went to the other anvil. The old man placed himself near and wanted to look on, and his white beard hung down. Then the youth seized the axe, split the anvil with one blow, and in it caught the old man's beard. 'Now I have you,' said the youth. 'Now it is your turn to die.' Then he seized an iron bar and beat the old man till he moaned and entreated him to stop, when he would give him great riches. The youth drew out the axe and let him go. The old man led him back into the castle, and in a cellar showed him three chests full of gold. 'Of these,' said he, 'one part is for the poor, the other for the king, the third yours.' In the meantime it struck twelve, and the spirit disappeared, so that the youth stood in darkness. 'I shall still be able to find my way out,' said he, and felt about, found the way into the room, and slept there by his fire. Next morning the king came and said: 'Now you must have learnt what shuddering is?' 'No,' he answered; 'what can it be? My dead cousin was here, and a bearded man came and showed me a great deal of money down below, but no one told me what it was to shudder.' 'Then,' said the king, 'you have saved the castle, and shall marry my daughter.' 'That is all very well,' said he, 'but still I do not know what it is to shudder!'

Then the gold was brought up and the wedding celebrated; but howsoever much the young king loved his wife, and however happy he was, he still said always: 'If I could but shudder—if I could but shudder.' And this at last angered her. Her waiting-maid said: 'I will find a cure for him; he shall soon learn what it is to shudder.' She went out to the stream which flowed through the garden, and had a whole bucketful of gudgeons brought to her. At night when the young king was sleeping, his wife was to draw the clothes off him and empty the bucket full of cold water with the gudgeons in it over him, so that the little fishes would sprawl about him. Then he woke up and cried: 'Oh, what makes me shudder so?—what makes me shudder so, dear wife? Ah! now I know what it is to shudder!'

KING GRISLY-BEARD

A great king of a land far away in the East had a daughter who was very beautiful, but so proud, and haughty, and conceited, that none of the princes who came to ask her in marriage was good enough for her, and she only made sport of them.

Once upon a time the king held a great feast, and asked thither all her suitors; and they all sat in a row, ranged according to their rank—kings, and princes, and dukes, and earls, and counts, and barons, and knights. Then the princess came in, and as she passed by them she had something spiteful to say to every one. The first was too fat: 'He's as round as a tub,' said she. The next was too tall: 'What a maypole!' said she. The next was too short: 'What a dumpling!' said she. The fourth was too pale, and she called him 'Wallface'. The fifth was too red, so she called him 'Coxcomb'. The sixth was not straight enough; so she said he was like a green stick, that had been laid to dry over a baker's oven. And thus she had some joke to crack upon every one: but she laughed more than all at a good king who was there. 'Look at him,' said she; 'his beard is like an old mop; he shall be called Grisly-beard.' So the king got the nickname of Grisly-beard.

But the old king was very angry when he saw how his daughter behaved, and how she ill-treated all his guests; and he vowed that, willing or unwilling, she should marry the first man, be he prince or beggar, that came to the door.

Two days after there came by a travelling fiddler, who began to play under the window and beg alms; and when the king heard him, he said, 'Let him come in.' So they brought in a dirty-looking fellow; and when he had sung before the king and the princess, he begged a boon. Then the king said, 'You have sung so well, that I will give you my daughter for your wife.' The princess begged and prayed; but the king said, 'I have sworn to give you to the first comer, and I will keep my word.' So words and tears were of no avail; the parson was sent for, and she was married to the fiddler. When this was over the king said, 'Now get ready to go—you must not stay here—you must travel on with your husband.'

Then the fiddler went his way, and took her with him, and they soon came to a great wood. 'Pray,' said she, 'whose is this wood?' 'It belongs to King Grisly-beard,' answered he; 'hadst thou taken him, all had been thine.' 'Ah! unlucky wretch that I am!' sighed she; 'would that I had married King Grisly-beard!' Next they came to some fine meadows. 'Whose are these beautiful green meadows?' said she. 'They belong to King Grisly-beard, hadst thou taken him, they had all been thine.' 'Ah! unlucky wretch that I am!' said she; 'would that I had married King Grisly-beard!'

Then they came to a great city. 'Whose is this noble city?' said she. 'It belongs to King Grisly-beard; hadst thou taken him, it had all been thine.' 'Ah! wretch that I am!' sighed she; 'why did I not marry King Grisly-beard?' 'That is no business of mine,' said the fiddler: 'why should you wish for another husband? Am not I good enough for you?'

At last they came to a small cottage. 'What a paltry place!' said she; 'to whom does that little dirty hole belong?' Then the fiddler said, 'That is your and my house, where we are to live.' 'Where are your servants?' cried she. 'What do we want with servants?' said he; 'you must do for yourself whatever is to be done. Now make the fire, and put on water and cook my supper, for I am very tired.' But the princess knew nothing of making fires and cooking, and the fiddler was forced to help her. When they had eaten a very scanty meal they went to bed; but the fiddler called her up very early in the morning to clean the house. Thus they lived for two days: and when they had eaten up all there was in the cottage, the man said, 'Wife, we can't go on thus, spending money and earning nothing. You must learn to weave baskets.' Then he went out and cut willows, and brought them home, and she began to weave; but it made her fingers very sore. 'I see this work won't do,' said he: 'try and spin; perhaps you will do that better.' So she sat down and tried to spin; but the threads cut her tender fingers till the blood ran. 'See now,' said the fiddler, 'you are good for nothing; you can do no work: what a bargain I have got! However, I'll try and set up a trade in pots and pans, and you shall stand in the market and sell them.' 'Alas!' sighed she, 'if any of my father's court should pass by and see me standing in the market, how they will laugh at me!'

But her husband did not care for that, and said she must work, if she did not wish to die of hunger. At first the trade went well; for many people, seeing such a beautiful woman, went to buy her wares, and paid their money without thinking of taking away the goods. They lived on this as long as it lasted; and then her husband bought a fresh lot of ware, and she sat herself down with it in the corner of the market; but a drunken soldier soon came by, and rode his horse against her stall, and broke all her goods into a thousand pieces. Then she began to cry, and knew not what to do. 'Ah! what will become of me?' said she; 'what will my husband say?' So she ran home and told him all. 'Who would have thought you would have been so silly,' said he, 'as to put an earthenware stall in the corner of the market, where everybody passes? but let us have no more crying; I see you are not fit for this sort of work, so I have been to the king's palace, and asked if they did not want a kitchen-maid; and they say they will take you, and there you will have plenty to eat.'

Thus the princess became a kitchen-maid, and helped the cook to do all the dirtiest work; but she was allowed to carry home some of the meat that was left, and on this they lived.

She had not been there long before she heard that the king's eldest son was passing by, going to be married; and she went to one of the windows and looked out. Everything was ready, and all the pomp and brightness of the court was there. Then she bitterly grieved for the pride and folly which had brought her so low. And the servants gave her some of the rich meats, which she put into her basket to take home.

All on a sudden, as she was going out, in came the king's son in golden clothes; and when he saw a beautiful woman at the door, he took her by the hand, and said she should be his partner in the dance; but she trembled for fear, for she saw that it was King Grisly-beard, who was making sport of her. However, he kept fast hold, and led her in; and the cover of the basket came off, so that the meats in it fell about. Then everybody laughed and jeered at her; and she was so abashed, that she wished herself a thousand feet deep in the earth. She sprang to the door to run away; but on the steps King Grisly-beard overtook her, and brought her back and said, 'Fear me not! I am the fiddler who has lived with you in the hut. I brought you there because I really loved you. I am also the soldier that overset your stall. I have done all this only to cure you of your silly pride, and to show you the folly of your ill-treatment of me. Now all is over: you have learnt wisdom, and it is time to hold our marriage feast.'

Then the chamberlains came and brought her the most beautiful robes; and her father and his whole court were there already, and welcomed her home on her marriage. Joy was in every face and every heart. The feast was grand; they danced and sang; all were merry; and I only wish that you and I had been of the party.

IRON HANS

There was once upon a time a king who had a great forest near his palace, full of all kinds of wild animals. One day he sent out a huntsman to shoot him a roe, but he did not come back. 'Perhaps some accident has befallen him,' said the king, and the next day he sent out two more huntsmen who were to search for him, but they too stayed away. Then on the third day, he sent for all his huntsmen, and said: 'Scour the whole forest through, and do not give up until you have found all three.' But of these also, none came home again, none were seen again. From that time forth, no one would any longer venture into the forest, and it lay there in deep stillness and solitude, and nothing was seen of it, but sometimes an eagle or a hawk flying over it. This lasted for many years, when an unknown huntsman announced himself to the king as seeking a situation, and offered to go into the dangerous forest. The king, however, would not give his consent, and said: 'It is not safe in there; I fear it would fare with you no better than with the others, and you would never come out again.' The huntsman replied: 'Lord, I will venture it at my own risk, of fear I know nothing.'

The huntsman therefore betook himself with his dog to the forest. It was not long before the dog fell in with some game on the way, and wanted to pursue it; but hardly had the dog run two steps when it stood before a deep pool, could go no farther, and a naked arm stretched itself out of the water, seized it, and drew it under. When the huntsman saw that, he went back and fetched three men to come with buckets and bale out the water. When they could see to the bottom there lay a wild man whose body was brown like rusty iron, and whose hair hung over his face down to his knees. They bound him with cords, and led him away to the castle. There was great astonishment over the wild man; the king, however, had him put in an iron cage in his courtyard, and forbade the door to be opened on pain of death, and the queen herself was to take the key into her keeping. And from this time forth everyone could again go into the forest with safety.

The king had a son of eight years, who was once playing in the courtyard, and while he was playing, his golden ball fell into the cage. The boy ran thither and said: 'Give me my ball out.' 'Not till you have opened the door for me,' answered the man. 'No,' said the boy, 'I will not do that; the king has forbidden it,' and ran away. The next day he again went and asked for his ball; the wild man said: 'Open my door,' but the boy would not. On the third day the king had ridden out hunting, and the boy went once more and said: 'I cannot open the door even if I wished, for I have not the key.' Then the wild man said: 'It lies under your mother's pillow, you can get it there.' The boy, who wanted to have his ball back, cast all thought to the winds, and brought the key. The door opened with difficulty, and the boy pinched his fingers. When it was open the wild man stepped out, gave him the golden ball, and hurried away. The boy had become afraid; he called and cried after him: 'Oh, wild man, do not go away, or I shall be beaten!' The wild man turned back, took him up, set him on his shoulder, and went with hasty steps into the forest. When the king came home, he observed the empty cage, and asked the queen how that had happened. She knew nothing about it, and sought the key, but it was gone. She called the boy, but no one answered. The king sent out people to seek for him in the fields, but they did not find him. Then he could easily guess what had happened, and much grief reigned in the royal court.

When the wild man had once more reached the dark forest, he took the boy down from his shoulder, and said to him: 'You will never see your father and mother again, but I will keep you with me, for you have set me free, and I have compassion on you. If you do all I bid you, you shall fare well. Of treasure and gold have I enough, and more than anyone in the world.' He made a bed of moss for the boy on which he slept, and the next morning the man took him to a well, and said: 'Behold, the gold well is as bright and clear as crystal, you shall sit beside it, and take care that nothing falls into it, or it will be polluted. I will come every evening to see if you have obeyed my order.' The boy placed himself by the brink of the well, and often saw a golden fish or a golden snake show itself therein, and took care that nothing fell in. As he was thus sitting, his finger hurt him so violently that he involuntarily put it in the water. He drew it quickly out again, but saw that it was quite gilded, and whatsoever pains he took to wash the gold off again, all was to no purpose. In the evening Iron Hans came back, looked at the boy, and said: 'What has happened to the well?' 'Nothing, nothing,' he answered, and held his finger behind his back, that the man might not see it. But he said: 'You have dipped your finger into the water, this time it may pass, but take care you do not again let anything go in.' By daybreak the boy was already sitting by the well and watching it. His finger hurt him again and he passed it over his head, and then unhappily a hair fell down into the well. He took it quickly out, but it was already quite gilded. Iron Hans came, and already knew what had happened. 'You have let a hair fall into the well,' said he. 'I will allow you to watch by it once more, but if this happens for the third time then the well is polluted and you can no longer remain with me.' On the third day, the boy sat by the well, and did not stir his finger, however much it hurt him. But the time was long to him, and he looked at the reflection of his face on the surface of the water. And as he still bent down more and more while he was doing so, and trying to look straight into the eyes, his long hair fell down from his shoulders into the water. He raised himself up quickly, but the whole of the hair of his head was already golden and shone like the sun. You can imagine how terrified the poor boy was! He took his pocket-handkerchief and tied it round his head, in order that the man might not see it. When he came he already knew everything, and said: 'Take the handkerchief off.' Then the golden hair streamed forth, and let the boy excuse himself as he might, it was of no use. 'You have not stood the trial and can stay here no longer. Go forth into the world, there you will learn what poverty is. But as you have not a bad heart, and as I mean well by you, there is one thing I will grant you; if you fall into any difficulty, come to the forest and cry: "Iron Hans," and then I will come and help you. My power is great, greater than you think, and I have gold and silver in abundance.'

Then the king's son left the forest, and walked by beaten and unbeaten paths ever onwards until at length he reached a great city. There he looked for work, but could find none, and he learnt nothing by which he could help himself. At length he went to the palace, and asked if they would take him in. The people about court did not at all know what use they could make of him, but they liked him, and told him to stay. At length the cook took him into his service, and said he might carry wood and water, and rake the cinders together. Once when it so happened that no one else was at hand, the cook ordered him to carry the food to the royal table, but as he did not like to let his golden hair be seen, he kept his little cap on. Such a thing as that had never yet come under the king's notice, and he said: 'When you come to the royal table you must take your hat off.' He answered: 'Ah, Lord, I cannot; I have a bad sore place on my head.' Then the king had the cook called before him and scolded him, and asked how he could take such a boy as that into his service; and that he was to send him away at once. The cook, however, had pity on him, and exchanged him for the gardener's boy.

And now the boy had to plant and water the garden, hoe and dig, and bear the wind and bad weather. Once in summer when he was working alone in the garden, the day was so warm he took his little cap off that the air might cool him. As the sun shone on his hair it glittered and flashed so that the rays fell into the bedroom of the king's daughter, and up she sprang to see what that could be. Then she saw the boy, and cried to him: 'Boy, bring me a wreath of flowers.' He put his cap on with all haste, and gathered wild field-flowers and bound them together. When he was ascending the stairs with them, the gardener met him, and said: 'How can you take the king's daughter a garland of such common flowers? Go quickly, and get another, and seek out the prettiest and rarest.' 'Oh, no,' replied the boy, 'the wild ones have more scent, and will please her better.' When he got into the room, the king's daughter said: 'Take your cap off, it is not seemly to keep it on in my presence.' He again said: 'I may not, I have a sore head.' She, however, caught at his cap and pulled it off, and then his golden hair rolled down on his shoulders, and it was splendid to behold. He wanted to run out, but she held him by the arm, and gave him a handful of ducats. With these he departed, but he cared nothing for the gold pieces. He took them to the gardener, and said: 'I present them to your children, they can play with them.' The following day the king's daughter again called to him that he was to bring her a wreath of field-flowers, and then he went in with it, she instantly snatched at his cap, and wanted to take it away from him, but he held it fast with both hands. She again gave him a handful of ducats, but he would not keep them, and gave them to the gardener for playthings for his children. On the third day things went just the same; she could not get his cap away from him, and he would not have her money.

Not long afterwards, the country was overrun by war. The king gathered together his people, and did not know whether or not he could offer any opposition to the enemy, who was superior in strength and had a mighty army. Then said the gardener's boy: 'I am grown up, and will go to the wars also, only give me a horse.' The others laughed, and said: 'Seek one for yourself when we are gone, we will leave one behind us in the stable for you.' When they had gone forth, he went into the stable, and led the horse out; it was lame of one foot, and limped hobblety jib, hobblety jib; nevertheless he mounted it, and rode away to the dark forest. When he came to the outskirts, he called 'Iron Hans' three times so loudly that it echoed through the trees. Thereupon the wild man appeared immediately, and said: 'What do you desire?' 'I want a strong steed, for I am going to the wars.' 'That you shall have, and still more than you ask for.' Then the wild man went back into the forest, and it was not long before a stable-boy came out of it, who led a horse that snorted with its nostrils, and could hardly be restrained, and behind them followed a great troop of warriors entirely equipped in iron, and their swords flashed in the sun. The youth made over his three-legged horse to the stable-boy, mounted the other, and rode at the head of the soldiers. When he got near the battlefield a great part of the king's men had already fallen, and little was wanting to make the rest give way. Then the youth galloped thither with his iron soldiers, broke like a hurricane over the enemy, and beat down all who opposed him. They began to flee, but the youth pursued, and never stopped, until there was not a single man left. Instead of returning to the king, however, he conducted his troop by byways back to the forest, and called forth Iron Hans. 'What do you desire?' asked the wild man. 'Take back your horse and your troops, and give me my three-legged horse again.' All that he asked was done, and soon he was riding on his three-legged horse. When the king returned to his palace, his daughter went to meet him, and wished him joy of his victory. 'I am not the one who carried away the victory,' said he, 'but a strange knight who came to my assistance with his soldiers.' The daughter wanted to hear who the strange knight was, but the king did not know, and said: 'He followed the enemy, and I did not see him again.' She inquired of the gardener where his boy was, but he smiled, and said: 'He has just come home on his three-legged horse, and the others have been mocking him, and crying: "Here comes our hobblety jib back again!" They asked, too: "Under what hedge have you been lying sleeping all the time?" So he said: "I did the best of all, and it would have gone badly without me." And then he was still more ridiculed.'

The king said to his daughter: 'I will proclaim a great feast that shall last for three days, and you shall throw a golden apple. Perhaps the unknown man will show himself.' When the feast was announced, the youth went out to the forest, and called Iron Hans. 'What do you desire?' asked he. 'That I may catch the king's daughter's golden apple.' 'It is as safe as if you had it already,' said Iron Hans. 'You shall likewise have a suit of red armour for the occasion, and ride on a spirited chestnut-horse.' When the day came, the youth galloped to the spot, took his place amongst the knights, and was recognized by no one. The king's daughter came forward, and threw a golden apple to the knights, but none of them caught it but he, only as soon as he had it he galloped away.

On the second day Iron Hans equipped him as a white knight, and gave him a white horse. Again he was the only one who caught the apple, and he did not linger an instant, but galloped off with it. The king grew angry, and said: 'That is not allowed; he must appear before me and tell his name.' He gave the order that if the knight who caught the apple, should go away again they should pursue him, and if he would not come back willingly, they were to cut him down and stab him.

On the third day, he received from Iron Hans a suit of black armour and a black horse, and again he caught the apple. But when he was riding off with it, the king's attendants pursued him, and one of them got so near him that he wounded the youth's leg with the point of his sword. The youth nevertheless escaped from them, but his horse leapt so violently that the helmet fell from the youth's head, and they could see that he had golden hair. They rode back and announced this to the king.

The following day the king's daughter asked the gardener about his boy. 'He is at work in the garden; the queer creature has been at the festival too, and only came home yesterday evening; he has likewise shown my children three golden apples which he has won.'

The king had him summoned into his presence, and he came and again had his little cap on his head. But the king's daughter went up to him and took it off, and then his golden hair fell down over his shoulders, and he was so handsome that all were amazed. 'Are you the knight who came every day to the festival, always in different colours, and who caught the three golden apples?' asked the king. 'Yes,' answered he, 'and here the apples are,' and he took them out of his pocket, and returned them to the king. 'If you desire further proof, you may see the wound which your people gave me when they followed me. But I am likewise the knight who helped you to your victory over your enemies.' 'If you can perform such deeds as that, you are no gardener's boy; tell me, who is your father?' 'My father is a mighty king, and gold have I in plenty as great as I require.' 'I well see,' said the king, 'that I owe my thanks to you; can I do anything to please you?' 'Yes,' answered he, 'that indeed you can. Give me your daughter to wife.' The maiden laughed, and said: 'He does not stand much on ceremony, but I have already seen by his golden hair that he was no gardener's boy,' and then she went and kissed him. His father and mother came to the wedding, and were in great delight, for they had given up all hope of ever seeing their dear son again. And as they were sitting at the marriage-feast, the music suddenly stopped, the doors opened, and a stately king came in with a great retinue. He went up to the youth, embraced him and said: 'I am Iron Hans, and was by enchantment a wild man, but you have set me free; all the treasures which I possess, shall be your property.'

CAT-SKIN

There was once a king, whose queen had hair of the purest gold, and was so beautiful that her match was not to be met with on the whole face of the earth. But this beautiful queen fell ill, and when she felt that her end drew near she called the king to her and said, 'Promise me that you will never marry again, unless you meet with a wife who is as beautiful as I am, and who has golden hair like mine.' Then when the king in his grief promised all she asked, she shut her eyes and died. But the king was not to be comforted, and for a long time never thought of taking another wife. At last, however, his wise men said, 'this will not do; the king must marry again, that we may have a queen.' So messengers were sent far and wide, to seek for a bride as beautiful as the late queen. But there was no princess in the world so beautiful; and if there had been, still there was not one to be found who had golden hair. So the messengers came home, and had had all their trouble for nothing.

Now the king had a daughter, who was just as beautiful as her mother, and had the same golden hair. And when she was grown up, the king looked at her and saw that she was just like this late queen: then he said to his courtiers, 'May I not marry my daughter? She is the very image of my dead wife: unless I have her, I shall not find any bride upon the whole earth, and you say there must be a queen.' When the courtiers heard this they were shocked, and said, 'Heaven forbid that a father should marry his daughter! Out of so great a sin no good can come.' And his daughter was also shocked, but hoped the king would soon give up such thoughts; so she said to him, 'Before I marry anyone I must have three dresses: one must be of gold, like the sun; another must be of shining silver, like the moon; and a third must be dazzling as the stars: besides this, I want a mantle of a thousand different kinds of fur put together, to which every beast in the kingdom must give a part of his skin.' And thus she though he would think of the matter no more. But the king made the most skilful workmen in his kingdom weave the three dresses: one golden, like the sun; another silvery, like the moon; and a third sparkling, like the stars: and his hunters were told to hunt out all the beasts in his kingdom, and to take the finest fur out of their skins: and thus a mantle of a thousand furs was made.

When all were ready, the king sent them to her; but she got up in the night when all were asleep, and took three of her trinkets, a golden ring, a golden necklace, and a golden brooch, and packed the three dresses—of the sun, the moon, and the stars—up in a nutshell, and wrapped herself up in the mantle made of all sorts of fur, and besmeared her face and hands with soot. Then she threw herself upon Heaven for help in her need, and went away, and journeyed on the whole night, till at last she came to a large wood. As she was very tired, she sat herself down in the hollow of a tree and soon fell asleep: and there she slept on till it was midday.

Now as the king to whom the wood belonged was hunting in it, his dogs came to the tree, and began to snuff about, and run round and round, and bark. 'Look sharp!' said the king to the huntsmen, 'and see what sort of game lies there.' And the huntsmen went up to the tree, and when they came back again said, 'In the hollow tree there lies a most wonderful beast, such as we never saw before; its skin seems to be of a thousand kinds of fur, but there it lies fast asleep.' 'See,' said the king, 'if you can catch it alive, and we will take it with us.' So the huntsmen took it up, and the maiden awoke and was greatly frightened, and said, 'I am a poor child that has neither father nor mother left; have pity on me and take me with you.' Then they said, 'Yes, Miss Cat-skin, you will do for the kitchen; you can sweep up the ashes, and do things of that sort.' So they put her into the coach, and took her home to the king's palace. Then they showed her a little corner under the staircase, where no light of day ever peeped in, and said, 'Cat-skin, you may lie and sleep there.' And she was sent into the kitchen, and made to fetch wood and water, to blow the fire, pluck the poultry, pick the herbs, sift the ashes, and do all the dirty work.

Thus Cat-skin lived for a long time very sorrowfully. 'Ah! pretty princess!' thought she, 'what will now become of thee?' But it happened one day that a feast was to be held in the king's castle, so she said to the cook, 'May I go up a little while and see what is going on? I will take care and stand behind the door.' And the cook said, 'Yes, you may go, but be back again in half an hour's time, to rake out the ashes.' Then she took her little lamp, and went into her cabin, and took off the fur skin, and washed the soot from off her face and hands, so that her beauty shone forth like the sun from behind the clouds. She next opened her nutshell, and brought out of it the dress that shone like the sun, and so went to the feast. Everyone made way for her, for nobody knew her, and they thought she could be no less than a king's daughter. But the king came up to her, and held out his hand and danced with her; and he thought in his heart, 'I never saw any one half so beautiful.'

When the dance was at an end she curtsied; and when the king looked round for her, she was gone, no one knew wither. The guards that stood at the castle gate were called in: but they had seen no one. The truth was, that she had run into her little cabin, pulled off her dress, blackened her face and hands, put on the fur-skin cloak, and was Cat-skin again. When she went into the kitchen to her work, and began to rake the ashes, the cook said, 'Let that alone till the morning, and heat the king's soup; I should like to run up now and give a peep: but take care you don't let a hair fall into it, or you will run a chance of never eating again.'

As soon as the cook went away, Cat-skin heated the king's soup, and toasted a slice of bread first, as nicely as ever she could; and when it was ready, she went and looked in the cabin for her little golden ring, and put it into the dish in which the soup was. When the dance was over, the king ordered his soup to be brought in; and it pleased him so well, that he thought he had never tasted any so good before. At the bottom he saw a gold ring lying; and as he could not make out how it had got there, he ordered the cook to be sent for. The cook was frightened when he heard the order, and said to Cat-skin, 'You must have let a hair fall into the soup; if it be so, you will have a good beating.' Then he went before the king, and he asked him who had cooked the soup. 'I did,' answered the cook. But the king said, 'That is not true; it was better done than you could do it.' Then he answered, 'To tell the truth I did not cook it, but Cat-skin did.' 'Then let Cat-skin come up,' said the king: and when she came he said to her, 'Who are you?' 'I am a poor child,' said she, 'that has lost both father and mother.' 'How came you in my palace?' asked he. 'I am good for nothing,' said she, 'but to be scullion-girl, and to have boots and shoes thrown at my head.' 'But how did you get the ring that was in the soup?' asked the king. Then she would not own that she knew anything about the ring; so the king sent her away again about her business.

After a time there was another feast, and Cat-skin asked the cook to let her go up and see it as before. 'Yes,' said he, 'but come again in half an hour, and cook the king the soup that he likes so much.' Then she ran to her little cabin, washed herself quickly, and took her dress out which was silvery as the moon, and put it on; and when she went in, looking like a king's daughter, the king went up to her, and rejoiced at seeing her again, and when the dance began he danced with her. After the dance was at an end she managed to slip out, so slyly that the king did not see where she was gone; but she sprang into her little cabin, and made herself into Cat-skin again, and went into the kitchen to cook the soup. Whilst the cook was above stairs, she got the golden necklace and dropped it into the soup; then it was brought to the king, who ate it, and it pleased him as well as before; so he sent for the cook, who was again forced to tell him that Cat-skin had cooked it. Cat-skin was brought again before the king, but she still told him that she was only fit to have boots and shoes thrown at her head.

But when the king had ordered a feast to be got ready for the third time, it happened just the same as before. 'You must be a witch, Cat-skin,' said the cook; 'for you always put something into your soup, so that it pleases the king better than mine.' However, he let her go up as before. Then she put on her dress which sparkled like the stars, and went into the ball-room in it; and the king danced with her again, and thought she had never looked so beautiful as she did then. So whilst he was dancing with her, he put a gold ring on her finger without her seeing it, and ordered that the dance should be kept up a long time. When it was at an end, he would have held her fast by the hand, but she slipped away, and sprang so quickly through the crowd that he lost sight of her: and she ran as fast as she could into her little cabin under the stairs. But this time she kept away too long, and stayed beyond the half-hour; so she had not time to take off her fine dress, and threw her fur mantle over it, and in her haste did not blacken herself all over with soot, but left one of her fingers white.

Then she ran into the kitchen, and cooked the king's soup; and as soon as the cook was gone, she put the golden brooch into the dish. When the king got to the bottom, he ordered Cat-skin to be called once more, and soon saw the white finger, and the ring that he had put on it whilst they were dancing: so he seized her hand, and kept fast hold of it, and when she wanted to loose herself and spring away, the fur cloak fell off a little on one side, and the starry dress sparkled underneath it. Then he got hold of the fur and tore it off, and her golden hair and beautiful form were seen, and she could no longer hide herself: so she washed the soot and ashes from her face, and showed herself to be the most beautiful princess upon the face of the earth. But the king said, 'You are my beloved bride, and we will never more be parted from each other.' And the wedding feast was held, and a merry day it was, as ever was heard of or seen in that country, or indeed in any other.

SNOW-WHITE AND
ROSE-RED

There was once a poor widow who lived in a lonely cottage. In front of the cottage was a garden wherein stood two rose-trees, one of which bore white and the other red roses. She had two children who were like the two rose-trees, and one was called Snow-white, and the other Rose-red. They were as good and happy, as busy and cheerful as ever two children in the world were, only Snow-white was more quiet and gentle than Rose-red. Rose-red liked better to run about in the meadows and fields seeking flowers and catching butterflies; but Snow-white sat at home with her mother, and helped her with her housework, or read to her when there was nothing to do.

The two children were so fond of one another that they always held each other by the hand when they went out together, and when Snow-white said: 'We will not leave each other,' Rose-red answered: 'Never so long as we live,' and their mother would add: 'What one has she must share with the other.'

They often ran about the forest alone and gathered red berries, and no beasts did them any harm, but came close to them trustfully. The little hare would eat a cabbage-leaf out of their hands, the roe grazed by their side, the stag leapt merrily by them, and the birds sat still upon the boughs, and sang whatever they knew.

No mishap overtook them; if they had stayed too late in the forest, and night came on, they laid themselves down near one another upon the moss, and slept until morning came, and their mother knew this and did not worry on their account.

Once when they had spent the night in the wood and the dawn had roused them, they saw a beautiful child in a shining white dress sitting near their bed. He got up and looked quite kindly at them, but said nothing and went into the forest. And when they looked round they found that they had been sleeping quite close to a precipice, and would certainly have fallen into it in the darkness if they had gone only a few paces further. And their mother told them that it must have been the angel who watches over good children.

Snow-white and Rose-red kept their mother's little cottage so neat that it was a pleasure to look inside it. In the summer Rose-red took care of the house, and every morning laid a wreath of flowers by her mother's bed before she awoke, in which was a rose from each tree. In the winter Snow-white lit the fire and hung the kettle on the hob. The kettle was of brass and shone like gold, so brightly was it polished. In the evening, when the snowflakes fell, the mother said: 'Go, Snow-white, and bolt the door,' and then they sat round the hearth, and the mother took her spectacles and read aloud out of a large book, and the two girls listened as they sat and spun. And close by them lay a lamb upon the floor, and behind them upon a perch sat a white dove with its head hidden beneath its wings.

One evening, as they were thus sitting comfortably together, someone knocked at the door as if he wished to be let in. The mother said: 'Quick, Rose-red, open the door, it must be a traveller who is seeking shelter.' Rose-red went and pushed back the bolt, thinking that it was a poor man, but it was not; it was a bear that stretched his broad, black head within the door.

Rose-red screamed and sprang back, the lamb bleated, the dove fluttered, and Snow-white hid herself behind her mother's bed. But the bear began to speak and said: 'Do not be afraid, I will do you no harm! I am half-frozen, and only want to warm myself a little beside you.'

'Poor bear,' said the mother, 'lie down by the fire, only take care that you do not burn your coat.' Then she cried: 'Snow-white, Rose-red, come out, the bear will do you no harm, he means well.' So they both came out, and by-and-by the lamb and dove came nearer, and were not afraid of him. The bear said: 'Here, children, knock the snow out of my coat a little'; so they brought the broom and swept the bear's hide clean; and he stretched himself by the fire and growled contentedly and comfortably. It was not long before they grew quite at home, and played tricks with their clumsy guest. They tugged his hair with their hands, put their feet upon his back and rolled him about, or they took a hazel-switch and beat him, and when he growled they laughed. But the bear took it all in good part, only when they were too rough he called out: 'Leave me alive, children,

> *'Snow-white, Rose-red,*
> *Will you beat your wooer dead?'*

When it was bed-time, and the others went to bed, the mother said to the bear: 'You can lie there by the hearth, and then you will be safe from the cold and the bad weather.' As soon as day dawned the two children let him out, and he trotted across the snow into the forest.

Henceforth the bear came every evening at the same time, laid himself down by the hearth, and let the children amuse themselves with him as much as they liked; and they got so used to him that the doors were never fastened until their black friend had arrived.

When spring had come and all outside was green, the bear said one morning to Snow-white: 'Now I must go away, and cannot come back for the whole summer.' 'Where are you going, then, dear bear?' asked Snow-white. 'I must go into the forest and guard my treasures from the wicked dwarfs. In the winter, when the earth is frozen hard, they are obliged to stay below and cannot work their way through; but now, when the sun has thawed and warmed the earth, they break through it, and come out to pry and steal; and what once gets into their hands, and in their caves, does not easily see daylight again.'

Snow-white was quite sorry at his departure, and as she unbolted the door for him, and the bear was hurrying out, he caught against the bolt and a piece of his hairy coat was torn off, and it seemed to Snow-white as if she had seen gold shining through it, but she was not sure about it. The bear ran away quickly, and was soon out of sight behind the trees.

A short time afterwards the mother sent her children into the forest to get firewood. There they found a big tree which lay felled on the ground, and close by the trunk something was jumping backwards and forwards in the grass, but they could not make out what it was. When they came nearer they saw a dwarf with an old withered face and a snow-white beard a yard long. The end of the beard was caught in a crevice of the tree, and the little fellow was jumping about like a dog tied to a rope, and did not know what to do.

He glared at the girls with his fiery red eyes and cried: 'Why do you stand there? Can you not come here and help me?' 'What are you up to, little man?' asked Rose-red. 'You stupid, prying goose!' answered the dwarf: 'I was going to split the tree to get a little wood for cooking. The little bit of food that we people get is immediately burnt up with heavy logs; we do not swallow so much as you coarse, greedy folk. I had just driven the wedge safely in, and everything was going as I wished; but the cursed wedge was too smooth and suddenly sprang out, and the tree closed so quickly that I could not pull out my beautiful white beard; so now it is tight and I cannot get away, and the silly, sleek, milk-faced things laugh! Ugh! how odious you are!'

The children tried very hard, but they could not pull the beard out, it was caught too fast. 'I will run and fetch someone,' said Rose-red. 'You senseless goose!' snarled the dwarf; 'why should you fetch someone? You are already two too many for me; can you not think of something better?' 'Don't be impatient,' said Snow-white, 'I will help you,' and she pulled her scissors out of her pocket, and cut off the end of the beard.

As soon as the dwarf felt himself free he laid hold of a bag which lay amongst the roots of the tree, and which was full of gold, and lifted it up, grumbling to himself: 'Uncouth people, to cut off a piece of my fine beard. Bad luck to you!' and then he swung the bag upon his back, and went off without even once looking at the children.

Some time afterwards Snow-white and Rose-red went to catch a dish of fish. As they came near the brook they saw something like a large grasshopper jumping towards the water, as if it were going to leap in. They ran to it and found it was the dwarf. 'Where are you going?' said Rose-red; 'you surely don't want to go into the water?' 'I am not such a fool!' cried the dwarf; 'don't you see that the accursed fish wants to pull me in?' The little man had been sitting there fishing, and unluckily the wind had tangled up his beard with the fishing-line; a moment later a big fish made a bite and the feeble creature had not strength to pull it out; the fish kept the upper hand and pulled the dwarf towards him. He held on to all the reeds and rushes, but it was of little good, for he was forced to follow the movements of the fish, and was in urgent danger of being dragged into the water.

The girls came just in time; they held him fast and tried to free his beard from the line, but all in vain, beard and line were entangled fast together. There was nothing to do but to bring out the scissors and cut the beard, whereby a small part of it was lost. When the dwarf saw that he screamed out: 'Is that civil, you toadstool, to disfigure a man's face? Was it not enough to clip off the end of my beard? Now you have cut off the best part of it. I cannot let myself be seen by my people. I wish you had been made to run the soles off your shoes!' Then he took out a sack of pearls which lay in the rushes, and without another word he dragged it away and disappeared behind a stone.

It happened that soon afterwards the mother sent the two children to the town to buy needles and thread, and laces and ribbons. The road led them across a heath upon which huge pieces of rock lay strewn about. There they noticed a large bird hovering in the air, flying slowly round and round above them; it sank lower and lower, and at last settled near a rock not far away. Immediately they heard a loud, piteous cry. They ran up and saw with horror that the eagle had seized their old acquaintance the dwarf, and was going to carry him off.

The children, full of pity, at once took tight hold of the little man, and pulled against the eagle so long that at last he let his booty go. As soon as the dwarf had recovered from his first fright he cried with his shrill voice: 'Could you not have done it more carefully! You dragged at my brown coat so that it is all torn and full of holes, you clumsy creatures!' Then he took up a sack full of precious stones, and slipped away again under the rock into his hole. The girls, who by this time were used to his ingratitude, went on their way and did their business in town.

As they crossed the heath again on their way home they

surprised the dwarf, who had emptied out his bag of precious stones in a clean spot, and had not thought that anyone would come there so late. The evening sun shone upon the brilliant stones; they glittered and sparkled with all colours so beautifully that the children stood still and stared at them. 'Why do you stand gaping there?' cried the dwarf, and his ashen-grey face became copper-red with rage. He was still cursing when a loud growling was heard, and a black bear came trotting towards them out of the forest. The dwarf sprang up in a fright, but he could not reach his cave, for the bear was already close. Then in the dread of his heart he cried: 'Dear Mr Bear, spare me, I will give you all my treasures; look, the beautiful jewels lying there! Grant me my life; what do you want with such a slender little fellow as I? you would not feel me between your teeth. Come, take these two wicked girls, they are tender morsels for you, fat as young quails; for mercy's sake eat them!' The bear took no heed of his words, but gave the wicked creature a single blow with his paw, and he did not move again.

The girls had run away, but the bear called to them: 'Snow-white and Rose-red, do not be afraid; wait, I will come with you.' Then they recognized his voice and waited, and when he came up to them suddenly his bearskin fell off, and he stood there a handsome man, clothed all in gold. 'I am a king's son,' he said, 'and I was bewitched by that wicked dwarf, who had stolen my treasures; I have had to run about the forest as a savage bear until I was freed by his death. Now he has got his well-deserved punishment.

Snow-white was married to him, and Rose-red to his brother, and they divided between them the great treasure which the dwarf had gathered together in his cave. The old mother lived peacefully and happily with her children for many years. She took the two rose-trees with her, and they stood before her window, and every year bore the most beautiful roses, white and red.

Classic Literature: Words and Phrases
adapted from the **Collins English Dictionary**

Accoucheur NOUN a male midwife or doctor ❏ *I think my sister must have had some general idea that I was a young offender whom an Accoucheur Policemen had taken up (on my birthday) and delivered over to her* (*Great Expectations* by Charles Dickens)

addled ADJ confused and unable to think properly ❏ *But she counted and counted till she got that addled* (*The Adventures of Huckleberry Finn* by Mark Twain)

admiration NOUN amazement or wonder ❏ *lifting up his hands and eyes by way of admiration* (*Gulliver's Travels* by Jonathan Swift)

afeard ADJ afeard means afraid ❏ *shake it – and don't be afeard* (*The Adventures of Huckleberry Finn* by Mark Twain)

affected VERB affected means followed ❏ *Hadst thou affected sweet divinity* (*Doctor Faustus 5.2* by Christopher Marlowe)

aground ADV when a boat runs aground, it touches the ground in a shallow part of the water and gets stuck ❏ *what kep' you? – boat get aground?* (*The Adventures of Huckleberry Finn* by Mark Twain)

ague NOUN a fever in which the patient has alternate hot and cold shivering fits ❏ *his exposure to the wet and cold had brought on fever and ague* (*Oliver Twist* by Charles Dickens)

alchemy ADJ false or worthless ❏ *all wealth alchemy* (*The Sun Rising* by John Donne)

all alike PHRASE the same all the time ❏ *Love, all alike* (*The Sun Rising* by John Donne)

alow and aloft PHRASE alow means in the lower part or bottom, and aloft means on the top, so alow and aloft means on the top and in the bottom or throughout ❏ *Someone's turned the chest out alow and aloft* (*Treasure Island* by Robert Louis Stevenson)

ambuscade NOUN ambuscade is not a proper word. Tom means an ambush, which is when a group of people attack their enemies, after hiding and waiting for them ❏ *and so we would lie in ambuscade, as he called it* (*The Adventures of Huckleberry Finn* by Mark Twain)

amiable ADJ likeable or pleasant ❏ *Such amiable qualities must speak for themselves* (*Pride and Prejudice* by Jane Austen)

amulet NOUN an amulet is a charm thought to drive away evil spirits. ❏ *uttered phrases at once occult and familiar, like the amulet worn on the heart* (*Silas Marner* by George Eliot)

amusement NOUN here amusement means a strange and disturbing puzzle ❏ *this was an amusement the other way* (*Robinson Crusoe* by Daniel Defoe)

ancient NOUN an ancient was the flag displayed on a ship to show which country it belongs to. It is also called the ensign ❏ *her ancient and pendants out* (*Robinson Crusoe* by Daniel Defoe)

antic ADJ here antic means horrible or grotesque ❏ *armed and dressed after a very antic manner* (*Gulliver's Travels* by Jonathan Swift)

antics NOUN antics is an old word meaning clowns, or people who do silly things to make other people laugh ❏ *And point like antics at his triple crown* (*Doctor Faustus 3.2* by Christopher Marlowe)

appanage NOUN an appanage is a living allowance ❑ *As if loveliness were not the special prerogative of woman – her legitimate appanage and heritage! (Jane Eyre* by Charlotte Brontë)

appended VERB appended means attached or added to ❑ *and these words appended (Treasure Island* by Robert Louis Stevenson)

approver NOUN an approver is someone who gives evidence against someone he used to work with ❑ *Mr. Noah Claypole: receiving a free pardon from the Crown in consequence of being admitted approver against Fagin (Oliver Twist* by Charles Dickens)

areas NOUN the areas is the space, below street level, in front of the basement of a house ❑ *The Dodger had a vicious propensity, too, of pulling the caps from the heads of small boys and tossing them down areas (Oliver Twist* by Charles Dickens)

argument NOUN theme or important idea or subject which runs through a piece of writing ❑ *Thrice needful to the argument which now (The Prelude* by William Wordsworth) .

artificially ADJ artfully or cleverly ❑ *and he with a sharp flint sharpened very artificially (Gulliver's Travels* by Jonathan Swift)

artist NOUN here artist means a skilled workman ❑ *This man was a most ingenious artist (Gulliver's Travels* by Jonathan Swift)

assizes NOUN assizes were regular court sessions which a visiting judge was in charge of ❑ *you shall hang at the next assizes (Treasure Island* by Robert Louis Stevenson)

attraction NOUN gravitation, or Newton's theory of gravitation ❑ *he predicted the same fate to attraction (Gulliver's Travels* by Jonathan Swift)

aver VERB to aver is to claim something strongly ❑ *for Jem Rodney,*

the mole catcher, averred that one evening as he was returning homeward (Silas Marner by George Eliot)

baby NOUN here baby means doll, which is a child's toy that looks like a small person ❑ *and skilful dressing her baby (Gulliver's Travels* by Jonathan Swift)

bagatelle NOUN bagatelle is a game rather like billiards and pool ❑ *Breakfast had been ordered at a pleasant little tavern, a mile or so away upon the rising ground beyond the green; and there was a bagatelle board in the room, in case we should desire to unbend our minds after the solemnity. (Great Expectations* by Charles Dickens)

bah EXCLAM Bah is an exclamation of frustration or anger ❑ *"Bah," said Scrooge. (A Christmas Carol* by Charles Dickens)

bairn NOUN a northern word for child ❑ *Who has taught you those fine words, my bairn? (Wuthering Heights* by Emily Brontë)

bait VERB to bait means to stop on a journey to take refreshment ❑ *So, when they stopped to bait the horse, and ate and drank and enjoyed themselves, I could touch nothing that they touched, but kept my fast unbroken. (David Copperfield* by Charles Dickens)

balustrade NOUN a balustrade is a row of vertical columns that form railings ❑ *but I mean to say you might have got a hearse up that staircase, and taken it broadwise, with the splinter-bar towards the wall, and the door towards the balustrades: and done it easy (A Christmas Carol* by Charles Dickens)

bandbox NOUN a large lightweight box for carrying bonnets or hats ❑ *I am glad I bought my bonnet, if it is only for the fun of having another bandbox (Pride and Prejudice* by Jane Austen)

barren NOUN a barren here is a stretch or expanse of barren land ❑ *a line* *of upright stones, continued the length of the barren* (*Wuthering Heights* by Emily Brontë)

basin NOUN a basin was a cup without a handle ❑ *who is drinking his tea out of a basin* (*Wuthering Heights* by Emily Brontë)

battalia NOUN the order of battle ❑ *till I saw part of his army in battalia* (*Gulliver's Travels* by Jonathan Swift)

battery NOUN a Battery is a fort or a place where guns are positioned ❑ *You bring the lot to me, at that old Battery over yonder* (*Great Expectations* by Charles Dickens)

battledore and shuttlecock NOUN The game battledore and shuttlecock was an early version of the game now known as badminton. The aim of the early game was simply to keep the shuttlecock from hitting the ground. ❑ *Battledore and shuttlecock's a wery good game vhen you an't the shuttlecock and two lawyers the battledores, in which case it gets too excitin' to be pleasant* (*Pickwick Papers* by Charles Dickens)

beadle NOUN a beadle was a local official who had power over the poor ❑ *But these impertinences were speedily checked by the evidence of the surgeon, and the testimony of the beadle* (*Oliver Twist* by Charles Dickens)

bearings NOUN the bearings of a place are the measurements or directions that are used to find or locate it ❑ *the bearings of the island* (*Treasure Island* by Robert Louis Stevenson)

beaufet NOUN a beaufet was a sideboard ❑ *and sweet-cake from the beaufet* (*Emma* by Jane Austen)

beck NOUN a beck is a small stream ❑ *a beck which follows the bend of the glen* (*Wuthering Heights* by Emily Brontë)

bedight VERB decorated ❑ *and bedight with Christmas holly stuck into the top.* (*A Christmas Carol* by Charles Dickens)

Bedlam NOUN Bedlam was a lunatic asylum in London which had statues carved by Caius Gabriel Cibber at its entrance ❑ *Bedlam, and those carved maniacs at the gates* (*The Prelude* by William Wordsworth)

beeves NOUN oxen or castrated bulls which are animals used for pulling vehicles or carrying things ❑ *to deliver in every morning six beeves* (*Gulliver's Travels* by Jonathan Swift)

begot VERB created or caused ❑ *Begot in thee* (*On His Mistress* by John Donne)

behoof NOUN behoof means benefit ❑ *"Yes, young man," said he, releasing the handle of the article in question, retiring a step or two from my table, and speaking for the behoof of the landlord and waiter at the door* (*Great Expectations* by Charles Dickens)

berth NOUN a berth is a bed on a boat ❑ *this is the berth for me* (*Treasure Island* by Robert Louis Stevenson)

bevers NOUN a bever was a snack, or small portion of food, eaten between main meals ❑ *that buys me thirty meals a day and ten bevers* (*Doctor Faustus 2.1* by Christopher Marlowe)

bilge water NOUN the bilge is the widest part of a ship's bottom, and the bilge water is the dirty water that collects there ❑ *no gush of bilge-water had turned it to fetid puddle* (*Jane Eyre* by Charlotte Brontë)

bills NOUN bills is an old term meaning prescription. A prescription is the piece of paper on which your doctor writes an order for medicine and which you give to a chemist to get the medicine ❑ *Are not thy bills hung up as monuments* (*Doctor Faustus 1.1* by Christopher Marlowe)

black cap NOUN a judge wore a black cap when he was about to sentence a prisoner to death ❑ *The judge* assumed the black cap, and the prisoner still stood with the same air and gesture. (*Oliver Twist* by Charles Dickens)

black gentleman NOUN this was another word for the devil ❑ *for she is as impatient as the black gentleman* (*Emma* by Jane Austen)

boot-jack NOUN a wooden device to help take boots off ❑ *The speaker appeared to throw a boot-jack, or some such article, at the person he addressed* (*Oliver Twist* by Charles Dickens)

booty NOUN booty means treasure or prizes ❑ *would be inclined to give up their booty in payment of the dead man's debts* (*Treasure Island* by Robert Louis Stevenson)

Bow Street runner PHRASE Bow Street runners were the first British police force, set up by the author Henry Fielding in the eighteenth century ❑ *as would have convinced a judge or a Bow Street runner* (*Treasure Island* by Robert Louis Stevenson)

brawn NOUN brawn is a dish of meat which is set in jelly ❑ *Heaped up upon the floor, to form a kind of throne, were turkeys, geese, game, poultry, brawn, great joints of meat, sucking-pigs* (*A Christmas Carol* by Charles Dickens)

bray VERB when a donkey brays, it makes a loud, harsh sound ❑ *and she doesn't bray like a jackass* (*The Adventures of Huckleberry Finn* by Mark Twain)

break VERB in order to train a horse you first have to break it ❑*"If a high-mettled creature like this," said he, "can't be broken by fair means, she will never be good for anything"* (*Black Beauty* by Anna Sewell)

bullyragging VERB bullyragging is an old word which means bullying. To bullyrag someone is to threaten or force someone to do something they don't want to do ❑ *and a lot of loafers bullyragging him for sport* (*The Adventures of Huckleberry Finn* by Mark Twain)

but PREP except for (this) ❑ *but this, all pleasures fancies be* (*The Good-Morrow* by John Donne)

by hand PHRASE by hand was a common expression of the time meaning that baby had been fed either using a spoon or a bottle rather than by breast-feeding ❑ *My sister, Mrs. Joe Gargery, was more than twenty years older than I, and had established a great reputation with herself . . . because she had bought me up 'by hand'* (*Great Expectations* by Charles Dickens)

bye-spots NOUN bye-spots are lonely places ❑ *and bye-spots of tales rich with indigenous produce* (*The Prelude* by William Wordsworth)

calico NOUN calico is plain white fabric made from cotton ❑ *There was two old dirty calico dresses* (*The Adventures of Huckleberry Finn* by Mark Twain)

camp-fever NOUN camp-fever was another word for the disease typhus ❑ *during a severe camp-fever* (*Emma* by Jane Austen)

cant NOUN cant is insincere or empty talk ❑ *"Man," said the Ghost, "if man you be in heart, not adamant, forbear that wicked cant until you have discovered What the surplus is, and Where it is."* (*A Christmas Carol* by Charles Dickens)

canty ADJ canty means lively, full of life ❑ *My mother lived til eighty, a canty dame to the last* (*Wuthering Heights* by Emily Brontë)

canvas VERB to canvas is to discuss ❑ *We think so very differently on this point Mr Knightley, that there can be no use in canvassing it* (*Emma* by Jane Austen)

capital ADJ capital means excellent or extremely good ❑ *for it's capital, so shady, light, and big* (*Little Women* by Louisa May Alcott)

capstan NOUN a capstan is a device used on a ship to lift sails and anchors ❑ *capstans going, ships going out to sea, and unintelligible sea creatures* roaring curses over the bulwarks at respondent lightermen (*Great Expectations* by Charles Dickens)

case-bottle NOUN a square bottle designed to fit with others into a case ❑ *The spirit being set before him in a huge case-bottle, which had originally come out of some ship's locker* (*The Old Curiosity Shop* by Charles Dickens)

casement NOUN casement is a word meaning window. The teacher in Nicholas Nickleby misspells window showing what a bad teacher he is ❑ *W-i-n, win, d-e-r, der, winder, a casement.'* (*Nicholas Nickleby* by Charles Dickens)

cataleptic ADJ a cataleptic fit is one in which the victim goes into a trance-like state and remains still for a long time ❑ *It was at this point in their history that Silas's cataleptic fit occurred during the prayer-meeting* (*Silas Marner* by George Eliot)

cauldron NOUN a cauldron is a large cooking pot made of metal ❑ *stirring a large cauldron which seemed to be full of soup* (*Alice's Adventures in Wonderland* by Lewis Carroll)

cephalic ADJ cephalic means to do with the head ❑ *with ink composed of a cephalic tincture* (*Gulliver's Travels* by Jonathan Swift)

chaise and four NOUN a closed four-wheel carriage pulled by four horses ❑ *he came down on Monday in a chaise and four to see the place* (*Pride and Prejudice* by Jane Austen)

chamberlain NOUN the main servant in a household ❑ *In those times a bed was always to be got there at any hour of the night, and the chamberlain, letting me in at his ready wicket, lighted the candle next in order on his shelf* (*Great Expectations* by Charles Dickens)

characters NOUN distinguishing marks ❑ *Impressed upon all forms the characters* (*The Prelude* by William Wordsworth)

chary ADJ cautious ❑ *I should have been chary of discussing my guardian too freely even with her* (*Great Expectations* by Charles Dickens)

cherishes VERB here cherishes means cheers or brightens ❑ *some philosophic song of Truth that cherishes our daily life* (*The Prelude* by William Wordsworth)

chickens' meat PHRASE chickens' meat is an old term which means chickens' feed or food ❑ *I had shook a bag of chickens' meat out in that place* (*Robinson Crusoe* by Daniel Defoe)

chimeras NOUN a chimera is an unrealistic idea or a wish which is unlikely to be fulfilled ❑ *with many other wild impossible chimeras* (*Gulliver's Travels* by Jonathan Swift)

chines NOUN chine is a cut of meat that includes part or all of the backbone of the animal ❑ *and they found hams and chines uncut* (*Silas Marner* by George Eliot)

chits NOUN chits is a slang word which means girls ❑ *I hate affected, niminy-piminy chits!* (*Little Women* by Louisa May Alcott)

chopped VERB chopped means come suddenly or accidentally ❑ *if I had chopped upon them* (*Robinson Crusoe* by Daniel Defoe)

chute NOUN a narrow channel ❑ *One morning about day-break, I found a canoe and crossed over a chute to the main shore* (*The Adventures of Huckleberry Finn* by Mark Twain)

circumspection NOUN careful observation of events and circumstances; caution ❑ *I honour your circumspection* (*Pride and Prejudice* by Jane Austen)

clambered VERB clambered means to climb somewhere with difficulty, usually using your hands and your feet ❑ *he clambered up and down stairs* (*Treasure Island* by Robert Louis Stevenson)

clime NOUN climate ❑ *no season knows nor clime* (*The Sun Rising* by John Donne)

clinched VERB clenched ❑ *the tops whereof I could but just reach with my fist clinched* (*Gulliver's Travels* by Jonathan Swift)

close chair NOUN a close chair is a sedan chair, which is an covered chair which has room for one person. The sedan chair is carried on two poles by two men, one in front and one behind ❑ *persuaded even the Empress herself to let me hold her in her close chair* (*Gulliver's Travels* by Jonathan Swift)

clown NOUN clown here means peasant or person who lives off the land ❑ *In ancient days by emperor and clown* (*Ode on a Nightingale* by John Keats)

coalheaver NOUN a coalheaver loaded coal onto ships using a spade ❑ *Good, strong, wholesome medicine, as was given with great success to two Irish labourers and a coalheaver* (*Oliver Twist* by Charles Dickens)

coal-whippers NOUN men who worked at docks using machines to load coal onto ships ❑ *here, were colliers by the score and score, with the coal-whippers plunging off stages on deck* (*Great Expectations* by Charles Dickens)

cobweb NOUN a cobweb is the net which a spider makes for catching insects ❑ *the walls and ceilings were all hung round with cobwebs* (*Gulliver's Travels* by Jonathan Swift)

coddling VERB coddling means to treat someone too kindly or protect them too much ❑ *and I've been coddling the fellow as if I'd been his grand-mother* (*Little Women* by Louisa May Alcott)

coil NOUN coil means noise or fuss or disturbance ❑ *What a coil is there?* (*Doctor Faustus 4.7* by Christopher Marlowe)

collared VERB to collar something is a slang term which means to capture.

In this sentence, it means he stole it [the money] ❑ *he collared it* (*The Adventures of Huckleberry Finn* by Mark Twain)

colling VERB colling is an old word which means to embrace and kiss ❑ *and no clasping and colling at all* (*Tess of the D'Urbervilles* by Thomas Hardy)

colloquies NOUN colloquy is a formal conversation or dialogue ❑ *Such colloquies have occupied many a pair of pale-faced weavers* (*Silas Marner* by George Eliot)

comfit NOUN sugar-covered pieces of fruit or nut eaten as sweets ❑ *and pulled out a box of comfits* (*Alice's Adventures in Wonderland* by Lewis Carroll)

coming out VERB when a girl came out in society it meant she was of marriageable age. In order to 'come out' girls were expecting to attend balls and other parties during a season ❑ *The younger girls formed hopes of coming out a year or two sooner than they might otherwise have done* (*Pride and Prejudice* by Jane Austen)

commit VERB commit means arrest or stop ❑ *Commit the rascals* (*Doctor Faustus 4.7* by Christopher Marlowe)

commodious ADJ commodious means convenient ❑ *the most commodious and effectual ways* (*Gulliver's Travels* by Jonathan Swift)

commons NOUN commons is an old term meaning food shared with others ❑ *his pauper assistants ranged themselves behind him; the gruel was served out; and a long grace was said over the short commons.* (*Oliver Twist* by Charles Dickens)

complacency NOUN here complacency means a desire to please others. Today complacency means feeling pleased with oneself without good reason. ❑ *Twas thy power that raised the first complacency in me* (*The Prelude* by William Wordsworth)

complaisance NOUN complaisance was eagerness to please ❑ *we cannot wonder at his complaisance* (*Pride and Prejudice* by Jane Austen)

complaisant ADJ complaisant means polite ❑ *extremely cheerful and complaisant to their guest* (*Gulliver's Travels* by Jonathan Swift)

conning VERB conning means learning by heart ❑ *Or conning more* (*The Prelude* by William Wordsworth)

consequent NOUN consequence ❑ *as avarice is the necessary consequent of old age* (*Gulliver's Travels* by Jonathan Swift)

consorts NOUN concerts ❑ *The King, who delighted in music, had frequent consorts at Court* (*Gulliver's Travels* by Jonathan Swift)

conversible ADJ conversible meant easy to talk to, companionable ❑ *He can be a conversible companion* (*Pride and Prejudice* by Jane Austen)

copper NOUN a copper is a large pot that can be heated directly over a fire ❑ *He gazed in stupefied astonishment on the small rebel for some seconds, and then clung for support to the copper* (*Oliver Twist* by Charles Dickens)

copper-stick NOUN a copper-stick is the long piece of wood used to stir washing in the copper (or boiler) which was usually the biggest cooking pot in the house ❑ *It was Christmas Eve, and I had to stir the pudding for next day, with a copper-stick, from seven to eight by the Dutch clock* (*Great Expectations* by Charles Dickens)

counting-house NOUN a counting house is a place where accountants work ❑ *Once upon a time – of all the good days in the year, on Christmas Eve – old Scrooge sat busy in his countinghouse* (*A Christmas Carol* by Charles Dickens)

courtier NOUN a courtier is someone who attends the king or queen – a member of the court ❑ *next the ten courtiers;* (*Alice's Adventures in Wonderland* by Lewis Carroll)

covies NOUN covies were flocks of partridges ❑ *and will save all of the best covies for you* (*Pride and Prejudice* by Jane Austen)

cowed VERB cowed means frightened or intimidated ❑ *it cowed me more than the pain* (*Treasure Island* by Robert Louis Stevenson)

cozened VERB cozened means tricked or deceived ❑ *Do you remember, sir, how you cozened me* (*Doctor Faustus* 4.7 by Christopher Marlowe)

cravats NOUN a cravat is a folded cloth that a man wears wrapped around his neck as a decorative item of clothing ❑ *we'd'a' slept in our cravats to-night* (*The Adventures of Huckleberry Finn* by Mark Twain)

crock and dirt PHRASE crock and dirt is an old expression meaning soot and dirt ❑ *and the mare catching cold at the door, and the boy grimed with crock and dirt* (*Great Expectations* by Charles Dickens)

crockery NOUN here crockery means pottery ❑ *By one of the parrots was a cat made of crockery* (*The Adventures of Huckleberry Finn* by Mark Twain)

crooked sixpence PHRASE it was considered unlucky to have a bent sixpence ❑ *You've got the beauty, you see, and I've got the luck, so you must keep me by you for your crooked sixpence* (*Silas Marner* by George Eliot)

croquet NOUN croquet is a traditional English summer game in which players try to hit wooden balls through hoops ❑ *and once she remembered trying to box her own ears for having cheated herself in a game of croquet* (*Alice's Adventures in Wonderland* by Lewis Carroll)

cross PREP across ❑ *The two great streets, which run cross and divide it into four quarters* (*Gulliver's Travels* by Jonathan Swift)

culpable ADJ if you are culpable for something it means you are to blame ❏ *deep are the sorrows that spring from false ideas for which no man is culpable.* (*Silas Marner* by George Eliot)

cultured ADJ cultivated ❏ *Nor less when spring had warmed the cultured Vale* (*The Prelude* by William Wordsworth)

cupidity NOUN cupidity is greed ❏ *These people hated me with the hatred of cupidity and disappointment.* (*Great Expectations* by Charles Dickens)

curricle NOUN an open two-wheeled carriage with one seat for the driver and space for a single passenger ❏ *and they saw a lady and a gentleman in a curricle* (*Pride and Prejudice* by Jane Austen)

cynosure NOUN a cynosure is something that strongly attracts attention or admiration ❏ *Then I thought of Eliza and Georgiana; I beheld one the cynosure of a ballroom, the other the inmate of a convent cell* (*Jane Eyre* by Charlotte Brontë)

dalliance NOUN someone's dalliance with something is a brief involvement with it ❏ *nor sporting in the dalliance of love* (*Doctor Faustus Chorus* by Christopher Marlowe)

darkling ADV darkling is an archaic way of saying in the dark ❏ *Darkling I listen* (*Ode on a Nightingale* by John Keats)

delf-case NOUN a sideboard for holding dishes and crockery ❏ *at the pewter dishes and delf-case* (*Wuthering Heights* by Emily Brontë)

determined ■ VERB here determined means ended ❏ *and be out of vogue when that was determined* (*Gulliver's Travels* by Jonathan Swift) ■ VERB determined can mean to have been learned or found especially by investigation or experience ❏ *All the sensitive feelings it wounded so cruelly, all the shame and misery it kept alive within my breast, became more poignant as I thought of this; and I determined that the life was unendurable* (*David Copperfield* by Charles Dickens)

Deuce NOUN a slang term for the Devil ❏ *Ah, I dare say I did. Deuce take me, he added suddenly, I know I did. I find I am not quite unscrewed yet.* (*Great Expectations* by Charles Dickens)

diabolical ADJ diabolical means devilish or evil ❏ *and with a thousand diabolical expressions* (*Treasure Island* by Robert Louis Stevenson)

direction NOUN here direction means address ❏ *Elizabeth was not surprised at it, as Jane had written the direction remarkably ill* (*Pride and Prejudice* by Jane Austen)

discover VERB to make known or announce ❏ *the Emperor would discover the secret while I was out of his power* (*Gulliver's Travels* by Jonathan Swift)

dissemble VERB hide or conceal ❏ *Dissemble nothing* (*On His Mistress* by John Donne)

dissolve VERB dissolve here means to release from life, to die ❏ *Fade far away, dissolve, and quite forget* (*Ode on a Nightingale* by John Keats)

distrain VERB to distrain is to seize the property of someone who is in debt in compensation for the money owed ❏ *for he's threatening to distrain for it* (*Silas Marner* by George Eliot)

Divan NOUN a Divan was originally a Turkish council of state – the name was transferred to the couches they sat on and is used to mean this in English ❏ *Mr Brass applauded this picture very much, and the bed being soft and comfortable, Mr Quilp determined to use it, both as a sleeping place by night and as a kind of Divan by day.* (*The Old Curiosity Shop* by Charles Dickens)

divorcement NOUN separation ❏ *By all pains which want and divorcement* *hath* (*On His Mistress* by John Donne)

dog in the manger, PHRASE this phrase describes someone who prevents you from enjoying something that they themselves have no need for ❏ *You are a dog in the manger, Cathy, and desire no one to be loved but yourself* (*Wuthering Heights* by Emily Brontë)

dolorifuge NOUN dolorifuge is a word which Thomas Hardy invented. It means pain-killer or comfort ❏ *as a species of dolorifuge* (*Tess of the D'Urbervilles* by Thomas Hardy)

dome NOUN building ❏ *that river and that mouldering dome* (*The Prelude* by William Wordsworth)

domestic PHRASE here domestic means a person's management of the house ❏ *to give some account of my domestic* (*Gulliver's Travels* by Jonathan Swift)

dunce NOUN a dunce is another word for idiot ❏ *Do you take me for a dunce? Go on?* (*Alice's Adventures in Wonderland* by Lewis Carroll)

Ecod EXCLAM a slang exclamation meaning 'oh God!' ❏ *"Ecod," replied Wemmick, shaking his head, "that's not my trade."* (*Great Expectations* by Charles Dickens)

egg-hot NOUN an egg-hot (see also 'flip' and 'negus') was a hot drink made from beer and eggs, sweetened with nutmeg ❏ *She fainted when she saw me return, and made a little jug of egg-hot afterwards to console us while we talked it over.* (*David Copperfield* by Charles Dickens)

encores NOUN an encore is a short extra performance at the end of a longer one, which the entertainer gives because the audience has enthusiastically asked for it ❏ *we want a little something to answer encores with, anyway* (*The Adventures of Huckleberry Finn* by Mark Twain)

equipage NOUN an elegant and impressive carriage ❏ *and besides, the equipage did not answer to any of*

their neighbours (*Pride and Prejudice* by Jane Austen)

exordium NOUN an exordium is the opening part of a speech ❏ *"Now, Handel," as if it were the grave beginning of a portentous business exordium, he had suddenly given up that tone* (*Great Expectations* by Charles Dickens)

expect VERB here expect means to wait for ❏ *to expect his farther commands* (*Gulliver's Travels* by Jonathan Swift)

familiars NOUN familiars means spirits or devils who come to someone when they are called ❏ *I'll turn all the lice about thee into familiars* (*Doctor Faustus 1.4* by Christopher Marlowe)

fantods NOUN a fantod is a person who fidgets or can't stop moving nervously ❏ *It most give me the fantods* (*The Adventures of Huckleberry Finn* by Mark Twain)

farthing NOUN a farthing is an old unit of British currency which was worth a quarter of a penny ❏ *Not a farthing less. A great many back-payments are included in it, I assure you.* (*A Christmas Carol* by Charles Dickens)

farthingale NOUN a hoop worn under a skirt to extend it ❏ *A bell with an old voice – which I dare say in its time had often said to the house, Here is the green farthingale* (*Great Expectations* by Charles Dickens)

favours NOUN here favours is an old word which means ribbons ❏ *A group of humble mourners entered the gate: wearing white favours* (*Oliver Twist* by Charles Dickens)

feigned VERB pretend or pretending ❏ *not my feigned page* (*On His Mistress* by John Donne)

fence ■ NOUN a fence is someone who receives and sells stolen goods ❏ *What are you up to? Ill-treating the boys, you covetous, avaricious, in-sa-ti-a-ble old fence?* (*Oliver Twist* by

Charles Dickens) ■ NOUN defence or protection ❑ *but honesty hath no fence against superior cunning* (*Gulliver's Travels* by Jonathan Swift)

fess ADJ fess is an old word which means pleased or proud ❑ *You'll be fess enough, my poppet* (*Tess of the D'Urbervilles* by Thomas Hardy)

fettered ADJ fettered means bound in chains or chained ❑ *"You are fettered," said Scrooge, trembling. "Tell me why?"* (*A Christmas Carol* by Charles Dickens)

fidges VERB fidges means fidgets, which is to keep moving your hands slightly because you are nervous or excited ❑ *Look, Jim, how my fingers fidges* (*Treasure Island* by Robert Louis Stevenson)

finger-post NOUN a finger-post is a sign-post showing the direction to different places ❑ *"The gallows," continued Fagin, "the gallows, my dear, is an ugly finger-post, which points out a very short and sharp turning that has stopped many a bold fellow's career on the broad highway."* (*Oliver Twist* by Charles Dickens)

fire-irons NOUN fire-irons are tools kept by the side of the fire to either cook with or look after the fire ❑ *the fire-irons came first* (*Alice's Adventures in Wonderland* by Lewis Carroll)

fire-plug NOUN a fire-plug is another word for a fire hydrant ❑ *The pony looked with great attention into a fire-plug, which was near him, and appeared to be quite absorbed in contemplating it* (*The Old Curiosity Shop* by Charles Dickens)

flank NOUN flank is the side of an animal ❑ *And all her silken flanks with garlands dressed* (*Ode on a Grecian Urn* by John Keats)

flip NOUN a flip is a drink made from warmed ale, sugar, spice and beaten egg ❑ *The events of the day, in combination with the twins, if not with the flip, had made Mrs. Micawber hysterical, and she shed tears as she replied* (*David Copperfield* by Charles Dickens)

flit VERB flit means to move quickly ❑ *and if he had meant to flit to Thrushcross Grange* (*Wuthering Heights* by Emily Brontë)

floorcloth NOUN a floorcloth was a hard-wearing piece of canvas used instead of carpet ❑ *This avenging phantom was ordered to be on duty at eight on Tuesday morning in the hall (it was two feet square, as charged for floorcloth)* (*Great Expectations* by Charles Dickens)

fly-driver NOUN a fly-driver is a carriage drawn by a single horse ❑ *The fly-drivers, among whom I inquired next, were equally jocose and equally disrespectful* (*David Copperfield* by Charles Dickens)

fob NOUN a small pocket in which a watch is kept ❑ *"Certain," replied the man, drawing a gold watch from his fob* (*Oliver Twist* by Charles Dickens)

folly NOUN folly means foolishness or stupidity ❑ *the folly of beginning a work* (*Robinson Crusoe* by Daniel Defoe)

fond ADJ fond means foolish ❑ *Fond worldling* (*Doctor Faustus 5.2* by Christopher Marlowe)

fondness NOUN silly or foolish affection ❑ *They have no fondness for their colts or foals* (*Gulliver's Travels* by Jonathan Swift)

for his fancy PHRASE for his fancy means for his liking or as he wanted ❑ *and as I did not obey quick enough for his fancy* (*Treasure Island* by Robert Louis Stevenson)

forlorn ADJ lost or very upset ❑ *you are from that day forlorn* (*Gulliver's Travels* by Jonathan Swift)

foster-sister NOUN a foster-sister was someone brought up by the same nurse or in the same household ❑ *I had been his foster-sister* (*Wuthering Heights* by Emily Brontë)

fox-fire NOUN fox-fire is a weak glow that is given off by decaying, rotten wood ❑ *what we must have was a lot of them rotten chunks* *that's called fox-fire* (*The Adventures of Huckleberry Finn* by Mark Twain)

frozen sea PHRASE the Arctic Ocean ❑ *into the frozen sea* (*Gulliver's Travels* by Jonathan Swift)

gainsay VERB to gainsay something is to say it isn't true or to deny it ❑ *"So she had," cried Scrooge. "You're right. I'll not gainsay it, Spirit. God forbid!"* (*A Christmas Carol* by Charles Dickens)

gaiters NOUN gaiters were leggings made of a cloth or piece of leather which covered the leg from the knee to the ankle ❑ *Mr Knightley was hard at work upon the lower buttons of his thick leather gaiters* (*Emma* by Jane Austen)

galluses NOUN galluses is an old spelling of gallows, and here means suspenders. Suspenders are straps worn over someone's shoulders and fastened to their trousers to prevent the trousers falling down ❑ *and home-knit galluses* (*The Adventures of Huckleberry Finn* by Mark Twain)

galoot NOUN a sailor but also a clumsy person ❑ *and maybe a galoot on it chopping* (*The Adventures of Huckleberry Finn* by Mark Twain)

gayest ADJ gayest means the most lively and bright or merry ❑ *Beth played her gayest march* (*Little Women* by Louisa May Alcott)

gem NOUN here gem means jewellery ❑ *the mountain shook off turf and flower, had only heath for raiment and crag for gem* (*Jane Eyre* by Charlotte Brontë)

giddy ADJ giddy means dizzy ❑ *and I wish you wouldn't keep appearing and vanishing so suddenly; you make one quite giddy.* (*Alice's Adventures in Wonderland* by Lewis Carroll)

gig NOUN a light two-wheeled carriage ❑ *when a gig drove up to the garden gate: out of which there jumped a fat gentleman* (*Oliver Twist* by Charles Dickens)

gladsome ADJ gladsome is an old word meaning glad or happy ❑ *Nobody ever stopped him in the street to say, with gladsome looks* (*A Christmas Carol* by Charles Dickens)

glen NOUN a glen is a small valley; the word is used commonly in Scotland ❑ *a beck which follows the bend of the glen* (*Wuthering Heights* by Emily Brontë)

gravelled VERB gravelled is an old term which means to baffle or defeat someone ❑ *Gravelled the pastors of the German Church* (*Doctor Faustus 1.1* by Christopher Marlowe)

grinder NOUN a grinder was a private tutor ❑ *but that when he had had the happiness of marrying Mrs Pocket very early in his life, he had impaired his prospects and taken up the calling of a Grinder* (*Great Expectations* by Charles Dickens)

gruel NOUN gruel is a thin, watery corn-meal or oatmeal soup ❑ *and the little saucepan of gruel (Scrooge had a cold in his head) upon the hob.* (*A Christmas Carol* by Charles Dickens)

guinea, half a NOUN a half guinea was ten shillings and sixpence ❑ *but lay out half a guinea at Ford's* (*Emma* by Jane Austen)

gull VERB gull is an old term which means to fool or deceive someone ❑ *Hush, I'll gull him supernaturally* (*Doctor Faustus 3.4* by Christopher Marlowe)

gunnel NOUN the gunnel, or gunwhale, is the upper edge of a boat's side ❑ *But he put his foot on the gunnel and rocked her* (*The Adventures of Huckleberry Finn* by Mark Twain)

gunwale NOUN the side of a ship ❑ *He dipped his hand in the water over the boat's gunwale* (*Great Expectations* by Charles Dickens)

Gytrash NOUN a Gytrash is an omen of misfortune to the superstitious, usually taking the form of a hound ❑ *I remembered certain of Bessie's tales, wherein figured a*

North-of-England spirit, called a 'Gytrash' (Jane Eyre by Charlotte Brontë)

hackney-cabriolet NOUN a two-wheeled carriage with four seats for hire and pulled by a horse ❏ *A hackney-cabriolet was in waiting; with the same vehemence which she had exhibited in addressing Oliver, the girl pulled him in with her, and drew the curtains close. (Oliver Twist* by Charles Dickens)

hackney-coach NOUN a four-wheeled horse-drawn vehicle for hire ❏ *The twilight was beginning to close in, when Mr. Brownlow alighted from a hackney-coach at his own door, and knocked softly. (Oliver Twist* by Charles Dickens)

haggler NOUN a haggler is someone who travels from place to place selling small goods and items ❏ *when I be plain Jack Durbeyfield, the haggler (Tess of the D'Urbervilles* by Thomas Hardy)

halter NOUN a halter is a rope or strap used to lead an animal or to tie it up ❏ *I had of course long been used to a halter and a headstall (Black Beauty* by Anna Sewell)

hamlet NOUN a hamlet is a small village or a group of houses in the countryside ❏ *down from the hamlet (Treasure Island* by Robert Louis Stevenson)

hand-barrow NOUN a hand-barrow is a device for carrying heavy objects. It is like a wheelbarrow except that it has handles, rather than wheels, for moving the barrow ❏ *his sea chest following behind him in a hand-barrow (Treasure Island* by Robert Louis Stevenson)

handspike NOUN a handspike was a stick which was used as a lever ❏ *a bit of stick like a handspike (Treasure Island* by Robert Louis Stevenson)

haply ADV haply means by chance or perhaps ❏ *And haply the Queen-Moon is on her throne (Ode on a Nightingale* by John Keats)

harem NOUN the harem was the part of the house where the women lived ❏ *mostly they hang round the harem (The Adventures of Huckleberry Finn* by Mark Twain)

hautboys NOUN hautboys are oboes ❏ sausages and puddings resembling flutes and hautboys (Gulliver's Travels by Jonathan Swift)

hawker NOUN a hawker is someone who sells goods to people as he travels rather than from a fixed place like a shop ❏ *to buy some stockings from a hawker (Treasure Island* by Robert Louis Stevenson)

hawser NOUN a hawser is a rope used to tie up or tow a ship or boat ❏ *Again among the tiers of shipping, in and out, avoiding rusty chain-cables, frayed hempen hawsers (Great Expectations* by Charles Dickens)

headstall NOUN the headstall is the part of the bridle or halter that goes around a horse's head ❏ *I had of course long been used to a halter and a headstall (Black Beauty* by Anna Sewell)

hearken VERB hearken means to listen ❏ *though we sometimes stopped to lay hold of each other and hearken (Treasure Island* by Robert Louis Stevenson)

heartless ADJ here heartless means without heart or dejected ❏ *I am not heartless (The Prelude* by William Wordsworth)

hebdomadal ADJ hebdomadal means weekly ❏ *It was the hebdomadal treat to which we all looked forward from Sabbath to Sabbath (Jane Eyre* by Charlotte Brontë)

highwaymen NOUN highwaymen were people who stopped travellers and robbed them ❏ *We are highwaymen (The Adventures of Huckleberry Finn* by Mark Twain)

hinds NOUN hinds means farm hands, or people who work on a farm ❏ *He called his hinds about him (Gulliver's Travels* by Jonathan Swift)

histrionic ADJ if you refer to someone's behaviour as histrionic, you are being critical of it because it is dramatic and exaggerated ❑ *But the histrionic muse is the darling* (*The Adventures of Huckleberry Finn* by Mark Twain)

hogs NOUN hogs is another word for pigs ❑ *Tom called the hogs 'ingots'* (*The Adventures of Huckleberry Finn* by Mark Twain)

horrors NOUN the horrors are a fit, called delirium tremens, which is caused by drinking too much alcohol ❑ *I'll have the horrors* (*Treasure Island* by Robert Louis Stevenson)

huffy ADJ huffy means to be obviously annoyed or offended about something ❑ *They will feel that more than angry speeches or huffy actions* (*Little Women* by Louisa May Alcott)

hulks NOUN hulks were prison-ships ❑ *The miserable companion of thieves and ruffians, the fallen outcast of low haunts, the associate of the scourings of the jails and hulks* (*Oliver Twist* by Charles Dickens)

humbug NOUN humbug means nonsense or rubbish ❑ *"Bah," said Scrooge. "Humbug!"* (*A Christmas Carol* by Charles Dickens)

humours NOUN it was believed that there were four fluids in the body called humours which decided the temperament of a person depending on how much of each fluid was present ❑ *other peccant humours* (*Gulliver's Travels* by Jonathan Swift)

husbandry NOUN husbandry is farming animals ❑ *bad husbandry were plentifully anointing their wheels* (*Silas Marner* by George Eliot)

huswife NOUN a huswife was a small sewing kit ❑ *but I had put my huswife on it* (*Emma* by Jane Austen)

ideal ADJ ideal in this context means imaginary ❑ *I discovered the yell was not ideal* (*Wuthering Heights* by Emily Brontë)

If our two PHRASE if both our ❑ *If our two loves be one* (*The Good-Morrow* by John Donne)

ignis-fatuus NOUN ignis-fatuus is the light given out by burning marsh gases, which lead careless travellers into danger ❑ *it is madness in all women to let a secret love kindle within them, which, if unreturned and unknown, must devour the life that feeds it; and, if discovered and responded to, must lead ignis-fatuus-like, into miry wilds whence there is no extrication.* (*Jane Eyre* by Charlotte Brontë)

imaginations NOUN here imaginations means schemes or plans ❑ *soon drove out those imaginations* (*Gulliver's Travels* by Jonathan Swift)

impressible ADJ impressible means open or impressionable ❑ *for Marner had one of those impressible, self-doubting natures* (*Silas Marner* by George Eliot)

in good intelligence PHRASE friendly with each other ❑ *that these two persons were in good intelligence with each other* (*Gulliver's Travels* by Jonathan Swift)

inanity NOUN inanity is sillyness or dull stupidity ❑ *Do we not wile away moments of inanity* (*Silas Marner* by George Eliot)

incivility NOUN incivility means rudeness or impoliteness ❑ *if it's only for a piece of incivility like to-night's* (*Treasure Island* by Robert Louis Stevenson)

indigenae NOUN indigenae means natives or people from that area ❑ *an exotic that the surly indigenae will not recognise for kin* (*Wuthering Heights* by Emily Brontë)

indocible ADJ unteachable ❑ *so they were the most restive and indocible* (*Gulliver's Travels* by Jonathan Swift)

ingenuity NOUN inventiveness ❑ *entreated me to give him something as an encouragement to ingenuity*

(*Gulliver's Travels* by Jonathan Swift)

ingots NOUN an ingot is a lump of a valuable metal like gold, usually shaped like a brick ❏ *Tom called the hogs 'ingots'* (*The Adventures of Huckleberry Finn* by Mark Twain)

inkstand NOUN an inkstand is a pot which was put on a desk to contain either ink or pencils and pens ❏ *throwing an inkstand at the Lizard as she spoke* (*Alice's Adventures in Wonderland* by Lewis Carroll)

inordinate ADJ without order. Today inordinate means 'excessive'. ❏ *Though yet untutored and inordinate* (*The Prelude* by William Wordsworth)

intellectuals NOUN here intellectuals means the minds (of the workmen) ❏ *those instructions they give being too refined for the intellectuals of their workmen* (*Gulliver's Travels* by Jonathan Swift)

interview NOUN meeting ❏ *By our first strange and fatal interview* (*On His Mistress* by John Donne)

jacks NOUN jacks are rods for turning a spit over a fire ❏ *It was a small bit of pork suspended from the kettle hanger by a string passed through a large door key, in a way known to primitive housekeepers unpossessed of jacks* (*Silas Marner* by George Eliot)

jews-harp NOUN a jews-harp is a small, metal, musical instrument that is played by the mouth ❏ *A jews-harp's plenty good enough for a rat* (*The Adventures of Huckleberry Finn* by Mark Twain)

jorum NOUN a large bowl ❏ *while Miss Skiffins brewed such a jorum of tea, that the pig in the back premises became strongly excited* (*Great Expectations* by Charles Dickens)

jostled VERB jostled means bumped or pushed by someone or some people ❏ *being jostled himself into the kennel* (*Gulliver's Travels* by Jonathan Swift)

keepsake NOUN a keepsake is a gift which reminds someone of an event or of the person who gave it to them. ❏ *books and ornaments they had in their boudoirs at home: keepsakes that different relations had presented to them* (*Jane Eyre* by Charlotte Brontë)

kenned VERB kenned means knew ❏ *though little kenned the lamplighter that he had any company but Christmas!* (*A Christmas Carol* by Charles Dickens)

kennel NOUN kennel means gutter, which is the edge of a road next to the pavement, where rain water collects and flows away ❏ *being jostled himself into the kennel* (*Gulliver's Travels* by Jonathan Swift)

knock-knee ADJ knock-knee means slanted, at an angle. ❏ *LOT 1 was marked in whitewashed knock-knee letters on the brewhouse* (*Great Expectations* by Charles Dickens)

ladylike ADJ to be ladylike is to behave in a polite, dignified and graceful way ❏ *No, winking isn't ladylike* (*Little Women* by Louisa May Alcott)

lapse NOUN flow ❏ *Stealing with silent lapse to join the brook* (*The Prelude* by William Wordsworth)

larry NOUN larry is an old word which means commotion or noisy celebration ❏ *That was all a part of the larry!* (*Tess of the D'Urbervilles* by Thomas Hardy)

laths NOUN laths are strips of wood ❏ *The panels shrunk, the windows cracked; fragments of plaster fell out of the ceiling, and the naked laths were shown instead* (*A Christmas Carol* by Charles Dickens)

leer NOUN a leer is an unpleasant smile ❏ *with a kind of leer* (*Treasure Island* by Robert Louis Stevenson)

lenitives NOUN these are different kinds of drugs or medicines: lenitives and palliatives were pain relievers; aperitives were laxatives;

abstersives caused vomiting; corrosives destroyed human tissue; restringents caused constipation; cephalalgics stopped headaches; icterics were used as medicine for jaundice; apophlegmatics were cough medicine, and acoustics were cures for the loss of hearing ❑ *lenitives, aperitives, abstersives, corrosives, restringents, palliatives, laxatives, cephalalgics, icterics, apophlegmatics, acoustics* (*Gulliver's Travels* by Jonathan Swift)

lest CONJ in case. If you do something lest something (usually) unpleasant happens you do it to try to prevent it happening ❑ *She went in without knocking, and hurried upstairs, in great fear lest she should meet the real Mary Ann* (*Alice's Adventures in Wonderland* by Lewis Carroll)

levee NOUN a levee is an old term for a meeting held in the morning, shortly after the person holding the meeting has got out of bed ❑ *I used to attend the King's levee once or twice a week* (*Gulliver's Travels* by Jonathan Swift)

life-preserver NOUN a club which had lead inside it to make it heavier and therefore more dangerous ❑ *and with no more suspicious articles displayed to view than two or three heavy bludgeons which stood in a corner, and a 'life-preserver' that hung over the chimney-piece.* (*Oliver Twist* by Charles Dickens)

lighterman NOUN a lighterman is another word for sailor ❑ *in and out, hammers going in ship-builders' yards, saws going at timber, clashing engines going at things unknown, pumps going in leaky ships, capstans going, ships going out to sea, and unintelligible sea creatures roaring curses over the bulwarks at respondent lightermen* (*Great Expectations* by Charles Dickens)

livery NOUN servants often wore a uniform known as a livery ❑ *suddenly a footman in livery came running out of the wood* (*Alice's Adventures in Wonderland* by Lewis Carroll)

livid ADJ livid means pale or ash coloured. Livid also means very angry ❑ *a dirty, livid white* (*Treasure Island* by Robert Louis Stevenson)

lottery-tickets NOUN a popular card game ❑ *and Mrs. Philips protested that they would have a nice comfortable noisy game of lottery tickets* (*Pride and Prejudice* by Jane Austen)

lower and upper world PHRASE the earth and the heavens are the lower and upper worlds ❑ *the changes in the lower and upper world* (*Gulliver's Travels* by Jonathan Swift)

lustres NOUN lustres are chandeliers. A chandelier is a large, decorative frame which holds light bulbs or candles and hangs from the ceiling ❑ *the lustres, lights, the carving and the guilding* (*The Prelude* by William Wordsworth)

lynched VERB killed without a criminal trial by a crowd of people ❑ *He'll never know how nigh he come to getting lynched* (*The Adventures of Huckleberry Finn* by Mark Twain)

malingering VERB if someone is malingering they are pretending to be ill to avoid working ❑ *And you stand there malingering* (*Treasure Island* by Robert Louis Stevenson)

managing PHRASE treating with consideration ❑ *to think the honour of my own kind not worth managing* (*Gulliver's Travels* by Jonathan Swift)

manhood PHRASE manhood means human nature ❑ *concerning the nature of manhood* (*Gulliver's Travels* by Jonathan Swift)

man-trap NOUN a man-trap is a set of steel jaws that snap shut when trodden on and trap a person's leg ❑ *"Don't go to him," I called out of the window, "he's an assassin! A* man-trap!" (*Oliver Twist* by Charles Dickens)

maps NOUN charts of the night sky ❑ *Let maps to others, worlds on worlds have shown* (*The Good-Morrow* by John Donne)

mark VERB look at or notice ❑ *Mark but this flea, and mark in this* (*The Flea* by John Donne)

maroons NOUN A maroon is someone who has been left in a place which it is difficult for them to escape from, like a small island ❑ *if schooners, islands, and maroons* (*Treasure Island* by Robert Louis Stevenson)

mast NOUN here mast means the fruit of forest trees ❑ *a quantity of acorns, dates, chestnuts, and other mast* (*Gulliver's Travels* by Jonathan Swift)

mate VERB defeat ❑ *Where Mars did mate the warlike Carthigens* (*Doctor Faustus Chorus* by Christopher Marlowe)

mealy ADJ Mealy when used to describe a face meant palid, pale or colourless ❑ *I only know two sorts of boys. Mealy boys, and beef-faced boys* (*Oliver Twist* by Charles Dickens)

middling ADJ fairly or moderately ❑ *she worked me middling hard for about an hour* (*The Adventures of Huckleberry Finn* by Mark Twain)

mill NOUN a mill, or treadmill, was a device for hard labour or punishment in prison ❑ *Was you never on the mill?* (*Oliver Twist* by Charles Dickens)

milliner's shop NOUN a milliner's sold fabrics, clothing, lace and accessories; as time went on they specialized more and more in hats ❑ *to pay their duty to their aunt and to a milliner's shop just over the way* (*Pride and Prejudice* by Jane Austen)

minching un' munching PHRASE how people in the north of England used to describe the way people from the south speak ❑ *Minching*

un' munching! (*Wuthering Heights* by Emily Brontë)

mine NOUN gold ❑ *Whether both th'Indias of spice and mine* (*The Sun Rising* by John Donne)

mire NOUN mud ❑ *Tis my fate to be always ground into the mire under the iron heel of oppression* (*The Adventures of Huckleberry Finn* by Mark Twain)

miscellany NOUN a miscellany is a collection of many different kinds of things ❑ *under that, the miscellany began* (*Treasure Island* by Robert Louis Stevenson)

mistarshers NOUN mistarshers means moustache, which is the hair that grows on a man's upper lip ❑ *when he put his hand up to his mistarshers* (*Tess of the D'Urbervilles* by Thomas Hardy)

morrow NOUN here good-morrow means tomorrow and a new and better life ❑ *And now good-morrow to our waking souls* (*The Good-Morrow* by John Donne)

mortification NOUN mortification is an old word for gangrene which is when part of the body decays or 'dies' because of disease ❑ *Yes, it was a mortification – that was it* (*The Adventures of Huckleberry Finn* by Mark Twain)

mought PARTICIPLE mought is an old spelling of might ❑ *what you mought call me? You mought call me captain* (*Treasure Island* by Robert Louis Stevenson)

move VERB move me not means do not make me angry ❑ *Move me not, Faustus* (*Doctor Faustus 2.1* by Christopher Marlowe)

muffin-cap NOUN a muffin cap is a flat cap made from wool ❑ *the old one, remained stationary in the muffin-cap and leathers* (*Oliver Twist* by Charles Dickens)

mulatter NOUN a mulatter was another word for mulatto, which is a person with parents who are from different races ❑ *a mulatter, most as white as* *a white man* (*The Adventures of Huckleberry Finn* by Mark Twain)

mummery NOUN mummery is an old word that meant meaningless (or pretentious) ceremony ❑ *When they were all gone, and when Trabb and his men – but not his boy: I looked for him – had crammed their mummery into bags, and were gone too, the house felt wholesomer.* (*Great Expectations* by Charles Dickens)

nap NOUN the nap is the woolly surface on a new item of clothing. Here the surface has been worn away so it looks bare ❑ *like an old hat with the nap rubbed off* (*The Adventures of Huckleberry Finn* by Mark Twain)

natural ■ NOUN a natural is a person born with learning difficulties ❑ *though he had been left to his particular care by their deceased father, who thought him almost a natural.* (*David Copperfield* by Charles Dickens) ■ ADJ natural meant illegitimate ❑ *Harriet Smith was the natural daughter of somebody* (*Emma* by Jane Austen)

navigator NOUN a navigator was originally someone employed to dig canals. It is the origin of the word 'navvy' meaning a labourer ❑ *She ascertained from me in a few words what it was all about, comforted Dora, and gradually convinced her that I was not a labourer – from my manner of stating the case I believe Dora concluded that I was a navigator, and went balancing myself up and down a plank all day with a wheelbarrow – and so brought us together in peace.* (*David Copperfield* by Charles Dickens)

necromancy NOUN necromancy means a kind of magic where the magician speaks to spirits or ghosts to find out what will happen in the future ❑ *He surfeits upon cursed necromancy* (*Doctor Faustus chorus* by Christopher Marlowe)

negus NOUN a negus is a hot drink made from sweetened wine and water ❑ *He sat placidly perusing the newspaper, with his little head on one side, and a glass of warm sherry negus at his elbow.* (*David Copperfield* by Charles Dickens)

nice ADJ discriminating. Able to make good judgements or choices ❑ *consequently a claim to be nice* (*Emma* by Jane Austen)

nigh ADV nigh means near ❑ *He'll never know how nigh he come to getting lynched* (*The Adventures of Huckleberry Finn* by Mark Twain)

nimbleness NOUN nimbleness means being able to move very quickly or skillfully ❑ *and with incredible accuracy and nimbleness* (*Treasure Island* by Robert Louis Stevenson)

noggin NOUN a noggin is a small mug or a wooden cup ❑ *you'll bring me one noggin of rum* (*Treasure Island* by Robert Louis Stevenson)

none ADJ neither ❑ *none can die* (*The Good-Morrow* by John Donne)

notices NOUN observations ❑ *Arch are his notices* (*The Prelude* by William Wordsworth)

occiput NOUN occiput means the back of the head ❑ *saw off the occiput of each couple* (*Gulliver's Travels* by Jonathan Swift)

officiously ADJ kindly ❑ *the governess who attended Glumdalclitch very officiously lifted me up* (*Gulliver's Travels* by Jonathan Swift)

old salt PHRASE old salt is a slang term for an experienced sailor ❑ *a 'true sea-dog', and a 'real old salt'* (*Treasure Island* by Robert Louis Stevenson)

or ere PHRASE before ❑ *or ere the Hall was built* (*The Prelude* by William Wordsworth)

ostler NOUN one who looks after horses at an inn ❑ *The bill paid, and the waiter remembered, and the ostler not forgotten, and the chambermaid taken into consideration* (*Great Expectations* by Charles Dickens)

ostry NOUN an ostry is an old word for a pub or hotel ❑ *lest I send you into the ostry with a vengeance* (*Doctor Faustus 2.2* by Christopher Marlowe)

outrunning the constable PHRASE outrunning the constable meant spending more than you earn ❑ *but I shall by this means be able to check your bills and to pull you up if I find you outrunning the constable.* (*Great Expectations* by Charles Dickens)

over ADJ across ❑ *It is in length six yards, and in the thickest part at least three yards over* (*Gulliver's Travels* by Jonathan Swift)

over the broomstick PHRASE this is a phrase meaning 'getting married without a formal ceremony' ❑ *They both led tramping lives, and this woman in Gerrard-street here, had been married very young, over the broomstick (as we say), to a tramping man, and was a perfect fury in point of jealousy.* (*Great Expectations* by Charles Dickens)

own VERB own means to admit or to acknowledge ❑ *It's my old girl that advises. She has the head. But I never own to it before her. Discipline must be maintained* (*Bleak House* by Charles Dickens)

page NOUN here page means a boy employed to run errands ❑ *not my feigned page* (*On His Mistress* by John Donne)

paid pretty dear PHRASE paid pretty dear means paid a high price or suffered quite a lot ❑ *I paid pretty dear for my monthly fourpenny piece* (*Treasure Island* by Robert Louis Stevenson)

pannikins NOUN pannikins were small tin cups ❑ *of lifting light glasses and cups to his lips, as if they were clumsy pannikins* (*Great Expectations* by Charles Dickens)

pards NOUN pards are leopards ❑ *Not charioted by Bacchus and his pards* (*Ode on a Nightingale* by John Keats)

parlour boarder NOUN a pupil who lived with the family ❑ *and somebody had lately raised her from the condition of scholar to parlour boarder* (*Emma* by Jane Austen)

particular, a London PHRASE London in Victorian times and up to the 1950s was famous for having very dense fog – which was a combination of real fog and the smog of pollution from factories ❑ *This is a London particular . . . A fog, miss'* (*Bleak House* by Charles Dickens)

patten NOUN pattens were wooden soles which were fixed to shoes by straps to protect the shoes in wet weather ❑ *carrying a basket like the Great Seal of England in plaited straw, a pair of pattens, a spare shawl, and an umbrella, though it was a fine bright day* (*Great Expectations* by Charles Dickens)

paviour NOUN a paviour was a labourer who worked on the street pavement ❑ *the paviour his pickaxe* (*Oliver Twist* by Charles Dickens)

peccant ADJ peccant means unhealthy ❑ *other peccant humours* (*Gulliver's Travels* by Jonathan Swift)

penetralium NOUN penetralium is a word used to describe the inner rooms of the house ❑ *and I had no desire to aggravate his impatience previous to inspecting the penetralium* (*Wuthering Heights* by Emily Brontë)

pensive ADV pensive means deep in thought or thinking seriously about something ❑ *and she was leaning pensive on a tomb-stone on her right elbow* (*The Adventures of Huckleberry Finn* by Mark Twain)

penury NOUN penury is the state of being extremely poor ❑ *Distress, if not penury, loomed in the distance* (*Tess of the D'Urbervilles* by Thomas Hardy)

perspective NOUN telescope ❑ *a pocket perspective* (*Gulliver's Travels* by Jonathan Swift)

phaeton NOUN a phaeton was an open carriage for four people ❑ *often* condescends to drive by my humble abode in her little phaeton and ponies (*Pride and Prejudice* by Jane Austen)

phantasm NOUN a phantasm is an illusion, something that is not real. It is sometimes used to mean ghost ❑ *Experience had bred no fancies in him that could raise the phantasm of appetite* (*Silas Marner* by George Eliot)

physic NOUN here physic means medicine ❑ *there I studied physic two years and seven months* (*Gulliver's Travels* by Jonathan Swift)

pinioned VERB to pinion is to hold both arms so that a person cannot move them ❑ *But the relentless Ghost pinioned him in both his arms, and forced him to observe what happened next.* (*A Christmas Carol* by Charles Dickens)

piquet NOUN piquet was a popular card game in the C18th ❑ *Mr Hurst and Mr Bingley were at piquet* (*Pride and Prejudice* by Jane Austen)

plaister NOUN a plaister is a piece of cloth on which an apothecary (or pharmacist) would spread ointment. The cloth is then applied to wounds or bruises to treat them ❑ *Then, she gave the knife a final smart wipe on the edge of the plaister, and then sawed a very thick round off the loaf: which she finally, before separating from the loaf, hewed into two halves, of which Joe got one, and I the other.* (*Great Expectations* by Charles Dickens)

plantations NOUN here plantations means colonies, which are countries controlled by a more powerful country ❑ *besides our plantations in America* (*Gulliver's Travels* by Jonathan Swift)

plastic ADV here plastic is an old term meaning shaping or a power that was forming ❑ *A plastic power abode with me* (*The Prelude* by William Wordsworth)

players NOUN actors ❑ *of players which*

upon the world's stage be (*On His Mistress* by John Donne)

plump ADV all at once, suddenly ❑ *But it took a bit of time to get it well round, the change come so uncommon plump, didn't it?* (*Great Expectations* by Charles Dickens)

plundered VERB to plunder is to rob or steal from ❑ *These crosses stand for the names of ships or towns that they sank or plundered* (*Treasure Island* by Robert Louis Stevenson)

pommel ■ VERB to pommel someone is to hit them repeatedly with your fists ❑ *hug him round the neck, pommel his back, and kick his legs in irrepressible affection!* (*A Christmas Carol* by Charles Dickens) ■ NOUN a pommel is the part of a saddle that rises up at the front ❑ *He had his gun across his pommel* (*The Adventures of Huckleberry Finn* by Mark Twain)

poor's rates NOUN poor's rates were property taxes which were used to support the poor ❑ *"Oh!" replied the undertaker; "why, you know, Mr. Bumble, I pay a good deal towards the poor's rates."* (*Oliver Twist* by Charles Dickens)

popular ADJ popular means ruled by the people, or Republican, rather than ruled by a monarch ❑ *With those of Greece compared and popular Rome* (*The Prelude* by William Wordsworth)

porringer NOUN a porringer is a small bowl ❑ *Of this festive composition each boy had one porringer, and no more* (*Oliver Twist* by Charles Dickens)

postboy NOUN a postboy was the driver of a horse-drawn carriage ❑ *He spoke to a postboy who was dozing under the gateway* (*Oliver Twist* by Charles Dickens)

post-chaise NOUN a fast carriage for two or four passengers ❑ *Looking round, he saw that it was a post-chaise, driven at great speed* (*Oliver Twist* by Charles Dickens)

postern NOUN a small gate usually at the back of a building ❑ *The little servant happening to be entering the fortress with two hot rolls, I passed through the postern and crossed the drawbridge, in her company* (*Great Expectations* by Charles Dickens)

pottle NOUN a pottle was a small basket ❑ *He had a paper-bag under each arm and a pottle of strawberries in one hand . . .* (*Great Expectations* by Charles Dickens)

pounce NOUN pounce is a fine powder used to prevent ink spreading on untreated paper ❑ *in that grim atmosphere of pounce and parchment, red-tape, dusty wafers, inkjars, brief and draft paper, law reports, writs, declarations, and bills of costs* (*David Copperfield* by Charles Dickens)

pox NOUN pox means sexually transmitted diseases like syphilis ❑ *how the pox in all its consequences and denominations* (*Gulliver's Travels* by Jonathan Swift)

prelibation NOUN prelibation means a foretaste of or an example of something to come ❑ *A prelibation to the mower's scythe* (*The Prelude* by William Wordsworth)

prentice NOUN an apprentice ❑ *and Joe, sitting on an old gun, had told me that when I was 'prentice to him regularly bound, we would have such Larks there!* (*Great Expectations* by Charles Dickens)

presently ADV immediately ❑ *I presently knew what they meant* (*Gulliver's Travels* by Jonathan Swift)

pumpion NOUN pumpkin ❑ *for it was almost as large as a small pumpion* (*Gulliver's Travels* by Jonathan Swift)

punctual ADJ kept in one place ❑ *was not a punctual presence, but a spirit* (*The Prelude* by William Wordsworth)

quadrille ■ NOUN a quadrille is a dance invented in France which is usually performed by four couples ❑ *However, Mr Swiveller had Miss Sophy's hand for the first quadrille (country-dances being low, were utterly proscribed)* (*The Old Curiosity Shop* by Charles Dickens) ■ NOUN quadrille was a card game for four people ❑ *to make up her pool of quadrille in the evening* (*Pride and Prejudice* by Jane Austen)

quality NOUN gentry or upper-class people ❑ *if you are with the quality* (*The Adventures of Huckleberry Finn* by Mark Twain)

quick parts PHRASE quick-witted ❑ *Mr Bennet was so odd a mixture of quick parts* (*Pride and Prejudice* by Jane Austen)

quid NOUN a quid is something chewed or kept in the mouth, like a piece of tobacco ❑ *rolling his quid* (*Treasure Island* by Robert Louis Stevenson)

quit VERB quit means to avenge or to make even ❑ *But Faustus's death shall quit my infamy* (*Doctor Faustus 4.3* by Christopher Marlowe)

rags NOUN divisions ❑ *Nor hours, days, months, which are the rags of time* (*The Sun Rising* by John Donne)

raiment NOUN raiment means clothing ❑ *the mountain shook off turf and flower, had only heath for raiment and crag for gem* (*Jane Eyre* by Charlotte Brontë)

rain cats and dogs PHRASE an expression meaning rain heavily. The origin of the expression is unclear ❑ *But it'll perhaps rain cats and dogs to-morrow* (*Silas Marner* by George Eliot)

raised Cain PHRASE raised Cain means caused a lot of trouble. Cain is a character in the Bible who killed his brother Abel ❑ *and every time he got drunk he raised Cain around town* (*The Adventures of Huckleberry Finn* by Mark Twain)

rambling ADJ rambling means confused and not very clear ❑ *my* *head began to be filled very early with rambling thoughts* (*Robinson Crusoe* by Daniel Defoe)

raree-show NOUN a raree-show is an old term for a peep-show or a fairground entertainment ❑ *A raree-show is here, with children gathered round* (*The Prelude* by William Wordsworth)

recusants NOUN people who resisted authority ❑ *hardy recusants* (*The Prelude* by William Wordsworth)

redounding VERB eddying. An eddy is a movement in water or air which goes round and round instead of flowing in one direction ❑ *mists and steam-like fogs redounding everywhere* (*The Prelude* by William Wordsworth)

redundant ADJ here redundant means overflowing but Wordsworth also uses it to mean excessively large or too big ❑ *A tempest, a redundant energy* (*The Prelude* by William Wordsworth)

reflex NOUN reflex is a shortened version of reflexion, which is an alternative spelling of reflection ❑ *To cut across the reflex of a star* (*The Prelude* by William Wordsworth)

Reformatory NOUN a prison for young offenders/criminals ❑ *Even when I was taken to have a new suit of clothes, the tailor had orders to make them like a kind of Reformatory, and on no account to let me have the free use of my limbs.* (*Great Expectations* by Charles Dickens)

remorse NOUN pity or compassion ❑ *by that remorse* (*On His Mistress* by John Donne)

render VERB in this context render means give. ❑ *and Sarah could render no reason that would be sanctioned by the feeling of the community.* (*Silas Marner* by George Eliot)

repeater NOUN a repeater was a watch that chimed the last hour when a button was pressed – as a result it was useful in the dark ❑ *And his watch is a gold repeater, and worth a hundred pound if it's worth a penny.* (*Great Expectations* by Charles Dickens)

repugnance NOUN repugnance means a strong dislike of something or someone ❑ *overcoming a strong repugnance* (*Treasure Island* by Robert Louis Stevenson)

reverence NOUN reverence means bow. When you bow to someone, you briefly bend your body towards them as a formal way of showing them respect ❑ *made my reverence* (*Gulliver's Travels* by Jonathan Swift)

reverie NOUN a reverie is a day dream ❑ *I can guess the subject of your reverie* (*Pride and Prejudice* by Jane Austen)

revival NOUN a religious meeting held in public ❑ *well I'd ben a-running' a little temperance revival thar' bout a week* (*The Adventures of Huckleberry Finn* by Mark Twain)

revolt VERB revolt means turn back or stop your present course of action and go back to what you were doing before ❑ *Revolt, or I'll in piecemeal tear thy flesh* (*Doctor Faustus 5.1* by Christopher Marlowe)

rheumatics/rheumatism NOUN rheumatics [rheumatism] is an illness that makes your joints or muscles stiff and painful ❑ *a new cure for the rheumatics* (*Treasure Island* by Robert Louis Stevenson)

riddance NOUN riddance is usually used in the form good riddance which you say when you are pleased that something has gone or been left behind ❑ *I'd better go into the house, and die and be a riddance* (*David Copperfield* by Charles Dickens)

rimy ADJ rimy is an ADJECTIVE which means covered in ice or frost ❑ *It was a rimy morning, and very damp* (*Great Expectations* by Charles Dickens)

riper ADJ riper means more mature or older ❑ *At riper years to Wittenberg he went* (*Doctor Faustus chorus* by Christopher Marlowe)

rubber NOUN a set of games in whist or backgammon ❑ *her father was sure of his rubber* (*Emma* by Jane Austen)

ruffian NOUN a ruffian is a person who behaves violently ❑ *and when the ruffian had told him* (*Treasure Island* by Robert Louis Stevenson)

sadness NOUN sadness is an old term meaning seriousness ❑ *But I prithee tell me, in good sadness* (*Doctor Faustus 2.2* by Christopher Marlowe)

sailed before the mast PHRASE this phrase meant someone who did not look like a sailor ❑ *he had none of the appearance of a man that sailed before the mast* (*Treasure Island* by Robert Louis Stevenson)

scabbard NOUN a scabbard is the covering for a sword or dagger ❑ *Girded round its middle was an antique scabbard; but no sword was in it, and the ancient sheath was eaten up with rust* (*A Christmas Carol* by Charles Dickens)

schooners NOUN A schooner is a fast, medium-sized sailing ship ❑ *if schooners, islands, and maroons* (*Treasure Island* by Robert Louis Stevenson)

science NOUN learning or knowledge ❑ *Even Science, too, at hand* (*The Prelude* by William Wordsworth)

scrouge VERB to scrouge means to squeeze or to crowd ❑ *to scrouge in and get a sight* (*The Adventures of Huckleberry Finn* by Mark Twain)

scrutore NOUN a scrutore, or escritoire, was a writing table ❑ *set me gently on my feet upon the scrutore* (*Gulliver's Travels* by Jonathan Swift)

scutcheon/escutcheon NOUN an escutcheon is a shield with a coat of arms, or the symbols of a family name, engraved on it ❑ *On the*

scutcheon we'll have a bend (*The Adventures of Huckleberry Finn* by Mark Twain)

sea-dog PHRASE sea-dog is a slang term for an experienced sailor or pirate ❑ *a 'true sea-dog', and a 'real old salt,'* (*Treasure Island* by Robert Louis Stevenson)

see the lions PHRASE to see the lions was to go and see the sights of London. Originally the phrase referred to the menagerie in the Tower of London and later in Regent's Park ❑ *We will go and see the lions for an hour or two – it's something to have a fresh fellow like you to show them to, Copperfield* (*David Copperfield* by Charles Dickens)

self-conceit NOUN self-conceit is an old term which means having too high an opinion of oneself, or deceiving yourself ❑ *Till swollen with cunning, of a self-conceit* (*Doctor Faustus chorus* by Christopher Marlowe)

seneschal NOUN a steward ❑ *where a grey-headed seneschal sings a funny chorus with a funnier body of vassals* (*Oliver Twist* by Charles Dickens)

sensible ADJ if you were sensible of something you are aware or conscious of something ❑ *If my children are silly I must hope to be always sensible of it* (*Pride and Prejudice* by Jane Austen)

sessions NOUN court cases were heard at specific times of the year called sessions ❑ *He lay in prison very ill, during the whole interval between his committal for trial, and the coming round of the Sessions.* (*Great Expectations* by Charles Dickens)

shabby ADJ shabby places look old and in bad condition ❑ *a little bit of a shabby village named Pikesville* (*The Adventures of Huckleberry Finn* by Mark Twain)

shay-cart NOUN a shay-cart was a small cart drawn by one horse ❑ *"I were at the Bargemen t'other night, Pip;"*

whenever he subsided into affection, he called me Pip, and whenever he relapsed into politeness he called me Sir; "when there come up in his shay-cart Pumblechook." (Great Expectations by Charles Dickens)

shilling NOUN a shilling is an old unit of currency. There were twenty shillings in every British pound ❑ *"Ten shillings too much," said the gentleman in the white waistcoat.* (*Oliver Twist* by Charles Dickens)

shines NOUN tricks or games ❑ *well, it would make a cow laugh to see the shines that old idiot cut* (*The Adventures of Huckleberry Finn* by Mark Twain)

shirking VERB shirking means not doing what you are meant to be doing, or evading your duties ❑ *some of you shirking lubbers* (*Treasure Island* by Robert Louis Stevenson)

shiver my timbers PHRASE shiver my timbers is an expression which was used by sailors and pirates to express surprise ❑ *why, shiver my timbers, if I hadn't forgotten my score!* (*Treasure Island* by Robert Louis Stevenson)

shoe-roses NOUN shoe-roses were roses made from ribbons which were stuck on to shoes as decoration ❑ *the very shoe-roses for Netherfield were got by proxy* (*Pride and Prejudice* by Jane Austen)

singular ADJ singular means very great and remarkable or strange ❑ *"Singular dream," he says* (*The Adventures of Huckleberry Finn* by Mark Twain)

sire NOUN sire is an old word which means lord or master or elder ❑ *She also defied her sire* (*Little Women* by Louisa May Alcott)

sixpence NOUN a sixpence was half of a shilling ❑ *if she had only a shilling in the world, she would be very lilkely to give away sixpence of it* (*Emma* by Jane Austen)

slavey NOUN the word slavey was used when there was only one servant in a house or boarding-house – so she had to perform all the duties of a larger staff ❑ *Two distinct knocks, sir, will produce the slavey at any time* (*The Old Curiosity Shop* by Charles Dickens)

slender ADJ weak ❑ *In slender accents of sweet verse* (*The Prelude* by William Wordsworth)

slop-shops NOUN slop-shops were shops where cheap ready-made clothes were sold. They mainly sold clothes to sailors ❑ *Accordingly, I took the jacket off, that I might learn to do without it; and carrying it under my arm, began a tour of inspection of the various slop-shops.* (*David Copperfield* by Charles Dickens)

sluggard NOUN a lazy person ❑ *"Stand up and repeat 'Tis the voice of the sluggard,'" said the Gryphon.* (*Alice's Adventures in Wonderland* by Lewis Carroll)

smallpox NOUN smallpox is a serious infectious disease ❑ *by telling the men we had smallpox aboard* (*The Adventures of Huckleberry Finn* by Mark Twain)

smalls NOUN smalls are short trousers ❑ *It is difficult for a large-headed, small-eyed youth, of lumbering make and heavy countenance, to look dignified under any circumstances; but it is more especially so, when superadded to these personal attractions are a red nose and yellow smalls* (*Oliver Twist* by Charles Dickens)

sneeze-box NOUN a box for snuff was called a sneeze-box because sniffing snuff makes the user sneeze ❑ *To think of Jack Dawkins — lummy Jack — the Dodger — the Artful Dodger — going abroad for a common twopenny-halfpenny sneeze-box!* (*Oliver Twist* by Charles Dickens)

snorted VERB slept ❑ *Or snorted we in the Seven Sleepers' den?* (*The Good-Morrow* by John Donne)

snuff NOUN snuff is tobacco in powder form which is taken by sniffing ❑

as he thrust his thumb and fore-finger into the proffered snuff-box of the undertaker: which was an ingenious little model of a patent coffin. (*Oliver Twist* by Charles Dickens)

soliloquized VERB to soliloquize is when an actor in a play speaks to himself or herself rather than to another actor ❑ *"A new servitude! There is something in that," I soliloquized (mentally, be it understood; I did not talk aloud)* (*Jane Eyre* by Charlotte Brontë)

sough NOUN sough is a drain or a ditch ❑ *as you may have noticed the sough that runs from the marshes* (*Wuthering Heights* by Emily Brontë)

spirits NOUN a spirit is the nonphysical part of a person which is believed to remain alive after their death ❑ *that I might raise up spirits when I please* (*Doctor Faustus 1.5* by Christopher Marlowe)

spleen ■ NOUN here spleen means a type of sadness or depression which was thought to only affect the wealthy ❑ *yet here I could plainly discover the true seeds of spleen* (*Gulliver's Travels* by Jonathan Swift) ■ NOUN irritability and low spirits ❑ *Adieu to disappointment and spleen* (*Pride and Prejudice* by Jane Austen)

spondulicks NOUN spondulicks is a slang word which means money ❑ *not for all his spondulicks and as much more on top of it* (*The Adventures of Huckleberry Finn* by Mark Twain)

stalled of VERB to be stalled of something is to be bored with it ❑ *I'm stalled of doing naught* (*Wuthering Heights* by Emily Brontë)

stanchion NOUN a stanchion is a pole or bar that stands upright and is used as a buidling support ❑ *and slid down a stanchion* (*The Adventures of Huckleberry Finn* by Mark Twain)

stang NOUN stang is another word for pole which was an old measurement ❑ *These fields were intermingled with woods of half a stang* (*Gulliver's Travels* by Jonathan Swift)

starlings NOUN a starling is a wall built around the pillars that support a bridge to protect the pillars ❑ *There were states of the tide when, having been down the river, I could not get back through the eddy-chafed arches and starlings of old London Bridge* (*Great Expectations* by Charles Dickens)

startings NOUN twitching or night-time movements of the body ❑ *with midnight's startings* (*On His Mistress* by John Donne)

stomacher NOUN a panel at the front of a dress ❑ *but send her aunt the pattern of a stomacher* (*Emma* by Jane Austen)

stoop VERB swoop ❑ *Once a kite hovering over the garden made a swoop at me* (*Gulliver's Travels* by Jonathan Swift)

succedaneum NOUN a succedaneum is a substitute ❑ *But as a succedaneum* (*The Prelude* by William Wordsworth)

suet NOUN a hard animal fat used in cooking ❑ *and your jaws are too weak For anything tougher than suet* (*Alice's Adventures in Wonderland* by Lewis Carroll)

sultry ADJ sultry weather is hot and damp. Here sultry means unpleasant or risky ❑ *for it was getting pretty sultry for us* (*The Adventures of Huckleberry Finn* by Mark Twain)

summerset NOUN summerset is an old spelling of somersault. If someone does a somersault, they turn over completely in the air ❑ *I have seen him do the summerset* (*Gulliver's Travels* by Jonathan Swift)

supper NOUN supper was a light meal taken late in the evening. The main meal was dinner which was eaten at four or five in the afternoon ❑ *and the supper table was all set out* (*Emma* by Jane Austen)

surfeits VERB to surfeit in something is to have far too much of it, or to overindulge in it to an unhealthy degree ❏ *He surfeits upon cursed necromancy* (*Doctor Faustus chorus* by Christopher Marlowe)

surtout NOUN a surtout is a long close-fitting overcoat ❏ *He wore a long black surtout reaching nearly to his ankles* (*The Old Curiosity Shop* by Charles Dickens)

swath NOUN swath is the width of corn cut by a scythe ❏ *while thy hook Spares the next swath* (*Ode to Autumn* by John Keats)

sylvan ADJ sylvan means belonging to the woods ❏ *Sylvan historian* (*Ode on a Grecian Urn* by John Keats)

taction NOUN taction means touch. This means that the people had to be touched on the mouth or the ears to get their attention ❏ *without being roused by some external taction upon the organs of speech and hearing* (*Gulliver's Travels* by Jonathan Swift)

Tag and Rag and Bobtail PHRASE the riff-raff, or lower classes. Used in an insulting way ❏ *"No," said he; "not till it got about that there was no protection on the premises, and it come to be considered dangerous, with convicts and Tag and Rag and Bobtail going up and down."* (*Great Expectations* by Charles Dickens)

tallow NOUN tallow is hard animal fat that is used to make candles and soap ❏ *and a lot of tallow candles* (*The Adventures of Huckleberry Finn* by Mark Twain)

tan VERB to tan means to beat or whip ❏ *and if I catch you about that school I'll tan you good* (*The Adventures of Huckleberry Finn* by Mark Twain)

tanyard NOUN the tanyard is part of a tannery, which is a place where leather is made from animal skins ❏ *hid in the old tanyard* (*The Adventures of Huckleberry Finn* by Mark Twain)

tarry ADJ tarry means the colour of tar or black ❏ *his tarry pig-tail* (*Treasure Island* by Robert Louis Stevenson)

thereof PHRASE from there ❏ *By all desires which thereof did ensue* (*On His Mistress* by John Donne)

thick with, be PHRASE if you are 'thick with someone' you are very close, sharing secrets – it is often used to describe people who are planning something secret ❏ *Hasn't he been thick with Mr Heathcliff lately?* (*Wuthering Heights* by Emily Brontë)

thimble NOUN a thimble is a small cover used to protect the finger while sewing ❏ *The paper had been sealed in several places by a thimble* (*Treasure Island* by Robert Louis Stevenson)

thirtover ADJ thirtover is an old word which means obstinate or that someone is very determined to do want they want and can not be persuaded to do something in another way ❏ *I have been living on in a thirtover, lackadaisical way* (*Tess of the D'Urbervilles* by Thomas Hardy)

timbrel NOUN timbrel is a tambourine ❏ *What pipes and timbrels?* (*Ode on a Grecian Urn* by John Keats)

tin NOUN tin is slang for money/cash ❏ *Then the plain question is, an't it a pity that this state of things should continue, and how much better would it be for the old gentleman to hand over a reasonable amount of tin, and make it all right and comfortable* (*The Old Curiosity Shop* by Charles Dickens)

tincture NOUN a tincture is a medicine made with alcohol and a small amount of a drug ❏ *with ink composed of a cephalic tincture* (*Gulliver's Travels* by Jonathan Swift)

tithe NOUN a tithe is a tax paid to the church ❏ *and held farms which, speaking from a spiritual point of view, paid highly-desirable tithes* (*Silas Marner* by George Eliot)

towardly ADJ a towardly child is dutiful or obedient ❏ *and a towardly child* (*Gulliver's Travels* by Jonathan Swift)

toys NOUN trifles are things which are considered to have little importance, value, or significance ❏ *purchase my life from them bysome bracelets, glass rings, and other toys* (*Gulliver's Travels* by Jonathan Swift)

tract NOUN a tract is a religious pamphlet or leaflet ❏ *and Joe Harper got a hymn-book and a tract* (*The Adventures of Huckleberry Finn* by Mark Twain)

train-oil NOUN train-oil is oil from whale blubber ❏ *The train-oil and gunpowder were shoved out of sight in a minute* (*Wuthering Heights* by Emily Brontë)

tribulation NOUN tribulation means the suffering or difficulty you experience in a particular situation ❏ *Amy was learning this distinction through much tribulation* (*Little Women* by Louisa May Alcott)

trivet NOUN a trivet is a three-legged stand for resting a pot or kettle ❏ *a pocket-knife in his right; and a pewter pot on the trivet* (*Oliver Twist* by Charles Dickens)

trot line NOUN a trot line is a fishing line to which a row of smaller fishing lines are attached ❏ *when he got along I was hard at it taking up a trot line* (*The Adventures of Huckleberry Finn* by Mark Twain)

troth NOUN oath or pledge ❏ *I wonder, by my troth* (*The Good-Morrow* by John Donne)

truckle NOUN a truckle bedstead is a bed that is on wheels and can be slid under another bed to save space ❏ *It rose under my hand, and the door yielded. Looking in, I saw a lighted candle on a table, a bench, and a mattress on a truckle bedstead.* (*Great Expectations* by Charles Dickens)

trump NOUN a trump is a good, reliable person wo can be trusted ❏ *This lad Hawkins is a trump, I*

perceive (*Treasure Island* by Robert Louis Stevenson)

tucker NOUN a tucker is a frilly lace collar which is worn around the neck ❏ *Whereat Scrooge's niece's sister the plump one with the lace tucker: not the one with the roses blushed.* (*A Christmas Carol* by Charles Dickens)

tureen NOUN a large bowl with a lid from which soup or vegetables are served ❏ *Waiting in a hot tureen!* (*Alice's Adventures in Wonderland* by Lewis Carroll)

turnkey NOUN a prison officer; jailer ❏ *As we came out of the prison through the lodge, I found that the great importance of my guardian was appreciated by the turnkeys, no less than by those whom they held in charge.* (*Great Expectations* by Charles Dickens)

turnpike NOUN the upkeep of many roads of the time was paid for by tolls (fees) collected at posts along the road. There was a gate to prevent people travelling further along the road until the toll had been paid. ❏ *Traddles, whom I have taken up by appointment at the turnpike, presents a dazzling combination of cream colour and light blue; and both he and Mr. Dick have a general effect about them of being all gloves.* (*David Copperfield* by Charles Dickens)

twas PHRASE it was ❏ *twas but a dream of thee* (*The Good-Morrow* by John Donne)

tyrannized VERB tyrannized means bullied or forced to do things against their will ❏ *for people would soon cease coming there to be tyrannized over and put down* (*Treasure Island* by Robert Louis Stevenson)

'un NOUN 'un is a slang term for one – usually used to refer to a person ❏ *She's been thinking the old 'un* (*David Copperfield* by Charles Dickens)

undistinguished ADJ undiscriminating or incapable of making a distinction between good and bad things ❑ *their undistinguished appetite to devour everything* (*Gulliver's Travels* by Jonathan Swift)

use NOUN habit ❑ *Though use make you apt to kill me* (*The Flea* by John Donne)

vacant ADJ vacant usually means empty, but here Wordsworth uses it to mean carefree ❑ *To vacant musing, unreproved neglect* (*The Prelude* by William Wordsworth)

valetudinarian NOUN one too concerned with his or her own health. ❑ *for having been a valetudinarian all his life* (*Emma* by Jane Austen)

vamp VERB vamp means to walk or tramp to somewhere ❑ *Well, vamp on to Marlott, will 'ee* (*Tess of the D'Urbervilles* by Thomas Hardy)

vapours NOUN the vapours is an old term which means unpleasant and strange thoughts, which make the person feel nervous and unhappy ❑ *and my head was full of vapours* (*Robinson Crusoe* by Daniel Defoe)

vegetables NOUN here vegetables means plants ❑ *the other vegetables are in the same proportion* (*Gulliver's Travels* by Jonathan Swift)

venturesome ADJ if you are venturesome you are willing to take risks ❑ *he must be either hopelessly stupid or a venturesome fool* (*Wuthering Heights* by Emily Brontë)

verily ADJ verily means really or truly ❑ *though I believe verily* (*Robinson Crusoe* by Daniel Defoe)

vicinage NOUN vicinage is an area or the residents of an area ❑ *and to his thought the whole vicinage was haunted by her.* (*Silas Marner* by George Eliot)

victuals NOUN victuals means food ❑ *grumble a little over the victuals* (*The Adventures of Huckleberry Finn* by Mark Twain)

vintage NOUN vintage in this context means wine ❑ *Oh, for a draught of vintage!* (*Ode on a Nightingale* by John Keats)

virtual ADJ here virtual means powerful or strong ❑ *had virtual faith* (*The Prelude* by William Wordsworth)

vittles NOUN vittles is a slang word which means food ❑ *There never was such a woman for givin' away vittles and drink* (*Little Women* by Louisa May Alcott)

voided straight PHRASE voided straight is an old expression which means emptied immediately ❑ *see the rooms be voided straight* (*Doctor Faustus 4.1* by Christopher Marlowe)

wainscot NOUN wainscot is wood panel lining in a room so wainscoted means a room lined with wooden panels ❑ *in the dark wainscoted parlor* (*Silas Marner* by George Eliot)

walking the plank PHRASE walking the plank was a punishment in which a prisoner would be made to walk along a plank on the side of the ship and fall into the sea, where they would be abandoned ❑ *about hanging, and walking the plank* (*Treasure Island* by Robert Louis Stevenson)

want VERB want means to be lacking or short of ❑ *The next thing wanted was to get the picture framed* (*Emma* by Jane Austen)

wanting ADJ wanting means lacking or missing ❑ *wanting two fingers of the left hand* (*Treasure Island* by Robert Louis Stevenson)

wanting, I was not PHRASE I was not wanting means I did not fail ❑ *I was not wanting to lay a foundation of religious knowledge in his mind* (*Robinson Crusoe* by Daniel Defoe)

ward NOUN a ward is, usually, a child who has been put under the protection of the court or a guardian for his or her protection ❑ *I call the Wards in Jarndcye. The* *are caged up with all the others.* (*Bleak House* by Charles Dickens)

waylay VERB to waylay someone is to lie in wait for them or to intercept them ❑ *I must go up the road and waylay him* (*The Adventures of Huckleberry Finn* by Mark Twain)

weazen NOUN weazen is a slang word for throat. It actually means shrivelled ❑ *You with a uncle too! Why, I knowed you at Gargery's when you was so small a wolf that I could have took your weazen betwixt this finger and thumb and chucked you away dead* (*Great Expectations* by Charles Dickens)

wery ■ ADV very ❑ *Be wery careful o' vidders all your life* (*Pickwick Papers* by Charles Dickens) ■ *See* wibrated

wherry NOUN wherry is a small swift rowing boat for one person ❑ *It was flood tide when Daniel Quilp sat himself down in the wherry to cross to the opposite shore.* (*The Old Curiosity Shop* by Charles Dickens)

whether PREP whether means which of the two in this example ❑ *we came in full view of a great island or continent (for we knew not whether)* (*Gulliver's Travels* by Jonathan Swift)

whetstone NOUN a whetstone is a stone used to sharpen knives and other tools ❑ *I dropped pap's whet-stone there too* (*The Adventures of Huckleberry Finn* by Mark Twain)

wibrated VERB in Dickens's use of the English language 'w' often replaces 'v' when he is reporting speech. So here 'wibrated' means 'vibrated'. In Pickwick Papers a judge asks Sam Weller (who constantly confuses the two letters) 'Do you spell it with a 'v' or a 'w'?' to which Weller replies 'That depends upon the taste and fancy of the speller, my Lord' ❑ *There are strings . . . in the human heart that had better not be wibrated'* (*Barnaby Rudge* by Charles Dickens)

wicket NOUN a wicket is a little door in a larger entrance ❑ *Having rested here, for a minute or so, to collect a good burst of sobs and an imposing show of tears and terror, he knocked loudly at the wicket;* (*Oliver Twist* by Charles Dickens)

without CONJ without means unless ❑ *You don't know about me, without you have read a book by the name of The Adventures of Tom Sawyer* (*The Adventures of Huckleberry Finn* by Mark Twain)

wittles ■ NOUN vittles is a slang word which means food ❑ *I live on broken wittles – and I sleep on the coals* (*David Copperfield* by Charles Dickens) ■ *See* wibrated

woo VERB courts or forms a proper relationship with ❑ *before it woo* (*The Flea* by John Donne)

words, to have PHRASE if you have words with someone you have a disagreement or an argument ❑ *I do not want to have words with a young thing like you.* (*Black Beauty* by Anna Sewell)

workhouse NOUN workhouses were places where the homeless were given food and a place to live in return for doing very hard work ❑ *And the Union workhouses? demanded Scrooge. Are they still in operation?* (*A Christmas Carol* by Charles Dickens)

yawl NOUN a yawl is a small boat kept on a bigger boat for short trips. Yawl is also the name for a small fishing boat ❑ *She sent out her yawl, and we went aboard* (*The Adventures of Huckleberry Finn* by Mark Twain)

yeomanry NOUN the yeomanry was a collective term for the middle classes involved in agriculture ❑ *The yeomanry are precisely the order of people with whom I feel I can have nothing to do* (*Emma* by Jane Austen)

yonder ADV yonder means over there ❑ *all in the same second we seem to hear low voices in yonder!* (*The Adventures of Huckleberry Finn* by Mark Twain)